SLIGHTLY WICKED
"Sympathetic characters and scalding sexual tension
make the second installment [in the Slightly series] a
truly engrossing read. . . . Balogh's sure-footed story
possesses an abundance of character and class."
—*Publishers Weekly*

SLIGHTLY MARRIED
"[A Perfect 10] . . . *Slightly Married* is a masterpiece!
Mary Balogh has an unparalleled gift for creating
complex, compelling characters who come alive
on the pages." —*Romance Reviews Today*

A SUMMER TO REMEMBER
"Balogh outdoes herself with this romantic romp,
crafting a truly seamless plot and peopling it with
well-rounded, winning characters." —*Publishers Weekly*

"The most sensuous romance of the year." —*Booklist*

"This one will rise to the top." —*Library Journal*

"Filled with vivid descriptions, sharp dialogue, and
fantastic characters, this passionate, adventurous tale
will remain memorable for readers who love an
entertaining read." —*Rendezvous*

# PRAISE FOR THE NOVELS OF MARY BALOGH

### SIMPLY PERFECT

"A warm-hearted and feel-good story . . . Readers will want to add this wonderful story to their collection. *Simply Perfect* is another must-read from this talented author, and a Perfect 10." —*Romance Reader*

"With her signature exquisite sense of characterization and subtle wit, Balogh brings her sweetly sensual, thoroughly romantic Simply quartet to a truly triumphant conclusion." —*Booklist*

### WEB OF LOVE

"A beautiful tale of how grief and guilt can lead to love." —*Library Journal*

### SIMPLY MAGIC

"Absorbing and appealing. This is an unusually subtle approach in a romance, and it works to great effect." —*Publishers Weekly*

"Balogh continues her superb Simply romance . . . with another exquisitely crafted Regency historical that brilliantly blends deliciously clever writing, subtly nuanced characters, and simmering sensuality into a simply sublime romance." —*Booklist*

### SIMPLY UNFORGETTABLE

"When an author has created a series as beloved to readers as Balogh's Bedwyn saga, it is hard to believe that she can surpass the delights with the first installment in a new quartet. But Balogh has done just that." —*Booklist*

"A memorable cast . . . refresh[es] a classic Regency plot with humor, wit, and the sizzling romantic chemistry that one expects from Balogh. Well written and emotionally complex." —*Library Journal*

SIMPLY LOVE
"One of the things that make Ms. Balogh's books so memorable is the emotion she pours into her stories. The writing is superb, with realistic dialogue, sexual tension, and a wonderful heart-wrenching story. *Simply Love* is a book to savor, and to read again. It is a Perfect 10. Romance doesn't get any better than this."
—*Romance Reviews Today*

"With more than her usual panache, Balogh returns to Regency England for a satisfying adult love story."
—*Publishers Weekly*

SLIGHTLY DANGEROUS
"*Slightly Dangerous* is the culmination of Balogh's wonderfully entertaining Bedwyn series. . . . Balogh, famous for her believable characters and finely crafted Regency-era settings, forges a relationship that leaps off the page and into the hearts of her readers."
—*Booklist*

"With this series, Balogh has created a wonderfully romantic world of Regency culture and society. Readers will miss the honorable Bedwyns and their mates; ending the series with Wulfric's story is icing on the cake. Highly recommended." —*Library Journal*

# First Comes Marriage

## MARY BALOGH

A DELL BOOK

FIRST COMES MARRIAGE
A Dell Book/ March 2009

Published by Bantam Dell
A Division of Random House, Inc.
New York, New York

This is a work of fiction. Names, characters, places, and incidents
either are the product of the author's imagination or are used
fictitiously. Any resemblance to actual persons, living or dead,
events, or locales is entirely coincidental.

*Book design by Diane Hobbing*

Dell is a registered trademark of Random House, Inc., and the
colophon is a trademark of Random House, Inc.

ISBN 978-0-440-24585-8

Printed in the United States of America
Published simultaneously in Canada

www.bantamdell.com

OPM 10 9 8 7 6 5 4 3 2 1

# First Comes Marriage

# PROLOGUE

WARREN Hall in Hampshire, principal country seat for generations past of the Earls of Merton, was surrounded by a large, well-landscaped park, in one secluded corner of which there was a small chapel, used nowadays almost exclusively for family weddings, christenings, and funerals since there was a sizable church in the village nearby for regular worship. It was generally a picturesque spot, especially during spring and summer, when the trees were laden with leaves and blossoms and the grass was green and flowers bloomed wild in the hedgerows and tame in the beds flanking the path leading to the church doors.

But this was early February, too early in the year even for the first of the snowdrops and primroses. And today it was raining. A chill wind tossed the bare branches of the trees against a leaden sky. It was the sort of day on which sensible folk remained indoors unless pressing business forced them out.

The man standing in the churchyard appeared to feel neither the cold nor the rain nor the call of the indoors. Nor was he admiring the scenery. He was holding his tall hat in one hand, and his dark, longish hair was plastered to his head and forehead. Water ran in rivulets down his face and neck to be absorbed by the fabric of his long black riding coat. Everything about him was black, in fact, except his face, and even that was dark-complexioned and quite un-English.

Given his surroundings, he looked somewhat sinister.

He was a young man, tall, long-limbed, lithe. His face was too rugged to be called handsome—it was long and narrow with high cheekbones and very dark eyes and a nose that had at some point in his life been broken and not set perfectly straight. The expression on his face was stern and forbidding. He was tapping a riding crop against his thigh.

If there had been any strangers close by, they would surely have given him a wide berth.

But there was no one, only his horse, which was grazing untethered nearby, apparently as oblivious to the cold and rain as its master.

He was standing at the foot of one particular grave—the newest, though a winter's frost and wind had obscured the freshness of its turned soil and given it a look little different from the others around it. Except that the gray headstone still looked very new.

The man's eyes were fixed on the second to last line of the inscription—"Aged Sixteen Years." And then beneath it, "Rest in Peace."

"He has found the man he was looking for, Jon," he said softly to the headstone. "And the odd thing is that you would have been delighted, would you not? You would have been happy and excited. You would have demanded to meet him, to befriend him, to love him. But no one thought to look for him until after you were dead."

The headstone offered no reply, and the corners of the man's mouth lifted in an expression that was more grimace than smile.

"You loved indiscriminately," he said. "You even loved me. *Especially* me."

He looked broodingly at the slight mound of earth beneath the headstone and thought of his brother buried six feet under it.

They had celebrated Jon's sixteenth birthday, the two of them, with all his favorite foods, including custard tarts and fruitcake, and with his favorite card games and a vigorous game of hide-and-seek that had continued for two whole hours until Jon had been exhausted and helpless with laughter—a fact that had made him ridiculously easy to find when it was his turn to hide. An hour later he had beamed up happily from beneath the covers of his bed before his brother blew out the candle and withdrew to his own room.

"Thank you for a lovely birthday party, Con," he had said in his newly deep voice, whose words and expression sounded incongruously childish. "It was the best ever."

It was something he said every year.

"I love you, Con," he had said as his brother bent over the candle. "I love you more than anyone else in the whole wide world. I love you forever and ever. Amen." He had giggled at the old joke. "Can we play again tomorrow?"

But when his brother had gone into his room the following morning to tease him about sleeping late now that he was sixteen and almost an old man, he had found Jon cold. He had been dead for several hours.

It had been a devastating shock.

But not really a surprise.

Children like Jon, the physician had warned their father soon after his birth, did not usually live much beyond their twelfth year. The child had had a large head and features that were flat and looked strangely mongoloid. He had been plump and ungainly. He had been slow to learn all the basic skills most children absorbed easily in early infancy. He had been slow-minded, though not by any means stupid.

He had, of course, always been called an idiot by almost everyone who encountered him—including his father.

There was perhaps only one thing at which he had excelled, and in that he had excelled utterly. He had loved. Always and unconditionally.

Forever and ever.

Amen.

Now he was dead.

And Con was going to be able to leave home—at last. He had left numerous times before, of course, though never for very long. There had always been the irresistible pull to return, especially as no one else at Warren Hall could be trusted to give Jon the time and the patience needed to keep him happy, though it had been an absurdly easy thing to do. Besides, Jon had always grieved and fretted if he was absent too long and had driven everyone to distraction with his incessant questions about the expected date of his return.

Now spring was coming and there was nothing to keep him here.

This time he would leave for good.

Why had he lingered even so long? Why had he not left the day after the funeral? Why had he come here every day of the winter since then? A dead boy did not need him.

Was it that *he* needed the dead?

His smile—or grimace—became more twisted.

He did not need anyone or anything. He had spent his whole life cultivating such a detachment. His instinct for survival had demanded it of him. He had lived here most of his life. His mother and father, who had raised him here, their firstborn son, were lying in their graves just beyond Jon's. He did not look in their direction. So were numerous brothers and sisters, none of whom had survived early infancy—only he, the eldest, and Jon, the youngest. Strange irony, that. The two undesirables had survived.

But now Jon too was gone.

Soon there would be another man here in his place.

"You will be able to do without me, Jon?" he asked softly.

He leaned forward and touched the hand that held the riding crop to the top of the headstone. It was cold and wet and hard and unyielding.

He could hear the approach of another horse—his own whinnied in greeting. His jaw tightened. It would be *him*. He could not leave him alone even here. Con did not turn. He would not acknowledge the man's presence.

But it was another voice that hailed him.

"*Here* you are, Con." The voice was cheerful. "I might have guessed it. I have been searching everywhere. Am I intruding?"

"No." Con straightened up and turned to squint up at Phillip Grainger, his neighbor and friend. "I came here to celebrate good news with Jon. The search has been successful."

"Ah." Phillip did not ask *which* search. He leaned forward to pat his horse's neck and stop it from prancing about. "Well, it was inevitable, I suppose. But this is devilish weather in which to be standing around in a churchyard. Come to the Three Feathers and I'll buy you a mug of ale. Maybe two. Or twenty. *You* can buy the twenty-first."

"An offer not to be resisted." Con set his hat back on his head, whistled for his horse, and swung into the saddle when it came trotting up.

"You will be leaving here, then?" Phillip asked.

"I have already been given my marching orders," Con told him, grinning rather wolfishly. "I am to leave within the week."

"Oh, I say." His friend grimaced.

"I'll not, though," Con added. "I'll not give him the satisfaction. I'll leave in my own good time."

He would stay against his own inclination and against a direct command in order to make a nuisance of himself. He had been doing that with considerable success for a whole year now.

He had done it all his life, in fact. It had been the surest way to draw his father's attention. Juvenile motive that, now that he came to think of it.

Phillip was chuckling.

"Deuce take it," he said, "but I'll miss you, Con. Though I could have lived quite happily this morning without having to hunt all over the countryside for you after being told at the house that you were out."

As they rode off, Con turned his head for one last look at his brother's grave.

Foolishly, he wondered if Jon would be lonely after he had gone.

And if *he* would be lonely.

# 1

EVERYONE within five miles of the village of Throckbridge in Shropshire had been in a spirit of heightened sensibilities for the week or so preceding February 14. Someone—the exact identity of the person was undecided though at least half a dozen laid claim to the distinction—had suggested that an assembly be held at the rooms above the village inn this year in celebration of St. Valentine's Day since it seemed like forever since Christmas, and summer—the occasion of the annual fete and ball at Rundle Park—was way off in the future.

The suggestion having been made—by Mrs. Waddle, the apothecary's wife, or Mr. Moffett, Sir Humphrey Dew's steward, or Miss Aylesford, spinster sister of the vicar, or by one of the other claimants—no one could quite explain why such an entertainment had never been thought of before. But since it *had* been thought of this year, no one was in any doubt that the Valentine's assembly would become an annual event in the village.

All were agreed that it was an inspired idea, even— or perhaps especially—those children who were not quite old enough to attend this year despite vociferous protests to the adults who made the rules. The youngest attendee was to be Melinda Rotherhyde, fifteen years old and allowed to go only because she was the youngest of the Rotherhyde brood and there could be no question of leaving her at home alone. And also allowed to attend, a few more critical voices added, because the Rotherhydes had always been overindulgent with all their offspring.

The youngest male was to be Stephen Huxtable. He was only seventeen, though there was never really any question of his *not* attending. Despite his youth, he was a favorite of females of all ages. Melinda in particular had sighed over him since the very moment three years before when she had been forced to renounce him as a frequent playmate because her mama had deemed their romping together no longer fitting considering their advancing ages and differing genders.

On the day of the assembly there was intermittent rain throughout the daylight hours, though nothing worse than that despite the dire prediction of six feet of snow that elderly Mr. Fuller had prophesied with much squinting and head nodding after church the previous Sunday. The assembly rooms above the inn had been dusted and swept, the wall sconces fitted with new candles, fires laid in the large hearths that faced each other across the room, and the pianoforte tested to see that it was still in tune—though no one had thought to wonder what would happen if it were not since the tuner lived twenty miles distant. Mr. Rigg brought his violin, tuned it, and played it for a while to limber up his fingers and get the feel of the room and its acoustics. Women brought food in quantities sufficient to stuff the five thousand so full that they would be prostrate for a week—or so Mr. Rigg declared as he sampled a jam tart and a few slices of cheese before having his hand slapped only half playfully by his daughter-in-law.

Throughout the village women and girls crimped and curled all day long and changed their minds half a dozen times about the gowns they would wear before inevitably settling upon their original choice. Almost all the unmarried women below the age of thirty—and a number of those of more advanced years—dreamed of St. Valentine and the possibilities of romance his day might bring this year if only . . .

Well, if only some Adonis would appear out of nowhere to sweep them off their feet. Or, failing that, if only some favored male acquaintance would deign to dance with them and notice their superior charms and . . .

Well, it *was* Valentine's Day.

And throughout the village men pretended to a yawning indifference to the whole tedious business of the assembly but made sure that their dancing shoes were polished and their evening coats brushed and the hands of the women of their choice solicited for the opening set. After all, the fact that this was St. Valentine's Day was sure to make the ladies a little more amenable to flirtation than they usually were.

Those too elderly either to dance or to flirt or to dream of romance on their own account looked forward to a good-sized gathering of gossips and card players—and to the sumptuous feast that was always the best part of village assemblies.

Apart from a few disgruntled older children, then, there was scarcely anyone who did not look forward to the evening's revelries with either open excitement or suppressed enthusiasm.

\* \* \*

There was one notable exception.

"A village *assembly,* for the love of God!" Elliott Wallace, Viscount Lyngate, was sprawled in his chair an hour before the event was due to begin, one long, booted leg hooked over the arm and swinging impatiently. "Could we have chosen a less auspicious day for our arrival here if we had tried, George?"

George Bowen, who was standing before the fire warming his hands, grinned at the coals.

"Tripping the light fantastic with a roomful of village maidens is not your idea of fine entertainment?" he asked. "Perhaps it is just what we need, though, to blow away the cobwebs after the long journey."

Viscount Lyngate fixed his secretary and friend with a steady gaze.

"*We?* The wrong pronoun, my dear fellow," he said. "*You* may feel the need to jig the night away. *I* would prefer a bottle of good wine, if any such commodity is available at this apology for an inn, the fire blazing up the chimney, and an early bed if no more congenial occupation presents itself. A village hop is *not* my idea of a more congenial occupation. In my experience those pastoral idylls one reads in which village maidens are not only numerous but also fair and buxom and rosy-cheeked *and* willing are entirely fictitious and not worth the paper they are written on. You will be dancing with ferret-faced matrons and their plain, simpering daughters, George, be warned. And making lame conversation with a dozen gentlemen with even duller minds than that of Sir Humphrey Dew."

That was admittedly a nasty thing to say. Sir Humphrey had been genial and hospitable. And dull.

"You will keep to your rooms, then?" George was still

grinning. "They might be vibrating to the sounds of fiddles and laughter for half the night, old chap."

Viscount Lyngate combed the fingers of one hand through his hair, sighing audibly as he did so. His leg continued to swing.

"Even that might be preferable to being led about on display like a performing monkey," he said. "Why could we not have come tomorrow, George? Tomorrow would have done just as well."

"So would yesterday," his friend pointed out with great good sense. "But the fact is that we came today."

Elliott scowled. "But if we had come yesterday," he said, "we might have been on our way home by now, our business accomplished, our young cub in tow."

"I doubt it will be as easy as you seem to expect," George Bowen said. "Even cubs need time to digest news they are not expecting and to pack their bags and bid their fond farewells. Besides, there are his sisters."

"Three of them." Elliott rested his elbow on the arm of the chair and propped his face in his hand. "But they are bound to be every bit as delighted as he. How could they not? They will be ecstatic. They will fall all over themselves in their haste to get him ready to leave with us at the earliest possible moment."

"For a man who has sisters of his own," George said dryly, "you are remarkably optimistic, Elliott. Do you really believe they will happily gather on their doorsill within the next day or two to wave their only brother on his way forever? And that then they will be willing to carry on with their lives here as if nothing untoward had happened? Is it not far more likely they will want to darn all his stockings and sew him half a dozen new shirts and . . . Well, and perform a thousand and one other useful and useless tasks?"

"Dash it all!" Elliott drummed his fingers on his raised thigh. "I have been trying to ignore the possibility that they might be an inconvenience, George. As females are more often than not. How simple and easy life would be without them. Sometimes I feel the distinct call of the monastery."

His friend looked at him incredulously and then laughed in open amusement mingled with derision.

"I know a certain widow who would go into deep mourning and an irreversible decline if you were to do that," he said. "Not to mention every unmarried lady of the *ton* below the age of forty. *And* their mamas. And did you not inform me as recently as yesterday on the journey down here that your main order of business during the coming Season is going to have to be the choosing of a bride?"

Elliott grimaced. "Yes, well," he said, his fingers pausing for a moment and then drumming faster. "The monastery may call with wistful invitation, George, but you are quite right—duty positively shouts it down, in the unmistakable voice of my grandfather. I promised him at Christmas . . . And of course he was quite right. It is time I married, and the deed will be done this year to coincide more or less with my thirtieth birthday. Nasty things, thirtieth birthdays."

He scowled in anticipation of the happy event, and his fingers beat a positive tattoo against his thigh.

"Perish the thought," he added.

Especially since his grandfather had made a specific point of informing him that Mrs. Anna Bromley-Hayes, Elliott's mistress of two years, simply would not do as his bride. Not that he had needed his grandfather to tell him that. Anna was beautiful and voluptuous and marvelously skilled in the bedroom arts, but she had also had a string of lovers before him, some of them while Bromley-Hayes was still alive. And she never made a secret of her amours. She was proud of them. Doubtless she intended to continue them with more lovers than just him at some time in the future.

"This is good," George said. "If you went into the monastery, Elliott, you would doubtless not need a secretary and I would be out of lucrative employment. I should hate that."

"Hmm." Elliott returned his foot to the floor and then crossed it over the other leg to rest his booted ankle above the knee.

He wished he had not thought of Anna. He had not seen her—or, more important, bedded her—since before Christmas. It was a damnably long time. Man was not made to be celibate, he had concluded long ago—another reason for avoiding the lure of the monastery.

"The three sisters will very probably be at the assembly tonight," George said. "Did not Sir Humphrey say that everyone and his dog will be attending—or words to that effect? Perhaps the cub will be there too."

"He is far too young," Elliott said.

"But we *are* deep in the country," his friend reminded him, "and far from the influence of all things *ton*nish. I'll wager on his being here."

"If you think that possibility will persuade me to attend," Elliott said, "you are much mistaken, George. I am not talking business with him tonight beneath the interested gaze of a villageful of gossips, for the love of God."

"But you can scout him out," George said. "We both can. And his sisters too. Besides, old chap, would it be quite the thing to absent yourself when Sir Humphrey Dew made such a point of waiting on you as soon as word reached him that you were here? And when he came in person specifically to invite us to the assembly and to offer to escort us upstairs and present us to everyone worthy of the honor? My guess is that that will be *everyone* without exception. He will not be able to resist."

"Do I pay you to be my conscience, George?" Elliott asked.

But George Bowen, far from looking cowed, only chuckled.

"How the devil did he discover that we were here, anyway?" Elliott asked, having worked himself into a thorough bad temper. "We arrived in this village and at this inn less than two hours ago, and no one knew we were coming."

George rubbed his hands together close to the heat of the fire and then turned resolutely away in the direction of his room.

"We are in the *country*, Elliott," he said again, "where news travels on the wind and on every blade of grass and every dust mote and every human tongue. Doubtless the lowliest scullery maid knows by now that you are in Throckbridge and is trying desperately—and in vain—to find another mortal who does *not* know. And everyone will have heard that you have been invited to the assembly as Sir Humphrey Dew's particular guest. Are you going to disappoint them all by keeping to your room?"

"Wrong pronoun again," Elliott said, pointing a finger. "I am not the only one everyone will have heard of. There is you too. *You* go and entertain them if you feel you must."

George clucked his tongue before opening the door to his room.

"I am a mere mister," he said. "Of mild interest as a stranger, perhaps, especially if I had arrived alone. But you are a *viscount,* Elliott, several rungs higher on the social ladder even than Dew. It will seem as if God himself had condescended to step into their midst." He paused a moment and then chuckled. "The Welsh word for God is *Duw*—my grandmother was always saying it—D-U-W, but pronounced the same way as our dear baronet's name. And yet you outrank him, Elliott. That is heady stuff, old boy, for a sleepy village. They have probably never set eyes upon a viscount before or ever expected to. Would it be sporting of you to deny them a glimpse of you? I am off to don my evening togs."

He was still chuckling merrily as he closed his door behind him.

Elliott scowled at its blank surface.

They had traveled here, the two of them, on business. Elliott deeply resented the whole thing. After a long, frustrating year during which his life had been turned upside down and inside out, he had expected soon to be free of the most irksome of the obligations his father's sudden death had landed on his shoulders. But that obligation, George's search and discovery had recently revealed, was actually far from over. It was not a discovery that had done anything to improve Elliott's almost perpetually sour mood.

He had not expected his father to die so young. His father's father, after all, was still alive and in vigorous good health, and the male line had been renowned for longevity for generations past. Elliott had expected many more years in which to be free to kick his heels and enjoy the carefree life of a young buck about town without any of the burdens of sober responsibility.

But suddenly he had had them, ready or not—just like the childhood game of hide-and-seek.

*Coming, ready or not.*

His father had died ignominiously in the bed of his mistress—a fact that had become one of the more enduring jokes among the *ton*. It had been less funny to Elliott's mother—not funny at all, in fact, even though she had long known, as everyone had, of her husband's infidelity.

Everyone but Elliott.

As well as longevity, the males of their line were also renowned for the long-term mistresses and their children that they kept in addition to their wives and legitimate offspring. His grandfather's liaison had come to an end only with the death of his mistress ten years or so ago. There had been eight children of that relationship. His father had left five behind, all comfortably provided for.

No one could accuse the Wallace men of not doing their part to populate the country.

Anna had no children—his or anyone else's. Elliott suspected that she knew a way of preventing conception, and he was glad of it. He had no children of other mistresses either.

He might have sent George down here alone, he reflected, bringing his mind back to the present situation. Bowen was perfectly capable of carrying out the business himself. Elliott had not needed to come in person.

But duty once embarked upon, he had found, imposed its own dreary code of honor, and so here he was in a part of the country that must be the very middle of nowhere even if it *was* picturesque—or would be once spring decided to show its face if George was to be believed.

They had put up at the only inn in Throckbridge, though it was but a country establishment with no pretension to elegance—it was not even a posting inn. They had intended to proceed to business before the afternoon was out. Elliott had hoped to begin the return journey tomorrow though George had predicted that another day, perhaps even two, was a distinct probability—and even that might be an overoptimistic estimate.

But the inn had proved to boast one fatal feature, as so many village inns did, dash it all. It had assembly rooms on the upper floor. And those rooms were to be put to use this very evening. He and George had had the singular misfortune of arriving on the day of a village dance. It really had not occurred to either of them that the inhabitants of a remote English village might take it into their heads to celebrate St. Valentine's Day. It had not even struck Elliott that this *was* St. Valentine's Day, for God's sake.

The assembly rooms were directly above his head as he continued to recline in his chair beside the fire despite the fact that it was not a vastly comfortable piece of furniture and the fire needed more coal and the bell rope was just out of his reach. The assembly rooms were also directly above his bedchamber. They were directly above *everything*. There would be no escaping the sounds and vibrations of prancing feet thumping over his bed for half the night. His ears would be assailed by merry music—doubtless inferior and inexpertly played—and loud voices and louder laughter.

He would be fortunate indeed if he were able to snatch one wink of sleep. Yet what else was there to do in this godforsaken place but try? He had not even brought a book with him—a massive oversight.

Sir Humphrey Dew, whom Elliott had never met before this afternoon, was the sort of gentleman who asked a thousand questions and answered nine hundred and ninety of them himself. He had asked them if they would do the village the honor of attending the ball and assured them that he was much obliged to them for their kind condescension in so honoring his humble self and neighborhood. He had asked them if he might call for them at eight and assured them that they were doing him far more honor than he would be doing them a favor. He asked if he might then present them to a select number of his neighbors and assured them that they would not be sorry to make the acquaintance of such agreeable and distinguished persons—though none as agreeable and distinguished as themselves, of course. Lady Dew would be ecstatic at their kind condescension. So would his daughters and daughter-in-law. He would live in pleasurable anticipation of the advent of eight o'clock.

Elliott might have said a firm no. He did not usually suffer fools gladly. But he had intended merely not to attend the assembly but to remain closeted in his room when the baronet arrived and to send his excuses via George. What were secretaries for, after all?

Sometimes they were for prodding their employers' conscience—damn their eyes.

For of course George was quite right. Elliott

Wallace, Viscount Lyngate, was—dash it all!—a gentle-man. He had given tacit acceptance to the invitation by not uttering a firm refusal. It would be ungentlemanly now to barricade himself inside the dubious privacy of his inn room. And if he did not attend the revelries, he would be disturbed by them all night long anyway and be in just as bad a mood at the end of it all. Worse—he would feel guilty.

Damn *everyone's* eyes!

And the boy might indeed be at the assembly, if George was in the right of it. His sisters almost cer-tainly would be. It might be as well to look them over this evening now that the opportunity had presented it-self, to get some impression of them all before calling upon them tomorrow.

But God bless us, would he be expected to *dance*?

To romp with the village matrons and maidens?

On Valentine's Day?

Surely not. He could scarcely imagine a less agree-able fate.

He set the heel of his hand to his brow and tried to convince himself that he had a headache or some other irrefutable excuse for taking to his bed. It could not be done, though. He never had headaches.

He sighed aloud.

Despite what he had told George, he was going to have to put in an appearance at this infernal village hop after all, then, was he not? It would be just too ill-mannered to stay away, and he was never openly ill-mannered. No true gentleman was.

Sometimes—and more and more often these days— it was a tedious business being a gentleman.

There must now be considerably less than an hour in

which to make himself presentable for the evening entertainment. It often took his man half an hour just to tie his neckcloth in a knot that satisfied his exacting valet's standards.

Elliott heaved both another sigh and his body to its feet.

In the future he was not going to venture anywhere beyond his own doors on February 14—or beyond Anna's doors anyway.

St. Valentine's, for God's sake!

Whatever next?

But the answer was all too painfully obvious.

A village assembly was next, that was what!

# 2

THE Huxtable family lived in a thatched, whitewashed cottage at one end of the main village street. Viscount Lyngate and his secretary would have driven past it on their way to the inn. It is doubtful they would have noticed it, though. Picturesque as it was, it was modest in size.

Small, in other words.

Three members of the family lived there. They had inhabited the grander, more spacious vicarage until eight years ago, until the Reverend Huxtable had gone to his heavenly reward—or so the new vicar had assured his congregation at the funeral. His children had moved out the day after the funeral to make way for the Reverend Aylesford and his sister.

Margaret Huxtable was now twenty-five years old. As the eldest of the family—their mother had died six years before their father—she was the one who, at the age of seventeen, had taken charge of the home and her siblings. She was still unmarried as a consequence and was likely to remain so for at least a few more years since Stephen, the youngest, was still only seventeen. No one had thought, perhaps, to point out to her that he was the same age now as she had been when she had shouldered such a huge responsibility. To her he was still just a boy. And heaven knew he needed *someone* to look after him.

Margaret was a rare beauty. Tall and generously proportioned, she had shining hair of a chestnut brown, large blue eyes fringed with dark lashes, and a classically lovely face. She was reserved and dignified in manner, though there was a time when she had been known more for the warmth and generosity of her character. There was also a thread of steel in her that was all too ready to show itself if anyone threatened the happiness or well-being of any of her siblings.

Because they had only one servant—Mrs. Thrush had remained with them after their move even though they could not really afford her, because she refused to leave or to accept more than her room and board in payment for her services—Margaret did a great deal of the housework herself and all the gardening. Her garden in summer was her pride and joy, one of the few outlets for the more sensual, spontaneous side of her nature. It was also the envy and delight of the village. She helped anyone who needed her and was often called out to assist the village physician in changing bandages or setting broken limbs or delivering babies or feeding gruel to the elderly and infirm.

Margaret had had a number of would-be suitors over the years, even a few who were willing to take her *and* her siblings, but she had quietly and firmly discouraged them all. Even the man she had loved all her life and would probably love until she went to her grave.

Katherine Huxtable was twenty. She too was beautiful in the tall, slender, willowy way of youth. She had a figure, though, that would mature well. Her hair was lighter than her sister's—a dark blond highlighted with golden threads that glinted in the sunlight. She had an eager, mobile, lovely face, her best feature being dark blue eyes that often seemed fathomless. For though she was good-natured and almost always cheerful in company, she loved also to be alone, to take solitary walks, to lose herself within her own imagination. She wrote poetry and stories whenever she had the time.

She taught the infants—the children aged four to five—at the village school three days a week and often helped the schoolmaster with older pupils on the other days.

Katherine too was unmarried though she was beginning to feel a little uneasy about her single state. She wanted to marry—of course she did. What else was there for a woman except to be a burden upon her relatives for the rest of her life? But though she had admirers galore and liked most of them, she could never decide which one she liked best. And that, she realized, probably meant she did not like any one of them sufficiently to marry him.

She had decided that it was sometimes a distinct disadvantage to be a dreamer. It would be far more comfortable to be a practical person without any imagination. Then she could simply choose the best candidate and settle into a worthy life with him. But she could not simply wave a magic wand and make herself into what she was not.

And so she could not make a choice. Not even a sensible one. Not yet, anyway, though the day would come, she supposed, when she would have to decide—or remain forever a spinster—and there would be an end of the matter.

Stephen Huxtable was tall and very slender, not

having yet quite grown into his man's body. And yet there was an energy and natural grace about him that saved him from appearing either thin or awkward. His hair was almost purely golden, and it fell about his head in soft curls that defied taming—much to his occasional despair and just as much to the eternal satisfaction of almost all who knew him. His face was handsome and brooding when it was not filled with laughter. His blue eyes gazed intensely at the world, the outer sign of a restless nature that had as yet not found sufficient outlet for his energy and curiosity and need to master his world.

He played hard. He rode and fished and swam and played sports and indulged in 101 other energetic activities with his peers. If there was any scrape to be got into, he was sure to be there. If there was any scheme to be dreamed up, he was sure to be the chief dreamer. He was liked and admired and followed almost worshipfully by all the boys and young men in the neighborhood. He was adored by women of all ages, who were charmed by his good looks and his smiles but were captivated most of all by the brooding restlessness of his eyes and lips. For what self-respecting woman can resist the challenge of taming a potential bad boy?

Not that he was bad . . . yet. He worked as diligently as he played. For as the only boy of the family, he was the privileged one. It was for him that Margaret had set aside the portion their mother had brought to her marriage so that when he was eighteen he would be able to go to university and thus secure a good future for himself in steady and perhaps even lucrative employment.

Much as Stephen sometimes chafed against the yoke of his eldest sister's authority, he understood too the sacrifice she was making for his sake. There was very little money left for her daily needs or for Katherine's.

He studied with the vicar and worked long and hard at his books. The career that a good education might bring him would be his means of escape from the confinement of life in the country. But because his was not an entirely selfish nature, he planned one day to repay his sisters for all they had done for him. Or, if they were married by then and did not need his support, then he would shower them and their children with gifts and favors.

That, at least, was his dream of the future. But in the meanwhile he worked to make his dream come true. And played hard too.

There was a fourth member of the family.

Vanessa, formerly Huxtable, now Dew, was twenty-four years old. She had married Hedley Dew, Sir Humphrey's younger son, when she was twenty-one and lost him a year later. She had been a widow for a year and a half now, but had remained at Rundle Park with her in-laws rather than return to the cottage to be an added financial burden there. Besides, her in-laws had wanted her to stay. They had needed her. She was a comfort to them, they had always assured her. How could anyone resist being needed? Besides, she was fond of them too.

Vanessa was the plain one of the family. She had always known it and had accepted it with cheerful resignation. She was not as tall as Margaret or Katherine. Neither was she small enough to be called petite. She was not as shapely as Margaret or as willowy as Katherine. The least said of her figure the better, in fact, since really there was nothing much to say. If the family hair color went in a descending scale from Margaret's vibrant chestnut through Katherine's gold-flecked dark blond to Stephen's golden, then Vanessa's fell somewhere on the line that was difficult to describe with a single word—or even a word with an adjective added. Her hair color was really quite uninteresting. And the hair itself had the misfortune of waving without curling. If ever she wore it loose, it fell in heavy ridges down her back rather than in a single shiny column like Margaret's.

And her face—well, it was a face on which all the features were exactly where they ought to be, and all of them functioned just as they ought. But there was nothing outstanding, nothing memorable, about any of them. Her eyes fell short of being blue though no other color quite described them either. Perhaps the best that could be said of her face was that it was not exactly ugly.

None of her family had ever called her ugly—they *loved* her. But she had been her father's favorite because she was willing to curl up in his study, reading, while he worked. And he had often told her that reading was a pastime she should continue to cultivate since it was very possible she would never have a home of her own to run. It was a roundabout way of telling her that she could never expect to marry. Her mother had stated the fact more baldly and had encouraged her to acquire housekeeping skills that she could offer Stephen and his wife after he married—or Margaret or Katherine after *they* married. She had been her mother's favorite too.

Her parents had felt a special tenderness for their plain Jane—her father had sometimes called her that with a fondness that had taken any sting out of the words.

But she *had* married. She was the only one of the family to have done so thus far, in fact.

She had always marveled over the fact that Hedley Dew had loved her so passionately, since he had been as beautiful as a god. But he had. Loved her passionately, that was.

Vanessa was not the sort of person to resent her sisters—or even her brother—for being better-looking than she. And she was certainly not the sort to hate herself merely because she was not beautiful.

She was as she was.

Plain.

And she adored her siblings. She would do anything in the world to secure their happiness.

She left Rundle Park on foot early in the afternoon of St. Valentine's Day, as she did three or four times every week, in order to call upon Margaret at the cottage. They had always been each other's best friend.

She set out on her walk at perhaps almost the exact time when Viscount Lyngate and George Bowen were settling into their rooms at the inn, blissfully unaware of what was in store for them for the rest of the day.

And Vanessa herself was unaware of their arrival—of their very existence, in fact.

Fate very often creeps up upon people without any warning.

She walked briskly. It was a chilly day. And she had something particular to tell her sister.

"I am *going*," she announced as soon as she had removed her winter cloak and bonnet inside the cottage door and greeted her sister in the parlor.

"To the assembly?" Margaret was seated beside the fire, busy as usual with her needlework, though she looked up to smile warmly at her sister. "I am so glad you have decided, Nessie. It would have been a shame for you to stay away."

"Mama-in-law has been urging me for the past week to go," Vanessa said. "And last evening Papa-in-law himself told me that I must attend and moreover that I must dance."

"That was very kind of him," Margaret said, "but no more than I would expect him to say. And it is high time. Hedley has been gone for well over a year."

"I know." Tears threatened, but Vanessa blinked them away. "Which is exactly what Papa-in-law said. I cannot mourn forever, he told me, and Mama-in-law nodded her agreement. And then we all had a little weep and the matter was settled. I am going." She smiled a slightly watery smile as she took a chair close to the fire.

"What do you think?" her sister asked, shaking out the garment she had been working on and holding it up for Vanessa's inspection.

It was Katherine's primrose yellow evening gown, which had been looking slightly limp and tired when she wore it at Christmas. It was at least three years old. Now it sported shining blue ribbon sewn in two bands close to the hem and in one thin band around the edges of the short sleeves.

"Oh, very smart indeed," Vanessa said. "It makes the dress look almost new again. Did you find the ribbon in Miss Plumtree's shop?"

"I did," Margaret said. "And a pretty penny it cost too. Cheaper than a new gown, however."

"And did you buy some for yourself too?" Vanessa asked.

"No," her sister said. "My blue gown is just fine as it is."

Except that it was even older than Katherine's yellow—and more faded. But Vanessa made no comment. Even the one length of ribbon was an extravagance that would have put a dent in Margaret's purse. *Of course* she would not have spent so recklessly on herself.

"It is," she agreed cheerfully. "And who notices your dresses anyway when the person inside them is so beautiful?"

Margaret laughed as she got to her feet to drape the dress over the back of an empty chair.

"And all of twenty-five years old," she said. "Goodness, Nessie, where has the time gone?"

For Margaret it had gone in caring for her siblings. On being unswervingly unselfish in her devotion to them. She had rejected a number of marriage offers, including the one from Crispin Dew, Hedley's older brother.

And so Crispin, who had always wanted to be a military officer, had gone off to war without her. That was four years ago. Vanessa was as sure as she could be that there had been an understanding between them before he left, but apart from a few messages in his letters to Hedley, Crispin had not communicated directly with Margaret in all that time. Nor had he been back home. One could say that he had not had any chance to come home with the country constantly at war as it was, and that it would have been improper anyway for a single gentleman to engage in a correspondence with a single lady. But even so, four years of near-silence was a very long time. Surely a really ardent lover would have found a way.

Crispin had not found one.

Vanessa strongly suspected that her sister was nursing a severely bruised heart. But it was one thing they never spoke of, close as they were.

"What will *you* be wearing this evening?" Margaret asked when her question was not answered. But how could one answer such a question? Where *did* time go?

"Mama-in-law wants me to wear my green," Vanessa said.

"And will you?" Margaret settled in her chair again and for once sat with idle hands.

Vanessa shrugged and looked down at her gray wool dress. She had still not been able to persuade herself to leave off her mourning entirely.

"It might appear that I had forgotten him," she said.

"And yet," Margaret reminded her—as if she needed reminding, "Hedley bought you the green because he thought the color particularly suited you."

He had bought it for the summer fete a year and a half ago. She had worn it only once—to sit beside his sickbed on that day while the revelries proceeded in the garden below.

He had died two days later.

"Perhaps I will wear it tonight," she said. Or perhaps she would wear the lavender, which did not suit her at all but was at least half mourning.

"Here comes Kate," Margaret said, looking through the window and smiling, "in more of a hurry than usual."

Vanessa turned her head to see their youngest sister waving to them from the garden path.

A minute later she burst in upon them, having divested herself of her outdoor garments in the hallway.

"How was school today?" Margaret asked.

"Impossible!" Katherine declared. "Even the children are infected with excitement about this evening. Tom Hubbard stopped by to ask me for the opening set, but I had to say no because Jeremy Stoppard had already reserved it with me. I will dance the second set with Tom."

"He will ask you again to marry him," Vanessa warned.

"I suppose so," Katherine agreed, sinking into the chair closest to the door. "I suppose he would die of shock if I were to say yes one of these times."

"At least," Margaret said, "he would die happy."

They all laughed.

"But Tom brought startling news with him," Katherine said. "There is a *viscount* staying at the inn. Have you ever heard the like?"

"At *our* inn?" Margaret asked her. "No, I never have. Whatever for?"

"Tom did not know," Katherine said. "But I can imagine that he—the viscount, that is—will be the main topic of conversation this evening."

"Goodness me, yes," Vanessa agreed. "A viscount in Throckbridge! It may never be the same again. I wonder how he will enjoy the sounds of music and dancing above his head for half the night. It is to be hoped that he does not demand we stop."

But Katherine had spotted her dress. She jumped to her feet with an exclamation of delight.

"Meg!" she cried. "Did *you* do this? How absolutely lovely it looks! I will be the envy of everyone tonight. Oh, you really ought not to have. The ribbon must have cost the earth. But I am so glad you did. Oh, thank you, thank you."

She dashed across the room to hug Margaret, who beamed with pleasure.

"The ribbon caught my eye," she said, "and I could not possibly leave the shop before I had bought a length of it."

"You want me to believe it was an impulsive purchase?" Katherine said. "What a bouncer, Meg. You went there deliberately to look for some suitable trimming just because you wanted to do something nice for me. I know you of old."

Margaret looked sheepish.

"Here comes Stephen," Vanessa said, "in more of a hurry than Kate was."

Their brother saw Vanessa looking out at him and grinned and waved a greeting. He was wearing his old riding clothes, she could see, and boots that looked as if they were in dire need of a good brushing. Sir Humphrey Dew allowed him to ride the horses from the Rundle stables whenever he wished, a favor Stephen had accepted gladly, but in return he insisted upon doing some work in the stables.

"I say," he said, bursting into the parlor a minute later, smelling of horse, "have you heard the news?"

"Stephen." Margaret looked pained. "Is that *manure* on one of your boots?"

The smell alone would have answered her question.

"Oh, dash it." He looked down. "I thought I had

cleaned it all off. I'll do it right away. Have you heard about the viscount staying at the inn?"

"*I* told them," Katherine said.

"Sir Humphrey has gone to bid him welcome," Stephen told them.

"Oh," Vanessa said with a slight grimace.

"I daresay," Stephen said, "he will find out what the man is doing here. It is a strange thing, is it not?"

"I suppose," Margaret said, "he is just passing through, poor man."

"Lucky man," Stephen said. "But whoever *passes through* Throckbridge? *From* where *to* where? And *why*?"

"Perhaps Papa-in-law will find out," Vanessa said. "And perhaps he will not. But doubtless we will all live on even if our curiosity is never satisfied."

"Perhaps," Katherine said, clasping her hands to her bosom and batting her eyelids theatrically as she twirled once about, "he has heard of the Valentine's ball and has come here to seek a bride."

"Oh, Lord," Stephen said. "Has Valentine's Day turned you daft, Kate?"

He laughed and ducked away from the cushion she hurled at his head.

The parlor door opened again to admit Mrs. Thrush. She had Stephen's best shirt over one arm.

"I have just ironed it, Mr. Stephen," she told him as he thanked her and took it from her. "You take it up to your room immediately and lay it flat on your bed. I do not want to see it all creases again even before you put it on."

"No, ma'am," he said, winking at her. "I mean, yes, ma'am. I did not even realize it needed ironing."

"No." She clucked her tongue. "I don't suppose you

did. But if all the young girls are going to be swooning over you, as I daresay they will, you might as well be wearing a freshly ironed shirt. And *not* those boots. Phew! I'll have you down scrubbing my floors with your own hands if you do not take them off and set them outside the door before you go upstairs."

"The ironing was to be my next task," Margaret said. "Thank you, Mrs. Thrush. Now I think it is time we all thought about getting ready for the assembly. Nessie, it is certainly time you went home before Lady Dew sends out a search party. Stephen, do get those disgusting boots out of this parlor. Mrs. Thrush, please make yourself a cup of tea and put your feet up for a while. You have been busy all day."

"And you have been sitting around doing nothing, I suppose," Mrs. Thrush retorted. "Oh, I must tell you all. Mrs. Harris knocked on the back door not five minutes since. There is a viscount staying at the inn. Sir Humphrey went to call on him there and has invited him to the assembly as his particular guest. What do you think of *that*?"

She looked a little surprised when they all burst out laughing, but then she joined them.

"Poor man," she said. "He probably didn't have any choice with Sir Humphrey. And I suppose it is just as well if he does go to the dance. The inn would be pretty noisy for anyone trying to get some rest."

"There you are, Kate," Stephen said. "If he has come looking for a bride, this is your chance."

"Or Miss Margaret's," Mrs. Thrush said. "She is as pretty as a picture. It is time her prince came riding by."

Margaret laughed.

"But this man is only a *viscount*," she said, "and I absolutely insist upon waiting for a prince to ride by. Now move, everyone, or we are going to be late."

She hugged Vanessa as her sister prepared to leave the room.

"Don't change your mind about this evening," she said. "Come, Nessie. Indeed, if you do not, I may well have to leave the inn and come to get you. It is time for you to enjoy life again."

Vanessa walked alone back to Rundle Park, having refused Stephen's offer to escort her. She was definitely going to the assembly, she thought, though she had not been *quite* sure about it even when she had arrived at the cottage. She was going. And despite herself—despite lingering grief for Hedley and a certain guilt over even *thinking* of enjoying herself again—she was looking forward to the evening with some eagerness. Dancing had always been one of her favorite activities, yet she had not danced for more than two years.

Was it selfish, heartless, to want to live again?

Her mother-in-law wanted her to go. So did her sisters-in-law. And Sir Humphrey—Hedley's *father*—had even told her she must dance.

Would anyone offer to partner her, though?

Surely *someone* would.

She would dance if someone asked her.

Perhaps the viscount . . .

She chuckled aloud at the absurd thought as she turned onto the footpath that was a shortcut to the house.

Perhaps the viscount was ninety years old and bald and toothless.

*And* married.

# 3

"I WISH," Louisa Rotherhyde said as she stood with Vanessa in the assembly rooms watching all the late arrivals and nodding and smiling in greeting at any acquaintance—at *everyone,* in other words—who passed close to them, "Viscount Lyngate would turn out to be tall, blond, and handsome and no more than twenty-five years old and charming and amiable and not at all high in the instep. And I wish he would turn out to like dumpy, mousy-haired females of very modest fortunes—well, no fortune at all, in fact—and marginally agreeable manners and years to match his own. I suppose I need not wish that he were rich. Doubtless he is."

Vanessa fanned her face and laughed.

"You are not dumpy," she assured her friend. "And your hair is a pretty shade of light brown. Your manners are very agreeable indeed, and your character is your fortune. And you have a lovely smile. Hedley used to say so."

"Bless his heart," Louisa said. "But the viscount has a friend with him. Perhaps *he* will see fit to become passionately attached to me—if he should happen to be personable, that is. And it would help if he were in possession of a sizable fortune too. It is all very well, Nessie, to have dances and assemblies and dinners and parties and picnics galore, but one always sees exactly the same faces at every entertainment. Do you never wish for London and a Season and beaux and . . . Ah, but of course you do not. You had Hedley. He was beautiful."

"Yes, he was," Vanessa agreed.

"Did Sir Humphrey describe Viscount Lyngate to you?" Louisa asked hopefully.

"He described him as an agreeable young gentleman," Vanessa said. "But to Father-in-law anyone below the age of his own sixty-four years is young, and almost everyone is agreeable. He sees his own good nature in everyone. And no, Louisa, he did *not* describe the viscount's looks. Gentlemen do not, you know. I do believe we are about to find out for ourselves, however."

Her father-in-law had entered the assembly rooms, looking important in his genial way, his chest thrust out with pride, his palms rubbing together, his complexion ruddy with pleasure. Behind him were two gentlemen, and there was no doubting who they were. There were very rarely any strangers in Throckbridge. Of the few there had been in living memory, none—not a single one—had ever attended a dance at the assembly rooms and precious few had ever been to the annual summer ball at Rundle Park.

These two were strangers—*and* they were at the assembly.

And one of them, of course, was a *viscount*.

The one who stepped into the room first behind Sir Humphrey was of medium height and build, though there was perhaps a suggestion of portliness about his middle. He had brown hair that was short and neatly combed, and a face that was saved from ordinariness by the open, pleasing amiability with which he observed the scene about him. He looked as if he were genuinely glad to be here. He was conservatively dressed in a dark blue coat with gray breeches and white linen. While probably past the age of twenty-five, he certainly still qualified for the epithet *young*.

Louisa plied her fan and sighed audibly. So did a number of the other ladies present.

But Vanessa's eyes had moved to the other gentleman, and she knew immediately that it was he who had provoked the sigh. She did not participate in it. Her mouth had turned suddenly dry, and for a few timeless moments she lost all awareness of her surroundings.

He was about the same age as the other gentleman, but there all similarities ended. He was tall and slim without being in any way thin. Indeed, his shoulders and chest were solidly built while his waist and hips were slender. His legs were long and muscled in all the right places. He had very dark hair, almost black, in fact, and it was thick and shining and cut expertly to look both tidy and disheveled at the same time. His face was bronzed and classically handsome with an aquiline nose, well-defined cheekbones, and the hint of a cleft in his chin. He had a firmly set mouth. He looked slightly foreign, as if perhaps he had some Italian or Spanish blood.

He looked gorgeous.

He looked perfect.

She might have fallen headlong in love with him, along with at least half the other ladies present, if she had not noticed something else about him. Two things, in fact.

He looked insufferably arrogant.

And he looked bored.

His eyelids were half drooped over his eyes. He held a quizzing glass in his hand, though he did not raise it to his eye. He looked about the room as if he could not quite believe the shabbiness of his surroundings.

There was not even the faintest suggestion of a smile on his lips. Instead, there was a hint of disdain as if he could not wait to get back downstairs to his room. Or, better yet, far away from Throckbridge.

He looked as if this were the last place on earth he wanted to be.

And so she did *not* fall in love with him, magnificent and godlike as he undoubtedly was to the eyes. He had stepped into *her* world, into the world of her family and friends, uninvited, and found it inferior and undesirable. How dared he! Instead of brightening her evening, as the presence of any stranger ought to have done—especially a handsome gentleman—he was actually threatening to spoil it.

For everyone, of course, would fawn over him. No one would behave naturally. No one would relax and enjoy the dancing. And no one would talk of anyone else but him for days—or more likely weeks—to come.

As if some god had favored them by dropping into their midst.

And yet it seemed clear to her that he despised them all—or that at the very least he found them all a colossal bore.

She wished he had come tomorrow—or not at all.

He was dressed all in black and white, a fashion she had heard was all the crack in London. When she had heard it, she had thought *how very dull, how very unattractive.*

She had been wrong, of course.

He looked sleek, elegant, and perfect.

He looked like every woman's ideal of a romantic hero. Like that Adonis they all dreamed of, especially on St. Valentine's Day, come to sweep them off their feet and onto his prancing white courser and away to a happily-forever-after in his castle in the clouds—white, fluffy ones, not damp, gray, English ones.

But Vanessa deeply resented him. If he despised them and their offered entertainment so much, he could at least have had the decency to look like a gargoyle.

She heard the echo of the sigh that had wafted about the assembly rooms like a breeze and fervently hoped she had not shared in it.

"Which one do you suppose is Viscount Lyngate?" Louisa asked in a whisper—necessary in the hush that had fallen over the room—as she leaned closer to Vanessa's right ear.

"The handsome one, without a doubt," Vanessa said. "I would wager on it."

"Ah," Louisa said, regret in her voice. "I think so too. He is impossibly gorgeous even if he is *not* blond, but he does not look as if he would be bowled over by my charms, does he?"

No, he certainly did not. Or by anyone else's from this humble, obscure corner of the world. His whole bearing suggested a man with an enormous sense of his own consequence. He was probably only ever bowled over by his own charms.

*What on earth* was he doing in Throckbridge? Had he taken a wrong turn somewhere?

The gentlemen did not remain long in the doorway.

Sir Humphrey led them about, a broad smile of satisfaction on his face as if he were solely responsible for bringing them to the village on this of all days. He presented them to almost everyone present, beginning with Mrs. Hardy at the pianoforte, Jamie Latimer on the flute, and Mr. Rigg on the violin. Soon after, the gentlemen were bowing to Margaret and Katherine. And a few moments after that, they were nodding to Stephen and Melinda and Henrietta Dew, Vanessa's sister-in-law, and the group of other very young people gathered with them.

"I do think everyone ought to start talking again in more than whispers," Vanessa whispered.

The shorter gentleman exchanged a few words with everyone, she noticed. And he smiled and looked interested. The other gentleman—undoubtedly Viscount Lyngate—remained virtually silent and totally intimidated everyone. Vanessa suspected that it was quite deliberate. His eyebrows rose when he was introduced to Stephen, giving him a look of great aristocratic hauteur.

And of course Melinda was giggling.

"Why is he here?" Louisa asked, still in a whisper. "In Throckbridge, that is. Did Sir Humphrey say?"

"They told him they were here on business," Vanessa said. "They must not have explained what it was or Father-in-law would not have been able to resist telling us."

"Business?" Louisa sounded both puzzled and amazed. "In *Throckbridge*? Whatever can it be?"

Vanessa had, of course, been wondering the same thing ever since Katherine had brought word of his arrival this afternoon. How could she not? How could *anyone* not? Whatever business could anyone have in a sleepy backwater like Throckbridge, picturesque as it was, especially in the summer, and dear as it was to her?

What business could a *viscount* have here?

And what business did he have looking down upon them all as if they were mere worms beneath his expensive dancing shoes?

She did not know the answers and perhaps never would. But there was no time for further speculation—not now anyway. Her father-in-law was bringing the two gentlemen their way. Vanessa wished he would not, but she realized that it was inevitable.

Sir Humphrey smiled jovially from Vanessa to Louisa.

"And this is the eldest Miss Rotherhyde," he announced, and added, with a lamentable lack of tact and questionable truth, "and the beauty of the family."

Louisa hung her head in obvious mortification and curtsied low.

"And Mrs. Hedley Dew, my dear daughter-in-law," Sir Humphrey added, beaming at Vanessa. "She was married to my son until his unfortunate demise over a year ago. Viscount Lyngate, ladies, and Mr. Bowen."

Vanessa had made the right identification, then. But she had never doubted it. She curtsied.

"Ma'am," Mr. Bowen said, bowing and addressing her with a charming but sympathetic smile, "my deepest commiserations."

"Thank you," she said while she was aware of Viscount Lyngate's eyes fixed on her. She had worn her lavender gown after all as a slight salve to her conscience for deciding to come to enjoy herself—though she *knew* Hedley would have urged her to wear the green. It was not a vibrant lavender, and it had never fit quite right. She knew it was a dreary garment that did not become her at all.

She hated herself at that moment for minding, for wishing she had chosen the green after all.

"I insisted that she come to the assembly tonight," Sir Humphrey explained. "She is far too young and pretty to mourn forever, as I am sure you would agree, gentlemen. She was good to my boy while he lived, and that is what counts. I have insisted that she must dance too. Has anyone solicited your hand for the first set, Nessie?"

She had grimaced inwardly at his opening words. She could have sunk through the floor at his last. She *knew* what he was going to say next.

"No, Papa," she said hastily before it occurred to her that she might have lied. "But—"

"Then I do not doubt one of these gentlemen would be delighted to lead you into the opening set," he said, rubbing his hands together and beaming at her.

There was a tiny silence while Vanessa fervently wished she could join poor Hedley in the grave.

"Perhaps, Mrs. Dew," the viscount said—his voice was deep and velvet-toned, to add to his other physical perfections, "you would do me the honor?"

She was being asked to dance with a *viscount*. With *this* viscount, this most glorious of male creatures. This arrogant . . . popinjay. But sometimes her sense of the ridiculous came close to being her undoing. Whatever must the viscount be thinking? She almost laughed aloud and dared not glance Margaret's way. But mortification quickly outpaced any amusement she was feeling. How absolutely *awful* that the assembly should begin this way.

Was it her imagination that the whole room hung upon her response?

Of course it was not.

Oh, goodness gracious. She really ought to have insisted upon remaining at home with a book and her memories.

"Thank you." She curtsied again and regarded the hand stretched out for hers with some fascination. It was as fine and as well manicured as any lady's. And yet there was nothing remotely effeminate about it.

Or about him, of course. Close up, he looked even taller and more solid and powerful than he had from across the room. She could smell a subtle masculine cologne. She could feel the heat of his aura.

And there was one other thing about his face, she noticed as she set her hand on his and looked up at him. His eyes were not dark, as his hair and complexion had led her to expect, but were of the deepest, clearest blue. They looked back at her keenly from beneath those still-drooped lids.

His hand was solid and warm.

Well, she thought as he led her toward the lines that were forming and Mr. Rigg played a nervous little trill on his fiddle, this was an evening she was not going to forget in a hurry. She was to dance with a handsome, proud viscount—and the opening set, no less. She wished she could go home afterward and share the fun with Hedley.

*"Nessie?"* Viscount Lyngate said as he settled her in the line of ladies and prepared to depart for the gentlemen's line opposite. His eyebrows were raised again. He was not addressing her. He was asking a question.

"Vanessa," she explained, and then wished she had not said it in such an apologetic way.

She did not hear clearly what he said in response as he stepped into the line opposite her own, but she thought it was "Thank God!"

Had he really said it?

She looked keenly at him, but he did not repeat the words, whatever they had been.

She had never liked the shortened form of her name. Nessie Dew sounded like such a . . . plain woman. But even so, it was none of his business what her family and friends chose to call her.

The men on either side of Viscount Lyngate looked awed and slightly uncomfortable. So would the ladies on either side of her if she turned her head to look, Vanessa guessed.

He was going to ruin the assembly for them all. They had been looking forward to it so very much. Yet it meant less than nothing to him. He was looking up and down the lines, not even trying to hide his boredom.

Oh, dear. She was not usually so harsh in her judgments, especially of strangers—not that she saw many of those. Why were her thoughts about Viscount Lyngate so . . . well, spiteful? Was it because she felt too embarrassed to admit to herself that she had very nearly tumbled into love with him?

How very ridiculous *that* would have been—the classic case of Beauty and the Beast, with no one in any doubt at all about which was which.

She reminded herself suddenly that she had been all too eager to give in to the urging of her in-laws and Meg and Kate that she come to the assembly tonight. And after she *had* given in, she had hoped with bated breath and crossed fingers that someone would ask her to dance.

Well, someone had asked her even if he *had* been more or less coerced. And he could not possibly be more handsome or more distinguished in every way. One could say that her wildest dream for the evening had come true.

She would enjoy herself then, regardless.

Suddenly she was aware of her family and friends and neighbors about her, all dressed in their best finery, all in a festive mood. She was aware of the fires crackling in the two hearths and the candles guttering in the draft from the door. She was aware of the smells of perfumes and food.

And she was aware of the gentleman standing opposite her waiting for the music to begin. And looking at her from beneath those drooped eyelids.

She was *not* going to allow him to believe that she was in awe of him. She was *not* going to allow him to render her speechless and incoherent.

The music began, and Vanessa smiled with deliberate brilliance and prepared for as much conversation as the measures of the dance would allow.

But most of all she gave herself up to the sheer joy of dancing again.

Of all the partners with whom he might have chosen to dance, Elliott reflected as the music struck up and the line of gentlemen bowed while the line of ladies curtsied, Mrs. Vanessa Dew—*Nessie,* for the love of God!— would surely not have been one of them.

She was Sir Humphrey's daughter-in-law. That was

bad enough. She was also an insignificant dab of a woman of medium height, who was altogether too slender and too small-breasted for his taste, her hair too mousy, her features too plain. Her eyes were a nondescript gray. And lavender as a color definitely did not suit her. Even if it had, the dress itself was hideous. She was not in the first blush of youth either.

She was the very antithesis of Anna and indeed of any lady with whom he usually chose to dance at *ton* balls.

But here he was dancing with her anyway. George would have spoken up if he had not, he supposed, but it had been obvious whom Dew had expected to speak up. And so he had been the performing monkey after all.

That fact did not make him feel any more cheerful about the evening's revelries.

And then, just as they began to dance, Mrs. Dew smiled dazzlingly at him, and he was forced to admit that perhaps she was not quite the antidote he had taken her for. It was not a flirtatious smile, he was relieved to notice when after the first moment she looked away from him and smiled in the same way at everything and everyone, as if she had never enjoyed herself more in her life. She fairly sparkled.

How anyone could find even a small measure of delight in such an insipid rural entertainment escaped his understanding, but perhaps she had little with which to compare it.

The rooms were small and cramped, the walls and ceilings bare of ornament—except for one large and hideous sketch over the fireplace of an obese Cupid shooting his arrows. The air was slightly musty as if the rooms were shut up for most of the year—as they doubtless were. The music was enthusiastic but inferior—the violin was half a tone out of tune and the pianist had a tendency to gallop along as if she were anxious to finish the piece before she could hit any wrong notes. Several candles came close to dying every time a door was opened and a draft attacked them. Everyone talked at once—and at ear-shattering volume. And it seemed that everyone was very much aware of his presence and was at great pains not to show it.

Mrs. Dew danced well at least. She was light on her feet and there was rhythm and grace in her movements.

He wondered idly if her husband had been the eldest son. How had she attracted him? Did her father have money? Had she married him, perhaps, because she had expected to be Lady Dew one day?

George, he could see, was dancing with the lady who had been standing with Mrs. Dew—the eldest daughter of a family whose name Elliott could not recall. And if she was the beauty of the family, heaven help the rest of them.

The younger of the two Huxtable sisters—Miss Katherine Huxtable—was also dancing. The elder was not but stood watching with Lady Dew. He had not been introduced to the third sister. She must have remained at home.

The elder Miss Huxtable was extremely handsome but was certainly no young girl—just as one might expect, of course, of the senior sibling of a family in which the parents were both deceased. She had probably been responsible for the care of the others for a number of years. He could feel some sympathy for her. Miss Katherine Huxtable looked somewhat like her though she was considerably younger and more animated. She also was ravishingly beautiful despite a faded, shabby gown that someone had tried to disguise with new ribbon.

Stephen Huxtable was indeed a young cub. Tall and slender and coltish, he was seventeen years old and looked it. He was also very attractive to the young ladies despite his youth. They had clustered about him before the dancing began, and though he had chosen a partner, there were two other young ladies on either side of her in the line who were giving him at least as much attention as they were giving their own more plodding partners.

His laughter wafted down the line toward Elliott, causing him to purse his lips. He hoped the laughter did not denote a careless mind and a shallow character. He had already lived through a difficult year. Let there not be something equally trying in store for him for the next four.

"You came to Throckbridge at an auspicious time, my lord," Mrs. Dew said when the figures of the dance brought them together for a few moments.

Because it was St. Valentine's Day, he supposed, and there was a dance at the assembly rooms of the inn where he had the great good fortune to be staying.

"Indeed, ma'am." He raised his eyebrows.

"Auspicious for *us*, perhaps." She laughed as they parted company, and he understood that his tone, if not his words, had been less than gracious.

"I have not danced in more than two years," she told him when they came together again and joined hands in order to turn once about, "and am quite, quite determined to enjoy it no matter what. You are a good dancer."

He raised his eyebrows again but made no reply. What did one say to such an unexpected compliment? But then what had she meant by that *no matter what*?

She laughed once more as they returned to their places.

"You are not, I perceive," she said the next time, "a conversationalist, my lord."

"I find it impossible to converse meaningfully in thirty-second bursts, ma'am," he told her, an edge to his voice. Particularly when every villager appeared to be shrieking at every other villager with no one left to listen—and the orchestra played louder to drown them out. He had never heard such a hideous din in his whole life.

Predictably, she laughed.

"But if you wish," he said, "I will pay you a compliment each time we meet. Thirty seconds will suffice for that."

They parted before she could reply, but instead of being quelled by his words, as he had intended, she laughed across at him with her eyes while Huxtable twirled his partner down the set and they all prepared to dance the figures over again.

"Most ladies," he said the next time he met his partner and turned back-to-back with her, "have to wear jewels in their hair to make it sparkle. The natural gold in yours does it for you." It was a rather outrageous claim since her hair was distinctly mousy, though the candlelight *did* flatter it, it was true.

"Oh, well done," she said.

"You outshine every other lady present in every imaginable way," he told her the time after that.

"Ah, not so well done," she protested. "No lady of

sense likes to be so atrociously flattered. Only those who are conceited."

"You are not conceited, then?" he asked her. She had precious little to be conceited about, it was true.

"You may certainly tell me, if you wish, that I am ravishingly beautiful," she said, turning her laughing face up to his, "but not that I am more ravishingly beautiful than anyone else. That would be too obvious a lie and I might disbelieve you and fall into a decline."

He looked at her with unwilling appreciation as she danced away. She had a certain wit, it would appear. He almost laughed aloud, in fact.

"You are quite ravishingly beautiful, ma'am," he told her as they clasped hands at the top of the set.

"Thank you, sir." She smiled at him. "You are kind."

"But then," he said as he began to twirl her down between the lines, "so is every other lady present tonight—without exception."

She threw back her head and laughed with glee, and for a brief moment he smiled back.

Good Lord, was he *flirting* with her?

With a dab of a plain woman who was not dazzled by his rank or greedy for his compliments? But who danced for all the world as if life held no greater joy?

He was surprised when the set ended. What, *already*?

"Is there not a *third* Miss Huxtable?" he asked her as he was leading her back to the spot at which he had met her.

"A third?" She looked inquiringly at him.

"I was presented to Miss Huxtable, the dark-haired lady standing over there," he said, nodding in her direction, "and to Miss Katherine Huxtable, her younger sister. But I thought there was a third."

She looked keenly at him, saying nothing for a moment.

"There is not a third *Miss Huxtable*," she said, "though there *is* a third sister. I am she."

"Ah," he said, his hand going to the handle of his quizzing glass. "I was not informed that one of the sisters had been married."

And poor woman, she had certainly been passed by in the looks department in that family, had she not?

"*Ought* you to have?" Her eyebrows arched upward in evident surprise.

"Not at all," he said briskly. "It was merely idle curiosity on my part. Was your husband Sir Humphrey's eldest son?"

"No," she said. "He was the younger of two. Crispin is the elder."

"I am sorry about your husband's demise," he said. A foolish thing to say really since he had not known the man and it had happened quite a while ago. "It must have been a nasty shock."

"I knew when I married him," she said, "that he was dying. He had consumption."

"I am sorry," he said again.

How the devil had he got himself into this?

"So am I," she said, unfurling her fan and plying it before her face. "But Hedley is gone and I am still alive and you did not know him and do not know me and so there is no point in either of us becoming maudlin, is there? Thank you for the set. I will be the envy of all the other ladies, having been the first to dance with you."

She smiled dazzlingly at him as he bowed to her.

"You will not boast of it, though," he said. "You are not conceited."

She laughed.

"Good evening to you, Mrs. Dew," he said, and turned away.

Before Sir Humphrey could bear down upon him again and take it upon himself to force another dancing partner upon him, he strolled off in the direction of what he thought must be the card room.

Fortunately, he was right. And the din in there was marginally muted.

He had made himself visible in the ballroom and reasonably agreeable for quite long enough.

So Mrs. Vanessa Dew was the third sister, was she? Strange irony that one so plain had been the first to marry. Though there was admittedly a sparkle to her that sometimes belied her looks.

She had knowingly married a dying man, for the love of God.

## 4

THERE was still no one up at Rundle Park when Vanessa had finished her breakfast the following morning except for Sir Humphrey, who was preparing to ride into the village to call upon Viscount Lyngate and Mr. Bowen at the inn. He was, he told Vanessa as he rubbed his hands together and looked thoroughly pleased with life, going to invite them to dinner.

"Perhaps," he said, "if I were to call out the carriage, you would care to ride with me, Nessie, to visit your sister. *She* is an early riser like you, I daresay."

Vanessa was happy to accept. She was eager to discuss the assembly with Margaret. It had been *such* a wonderful evening. She had, of course, lain awake half the night thinking about the opening set. It was hardly surprising. No one else at the assembly had been willing to allow her to forget it. The viscount had danced with her and *only* with her.

She had made up her mind even before the dancing began that she would not maintain an awed silence with him. After a few minutes it had become obvious, though, that *he* had no intention of conversing with *her*, though surely any really polite gentleman would have made the effort. Obviously he was not a very polite gentleman—yet another fault she had found in him without really knowing him at all. And so *she* had started talking to *him*.

They had ended up almost joking with each other. Almost *flirting*. Perhaps, she had conceded, there was more to the man than she had thought. Goodness, she had never flirted with any other man. And no other man had ever flirted with her.

One dance with her, though, had obviously frightened him off from dancing with anyone else. He had spent the rest of the evening in the card room. It would all have been very lowering if she had felt that his good opinion was worth having. As it was, it had merely been disappointing for a dozen other women who had hoped to catch his eye and dance with him.

But it was what he had said to her after the set was over that had kept her awake more than anything else. It had puzzled her at the time and had continued to puzzle her ever since. She wondered what Margaret would make of it.

"Viscount Lyngate and Mr. Bowen are remarkably amiable young gentlemen, would you not agree, Nessie?" Sir Humphrey asked her when they were in the carriage.

"Indeed, Papa."

Mr. Bowen had been very amiable. He had danced with as many different partners as there had been sets, and he had conversed with them and with almost everyone else too between sets and during supper. Viscount Lyngate, Vanessa strongly suspected, had not really enjoyed the evening at all. And it was entirely his own fault if he had not, for he had arrived expecting to be bored. *That* had been perfectly obvious to her. Sometimes one got exactly what one wished for.

"I think, Nessie," Sir Humphrey said, chuckling merrily, "the viscount fancied you. He danced with no one else but you."

"I think, Papa," she said, smiling back at him, "he fancied a game of cards far more than he did me or anyone else. It was in the card room he spent most of the evening."

"That was dashed sporting of him," her father-in-law said. "The older people appreciated his condescension in playing with them. Rotherhyde relieved him of twenty guineas and will not talk of anything else for the next month, I daresay."

It was not raining, though it looked as if it might at any moment. It was also chilly. Vanessa was grateful for the ride, as she informed Sir Humphrey while his coachman handed her down from the carriage outside the cottage gates.

She found Katherine at home as well as Margaret, this being one of the days when the infants did not attend school. Stephen was there too, but he was upstairs in his room, toiling over a Latin translation since Margaret had told him at breakfast that he ought not to go out until it was done.

Vanessa hugged both sisters and took her usual chair close to the fire in the parlor. They talked, of course, about the assembly while Margaret stitched away at some mending.

"I was *so* relieved when I saw you come into the rooms with Lady Dew and Henrietta and Eva, Nessie," she said. "I thought you might talk yourself out of coming at the last moment. And I was more than delighted to see you dance every single set. It quite exhausted me just to watch you."

And yet Margaret herself had danced all but two sets.

"I did not sit down all evening either," Katherine said. "Was it not a delightful evening? Of course, *you* made the greatest conquest, Nessie. You danced the *opening set,* no less, with Viscount Lyngate, who is really so handsome that I daresay there was not a steady female heartbeat in the rooms all evening. If you had not come here this morning, I would have had to walk over to Rundle. *Tell all!*"

"There is not much to tell. He danced with me because Papa-in-law gave him little choice," Vanessa said. "He was *not,* alas, smitten by my charms, and if he came to the Valentine's assembly to find a bride, he gave up the search after one dance with me. How very lowering, to be sure."

They all chuckled.

"You belittle yourself, Nessie," Margaret said. "He did not ignore you. He conversed with you while you danced."

"Because I forced him into it," Vanessa said. "He told me that I was quite ravishingly beautiful."

"Nessie!" Katherine exclaimed.

"And then he went on to say that so was every other lady in the room without exception," Vanessa told them. "Which effectively negated the compliment, would you not say?"

"Was that when you threw back your head and laughed?" Margaret asked. "You had everyone in the room smiling, Nessie, and wishing they could eavesdrop. You *forced* him into speaking such nonsense? How do you do it? You have always had a gift for making people laugh. Even Hedley when he was . . . very ill."

Vanessa had used the last reserves of her energy during those final few weeks, making him laugh, keeping him smiling. She had collapsed afterward. She had scarcely been able to drag herself out of bed for two whole weeks after the funeral.

"Oh," she said, blinking away tears, "but it was Viscount Lyngate who made *me* laugh."

"Did he explain," Katherine asked, "why he is in Throckbridge?"

"He did not," Vanessa said. "But he did say something very peculiar. He asked me about the *third* Huxtable sister, having been presented only to the two of you. Did Papa-in-law mention my existence when he presented Viscount Lyngate to you last evening?"

"Not that I recall," Margaret said, looking up from the pillowcase she was mending.

"He did not," Katherine said decisively. "Perhaps he said something after they walked away from us, or when he was presenting Stephen. Did you answer him?"

"I told him *I* was the third sister," Vanessa said. "And he commented that he had not been informed that one of us had been married. Then he changed the subject and asked me about Hedley."

"How peculiar indeed," Katherine said.

"I wonder," Vanessa said, "what Viscount Lyngate *is* doing in Throckbridge—if he is not just innocently passing through, that is. But he told Papa-in-law that he has business here. How did he know there were *three* Huxtable sisters? And why would that fact be of any interest whatsoever to him?"

"Idle curiosity, I daresay," Margaret said. "Whatever does Stephen do to split the seams of every pillowcase I put on his bed?" She picked up another and tackled it with her needle and thread.

"Perhaps it was *not* idle curiosity," Katherine said, jumping suddenly to her feet, her eyes fixed beyond the parlor window. "He is coming here now. They *both* are." Her voice had risen to something resembling a squeak.

Margaret hastily set aside her mending and Vanessa turned her head sharply to look out the window and see that indeed Viscount Lyngate and Mr. Bowen were coming through the garden gate and proceeding up the path to the front door. Her father-in-law must have had an uncharacteristically short visit with them.

"I say!" They could hear Stephen clattering down the stairs, calling as he came, obviously glad of any excuse to escape from his books for a while. "Meg? We have visitors coming. Ah, are you here too, Nessie? I daresay the viscount was smitten with your charms last evening and has come to offer for you. I shall question him very sternly about his ability to support you before I give my consent." He grinned and winked at her.

"Oh, dear," Katherine said as a knock sounded at the door, "whatever does one say to a *viscount?*"

The two gentlemen had come here to Throckbridge, Vanessa realized suddenly in some shock, because of *them*. *They* were the business the viscount had spoken of. He had known of them before he came here, though he had not been informed that one of them had been married. What a strange and intriguing mystery this was! She was very glad she had come here this morning.

They waited for Mrs. Thrush to open the front door. And then they waited for the parlor door to open, as if they were presenting a silent tableau on a stage. After what was only a few moments but felt like several minutes, it opened and the two gentlemen were announced.

It was the viscount who entered first this time.

There was no concession to the country in his appearance this morning, Vanessa was quick to see. He wore a calf-length heavy greatcoat, which must have sported a dozen capes, a tall beaver hat, which he had already removed, tan leather gloves, which he was in the process of removing, and supple black leather boots, which must have cost a fortune. He looked larger, more imposing, more forbidding—and ten times more gorgeous—than he had appeared last evening as he glanced around the small parlor before bowing to Margaret. He was also frowning, as though this were a visit he did not relish. He looked far from joking and flirting this morning.

Why had he come here? *Why on earth?*

"Miss Huxtable," he said. He turned to them each in turn. "Mrs. Dew? Miss Katherine? Huxtable?"

Mr. Bowen bowed to them all, smiling genially.

"Ladies? Huxtable?" he said.

Vanessa told herself quite deliberately, as she had the evening before, that she was *not* going to be awed by a fashionable greatcoat and costly boots and a title. Or by a darkly handsome, finely chiseled, frowning face. Gracious heavens, her father-in-law was not a nobody. He was a baronet!

She *felt* awed nonetheless. Viscount Lyngate looked quite out of place in Meg's humble, not-quite-shabby parlor. He made it look many times smaller than usual. He seemed to have sucked half the air out of it.

"My lord? Mr. Bowen?" Margaret said with admirable composure as she indicated the two chairs that flanked the fireplace. "Won't you have a seat? Will you bring a tray of tea, please, Mrs. Thrush?"

They all seated themselves as Mrs. Thrush, looking decidedly relieved at being dismissed, whisked herself out of sight.

Mr. Bowen complimented them on the picturesque appearance of the cottage. He guessed that the garden was a picture of color and beauty during the summer. He commended the village on the success of last evening's assembly. He had spent a decidedly agreeable evening, he assured them.

Viscount Lyngate spoke again after the tray had been brought in and the tea poured.

"I am the bearer of news that concerns all of you," he said. "I am afraid it is my sad duty to inform you all of the recent demise of the Earl of Merton."

They all stared at him for a moment.

"That is sad news indeed," Margaret said, breaking the silence, "and I am much obliged to you for bringing it in person, my lord. I believe we do have a connection with the earl's family, though we have never had any communication with them. Our father discouraged any talk of them. Nessie may be better acquainted with the exact relationship." She looked inquiringly at her sister.

Vanessa had spent a great deal of time with her paternal grandparents as a child and had always listened enthralled to their endless stories of their younger years while Margaret had been less interested.

"Our grandfather was a younger son of the Earl of Merton," she said. "He was cut off from the family when they objected to his wild ways and his choice of our grandmother as his bride. He never saw them again. He used to tell me that our papa was first cousin to the current earl. Is it he who has just died, my lord? That would make us his first cousins once removed."

"I say," Stephen said, "that really is quite a close relationship. I had no idea, though I knew there was *some* connection. We are indeed obliged to you, my lord, for coming. Did the new earl ask you to find us? Is there some question of a family reconciliation?" He had brightened considerably.

"I am not sure I would *want* one," Katherine said with some feeling, "if they all turned their backs on Grandpapa because he married Grandmama. We would not even exist if he had not."

"I shall nevertheless write a letter of condolence to the new earl and his family," Margaret said. "It is the civil thing to do. Would you not agree, Nessie? Perhaps you would take it with you when you go, my lord."

"The earl who recently died was a mere boy of sixteen," Viscount Lyngate explained. "He survived his father by only three years. I was his guardian and the executor of his estates after the demise of my own father last year. Unfortunately the boy was always in precarious health and was never expected to live to adulthood."

"Ah, poor boy," Vanessa murmured.

His keen, unsettlingly blue eyes rested on her for a moment and she leaned farther back in her chair.

"The young earl had no son, of course," he said, turning back to Stephen, "and no brothers who could succeed him. No uncles either. The search for his successor moved back to his grandfather and *his* brother—your grandfather—and his descendants."

"Oh, I say," Stephen said as Vanessa pressed even

farther back into her chair and Katherine's hands came up to cover her cheeks.

Grandpapa had had only the one son—their father.

"It alit upon you, in fact," Viscount Lyngate said. "I have come here to inform you, Huxtable, that you are now the Earl of Merton and owner of Warren Hall in Hampshire among other properties, all of them prosperous, I am happy to report. My felicitations."

Stephen merely stared at him. His face had turned a pasty white.

"An *earl*?" Katherine whispered. "*Stephen?*"

Vanessa gripped the arms of her chair.

Margaret looked as if she were cast out of marble.

"Congratulations, lad," Mr. Bowen said with hearty good humor as he rose to his feet to offer Stephen his hand.

Stephen surged to his feet to take it.

"It is unfortunate," Viscount Lyngate continued, "that your upbringing has not prepared you for the life that is to be yours, Merton. There is much work involved and a large number of duties and responsibilities apart from just the glamour of possessing rank and fortune. You will need a great deal of training and education, all of which I will arrange and in which I will be pleased to involve myself. We will need to remove you to Warren Hall without further delay. It is already February. It is to be hoped that by the time Easter has come and gone, you will be ready to make an appearance in London. The *ton* will be gathered there in large numbers, you will understand, for the Season and the parliamentary session. They will be waiting to make your acquaintance, young as you are. Can you be ready to leave tomorrow morning?"

"Tomorrow morning?" Stephen said, releasing Mr. Bowen's hand in order to stare at the viscount in some astonishment. "That soon? But I—"

"Tomorrow morning, my lord?" Margaret said more firmly. Vanessa recognized the thread of steel in her voice. *"Alone?"*

"It is necessary, Miss Huxtable," the viscount explained. "We have already wasted several months discovering the new Merton's whereabouts. Easter will—"

"He is seventeen," Margaret said. "It is quite out of the question that he go with you alone. And *tomorrow?* It is impossible. There will be all sorts of preparations to make. The *ton* can wait to make his acquaintance."

"I am well aware, ma'am—" the viscount began.

"Oh, I think you are *not*," Margaret told him while Vanessa and Katherine gazed from one to the other in silent fascination and Stephen lowered himself to his chair again, looking as if he might be on the verge of collapse. "My brother has never been more than a few miles from home, and yet you expect him to leave alone with you, a perfect stranger, tomorrow in order to live in a new home among people he has never met and enter upon a life that is totally unexpected and totally foreign to him?"

"Meg—" Stephen's cheeks were suddenly flushed.

"When my father lay on his deathbed eight years ago," Margaret said, holding up a staying hand but not removing her eyes from the viscount, "I made him a solemn promise that I would see all my siblings to adulthood and care for them until they were all old enough and able to care for themselves. I have always held that promise sacred. Stephen is going nowhere tomorrow and nowhere the next day or the day after that. Not alone anyway."

Viscount Lyngate raised his eyebrows and looked very haughty indeed.

"I do assure you, ma'am," he said, impatience obvious in every line of his body, "that your brother will be very well cared for indeed under my guardianship. He is one of the wealthiest men in the land, and it is imperative—"

"Under your *guardianship*?" Margaret said. "I beg your pardon, my lord. Stephen is under *my* care even if it turns out that he is as rich as Croesus and the King of England."

"Meg," Stephen said, and pushed the fingers of one hand through his curls, which immediately restored themselves to their usual disorder. He looked horribly embarrassed. "I am seventeen, not seven. And I am the Earl of Merton unless this is some bizarre hoax. I had better go and find out what it is all about and learn how to do the job properly. It would be lowering to meet my peers and not have any idea how to go on. You have to agree with that."

He looked at them all in turn.

"Stephen—" Margaret began.

But he raised a hand palm out and addressed the viscount.

"The thing is," he said, "that we are a close-knit family, as you can see for yourself. I owe a great deal to *all* my sisters, but especially to Meg. Of course they must come with me if I go—which I daresay I will. They must come because I insist upon it. I will not go without them, in fact. What would I do rattling around in a large ancestral home on my own, anyway? I take it Warren Hall *is* large?"

The viscount inclined his head while Meg gazed at Stephen in some astonishment.

"And what sort of a wealthy, influential earl would I be," Stephen continued, "if I left my sisters behind in a cottage like this when they have been prepared to sacrifice almost their last penny to send me to university later this year when I am eighteen? No, Lord Lyngate, Meg and Kate will go with me. And Nessie too if she wishes or can be persuaded. I daresay she would not enjoy being left at Rundle Park if we were all gone."

They might all go without her? Vanessa thought, appalled. She might lose her whole family at once? *Of course* she would go with them.

"You must admit, Elliott," Mr. Bowen said, "that it is a sensible suggestion. The boy has his mind made up, and he will have a steady home life if his sisters are with him. He is going to need it. And they are now the sisters of an earl. It would be more fitting for them to live at Warren Hall than here."

Viscount Lyngate looked about the room with raised eyebrows and at each of them in turn.

"In time, yes," he said. "But preferably not yet. They would *all* need to be educated and clothed and a thousand and one other things. They would all have to be presented at court and then to the *ton*. The task would be monumental."

Vanessa drew a slow breath. If he had redeemed himself in her eyes just a fraction of a degree last evening while they danced, he had just plummeted to the depths again. He saw them—all of them, even Meg—as a *monumental* liability. A nuisance. Nobodies. Country bumpkins. She drew breath to speak.

But Stephen seemed not to have seen or heard anything amiss—or anything at all that the viscount had said. He had asserted himself, tested the wings of early

manhood in light of the almost incredible announcement that had just been made to him. But he was still
very much an exuberant boy too.

"I say." He got to his feet again and beamed around
on them all. "We are going to Warren Hall, Meg. You
will have a come-out Season in London among the *ton,*
Kate. And you will be back living with us, Nessie. Oh,
this is famous!" He rubbed his hands together and then
reached out to hug Katherine.

Vanessa could not spoil the moment for him. But
when she glanced at Viscount Lyngate, not even trying
to hide her annoyance, she found that he was looking
back at her, his eyebrows raised.

She pressed her lips tightly together.

But then she *did* smile and even laugh as Stephen
pulled her up from her chair, lifted her off her feet, and
twirled her once about.

"This is *famous!*" he exclaimed again.

"Indeed it is," she agreed fondly.

"We had better go over to Rundle Park," he said, "to
tell Sir Humphrey and Lady Dew. And to the vicarage
to tell the vicar. And to— Oh, Lord." He sat down
abruptly and turned pale again. "Oh, Lord."

Viscount Lyngate got to his feet.

"We will leave you all to digest the news," he said.
"But we will return this afternoon to discuss some of
the details. There is no time to delay."

Margaret had risen too.

"We will *not* delay, my lord," she said firmly. "But you
must not expect us to be ready to leave tomorrow or the
next day or even the next. We will leave as soon as we
are ready. We have lived here in Throckbridge all our
lives. We have roots here as deep as those *you* probably

have in *your* home. You must give us time to pull them free."

"Ma'am." The viscount bowed to her.

He had come here, Vanessa realized, expecting to use his power and consequence to strike awe into them so that he could bear Stephen off to his new life *tomorrow*. Without his sisters.

How foolish men were.

She smiled at Viscount Lyngate when he bowed to her. Country bumpkins, he would discover, were not necessarily as easy to handle as the minions he must be more accustomed to encounter and dominate.

But Stephen, she thought as the gentlemen stepped out of the room and then out of the house. Stephen was an earl.

*The Earl of Merton.*

"The Earl of Merton," he said, echoing her thought. "Pinch me, someone."

"Only if you will pinch me first," Katherine told him.

"Oh, goodness me," Margaret said, still on her feet and looking anxiously about the room. "Wherever am I to *start*?"

"At the beginning?" Vanessa suggested.

"If I only knew where that *was*," Meg said, her voice close to a wail.

And then Stephen spoke up again, his color returned, his eyes burning with intensity.

"I say!" he said. "Do you realize what this *means*? It means that I don't have to wait until after university and probably years after *that* before I can do everything I have dreamed of doing in life. I do not have to wait to support you all. I don't have to wait even a single minute longer. I am the Earl of Merton. I own property. I am a wealthy man. And I am going to give you all a grand new home and an even grander new life. And as for myself . . . Well."

Clearly he was lost for words.

"Oh, Stephen," Katherine said fondly.

Vanessa bit her upper lip.

Margaret burst into tears.

# 5

IT TOOK *six days*.

Six days of kicking their heels at a modest village inn. Six days of amusing themselves as best they could in a remote country village during February, when the sun did not once shine but a chilly rain drizzled down on their heads almost every time they decided to set foot out of doors. Six days of being wined and dined and called upon at all hours of the day by a persistently cheerful and hospitable Sir Humphrey Dew. Six days of observing the reactions of a sleepy English village to the astonishing news that one of their own had just inherited an earl's title and property and fortune.

Six days of fuming with impatience to be gone—or of *sulking* with impatience if one listened to George Bowen, who was perhaps the most insubordinate secretary any man had ever employed.

Six days of longing for Anna with a gnawing ache of unfulfilled lust.

It felt more like six weeks.

Or months.

They called a couple of times at the cottage, but each time they found everyone so busy getting ready to leave that Elliott hated to slow them down. Young Merton called upon them once at the inn to assure them that they would all be ready in no time at all.

Six days was *no time at all*?

He saw more of Mrs. Dew than of the others. But of course she lived at Rundle Park rather than at the cottage with her own family.

It did not take him long to discover that she was going to be a thorn in his flesh. He had guessed it on the morning of his first visit to the cottage, of course, when she had clearly taken umbrage at his objection to the three sisters accompanying young Merton to Warren Hall without giving him a chance to settle in first and learn a few things about his new life. She had not actually said anything on that occasion, but she had *looked* plenty. Perhaps she thought that marriage to the younger son of a country baronet had equipped her adequately to take on the *ton*.

She was not so silent when he ran into her three days later.

He and George were riding to Rundle Park in response to one of the wining and dining invitations and came upon her walking homeward, presumably from the cottage. Elliott dismounted, directed George to ride ahead and take his horse with him, and then wondered if either he or Mrs. Dew appreciated his impulsive gallantry. They walked for several minutes without saying anything of greater significance than that the weather remained stubbornly chilly, a fact that was made worse by the total lack of sunshine and the abundance of wind, which always seemed to blow in one's face no matter which direction one took. She buried her hands in her muff, and he wondered if they would now move on to predicting what sort of summer they were likely to have—or whether they would have one at all.

It was the sort of conversation that was enough to set his teeth on edge.

The chill air had whipped some color into her cheeks—and nose. As a result she looked quite wholesome in a countrified sort of way, he conceded reluctantly, even if she was *not* exactly pretty.

But she too had tired of the weather as a topic, it seemed.

"You must understand," she said, breaking a short silence, "that we are as worried as we are elated."

"Worried?" He looked at her, his eyebrows raised.

"Worried about Stephen," she said.

"Why would you worry about your brother?" he asked. "He has just come into an inheritance that brings with it untold wealth as well as position and property and prestige."

"*That* is what worries us," she said. "How will he handle it all? He loves life and he loves to be active. He is also attentive to his studies. He has been working conscientiously toward a meaningful future goal, both for his own sake and for Meg's, who has sacrificed so much for him—as she has for all of us. He is young and impressionable. I wonder if it is not the worst possible time for this to happen to him."

"You are afraid," he asked, "that all this will go to his head? That he will suddenly neglect his studies and run wild? And become grossly irresponsible? I will make it my mission to see that none of that happens, Mrs. Dew. A good education is essential for any gentleman. It—"

"It is not of any of that I am afraid," she said, interrupting him. "His character is good and his upbringing has been sound. A little wildness will not hurt him, I daresay. He has been wild enough even here. It is part of growing up for a man, it seems."

"What, then?" He looked at her inquiringly.

"I am afraid," she said, "that you will try to make him like yourself and that perhaps you will succeed. He is quite dazzled by you, you know."

Well.

"I am not a good enough model for him?" he asked, stopping walking abruptly in order to glare directly at her. He was not good enough for her brother, a country lad turned earl? After all he had sacrificed during the past year and was going to sacrifice for the next four? Anger bit into him. "And why not, may I ask?"

"Because," she said, not avoiding looking directly back into his eyes though he was frowning and not even trying to hide his annoyance, "you are proud and overbearing. Because you are impatient with all who are beneath you socially and somewhat contemptuous too. You expect to have your own way in everything and become bad-tempered when you do not—just because of who you are. You frown almost constantly and never smile. Perhaps all aristocrats are arrogant and unpleasant. Perhaps it is an inescapable effect of being wealthy and powerful. But I doubt it. It is *you,* though, who are now effectively Stephen's guardian despite what Meg may say. It is you who will try teaching him what it is to be an aristocrat. I do not want him to become like you. I should hate it of all things."

*Well!*

This little dab of a country mouse certainly did not mince words.

"I beg your pardon," he said, frowning even more ferociously as his mood deteriorated. "It seems to me we met only a few days ago, ma'am. Or have I mistaken? Do we have a longer acquaintance, which I have unfortunately forgotten? Do you, in fact, *know* me?"

She did not fight fair. She used the lamest—and perhaps the most effective—tactic of all. She answered a question with one of her own.

"And do *you* know *us?*" she asked. "Do you know Meg or Kate or me? Do you know us well enough to judge that we will be an embarrassment to you when we accompany Stephen into his new life?"

He leaned slightly toward her, his nostrils flaring.

"Have I missed something, ma'am?" he asked her. "Have I ever said—or *judged,* to use your word—that you will be an embarrassment to me or anyone else?"

"Of course you have," she said. "If I could remember your exact words, I would quote them to you. But I remember their meaning only too well. We will have to be educated and clothed and presented to the queen and society. It will be a *monumental task*."

He glared ferociously at her. Her eyes were wide and bright from the cold or battle and were undoubtedly her finest feature. She should flash them more often—though not at him, it was to be hoped. What a truly dreadful creature she was!

"And?" he said. "Are you taking issue with me, ma'am, for speaking the *truth* to you? Do you imagine that you and your sisters are ready to step into polite society and take the *ton* by storm? Do you think you could appear on Bond Street in London in that particular cloak and bonnet and not find yourself being treated as someone's servant? Do you think you are in any way even remotely prepared for life as the sister of an earl?"

"I *think*," she said, "that these matters are not your

concern, my lord. *We* are not your concern, even if Stephen is. I believe my sisters and I can be trusted to learn what we must in order to mingle in society and not embarrass Stephen in any way at all. Frankly, I do not care if we embarrass *you*. And *if* we do, I daresay you will take satisfaction from looking along the length of your nose at us and curling your lip and everyone will pity you for having been landed with such a parcel of bumpkins."

"And *how* are you to do this mingling with society?" he asked her, lowering his voice considerably and narrowing his eyes. "*Who* is to sponsor you at your court presentation? *Who* is to send you invitations? To whom will *you* send invitations?"

That silenced her.

"Perhaps, ma'am," he suggested, "we should proceed on our way before the dinner gets cold."

She sighed and they walked onward. But she had not given up the fight.

"How would *you* like it," she asked him, "if someone arrived on *your* doorstep out of the blue one day and turned your world upside down and inside out."

It had happened!

"If he presented me with a new and better world," he said, "I would be delighted."

"But how would you know," she asked, "that it *was* better?"

"I would go and find out," he said. "And in the meantime I would not take out my fears and misgivings on the messenger."

"Not even if he made you feel like a worm beneath his boot?" she asked.

"I would not presume to judge him until I knew him better," he said.

"And so I am chastised," she said. "Let us take *this* path. It will get us to the house and our dinner faster. I have offended you, have I not? I am sorry if I have been overhasty in my judgment. It is just that I worry about Stephen. He has always been restless and has wanted something more adventurous of life than he could possibly hope for. Now suddenly he has infinitely more than he ever thought to wish for. But he does not know who he is any longer or what his life is to be or his exact position in his new world. And so he will turn to you as a mentor and model, especially as he already admires you. I fear for him if you insist that he must become more—"

One hand came free of her muff and she made circling motions with it.

"Arrogant? Obnoxious?" he suggested.

She laughed suddenly and unexpectedly, a light, merry sound.

"Is that what I called you?" she said. "I daresay you are accustomed to being treated with obsequious deference by your inferiors. I was determined from the start not to stand in awe of you. It seemed so silly to do so."

"It must be gratifying for you," he said curtly, "to know that you have succeeded so well."

Good lord! That had been pure spite, something he never indulged in. And he still had the irritation of an evening spent as a guest of Sir Humphrey Dew to look forward to.

"Being an earl—or a viscount—is serious business, Mrs. Dew," he continued. "It is not all basking in one's consequence and spending one's pots of money and beaming geniality on one's minions and dependents. Or even striking awe into them. One is *responsible* for them."

As he had found to his cost during the past year. The very idea that he was settling down and would complete the process this year when he selected a bride and married her could plunge him into the deepest gloom. He *certainly* had not needed the added aggravation of finding himself guardian to a seventeen-year-old—especially when the boy happened to come encumbered with three sisters, none of whom had been farther than ten miles from Throckbridge, Shropshire, their entire lives if his guess was correct. Certainly the boy had not.

"And one of those people for whom *you* are responsible is Stephen?" she asked softly.

"Precisely," he said.

"How did that come about?" she asked him.

"The old earl was my uncle," he explained. "My father agreed to be appointed guardian to his nephew, my cousin and your brother's predecessor. But my father died last year, only two years after my uncle."

"Ah," she said. "And so you inherited the guardianship as well as everything else?"

"Yes," he said. "And then a few months ago my young cousin died and the hunt for your brother began. And *then* it was discovered that he too was a minor. May he live long. There has been enough death in my family to suffice for a long, long time."

"If you were a cousin," she began, "why—"

"A *maternal* cousin," he explained without waiting for her to finish her question. "My mother and Jonathan's mother were sisters."

"*Jonathan.* Poor boy." She sighed. "But now I can see

that I have done you something of an injustice, resenting you when all you have been doing is a duty you inherited from your father. How disappointed you must have been to learn that Stephen is so young."

It was perhaps an apology of sorts. But he was not appeased. The woman was sharp-tongued and offensive.

However had he put himself into this position anyway? He might simply have touched the brim of his hat as he passed her on his horse, inquired civilly into her health, and ridden onward with George.

He turned his head to look at her and found that she was turning hers at the same moment to look at *him*. She bit her lip as their eyes met, and hers filled with merriment.

"I have dared to quarrel with a *viscount*," she said. "Will it be written on my epitaph, do you suppose?"

"Only," he said, "if you boast of it to your family and never let them forget until your dying day."

She laughed and turned her head to the front again.

"You see?" she said. "We are almost at the house. I am sure we are both thankful for that."

"Amen," he said, and she laughed again.

Perhaps, he thought as they completed the walk without talking, she would think twice about her decision to move to Warren Hall with her family in light of this conversation and her opinion of him. Perhaps she would decide to stay here at Rundle Park, where she would not have to suffer his arrogance and contempt and bad temper. Sir Humphrey Dew was not a marvelously sensible man, but he was undeniably genial and he was obviously as fond of his daughter-in-law as he was of his own daughters. She must be comfortable here.

He hoped fervently she would think twice.

But of course she did not.

The long wait was finally over. Young Merton called at the inn on the fifth evening to announce that he and his sisters—all three of them, alas—would be ready to leave on the morrow, and the following morning they showed themselves to be as good as their word. Or almost. When Elliott and George rode their hired horses along the village street to the Huxtable cottage, having settled their account at the inn, all four travelers were out of doors, dressed for the journey. The baggage coach George had hired was loaded with all their baggage. Elliott's traveling coach was drawn up before the cottage gate, its door wide open, its steps down ready to receive the ladies.

But there was a delay. Not only were the three Huxtables and Mrs. Dew out of doors and gathered before the cottage. So also were surely all the rest of the inhabitants of the village of Throckbridge—*and* their dogs.

Miss Huxtable was on the garden path, hugging the housekeeper, who was to remain behind in the cottage. Miss Katherine Huxtable was outside the gate, hugging an unknown villager. Merton was shaking hands with the vicar while his left arm was draped about the shoulders of a sobbing young girl—the very one who had giggled her way through the Valentine's assembly just a week ago. And Mrs. Dew was in the arms of Sir Humphrey, while the rest of his family clustered about them, handkerchiefs in hand, all looking tragic. Tears trickled unabashedly down the baronet's cheeks.

Other persons appeared to be awaiting their turn with all four.

A terrier, a collie, and a canine of indeterminate breed were rushing hither and yon, barking and yipping with excitement and occasionally meeting and stopping to sniff noses.

"One wonders," Elliott said dryly as he drew his horse to a halt well short of the main action, "if there is a single villager who has remained at home this morning."

"It is an affecting sight," George agreed, "and a testament to the closeness of neighbors in a small village."

A village lad was holding the head of the horse Merton had purchased from the stables at Rundle, Elliott could see, and was fairly bursting with pride as two of his less fortunate peers gazed enviously on.

Foolishly, Elliott had expected to ride up to the cottage, assist the ladies into his carriage, and depart along a deserted street without further ado. Six days in Throckbridge should have forewarned him that the departure would not be that simple. The fact that young Stephen Huxtable was now the Earl of Merton was spectacular news enough, but the added fact that he and his sisters were to leave Throckbridge, perhaps forever, was of far more moment.

Lady Dew had stepped through the garden gate to exchange a few words with Miss Huxtable, and then the two of them were hugging each other. One of the Dew sisters was weeping rather noisily on Mrs. Dew's shoulder.

It was a scene to outdo even the most sentimental of melodramas on any London stage.

"We have changed all their lives forever," George observed. "One can only hope it is for the better."

"*We* have changed their lives? I had nothing whatsoever to do with Jonathan Huxtable's demise, George. Neither did you, it is to be hoped. And it was not I who agreed to be guardian to a boy who would never be a mature adult—and then to *another* boy, who will not achieve his majority for four more years. It was my father."

Elliott felt for the handle of the quizzing glass beneath his greatcoat and raised it to his eye. No, Mrs. Dew was not in tears, but there was a look of deep grief and affection on her face. Obviously it was not easy for her to say good-bye to her in-laws. Then why the devil was she doing it? She wore a gray cloak and bonnet. There were glimpses of a lavender dress beneath the cloak. She was still in partial mourning after more than a year. Perhaps she had been fond of the consumptive Dew whom she had married. Perhaps she had not married him just out of pity or from a desire to attach herself to the family of a baronet.

It would be as well for her when she left off her mourning. Those colors—if they could be called colors at all—did nothing whatsoever for her. They looked quite hideous on her, in fact.

And *why* was he allowing a woman with no pretensions to either beauty or conduct to ruffle his feathers?

He looked about him impatiently.

His arrival had been noted, he was relieved to see, and the remaining farewells were being said in some haste. Miss Huxtable nodded briskly to him, Miss Katherine Huxtable smiled and raised a hand in greeting, and Merton strode along the street to shake each of them by the hand, his eyes burning with some inner fire.

"We are ready," he told them. "But there are just a few more farewells to say, as you can see."

He turned back into the throng. Within minutes, though, he handed his eldest and youngest sisters into the carriage, while Sir Humphrey performed the courtesy for Mrs. Dew, patting her hand and pressing a wad of something that looked like money into her palm as he did so. He stepped back, drew a large handkerchief from his pocket, and blew his nose loudly.

And finally and miraculously they were on their way only half an hour or so later than Elliott had planned— or five days later, depending upon which plan one was considering.

He had expected all this to be relatively easy—a journey down to Throckbridge in two days, a day here to deliver the news and prepare the boy, a two-day journey back to Warren Hall with the new Merton, and then an immediate and intensive training program so that he would be fit for his new role before summer came.

But his plans had already gone awry, as he should have expected as soon as he knew there were women involved. He had sisters of his own and knew how they could hopelessly complicate the simplest of plans. Instead of allowing their brother to go with him and George and get settled before even thinking about joining him, these sisters had decided to accompany him now. Including Mrs. Nessie Dew.

He conveniently forgot that it was Merton himself who had insisted that they go to Warren Hall with him.

All he *did* know for sure was that he now had responsibility for Merton *and* his three sisters, all of whom were great-grandchildren of an earl, but none of whom had been brought up to the life they must now live. They had spent their lives in this village, for God's sake, the children of the late vicar. Until today they had been living in a cottage that would fit into the grand entrance of Warren Hall. They wore clothes they had obviously made—and mended—themselves. The youngest girl had been teaching in the village school. The eldest had done as much work about the house as the house-keeper. The widow—well, the least said about her the better.

But *one* thing that could be said of her was that she was incredibly naive. They were *all* going to have to be brought up to scratch, and it was not going to be easy. Neither was it something they could do alone without assistance.

They were going to need husbands, and those husbands were going to have to be gentlemen of the *ton* since they were now the sisters of an earl. In order to find respectable husbands among the *ton,* they were going to have to be formally presented to society. They were going to need a Season or two in London. And in order to be presented and taken about during a Season, they were going to need a sponsor.

A *lady* sponsor.

They could *not* do it alone.

And *he* could not do it. He could not take three ladies to London with him and start escorting them about to all the parties and balls with which the Season abounded. It was just not done. It would be scandalous. And though he had courted scandal quite outrageously on numerous occasions during the past ten years or so, he had not done so during the past year. He had been the epitome of strict respectability. He had had no choice. The days of his careless young manhood had come to an abrupt end with his father's death.

It was a thought that did nothing to improve his mood.

Neither could he leave the sisters to find their own way in their new world. For reasons he could not even explain to himself, he could not simply abandon them to the dismal discovery that it simply could not be done—though he might have been tempted if Mrs. Dew had been the only sister.

He had talked about the situation ad nauseam with George during the past several days. It was not as if they had had a great deal of other activity to distract their minds, after all.

Elliott's mother was the obvious choice as sponsor. She had experience at preparing young ladies for their come-out and at finding suitable husbands for them. She had already done it with the two eldest of his sisters. But the trouble was that there was still Cecily to fire off—this year, in fact.

His mother could not be burdened with three other females, the youngest of whom was already twenty, who had no experience at all of society and who were not even related to her. Cecily was enough of a handful in her own right.

And she would doubtless not appreciate it either.

There were his married sisters, of course, but Jessica was in a delicate condition again, and Averil, at the age of twenty-one, was hardly old enough to sponsor the Huxtable sisters, two of whom were older than she was.

That left his paternal aunts. But either possibility made him wince. Aunt Fanny, the elder, paraded out a whole litany of new maladies as well as all the old every time he was unfortunate enough to set eyes on her, and talked in a perpetual nasal whine, while Aunt Roberta, the younger, had missed her calling—or her gender— and ought to have been a sergeant-major. She would have excelled.

Much as he resented the Huxtables, he did not in all conscience feel he could inflict either aunt upon them—even if either was willing to accept the daunting responsibility. It had taken Aunt Fanny all of five ex-hausting seasons to fire off her own daughter, and Aunt Roberta was always busy bullying her hellion brood— all male—into toeing the line of respectability.

"I cannot simply leave them at Warren Hall to their own devices while I take their brother under my wing, can I?" he had said over a dinner of tough roast beef one evening. "It will be years before he can do anything for them himself, and by that time they will all be hope-lessly long in the tooth. The elder two must be in their middle twenties already. Marrying off the widow, of course, is definitely not my concern, though I suppose even she is going to have to be presented to society. It will be up to her whether she marries again—if anyone will have her, that is. She does not have anything like the looks of the other two, does she?"

"A little unfair, old boy," George had said. "She looks quite appealing when she smiles and is animated—as she frequently is. Apparently her husband was extraor-dinarily good-looking and freely chose her. It was a love match."

Hard to believe. Elliott snorted.

"What you ought to do," George said on another oc-casion, when they were riding along some country lanes for exercise and being coldly drizzled upon, "is marry soon—sooner even than you planned, that is. Your *wife* could sponsor Merton's sisters."

"*What?*" Elliott asked, turning his head rather too sharply and causing a shower of cold water to stream from his hat brim to his lap. "Without any time for deliberation, you mean?"

He had no candidate for bride in mind yet, though his mother would doubtless be able to count off all the most eligible young ladies on her ten fingers. But he need not think of that for another few months yet.

George shrugged. "It is not as if you would have any problem persuading any woman to say yes. Quite the contrary. You may have to beat them all back with a stick when they know you are going shopping at the marriage mart this year. But you could foil them all by marrying before the news spreads."

"Devil take it," Elliott said wrathfully, "has it come to this? Must I rush my fences over one of the most important decisions of my life—if not *the* most important—for the sake of an imagined responsibility to three females I scarcely even know? It is preposterous."

"All the more time in which to live happily ever after," George said.

"Then why the devil," Elliott asked, "are you still a single man? And since when has it been a part of any secretary's duties to advise his employer about when he ought to marry?"

But his friend, he saw when he turned his head again, was grinning. He was actually enjoying all this. As well he might. He had been able to leave behind his office at Finchley Park in order to travel all over the country, but had none of the responsibility that was weighing down Elliott's unwilling shoulders.

And those women *were*—dash it all!—his responsibility, Elliott thought now as his carriage containing them moved off from the cottage gate and the villagers raised hands and handkerchiefs in farewell.

His thoughts were interrupted when Merton himself maneuvered his horse between George's and his own.

"We have lived here all our lives," he said by way of apology for the delay. "Leaving is hard—for everyone we leave behind and for us too."

"I understand, lad," George assured him. "Even if the change in your circumstances is for the better, it is still not easy to leave behind all that is familiar and dear."

But the boy brightened as they rode clear of the village, the carriages ahead of them.

"I thought," he said, "I would have to wait until I had finished studying at university and had begun some career before I could do something for my sisters to repay them for all they have done for me and make their lives more comfortable. But now I will not have to wait. I will be able to give all of them the kind of life they deserve but have only been able to dream of until now."

Or *he* would, Elliott thought wryly even if it was Merton who was footing the bill. And he remembered something else George had said during that damp afternoon ride. He had been joking, of course, but the words had nevertheless stuck in Elliott's memory like a moth trapped inside a lamp.

"Of course," he had said, "you could always marry Miss Huxtable, Elliott, and allow *her* to sponsor her sisters as your wife. That would solve a lot of problems.

And she is dashed lovely to look at. I am only surprised that she is still on the market."

Duties, Elliott decided again now as he had decided a dozen times since the words had been spoken, did have their limits. Why should he even consider marrying the lovely but rather dour Miss Huxtable just because it would be convenient for everyone but him?

Except that he *was* about to be in search of a wife. And in many ways it *would* be a convenient thing to do. She was the sister of an earl, after all. And there was no denying that she came in a very delectable package.

Devil take it, he might well be fit only for Bedlam by the time all this was over. Although he never suffered from headaches, it seemed to him that one gigantic one had hovered over his head like a foggy halo for all of six days.

He thought wistfully of his mother and of his pregnant sister and gloomily of his two aunts, and wondered which of the last two might be the lesser evil.

But perhaps his mother would have some decent advice to give him even if she could not be expected to offer her services.

*Why* could his father not have lived another thirty years or so?

He could be in London now, carousing with his friends and spending his nights in Anna Bromley-Hayes's inviting arms. He could be without a care in the world. He could be . . .

But he was not.

And that was that.

# 6

T H E Y would be at Warren Hall in about two hours, Viscount Lyngate had said after luncheon about an hour and a half ago. They would be there soon, then.

The countryside was green and rolling. It looked like prosperous farming land. Warren Hall *was* prosperous, the viscount had said on that first morning. So were Stephen's other properties. There were three of them— in Dorset and Cornwall and Kent—but Warren Hall in Hampshire was his principal seat.

"Oh, this must be it," Katherine said suddenly, leaning forward in her seat and pressing her nose against the glass of the window, the better to see what was behind her.

The carriage was making a sharp left turn to pass between high stone gateposts, and Stephen appeared beside the carriage. He had ridden forward and was bending an eager face, reddened from the cold, to look in at them.

"This is it," he mouthed, pointing ahead.

Margaret smiled and nodded. Vanessa raised a hand in acknowledgment that they understood. Katherine was craning her neck to catch a glimpse of the house, though it was still out of sight beyond the dense grove of trees through which the driveway was winding.

But a few minutes later they could all see it as the

carriage drew away from the trees and, as if on cue, the sun struggled free of the clouds that had covered it most of the day.

Warren Hall.

Vanessa had expected a medieval heap, perhaps because it was called a hall. It was actually a neat and solidly square Palladian mansion of pale gray stone. There was a dome and a pillared portico at the front with what looked like marble steps leading up to the doors. There was a stable block off to one side—the driveway led toward it. Before the house there was a wide, flat terrace surrounded by a stone balustrade, with steps leading down to flower gardens beneath it, still bare now in February.

"Oh, goodness," Vanessa said, "this is all very real, is it not?"

Which was a foolish thing to say, though her sisters must have known what she meant since they did not question her words.

They all gawked in amazement.

"It is *beautiful*!" Katherine exclaimed.

"I will still have a garden to tend, then," Margaret said.

At any other time they might all have laughed with considerable merriment over the gross understatement. Even apart from the terrace and flower garden, they were surrounded by cultivated parkland for as far as the eye could see.

None of them laughed.

It was indeed suddenly all very real. None of them could ever have imagined such grandeur and such a total change in their lives. But here they were.

The driveway ascended a slope as it approached the

stables and then turned unexpectedly to take them across the terrace to the foot of the house steps. There was a stone fountain in the middle of the cobbled terrace, though there was no water in it this early in the year. There were also many stone urns, which were probably filled with flowers during the summer.

The carriage drew to a halt, the coachman opened the door and set down the steps, and Stephen himself reached inside to hand Margaret down and then to swing Katherine out without benefit of the steps. He was looking very exuberant indeed. Another hand appeared in the doorway before he could turn back for Vanessa—Viscount Lyngate's.

Vanessa had been in virtual hiding from him since the day on which she had lashed out at him and told him exactly what she thought of him. Afterward, part of her had been appalled at her temerity while another part had been proud that she had found the courage. And all of her had been horribly embarrassed at the thought of coming face-to-face with him again.

The moment had come.

Not that she had not looked at him in private a great deal more than she ought during their journey. He was undeniably good-looking—gross understatement—and virile and . . . well, and *masculine*. And she admired his effortless horsemanship—she had watched him often while trying to convince herself that it was Stephen she watched. It was all really not fair at all. Hedley had deserved everything good and wonderful this world had to offer and yet he had been thin and weak and very ill during the last couple of years of his life.

Indeed, she felt guilty about admiring someone who

was his antithesis—as if she still owed her husband her undivided loyalty.

Hedley was long dead.

"Thank you." She forced herself to look into the viscount's eyes as she set a hand in his and descended the carriage steps to the terrace. But then her eyes moved to the house. "Oh, it is far more vast than it looked on the approach."

She felt like a dwarf. But what gauche words to speak aloud!

"That is because from a distance one sees the house and terrace and flower gardens as a unit and is impressed more by the pleasing vista than by the size of the house," the viscount said. "One is meant to be impressed by the house itself when one arrives here."

"The steps *are* marble," she said.

"They are indeed," he agreed, "as are the pillars."

"And this is where our grandfather grew up," she said.

"No," he told her. "This house is no more than thirty years old. The old medieval hall was torn down and this built in its place. It was shabby and crumbling, I have been told. And this is certainly beautiful. I nevertheless wish I could have seen the house as it was. Much character and many memories must have been destroyed in the name of modernity."

Vanessa looked at him with appreciation for his feelings. But at the same moment she realized that her gloved hand was still in his. She snatched it away as if it had been scalded, drawing attention to the fact, and he raised his eyebrows.

A very superior-looking gentleman, dressed all in black, was bowing to Stephen and indicating the marble steps. Vanessa realized in some shock that he must be the butler. Halfway up the steps stood a plumpish woman, also in black, who was probably the housekeeper. And at the top of the steps, she noticed for the first time, were two lines of smartly dressed servants, one line on each side of the huge double doors, which stood open. The servants were being paraded for their new master.

Oh, goodness. Could their arrival at their new home have been more intimidating? How would Stephen be able to deal with it all?

But Stephen had offered one arm to Margaret and the other to Katherine and proceeded up the steps in the butler's wake after throwing a glance over his shoulder at Vanessa to see that she followed.

Viscount Lyngate offered his arm, and she took it.

The servants were not wearing cloaks and it was a chilly day despite the sunshine. Nevertheless, not one of them moved a muscle except to bow or curtsy to Stephen as each was introduced to him. He had a word with all of them—as if to the manner born, Vanessa thought with some pride.

She forced herself to smile and nod at all of the servants as she passed, and they bowed or curtsied in return. Rundle Park was like a rural cottage in comparison with this.

Mr. Bowen came behind them.

And then they were inside the great hall, which was great indeed and fairly robbed Vanessa of breath. It was round and pillared and stretched up the full height of the house and into the dome, which was gilded and painted with scenes from mythology. Light from its long, narrow windows streamed into the hall below, making patterns of light and shade on the pillars and checkered floor.

They all stood and gaped.

Viscount Lyngate was the first to speak.

"The devil!" he muttered while the rest of them were still standing with their necks craned backward, and the butler and housekeeper waited to escort them elsewhere.

Vanessa looked at him in some surprise. But then she saw that another gentleman was striding into the hall through one of the arches surrounding it, his boot heels ringing on the tiles.

Vanessa had an impression of tall, dark handsomeness, of a dark-complexioned face, a lock of dark hair fallen across his forehead, of black riding clothes that were well worn but nevertheless becoming on his athletic form. He stopped and clasped his hands at his back and smiled.

It was a smile of considerable charm.

He looked sufficiently like Viscount Lyngate that Vanessa would not have been surprised to learn that they were brothers.

"Ah," he said, "the new earl, I presume? And his . . . entourage?"

Viscount Lyngate released Vanessa's arm and strode forward, his heavy greatcoat swinging against his boots. He came to a halt only when he was almost toe to toe with the other man. They were almost exactly the same height.

"You were supposed to be gone by now," he said curtly and with undisguised annoyance.

"Was I?" the other gentleman said, his smile still in place but his voice transformed into a drawl of what sounded like boredom. "But I am not, am I, Elliott? Introduce me if you will be so good."

The viscount hesitated but then turned back to face them.

"Merton," he said, "Miss Huxtable, Mrs. Dew, Miss Katherine, may I present Mr. Huxtable?"

*Not* a brother, then?

"*Constantine* Huxtable," the gentleman said, making them all an elegant bow. "Con to my friends."

"Oh, I say!" Stephen exclaimed, stepping forward to shake the gentleman heartily by the hand while the ladies curtsied. "You have our name. You must be a relative."

"I must indeed," Mr. Huxtable agreed while Vanessa and her sisters looked on with interest. "Second cousin to be exact. We share a great-grandfather."

"Indeed?" Stephen said. "Nessie has been telling us about our family tree, something the rest of us have sadly neglected, I am afraid. Great-Grandpapa had just two sons, did he not?"

"Your grandfather and mine," Constantine Huxtable said. "And then there were your father and mine. And then my brother—my *younger* brother, who is recently deceased. And you. Earl of Merton. My felicitations."

He sketched Stephen another bow.

So Constantine Huxtable and Viscount Lyngate were first cousins—their mothers were sisters. But it was another relationship that Vanessa was working out in her head. So were her siblings by the looks on their faces. Stephen was staring at their second cousin, his brow knit in thought.

"There is something here I do not understand," he said. "You are the elder brother of the earl who just died? Ought not you to have been—? Ought not you to be—?"

"The Earl of Merton myself?" Mr. Huxtable laughed. "I missed my chance for glory by two days, lad. That is what comes of being too eager in this life. May it be a lesson to you. My mother was Greek, daughter of an ambassador to London. She met my father when she was visiting her sister, who had married Viscount Lyngate and lived with him at nearby Finchley Park. But it was not until after her return to Greece with her papa, my grandfather, that she confessed to being in an, ah, interesting condition. He marched her back across Europe in high dudgeon. He demanded that my father do the decent thing—which he did. But I would not wait for the fairy-tale ending—or beginning—to my own story. I bowed to the stress of a sea crossing that had incapacitated my mother, and I made my squalling appearance in this world two days before my father could procure a special license and marry her. Thus I was and am and forever will be an illegitimate son. My esteemed parents had to wait another ten years for the arrival of a live and legitimate heir. Jonathan. He would have been more than delighted to make the acquaintance of all these new cousins. Would he not, Elliott?"

He looked at Viscount Lyngate, one eyebrow cocked in what Vanessa suspected was mockery.

Clearly there was no love lost between the cousins.

"But he died a few months ago," Mr. Huxtable continued, "several years later than the physicians had predicted. And so, here you are, the new and legitimate Earl of Merton and his sisters. I assume these ladies *are* all sisters, including Mrs. Dew? Mrs. Forsythe, we will have tea in the drawing room."

He spoke with absolute authority and with an aristo-cratic ease of manner, as if after all he were the Earl of Merton and owner of Warren Hall.

"That is the saddest story I have ever heard," Katherine said, gazing at him wide-eyed. "I must write a story about it."

Constantine Huxtable turned his smile on her.

"In which I figure as the tragic hero?" he said. "But there are compensations for having been born two days too soon, I do assure you. A certain freedom, for exam-ple, which neither Merton nor my cousin Elliott here can enjoy." He bowed to Margaret. "Miss Huxtable, may I have the pleasure of escorting you upstairs?"

Margaret stepped forward and set a hand on his arm, and he led her through the arch by which he had entered the hall a few minutes ago. Stephen and Katherine fol-lowed close behind, gazing with eager interest at this newfound cousin. Viscount Lyngate exchanged a glance with Mr. Bowen before offering his arm to Vanessa again.

"I do apologize," he said. "He *was* asked to leave."

"But why?" she asked. "He *is* our cousin, is he not, and has welcomed us with considerable courtesy when he might have resented us—or Stephen anyway. His story *is* true, is it? He grew up here as the firstborn son of the Earl and Countess of Merton?"

"It is true. But English law is quite rigid in such mat-ters," he said. "There would be no way to make him le-gitimate even if there had been no other descendants of his line to inherit."

"But if there had not," Vanessa said as they walked through the arch and came to a magnificent marble staircase that wound its way upward, "he might have petitioned the king to grant him the title, might he not?"

Had she not read about such a thing somewhere?

"I suppose he might," Viscount Lyngate said. "A lawyer would know the legalities of such a claim and the likelihood of his petition being granted. But there *was* a descendant—your brother."

How could he *not* resent Stephen? Vanessa wondered as she looked up the stairs to where Constantine Huxtable was smiling at Margaret and bending his head to listen to something she said. It must seem to him that a crowd of strangers was invading his home.

He had been asked to leave his own home—by his younger brother's guardian. By his own first cousin— his mother and Viscount Lyngate's had been sisters.

"He is trouble, Mrs. Dew," Viscount Lyngate said, his voice low. "He can mean only mischief by remaining here. You must not allow yourself to be deceived by his charm, which he has always possessed in abundance. Your brother must be quite firm with him. He must be given a week's notice at the longest. He has had enough time to find another home and pack his belongings."

"But this *is* his home," Vanessa said, frowning. "This is where he has always belonged. It would have been his if he had been born two days later."

"But he was not," Viscount Lyngate said firmly as they followed the others into a drawing room. "And life is made up of what-ifs. There is no point in allowing ourselves to be distracted by them. What-ifs are not reality. The reality is, Mrs. Dew, that Con Huxtable is an illegitimate son of a former earl, while your brother is the Earl of Merton. It would be a mistake to be swayed by pity."

But if one never felt pity for a fellow human, Vanessa

thought, one was surely not fully human oneself, was one? That made Viscount Lyngate a little less than human. She looked at him, still frowning. Did he have *no* feeling for others, even his own cousin?

But he had moved away from her to stride forward to Stephen's side.

Stephen was gazing admiringly at Constantine Huxtable. So was Katherine. Margaret was regarding him kindly. Vanessa smiled at him, though he was not looking her way.

What a dreadful day this must be for him. The fact that he was meeting four new cousins, all of whom would surely be kindly disposed toward him, must seem poor comfort.

For a few minutes Vanessa had forgotten her initial awe at a mansion that was magnificent beyond anything she had dreamed of. But the awe returned suddenly. The drawing room was large and square with a high, coved ceiling, painted with some scene from mythology and trimmed lavishly with gold. The furniture was elegant and the draperies of wine-colored velvet. Paintings in heavy gold frames covered the walls. There was a large Persian carpet underfoot, fringed by wood so highly polished that surely one would see one's face in it if one bent forward.

Vanessa felt a surge of unexpected longing for Rundle Park—as if she had abandoned Hedley there.

She must not—she *would* not—forget him.

Her eyes rested upon Viscount Lyngate, who even without his greatcoat still looked large and imposing and virile and masculine. And handsome, of course. And very much alive.

She resented him greatly.

\* \* \*

Elliott and Con Huxtable had been the closest of friends all their lives—until just a year ago, in fact. The three-year gap in their ages—Elliott was the elder—had not mattered one whit. They had lived only five miles apart, they were cousins, neither had had many other playmates in their neighborhoods, and they had enjoyed doing the same sorts of things—mostly outdoor sports and other vigorous, energetic games that involved climbing trees and diving into pools and wading through muddy bogs and devising other such strenuous activities that had filled their days with exercise and fun and got them into a great deal of trouble with their respective nurses.

When they grew up, they had remained close friends and had continued to enjoy life together, even if doing so had meant frequently stirring up mischief and mayhem and putting themselves in danger and raking their way to an admiring reputation among their peers and a less approving notoriety among society in general. They had both been great favorites among the ladies.

They had been two young blades sowing their wild oats together, in fact, never doing anyone any great harm, including—by some miracle—themselves. They had been young gentlemen, after all, and had known where to draw the line.

Even after Con's father died they had remained friends though Con had started to spend more and more of his time at Warren Hall with Jonathan, of whom he had been inordinately fond. Elliott had missed him but admired his devotion to the handicapped boy. It had even struck him that Con was growing up and settling down faster than he was. Elliott's father had been the boy's guardian, of course, but he had been slack in his duties, trusting Con to look after the boy's needs and oversee the day-by-day running of his estates with the aid of a competent steward.

And then Elliott's father had died too.

And everything had changed. For Elliott had made the decision to take his new responsibilities seriously, and one of those responsibilities had been Jonathan. So he had spent some time at Warren Hall, acquainting himself with the nature of his duties there, though he had fully expected to be able to turn over the unofficial guardianship to Con again. He had even felt somewhat embarrassed that his uncle had not made Con the official guardian. He was old enough and quite capable enough, after all. And Jonathan had adored him.

But Elliott had soon made the painful discovery that Con had abused the trust Elliott's father had placed in him, embezzling funds and stealing costly family jewels for his own gain, safe in the knowledge that Jonathan would never know the difference. And then there were the debaucheries Elliott had become aware of—housemaids impregnated and dismissed, laborers' daughters ruined.

Con was not the person Elliott had always thought him to be. There was no honor in him after all. He preyed upon the weak. He was the very antithesis of a gentleman. It was no excuse that through no fault of his own he had narrowly missed being his father's heir.

His villainy had been an excruciatingly painful discovery.

*Not* that he had ever admitted to the thefts or the debaucheries. Though he had not denied them either. He had merely laughed when Elliott had confronted him with his findings.

"You may go to the devil, Elliott" was all he had said.

They had been bitter enemies for the last year. At least, for Elliott it had been bitter. He could not speak for Con.

Elliott had, of course, taken Jonathan's care and the running of his estates directly into his own hands and had spent as much time at Warren Hall as he had at Finchley Park, it had seemed. There had been precious little time left for himself.

Con had made that year almost intolerable for him. He had done all in his power to set obstacles in the path of his erstwhile friend and to influence Jonathan to defy Elliott's wishes. That had not been a hard thing to accomplish—the poor boy had not even realized he was doing it.

Naively perhaps, Elliott had hoped that the worst of his burden was now behind him, for even though the new Merton was a minor and totally unprepared for the life and duties that would be his, and even though he had three sisters who were equally unprepared, *at least* there would no longer be Con Huxtable as a thorn in his side.

Or so he had thought. He had told Con to leave.

But he was still here. And he had chosen to greet the new owner of Warren Hall and his sisters with all the power of his great charm.

Common decency ought to have dictated that he leave before the new earl took up residence, even if he *was* a distant relative. But one ought to have known by now not to expect common decency from Con Huxtable.

Elliott left Mrs. Dew's side and crossed the drawing room with determined steps.

"Indeed it *is* all rather splendid," Con was saying, apparently in answer to something one of his young cousins had said. "My esteemed father saw fit to pull down the old abbey-cum-fortress-cum-hall soon after he succeeded to the title and to put up this testament to his wealth and taste in its place. Later he filled it with treasures from his travels as a very young man."

"Oh, but I *wish*," Katherine Huxtable said, "I might have seen the abbey."

"It *was* nothing short of criminal," Con agreed, "to have pulled it down, though perhaps one would not really have enjoyed its drafty corridors and dark, narrow-windowed chambers and archaic sanitation rather than the opulent comforts of this building."

"If *I* had been doing it," Merton said, "I would have left the old hall standing and built this house close by. History is all very well, and historic buildings really ought to be preserved, as Nessie is always saying, but I confess to enjoying the comforts of modern living."

"Ah," Con said just as Elliott was about to try maneuvering him closer to the window, where he intended to have a private word with him, "here is the tea tray. Set it down in the usual place, Mrs. Forsythe. Perhaps Miss Huxtable will be so good as to pour."

But then he smiled ruefully and bowed to her.

"I do beg your pardon," he said. "As the eldest sister of young Merton, you are hostess here, Cousin, and do not need my permission to pour. Please proceed."

She inclined her head to him and took her seat behind the tray. Mrs. Dew joined her there in order to hand around the cups and saucers and the plate of dainties.

George, in silent communication with Elliott, drew Merton and his young sister toward the marble fireplace, where they held out their hands to the welcome warmth of the fire.

Elliott strolled in the direction of the window, virtually forcing Con to go with him. He did not mince his words when they were out of earshot of the others.

"This is in decidedly poor taste," he said, keeping his voice low.

"Putting aside my own inclination in order to remain here to greet my cousins' arrival and help them feel at home?" Con said, feigning surprise. "I would call it in the *best* of taste, Elliott. I congratulate myself on my unselfishness and thoughtfulness."

"You have greeted them and welcomed them," Elliott said curtly. "Now you may leave."

*"Now?"* Con's eyebrows arched upward. "At this very moment? Would it not appear somewhat abrupt, somewhat ill-mannered? I am amazed you would suggest such a thing, Elliott. You, who have turned into such a high stickler lately. You are in grave danger of turning into a dry old stick, you know. It fairly gives one the shudders."

"I will not spar verbally with you," Elliott said. "I want you gone."

"I beg your pardon." Con regarded him with a puzzled frown—and mocking eyes. "But do your wishes rule Warren Hall? Is it not rather those of Merton, my second cousin?"

"He is a *boy,*" Elliott said between half-clenched teeth. "And impressionable. And I am officially his guardian. You have already terrorized one child and there was precious little I could do about it—he was your brother and under your influence. It will not happen with *this* boy."

"Terrorized." For one moment the air of mockery slipped and something altogether more ugly gleamed in Con's eyes. "I *terrorized* Jon." And then he recovered. "But of course I did, and it was easy to do. He did not exactly have all his wits about him, did he? Or if he did, there were not very many of them behind which he might have sheltered himself from my pernicious influence. Ah, Mrs. Dew—an appropriate name. I am parched and you bring me tea."

His charming smile was back in place.

She carried two cups. Elliott took the other one and inclined his head in acknowledgment.

"Mrs. Dew," Con said. "But there is no *Mr.* Dew with you?"

"I am a widow," she told him. "My husband died a year and a half ago."

"Ah," Con said. "But you are yet so young. I am sorry. It is hard to lose loved ones—especially those who are as close as one's own heartbeat."

"It *was* hard," she agreed. "It *is* hard. I have come here to live with Stephen and my sisters. Where will *you* live, Mr. Huxtable? Here?"

"I will find somewhere to lay my weary head after I leave here, ma'am," Con said. "You must not worry about me."

"I am sure you will," she said. "It had not occurred to me to worry. But there is no hurry, surely. This house is more than large enough for all of us, and it *is* your home. And we really ought to get properly acquainted. An ancient family feud has kept us apart for too long. May I fetch you some dainties? And you, Lord Lyngate?"

Something in her eyes and her tone told Elliott that she had overheard at least a part of his conversation with Con. And, being one as usual to jump to conclusions, she was annoyed with him.

Merton came over to join them as she was leaving, obviously too restless to remain by the fire.

"I say," he said, looking out the window with bright, intense eyes, "there is a magnificent view from up here, is there not?"

"I believe it must have been this very view," Con said, "that impelled my father to build the new house on the exact site of the old."

The window faced south. From it one could see out over the terrace and the formal gardens below and across rolling parkland in every direction—lawns and woods and lake—to the distant patchwork of the fields of the home farm.

"Perhaps," Merton said, "you will ride out with me tomorrow, Cousin, and show me everything."

"And the house too," Katherine Huxtable added. She had come to join her brother. "Will you show it to us and describe all its treasures? You must know them so well."

"It will be my pleasure," Con said. "Anything to please my cousins. What an abomination family quarrels are, as your sister has just observed." His eyes came to rest on Elliott, and one of his eyebrows rose mockingly. "They are frequently about nothing at all of any moment and can drag on for generations, depriving cousins and second cousins of one another's acquaintance."

Theft and debauchery were of no moment? Elliott

held his gaze until Con looked away at something in the garden at which Katherine Huxtable was pointing.

Mrs. Dew was standing by the tea tray, cake plate in hand, conversing with her sister and George. She smiled at something George said and turned in the direction of the window with the plate. Her still-smiling eyes met Elliott's, and he looked back at her, tight-lipped.

Why did he find himself looking at her far more frequently than he looked at either of her sisters? They were far easier on the eyes than she was, after all. Though it was not in appreciation that he looked, was it? He was invariably irritated by her.

He wished, as he had a dozen times since leaving Throckbridge, that she had remained behind. He had the uneasy feeling, as he had there, that she was indeed going to be a constant thorn in his side.

She was going to court Con's friendship, he suspected, merely to spite him.

What an abominable woman she was.

## 7

VANESSA had always been of the opinion that conflict did not bring out the best in people.

There was definitely some sort of conflict between Viscount Lyngate and Constantine Huxtable. And while she might have been inclined to believe that the viscount was probably to blame simply because it was in his nature to be arrogant and bad-tempered and Mr. Huxtable was an illegitimate son of a former earl and was therefore beneath him socially, she was no longer sure that Mr. Huxtable was entirely blameless.

She overheard a part of what they said to each other as she approached with the tea. She did not feel guilty about overhearing what had not been meant for her ears. The drawing room—*Stephen's* drawing room—at teatime was not the place to be conducting a private feud if one wished to keep it from the other people present.

But while Viscount Lyngate was being his usual obnoxious self, Constantine Huxtable was showing a different side to his nature than he had demonstrated thus far. He was sneering, and he was goading the viscount, clearly enjoying the fact that he had him rattled.

He had been told to leave Warren Hall before their arrival but had stayed.

Because he had wanted to greet Stephen and his

sisters, long-lost cousins, and welcome them to the home that had been his until now? Or because he had known it would annoy Viscount Lyngate to find him still here?

If the latter had been his motive, she could still feel some sympathy for him though it would be a bit lowering for *them*. Why should he leave, after all, just because Viscount Lyngate had told him to?

But really the whole thing appeared to be petty. Good heavens, the two men were adults and they were cousins. They looked enough alike to be brothers except that the one cultivated an almost perpetual scowl while the other cultivated charm and smiles, revealing just how handsome he was despite his crooked nose. Though in truth he was not quite as handsome as Viscount Lyngate.

Vanessa did not care what their quarrel was about. Well, she *did*—most people, after all, feel a natural curiosity about such things. But she did not believe that she and Stephen and her sisters ought to be drawn into it today of all days. Today was probably one of the most exciting of Stephen's life. The two men might have the good manners to keep their quarrel for another time and place.

But Stephen's was a good fortune, after all, that had been achieved as a result of the misfortune of another. And during dinner Vanessa noted that Mr. Huxtable was clothed all in black, as he had been earlier when he was still dressed for riding. Like her, he was in mourning, though for him it was still full mourning. What must it be like to lose a brother? Her mind touched upon Stephen, but she firmly cut short her imaginings. It did not bear thinking of.

"Tell me about Jonathan," she said to Mr. Huxtable after they had all removed to the drawing room.

Meg had been saying something to Viscount Lyngate and Stephen, but they must all have heard her question and paused to listen to the answer.

Vanessa thought he was not going to reply. He gazed into the fire, a slight smile on his lips. But then he did speak.

"It is usually impossible to describe someone with one word," he said. "But with Jon only one word seems really appropriate. He was love. There was no one and nothing he did *not* love."

Vanessa smiled her sympathy and encouragement.

"He was a child in a young man's body," Mr. Huxtable continued. "He loved to play. And sometimes he loved to tease. He liked to hide even if it was perfectly obvious to the searcher where he was hidden. Is that not so, Elliott?"

He looked at Viscount Lyngate, and for a moment the mockery Vanessa had seen in his face earlier was back. It was a pity. It was an expression that did not suit him.

The viscount—of course—frowned.

"You must miss him dreadfully," Vanessa said.

Mr. Huxtable shrugged.

"He died on the night of his sixteenth birthday," he said. "He died in his sleep after a busy, happy day of play. We should all be so fortunate. I did not wish him dead, but now at least I am free to seek my fortune elsewhere. Sometimes love can be almost a burden."

It was shocking to hear the words spoken aloud. Vanessa could never have been so honest. But she felt a shiver of recognition in them. Was it not callous, though, to think thus? Though he had said *almost*. She knew all about the pain of loving.

"I say," Stephen said, breaking a short silence that everyone else might have been finding embarrassing, "I hope you are not planning to leave here soon, Cousin. There is much I wish to ask you. Besides, there is no reason to stop thinking of this as your home just because it is legally mine."

"You are all kindness, lad," Mr. Huxtable said, and the faint suggestion of mockery was there again in his voice and in one slightly arched eyebrow.

Was he a pleasant man hiding behind a mask of seeming carelessness, Vanessa wondered, or an unpleasant man hiding behind a mask of charm and smiles? Or, like most humans, was he a dizzying mix of contradictory characteristics?

And what of Viscount Lyngate? She turned her gaze on him and found him looking back at her. The blueness of his eyes was always a slight shock.

"It is not just kindness, Mr. Huxtable," she said, still looking at the viscount. "We are really very happy to find a cousin we did not even know we had. No one told us about you."

The viscount's lip curled ever so slightly at one corner, but the expression could not by any stretch of the imagination be called a smile.

"And since we *are* cousins," Mr. Huxtable said, "I beg you will all call me by my first name."

"Constantine," she said, turning her attention back to him. "And I am Vanessa, if you please. I am sorry about Jonathan. It is hard to watch a young person die, especially when one loves him."

He smiled back at her without making any verbal

comment, and she decided that he was at least partly a pleasant man. No one could fake that expression. It told her that he had loved his brother—though Jonathan had taken the title that might have been his.

"You told me at dinner, Constantine," Kate reminded him, "that you would teach me to ride. That cannot be done all in a day or so, I daresay. You must certainly stay longer."

"It may possibly take a week if you are a slow learner," he said. "Though I will wager you are not. I shall stay at least until you are an accomplished rider, then, Katherine."

"That will please us all," Meg said.

Vanessa wondered if Viscount Lyngate realized that the fingers of his right hand were beating a rhythmic tattoo against his thigh.

Why were he and Constantine enemies? she wondered. Had they always been?

Elliott had intended taking Merton in hand the very morning after his arrival at Warren Hall. He had business of his own to attend to at Finchley Park, his own home five miles away. And even apart from that, he was eager to be home again, though he would, of course, have to ride over to Warren Hall quite frequently for the next month or two. There was much to be done.

He had intended to introduce Merton to his steward, Samson, a competent man Elliott's father had hired two years or so ago. He had intended spending the morning indoors, going over a number of things with the boy in Samson's office. And then during the afternoon the three of them would go out riding to see the home farm and other places of importance to the new earl.

He had intended being busy all day long with the boy. There really was no time to lose.

But after breakfast Merton informed him that Con had agreed to take him and his sisters on a tour of the house and inner park.

It was a tour that lasted the whole morning.

And after luncheon Merton informed Elliott that Con had promised to take him riding about the outer park and home farm and to introduce him to the laborers and some of the tenants.

"It is very decent of him," Merton said, "to be willing to give up his whole day for my benefit. Will you come with us?"

"I'll stay here," Elliott told him dryly. "But tomorrow you will need to spend some time with Samson, your steward, Merton. I'll be with you too."

"But of course," Merton said. "There is much I need to know."

The next morning, though, Elliott had to go in search of him and found him in the stables with Con and the head groom, getting acquainted with all the horses and looking as if he was enjoying himself immensely. And then, of course, he had to go and change before coming to the office.

"Meg never likes the smell of horse in the house," he explained. "She fusses if she smells even a speck of manure on me."

He did apply himself to a whole pile of information in the office for a few hours before luncheon, and he showed an admirable eagerness to learn and asked a number of intelligent questions. After luncheon, though, he announced that Con was to take him to meet the vicar and the Graingers and one or two other of the more prominent families of the neighborhood.

"It is decent of him to be willing," the boy commented. "He might have resented me, I suppose. Instead, he is making every effort to make himself agreeable. He is going to take my sisters boating on the lake tomorrow if the fine weather holds. I daresay I will go too so that we can take out two boats. Come and join us if you will."

Elliott declined the offer.

Each evening after dinner Con conversed with a charm that was all too familiar to Elliott. He had always been able to wind people of all ages and both genders about his little finger whenever he chose. They had used to laugh over it. He had always been more skilled at it than Elliott had.

Con, of course, did not care the snap of his fingers for his newfound cousins. Or if he did, it was certainly not affection he felt. Good Lord, they had come, perfect strangers, to oust him from his own home or at the very least to make him feel like a guest in it. He probably hated them with a passion.

He had stayed only to irk Elliott.

The trouble was that they knew each other too well. Con knew just what would annoy his former best friend. And Elliott knew just what was going on in Con's mind.

Elliott, standing at the window of his guest bedchamber early on the morning of the proposed boat rides, watched Con step out of the main doors below and stride purposefully across the terrace and down the steps to the flower garden.

Elliott was already dressed. He had been contemplating an early morning ride, in fact. But it was time he and Con had a talk far away from the other occupants of the house. Merton was young and impressionable. His sisters were innocent and naive. Con had used poor Jon quite successfully to make Elliott's task as guardian more difficult than it might otherwise have been. He was not going to be given the chance to use the present Merton for the same purpose.

He went after Con. He had turned left out of the flower garden—Elliott had seen that before leaving his room. He had not been heading toward the lake, then, or the stables. But it soon became clear where he *had* gone.

Elliott followed him to the private family chapel and the churchyard surrounding it. And sure enough, there he was standing at the foot of Jonathan's grave.

For a moment Elliott regretted coming. If this was a private moment, he did not want to intrude upon it. But almost immediately he felt angry. For even if Con *had* loved Jonathan, he had also taken advantage of him in a most dishonorable manner, robbing him and making of his home a house of ill repute. It did not really matter that Jonathan had not known and would not have understood even if the facts had been explained to him. That was not the point at all.

And then the moment for turning back unseen—*if* he had wanted that moment—was gone. Con turned his head and looked steadily at him. He was not smiling now. There was no audience he might wish to charm.

"Is it not enough, Elliott," he asked, "that you must come prying into my father's and brother's home—and my cousin's—and throwing your weight around there as if it were your own? Must you now invade even the graveyard where they are all buried?"

"I have no quarrel with them," Elliott said. "And fortunately for you, they have no quarrel with you. They are all dead. But it amazes me that you choose to stand on such hallowed ground. They *would* have a quarrel with you if they were alive and knew what I know."

"What you *think* you know." Con laughed harshly. "You have become a sanctimonious bore, Elliott. There was a time when you were not."

"There was a time when I sowed some damnably wild oats," Elliott admitted. "But I was never a scoundrel, Con. I never relinquished my honor."

"Go back to the house," Con said harshly, "while you still have your health intact. Better yet, go home to Finchley. The cub will prosper well enough without your interference."

"But with *yours* he would doubtless be stripped of what remains of his inheritance," Elliott said. "I am not here to bandy words with you, Con. Leave here today. If you have a scrap of decency remaining, go away and leave these people alone. They are innocents. They know nothing."

Con sneered at him.

"Fancy one of them, do you, Elliott?" he asked. "The eldest is an eyeful, is she not? The youngest is mouthwatering too. Even the widow is not without appeal. She has fine, laughing eyes. Which one do you fancy? I suppose you are planning to be a good boy and marry soon and set up your nursery. It would be convenient to marry a Huxtable of Warren Hall."

Elliott took a couple of menacing steps toward him.

"Just make sure that *you* do not take a fancy to one of

them," he said. "I would not stand for it, you know. They are not for the likes of you."

Con sneered again.

"I ran into Cecily last week," he said. "She was out riding with the Campbells. She is making her come-out this year, she was telling me. She told me to be sure to be at her come-out ball. She is going to reserve a set for me. Sweet little Cece—she has grown into quite a beauty."

Elliott's hands balled into fists at his sides and he strode another few steps forward.

"You are not about to swing one of those are you, Elliott?" Con asked, cocking one eyebrow and laughing. "It is an age since we last came to fisticuffs. It was when you broke my nose, I believe—though I also seem to recall that I drew a pint or so of blood from yours *and* blackened one of your eyes. Come on, then. If it is a fight you are spoiling for, I am your man. Indeed, I will not even wait for you to make the first move. You always were slow to get started."

And he closed the short distance between them and planted Elliott a facer—or would have if Elliott had not blocked the blow with the side of one arm before taking a swing of his own. The blow glanced off Con's ear and *his* next blow caught Elliott on the shoulder instead of on the chin as intended.

They backed up, their fists at the ready, and circled and weaved, looking for an opening. Ready for the real fight—without pausing to divest themselves of their coats.

And this, Elliott thought, half exhilarated despite himself, was indeed what he had been spoiling for for a long time. It was time someone gave Con a good drubbing. And he had always been better with his fists than

Con, who had indeed once blackened his eye and drawn blood from his nose, though not nearly a pint, by Jove.

He saw his opening and—

"Oh, *please* do not," a voice said from behind him. "Violence never accomplishes anything. Can you not *talk* about your differences instead?"

A woman's voice.

Uttering absurdly asinine words.

Mrs. Dew's voice.

Of course.

Con dropped his fists and grinned.

Elliott turned his head over one shoulder and glared.

"Talk?" he said. "*Talk?* I would ask you to turn about and return to the house, ma'am, and stay away from what does not concern you."

"So that you can continue to hurt each other?" she said, drawing nearer. "Men are so foolish. They think themselves the superior sex, but whenever there is a difference between two of them or two groups of them or two *nations* of them, the only solution they can see is to fight. A fistfight, a war—there is really no difference between them."

Good Lord!

She had thrown her clothes on hastily, at a guess. She was not wearing either gloves or a bonnet, and her hair had been gathered into a rather untidy knot at the back of her head. Her cheeks were flushed and her eyes were bright.

She was the most abominable female it had ever been his displeasure to know.

"You are quite right, Vanessa," Con said, his voice shaking with laughter. "And I have always believed that in fact it is the female sex that is the superior of the two. But you see, we men *enjoy* a good bout of fisti-cuffs."

"You are not going to persuade me that this was to be a friendly sparring match," she said. "It was not. For some reason the two of you hate each other—or think you do. If you would just *talk* to each other, perhaps you could patch up your quarrel far more easily than you think and could be friends again. I suppose you were once friends. You grew up five miles apart and are cousins close to each other in age."

"If Elliott will agree to it," Con said, "we will kiss and make up."

"Mrs. Dew," Elliott said, "your impertinence knows no bounds. But I am sorry to have disturbed your walk. Allow me to escort you back to the house."

He glared fiercely at her to show her that he was very aware of the fact that she had not been out innocently walking. Like him, she must have been looking out of her bedchamber window and had seen first Con and then him disappear in this direction. She had drawn her own conclusions and come after them, the interfering baggage.

"Not," she said, standing her ground, "until I have had your assurance—and Constantine's—that you will not fight later today or tomorrow or some other time when I am not present to stop you."

"*I* will return to the house," Con said. "You must not upset yourself over this, Vanessa. As you have guessed, Elliott and I have been friends and enemies—mostly friends—all our lives. And whenever we have fought—even the time when he broke my nose and I black-ened his eye when I was fourteen—we have always laughed immediately afterward and agreed that it was all great fun."

She clucked her tongue, but Con kept on talking.

"I must be leaving within the next few days," he said. "I have business to attend to elsewhere. I promise not to initiate any fight with Elliott in the meantime."

He laughed, made her a bow, threw Elliott a mocking glance, and turned to stride away in the direction of the house.

"Which would put the blame squarely on *your* shoulders," Mrs. Dew said, turning to Elliott with a smile, "if there is a fight. It was cleverly done. Has he always been able to cast you in the light of the villain?"

"I am severely annoyed with you, ma'am," he said.

"I know." Her smile became more rueful. "But I am annoyed with you too. This is a happy week for my brother. And for my sisters too. I do not want that happiness marred by the quarrel that is between you and Constantine. How would they feel if the two of you were to appear at the house with blackened eyes or bloody noses or raw knuckles? They are already fond of Constantine, and they respect you. They do not deserve to be upset by some petty private quarrel."

"It is certainly not petty, ma'am," he said stiffly. "But your point is taken. Has *your* happiness been marred?"

"Not really." She smiled again, the bright, sunny expression he remembered from the Valentine's assembly. "Is this where my ancestors are buried? Constantine did not bring us here when he showed us the park."

"Perhaps," he said, "he thought it too gloomy a spot."

"Or perhaps," she said, "his grief for his brother is too new and too private a thing to be shared with cousins who did not know him. I wish I had. Was he as sweet as Constantine described him?"

"Oh, yes," he said. "He may have been handicapped in many ways and he may have looked different from other people, but we could all learn from persons like Jonathan. He was unfailingly affectionate, even toward those who were impatient with him."

"Were you?" she asked him. "Impatient, I mean?"

"Never with him," he said. "He used to hide from me when I came here—after my father died and I became his guardian, that was. Sometimes, if he could keep from giggling, I would have to waste precious time finding him. But he was always so delighted when I did that it would have been churlish to be annoyed with him. It was Con who put him up to it, after all."

"To amuse him?" she asked. "Or to annoy you?"

"Always the latter," he said.

"Did he resent the fact that you were Jonathan's guardian," she asked him, "even though you were not much older than he, if you are older at all, that is?"

"He did," he said curtly.

"But surely," she said, "he must have understood that it was not really you who had been appointed guardian, but your father, who was older and wiser and more experienced than either of you."

"I suppose he did," he said.

"Could you not," she asked, "have shown some sensitivity and turned over the guardianship to Constantine, even if only unofficially?"

"I could not," he said.

"Oh, dear." She looked steadily at him, her head tipped to one side. "You really are a most inflexible, uncommunicative man. It is just that it seems to me that the enmity that has grown between the two of you is unnecessary. And now you are demanding that Constantine leave here though it has always been his home. Can you feel no compassion for him?"

"Mrs. Dew." He clasped his hands behind his back and leaned a little toward her. "Life is not such a simple thing as you seem to believe it to be. Perhaps it would be as well for you not to try to advise me on matters about which you know virtually nothing."

"Life is often simpler than we give it credit for," she said. "But if you wish me to mind my own business, I will. Where is my great-grandfather buried?"

"There." He turned and pointed and they both moved toward the grave.

She gazed at the headstone and its flowery praise of the earl who was buried there.

"I wonder," she said, "what he would say now if he could see us here—the descendants of the son he cast off and the woman his son married."

"Life is never predictable," he said.

"And it was so unnecessary," she said, "all the conflict, all the suffering and loneliness there must have been on both sides. Here we are anyway, but with so many precious years missing."

Her eyes looked wistful. Con had been right about one thing, Elliott thought. She *did* have fine eyes—even when they were not laughing.

"Where is Jonathan buried?" she asked.

He took her to the newest grave. Its headstone was immaculately clean, the grass around it short and free of weeds. Someone had planted spring flowers there, and snowdrops were blooming and crocus leaves were pushing up through the soil.

Someone cared. Con, he supposed.

A guilt offering?

"I wish I had known him," she said. "I *do* wish it. I believe I would have loved him."

"One could not help being fond of him," he said.

"But not of his brother?" she said, turning her head to look at him. "Perhaps if you had laughed at his attempts to needle you every time he had Jonathan hide from you, you could all have laughed together and been friends. Perhaps what you need as much as anything is a sense of humor."

He felt his nostrils flare.

*"A sense of humor?"* he half barked at her. "In the handling of serious duties? In dealing with a rogue? In looking after the interests of a slow-witted innocent? And in dealing with impertinence too, I suppose?"

"The impertinence being mine?" she said to him. "I could not simply let you fight, you know, without at least trying to stop you. And now I was merely attempting to point out a way in which you might make your own life happier as well as easier. Constantine at least *smiles* much of the time even if there is sometimes an edge of mockery in the expression. You never smile. And if you continue to frown all the time, as you are doing now, you will have permanent lines between your brows before you grow old."

*"Smiles,"* he said. "Ah, now at last I understand the great secret of life. If one smiles, one will have an easy, happy time of it, no matter how much of a rogue one is. I must learn to *smile*, ma'am. Thank you for the advice."

And he smiled at her.

She looked steadily at him, her head cocked to one side again.

"*That* is not a smile," she said. "It is an angry grimace that makes you look a little like a wolf—though I have read that in many ways wolves are the gentlest, most admirable of beasts. You have twice referred to Constantine as a rogue. Just because he resented your guardianship and encouraged Jonathan to play tricks on you? And because he ignored your ultimatum and remained here until we came? *Rogue* is rather a harsh word to describe such a man, is it not? If there is no more to his perfidy than what you have told me, you cannot expect me to accept your opinion without question."

"It is a desirable thing, ma'am," he said, "to know whose word you can trust and whose you cannot."

"And I am supposed to trust yours?" she asked him. "I am supposed to take your word for it that my cousin is a rogue? I am supposed to disregard everything *he* says? I have no reason to trust you or to distrust him. I will make my own observations, my lord, and draw my own conclusions."

"I believe," he said, "our breakfast awaits, ma'am. Shall we walk back to the house?"

"Yes, I suppose so," she said with a sigh. "Oh, goodness, I have no gloves." She touched her head. "And no hat. Whatever must you think of me?"

Wisely, perhaps, he refrained from telling her.

So he had no sense of humor, did he?

Good Lord, he thought as they walked side by side in silence, was one supposed to be cracking jokes at every turn and laughing like a hyena even if no one else did?

Or was one supposed to ooze false charm as Con did?

*8*

ELLIOTT stayed for three more days before he returned home to Finchley Park. And it was during those days that he began to consider seriously the idea of marrying Miss Margaret Huxtable.

The sisters, even though they were more refined than he had at first feared, were desperately in need of some town bronze and some connections suitable to their new status. They needed it all now, this year, this Season. And the Season would be beginning in earnest as soon as Easter was over.

As it was, they were all very countrified and naive and an easy prey to practiced charmers like Con Huxtable.

Con left Warren Hall the day after the averted fight. He had mentioned leaving the evening before, insisting when there was a chorus of protests from his cousins that he really did have important business to attend to elsewhere. He left without fanfare, early in the morning before anyone was up.

Elliott was greatly relieved. But he did not trust Con to stay away. The Huxtables needed to be taken away instead, at least temporarily, to be educated in the ways of the *ton*.

Elliott observed them all during the days following Con's departure. And he was pleased with what he saw of Miss Huxtable. She was learning fast—from her consultations with the housekeeper and the cook—how to run such a large household. She was taking her duties seriously.

She was an intelligent and sensible woman.

She was also, of course, almost incredibly beautiful. With some grooming, which she would quickly acquire in town, she would be nothing short of stunning.

It was a dispassionate observation. He felt no stirring of desire for her. But then he had never expected to feel any such thing for his chosen bride. One married for reasons other than passion.

Marriage to Miss Huxtable would be convenient in a number of ways. And there was no point in paying any attention to the slight depression he felt at the prospect. Just the thought of marriage itself was depressing. It was also unfortunately necessary and could be delayed no longer.

He was still not sure when he left Warren Hall that he would make the offer, but he was seriously considering it.

Young Merton had concentrated more of his attention on his position once the distraction of Con's presence had been removed—though he was clearly disappointed to lose someone he admired a great deal. He and Samson took well to each other, and Samson was just the man to teach his young master much of what he needed to know. Elliott had talked with the boy about the necessity of hiring a tutor to teach him the rest—of hiring two tutors, in fact, one to teach him to be an aristocrat, the other to instruct him in the academics he would need in order to go to university. The boy had been somewhat taken aback by the suggestion that he continue with that plan, but Elliott had pointed out to him that a true gentleman was also an educated gentleman. Miss Huxtable had agreed with him, and Merton had succumbed.

Elliott was not displeased with the boy.

George Bowen had been sent on to London to interview suitable candidates for tutor, as well as one for the position of valet. Merton had protested that he did not need a personal servant since he had always looked after his own needs. But it was one of the first lessons he must learn. An earl must look the part when he went into society, in deportment and manner as well as in dress, and who better to see that he did than an experienced valet?

Finally Elliott felt it possible to leave Warren Hall, at least for a few days. He wanted to go home. He also wanted to give full consideration to what he had rejected out of hand a mere couple of weeks ago when George had first suggested it. But he thought he would probably decide to offer for Miss Huxtable.

There was really only one consideration that might give him serious pause. If he married her, he would be acquiring Mrs. Dew as a sister-in-law.

It was a depressing thought.

It was enough to cause him to live in a permanent bad temper.

The woman had smiled sunnily at him for three days, as if she thought him something of a joke.

It felt good to be home at last.

His youngest sister was the first person he saw when he arrived. She was on her way out of the house, dressed dashingly for riding. She smiled warmly and turned her cheek for his kiss.

"Well?" she asked him. "What is he like?"

"I am delighted to see you too, Cece," he said dryly. "You mean Merton? He is cheerful and bright and seventeen years old."

"And handsome?" she asked. "What color is his hair?"

"Blond," he said.

"I prefer men with dark hair," she told him. "But no matter. Is he tall? And slim?"

"Is he an Adonis in fact?" he asked her. "You will have to decide for yourself. Mama will doubtless take you over there soon. His sisters are there with him."

She brightened still further. "Are any of them my age?" she asked.

"I believe the youngest must be close," he said. "A year or two older, probably."

"And is she pretty?" she asked.

"Yes, very," he told her. "But so are you. And now you have had your compliment from me and can go on your way. You are not going to be riding alone, I hope?"

"No, of course not!" she said, pulling a face. "One of the grooms will ride with me. I am going to join the Campbells. They asked me yesterday and Mama said I might go provided it did not rain."

"Where *is* Mama?" he asked.

"In her rooms," she said.

A few minutes later he sank gratefully into a soft upholstered chair in his mother's private boudoir and accepted a cup of coffee from her hands.

"You really ought to have let me know that you were bringing Merton's three sisters as well as him, Elliott," she said in response to the brief report he had delivered as soon as he had hugged her and asked after her health. "Cecily and I would have gone to call on them yesterday or the day before."

"I judged that they needed some time to adjust to their new surroundings and circumstances, Mama," he said. "Throckbridge is a very small village quite off the beaten track. They lived there in near poverty in a small cottage. The youngest sister was teaching at the village school."

"And the widow?" she asked.

"She was living at Rundle Park, home of a baronet, her father-in-law," he said. "But it is not large, and Sir Humphrey Dew is a foolish, garrulous man, albeit good-natured and harmless. I doubt he has ever been farther than ten miles from home."

"They are all going to need to be brought up to scratch, then," she said.

"They are." He sighed. "I hoped to bring just Merton himself for now. The sisters could have followed later—preferably *much* later."

"But they *are* his sisters," she said, getting to her feet to pour him another cup. "And he *is* just a boy."

"Thank you, Mama," he said, taking his cup from her hands. "How peaceful it is in here."

He wished she did not have another daughter to bring out this year. It would save him from having to . . .

But he was going to have to marry *someone* this year.

"They are a noisy family?" she asked, raising her eyebrows.

"Oh, no, no, nothing like that." He sighed again. "It is just that I felt so—"

"Responsible?" she suggested. "You have done ever since you inherited that obligation, Elliott. Is the boy intelligent? Serious-minded? Willing to learn?"

"Definitely intelligent," he said, "though with something of a restless nature, I believe. He has wings and desperately wishes to use them without having much idea of how it might best be done."

"He is, then, a typical young man," she said with a smile.

"I suppose so," he said. "But he shows an interest in his land and its workings and in the prospect of taking on all the responsibilities of being a peer of the realm when he reaches his majority. He has agreed to continue with his plans to attend Oxford this autumn. He certainly has charm. I believe the servants at Warren Hall already adore him—not excluding Samson."

"Then your time and efforts will not be wasted," she said. "And the ladies? Are they hopelessly rustic? Vulgar? Dull-minded?"

"None of those things." He drained his cup, sighed with contentment as he stretched out his booted feet before him, and set it down at his elbow. "I believe they will go on well enough. But, Mama, they are going to need to be taken to town this spring and outfitted properly and introduced to all the right people and presented to society and . . . Well, I just do not know how it is to be done. *I* cannot do it—not for the sisters, at least."

"Certainly not," she agreed.

"And *you* cannot do it," he said. "You have Cecily to bring out this year."

He looked at her half hopefully.

"I do," she agreed.

"I did think perhaps Aunt Fanny or Aunt Roberta—" he began.

"Oh, Elliott." She interrupted him. "You *cannot* be serious."

"No," he said. "I suppose not. And Grandmama is far

too elderly. George says I ought to marry and have my wife sponsor them."

She brightened noticeably but then frowned.

"You told me after Christmas," she said, "that you intend to marry this year, before you turn thirty. I am delighted, of course, but I do hope you are not intending to choose coldly with your reason and forget that you also have a heart."

"And yet," he said, "marriages that are carefully planned and arranged often turn out more happily than love matches, Mama."

He wished he had not said that as soon as the words were out. His mother's marriage had been very carefully arranged. But though she had been young and beautiful—and was still handsome in middle age—it had not been a happy match. His father had remained firmly attached to the mistress and family that had preceded her and her own.

She smiled into her cup but did not look up at him.

"George suggested that I marry Miss Huxtable," he told her, watching her closely.

His mother had been lifting her cup to her lips, but her hand paused in midair.

"The eldest sister?" she asked.

"Of course," he said.

"A rustic girl who has been living in a rural cottage?" She frowned at him and set her cup back in the saucer. "And someone you scarcely know? How old is she?"

"Probably in her middle twenties," he said. "She is sensible and refined of manner despite her humble upbringing in a country vicarage—and she is the great-granddaughter and sister of an earl, Mama."

"*George* said." She looked fixedly at him. "But what do *you* say, Elliott?"

He shrugged. "It is time I married and set up my nursery," he said. "I am quite resigned to being a married man before the year is out and a father as soon as possible after that. I have no preference for any particular bride. Miss Huxtable is, I suppose, as eligible as anyone."

His mother sat back in her chair and said nothing for a while.

"Jessica and Averil both married advantageously," she said. "But just as important, Elliott, they both had an affection for their husbands even before they married them. It is what I will hope for with Cecily either this year or next. It is what I have always hoped for with you too."

"This is a discussion we have had before." He smiled at her. "I am *not* a romantic, Mama. I hope to marry someone with whom I can enjoy some comfort and companionship and even affection down the years. But most of all I hope to marry sensibly."

"And is Miss Huxtable a sensible choice?" she asked him.

"I trust so," he said.

"Is she beautiful?" his mother asked.

"Extremely," he said.

She set down her cup and saucer on the table beside her.

"It is high time Cecily and I took the carriage over to Warren Hall," she said, "to pay our respects to the new Earl of Merton and his sisters. They must think it remiss of us not to have done so already. Is Constantine still there?"

"He left three days ago." His jaw tightened.

"Cecily will be disappointed," she said. "She adores him. I daresay the new Earl of Merton will be inducement enough to persuade her to accompany me, though. She has asked a thousand questions about him, none of which I have been able to answer. I will take a look at Miss Huxtable. Are you quite determined to have her?"

"The more I think of it, the more I am in favor of the idea," he said.

"And will she have you?" his mother asked.

He could not see why not. Miss Huxtable was single and perilously close to being an old maid. He could understand why she had not married before now, though with her looks she must have had offers even in a backwater like Throckbridge. But she had made that promise to her father, and she had kept it. There was no further need to remain with her family now, though. Her two sisters were past girlhood, and Merton would have them for company—and his guardian and eldest sister for neighbors.

Nothing, in fact, could be more convenient—for any of them.

"I believe so," he said.

His mother leaned forward and touched his hand.

"I shall go and see Miss Huxtable for myself," she said. "Tomorrow."

"Thank you," he said. "I would appreciate your opinion, Mama."

"My opinion," she said, "ought not to matter, Elliott. If she is the woman of your choice, you ought to be willing to defy the devil himself if necessary in order to wed her."

She raised her eyebrows as if expecting him to

declare an undying passion for Miss Huxtable. He covered her hand with his own and patted it before getting to his feet.

Viscountess Lyngate called at Warren Hall with her daughter the next day.

There was very little warning of their coming.

Stephen came into the library from the steward's office, where he had been ensconced with Mr. Samson, to inform his sisters that Viscount Lyngate's carriage was approaching up the driveway. But there was nothing very remarkable in that. He had said when he left yesterday that he would return frequently. And his business would be with Stephen.

Margaret was examining the housekeeper's books, which Mrs. Forsythe had sent up at her request. Vanessa, having finished writing a letter to Lady Dew and her sisters-in-law, was examining all the leather-bound books on the shelves and thinking that this room was a little like heaven.

And then Katherine came flying up from the stables to announce the approach of the carriage *and* the viscount himself, who was on horseback.

"Whoever can be in the carriage, then?" Margaret asked in some alarm, closing the book on the desk in front of her and running her hands over her hair.

"Oh, my," Katherine said, looking down at her disheveled self—she had just been having a lesson with one of the grooms. "His *mother,* do you think?"

She dashed off again, presumably to wash her hands and face and make herself more presentable.

Margaret and Vanessa had no such opportunity. They

could hear the carriage already drawing to a halt before the doors beyond the window, and then they could hear voices in the hall. Stephen stepped out to greet the new arrivals. And they were indeed the viscountess and her daughter. Viscount Lyngate brought them into the library almost immediately and presented them.

They looked very grand indeed to Vanessa. Their dresses and pelisses and bonnets were obviously in the very height of fashion. She felt instantly transformed into a country mouse and looked reproachfully at the viscount, who might have sent a warning. She was still wearing the apron she had put on over her gray dress as protection against any dust on the bookshelves. Margaret's hair, like her own, was caught up in the simplest of knots and had not been brushed for hours.

He looked back and raised his eyebrows—and it was almost as if she could read his thoughts. True ladies, that disdainful look seemed to say, were always prepared for unexpected visitors during the afternoon. He, of course, was looking as immaculate as ever—and as handsome and virile.

"How kind of you to have called," Margaret was saying, behaving as if she were quite unruffled. "Do come up to the drawing room, where we can be more comfortable. Mrs. Forsythe will send tea."

"I was extremely happy to hear from Elliott that you had insisted upon bringing your sisters with you, Merton," Lady Lyngate said as they were ascending the stairs. "This is a large house for a young gentleman alone."

"If he had not insisted, *I* would," Margaret told her. "Stephen is only seventeen years old, and while he insists that he is as close to being an adult as makes no difference, I would not have known a moment's rest if I had allowed him to come alone, with only Viscount Lyngate and Mr. Bowen for company."

"That is quite understandable," Lady Lyngate said while Stephen looked sheepish and Miss Wallace eyed him with interest.

"*I* would not have guessed you were seventeen," that young lady said. "I would have thought you were older than I am, and I am eighteen."

Stephen smiled winningly at her.

Katherine joined them after they had been in the drawing room just a few minutes. She looked tidy and clean with a shiny, freshly washed face. She also looked lovely, as she always did. But Vanessa, gazing fondly and critically at her, could see that she appeared quite unpolished in contrast with Miss Wallace.

"Perhaps," Viscount Lyngate said, "we could excuse ourselves from taking tea with the ladies, Merton. I want to hear what you have accomplished since yesterday."

Miss Wallace looked openly disappointed, but she transferred her attention to Katherine.

"Elliott says you are to go to town after Easter for a come-out Season," she said. "It is to be my come-out too. We will be able to keep each other company. I wish my hair had golden highlights as yours does. It is lovely."

Miss Wallace was very dark—like her brother. It was obvious that they got their coloring primarily from their mother, who looked very Greek with her silvering dark hair and strong, handsome features.

"Thank you," Katherine said. "I am very much enjoying being at Warren Hall, I must confess. I am not so sure about London just yet, though. There is so much space to explore here and so much beauty to appreciate, and I am learning to ride."

"Only *learning*?" Miss Wallace asked, all incredulity.

"I am afraid so," Katherine said. "Meg learned when Papa was alive and we still had a horse. And Nessie rode at Rundle Park after she married Hedley, our brother-in-law. But I never had a chance. Constantine gave me a few lessons before he went away a few days ago, and now Mr. Taber, the head groom, is helping me."

"I am *so* vexed that Con has left," Miss Wallace said. "He never comes to Finchley these days and Mama will not allow me to come here alone. I adore him. Is he not the most handsome man you have ever seen?"

Katherine smiled and Lady Lyngate raised her eyebrows.

"Anyway," Miss Wallace continued, "you simply must come to town for the Season. I brought a book of fashion plates with me—it is in the carriage. Do let me show it to you. Some of the newest styles would look wonderful on you—you are so beautifully tall and slender. Indeed, I am sure they *all* would."

"Perhaps, Kate," Margaret suggested, "you and Miss Wallace would like to take the book into the library, where you may enjoy its contents without interruption."

They went off together, leaving Margaret and Vanessa alone with the viscountess. She smiled at them graciously but kindly enough, and they conversed politely on a number of topics while tea was served.

"You really do all need to make an appearance in town this spring," Lady Lyngate said eventually, "though I can understand that the prospect may be daunting to you. Your brother is too young, of course, to mingle freely with his peers as he will be able to do in a few years' time. Nevertheless, the *ton* will wish to have a look at him. They have been deprived of an Earl of Merton for long enough. Jonathan was a mere boy and incapable anyway of leaving here."

"It is nevertheless tragic that he died so young," Vanessa said. "He was your nephew, ma'am?"

"My sister's boy," the viscountess said. "Yes, it was sad indeed, especially as she died not long after his birth. But he was happy all his life, you know. Perhaps happiness compensates for a short life. I like to believe so. And he died suddenly and peacefully. It is your brother who belongs here now, however, and he seems to be a delightful young man."

"We think so, of course," Vanessa said.

"He owns a house in town," Margaret said. "And so there would be no problem of accommodation if we were to go there. But there are all sorts of other problems, as you can see, my lady, just from looking at us."

"You are extremely lovely," Lady Lyngate said frankly, looking, of course, just at Margaret.

"Thank you." Margaret flushed. "But that is not the point."

"No, it is not," Lady Lyngate agreed. "But if one of you were just married, your problem would be solved."

"My husband is dead, ma'am," Vanessa said. "He did not move in *ton*nish circles anyway, though his father is a baronet."

"No," the viscountess said, her eyes resting kindly upon Vanessa for a moment before moving back to Margaret. "The husband would have to be well placed in society, someone to give you position and countenance. And then with a presentation at court and the right clothes and a little polishing, you would be quite able to sponsor your sisters and find husbands for them too."

Margaret's hand crept to her bosom, and her flush returned. "*I*, my lady?" she asked.

"You have been caring for your brother and sisters for a number of years," Lady Lyngate said. "You have behaved admirably. But valuable years have gone by. You are still lovely, and you have a natural grace of manner that will make it relatively easy for you to take with the *ton*. But it is, my dear, time for you to marry—for your own sake as well as for that of your siblings."

"Meg does not have to marry for *my* sake," Vanessa said, her eyes upon Margaret, whose flush had disappeared, leaving her looking rather white.

"No," Lady Lyngate agreed. "But you have had your chance, Mrs. Dew. Your elder sister has not. And your younger sister will need her chance soon—she is older than Cecily. Forgive me. You may say that this is none of my business, and you would, of course, be quite right. However, you confess yourselves to be in need of help and advice. This is my advice to you, Miss Huxtable. Marry as soon as you may."

Margaret's color had returned and she looked suddenly amused.

"I am reminded of the old puzzle over the chicken and the egg," she said. "I need to marry in order that we may make an easier entrée into society. But you must agree, my lady, that I would need to be in society in order to find a husband."

"Not necessarily," Lady Lyngate said. "Perhaps there is a prospective husband—an eminently eligible one— closer than you think."

She did not elaborate but asked them if they had thought of sending to London for a lady's maid who could help them learn something of the newest fashions and who could dress them and style their hair more fashionably. She would be very willing to see to acquiring one on their behalf, she told them.

"I would be very grateful," Margaret told her. "I have only to look at you and Miss Wallace to understand how much we have to learn."

It was only later, when they had strolled out onto the terrace to look down at the formal gardens while waiting for the carriage to come up and Miss Wallace and the viscount to join their mother, that she said what perhaps she had been hinting at earlier.

"Elliott has decided to take a bride this year," she said. "He will be a brilliant catch for any lady, of course. As well as the obvious attributes, he also has a loyal heart—even a loving one if he would but realize it. But the right woman will teach him to discover that. It is his intention—and my hope—to find a lady of character and principle. Beauty and grace would not come amiss either, of course. Perhaps he will not have to look too far."

She spoke with her eyes on the empty flower beds below, as if she were thinking aloud.

Vanessa was not the only one who read the unspoken message. The carriage departed a few minutes later, Viscount Lyngate riding beside it. Katherine and Stephen walked off in the direction of the stables—they were going to ride into the village to visit the Graingers—leaving Vanessa and Margaret alone on the terrace.

"Nessie," Margaret said after a few moments, when

the clopping of the horses' hooves grew fainter, "was Lady Lyngate saying what I think she was saying?"

"It would seem," Vanessa said, "that she is trying to arrange a match between you and her son."

"But that is utterly absurd!" Margaret exclaimed.

"It is not actually," Vanessa said. "He is of an age to look about him for a wife—all gentlemen of property must marry, you know, whatever their personal inclination might be. And you are eligible. Not only are you single and beautiful and refined, but you are also the sister of an earl and the very earl over whom he is guardian. What could be more convenient than for him to marry you?"

"Convenient for *whom*?" Margaret asked.

"And *he* is very eligible," Vanessa continued. "Just two weeks ago we were filled with awe just to know he was staying at the village inn and would be attending the assembly. He is titled and wealthy and young and handsome. And you yourself explained to Lady Lyngate the awkwardness of our situation, with no lady to introduce us to society."

"And I would be able to do that for myself and for you and Kate if I were married?" Margaret asked, shivering and leading the way back toward the house.

"Yes," Vanessa said. "I suppose you would. You would be presented at court as Lady Lyngate explained and then you might do as you pleased. And Viscount Lyngate would be able to do all in his power for us without any appearance of impropriety. It would be entirely proper if he were your husband."

For some reason it was a ghastly thought—Meg and Viscount Lyngate. Vanessa tried to picture them together—at the altar during their nuptials, sitting on either side of a winter hearth in a domestic setting, and . . . No! She would not even try to picture *that*. She gave her head a little shake.

Margaret stopped beside the fountain. She set a hand on the edge of the stone basin, as if to steady herself.

"Nessie," she said, "you cannot be serious."

"The question is," Vanessa said, "whether *she* is serious. And whether she can persuade the viscount to be serious about it too."

"But would she even have dropped that less-than-subtle hint," Margaret asked, "if he knew nothing about it? And why would she even have *thought* of such a thing if he had not somehow mentioned it to her as a possibility? She had never set eyes on us before this afternoon. Is it not likely that she came here today to take a look at his proposed bride? The fact that she said what she just did would surely indicate that she approves of his choice. But how *could* she? I look positively *rustic*. And how could *he* have considered such a thing? He has never given even the smallest indication that he is interested in making a match with me. Have I walked into some bizarre nightmare, Nessie?"

Vanessa realized that Margaret must be right. Viscount Lyngate had known from the start that their coming to Warren Hall with Stephen was going to pose a problem. It was altogether possible that he had thought to solve at least part of the problem by marrying Margaret. And according to his mother he had already decided that he must marry this year.

"But even if he offers," she said, "you can say no, Meg. Would you wish to, though?"

"To say no?" Margaret frowned and said nothing for a long time.

*. . . have I walked into some bizarre nightmare?*

"Is it Crispin?" Vanessa asked softly.

It was the first time his name had been spoken between them for a long, long time.

Margaret looked sharply at her and then away again, but not before Vanessa had seen tears well into her eyes.

"Who?" Meg asked. "Do I know anyone of that name?"

There was such pain and such bitterness in her voice that Vanessa could think of no answer to give. Obviously the questions were rhetorical anyway.

"If I once did," Margaret said eventually, "I know him no longer."

Vanessa swallowed. She felt close to tears herself.

"If I were to marry," Margaret said, "*if* Viscount Lyngate were to ask, that is, I would be able to make life considerably easier for Kate, would I not? And for you. And for Stephen."

"But you cannot marry just for our sakes," Vanessa said, aghast.

"Why not?" Margaret looked at her with bleak, empty eyes. "I love you all. You are everything to me, the three of you. You are my reason for living."

Vanessa was appalled. She had never heard Margaret speak with such despair before now. She was always calm and cheerful, the anchor upon whom they all depended. But then Vanessa had always known about her broken heart. She had just not had the imagination to understand quite how it had emptied out her sister's very soul. She *ought* to have understood.

"But now your obligation to us has been considerably

eased," she said. "Stephen is in a position to care for us and provide for us. All we need from you is your love, Meg—and your happiness. Do not do this. *Please.*"

Margaret smiled.

"Such a Cheltenham tragedy," she said, "though we do not even know for sure that Lady Lyngate has picked me out as the viscount's prospective bride. We do not know how *he* feels about the idea, or even if it has occurred to him. How lowering now, Nessie, if he does *not* come here offering for me."

She laughed lightly, but her eyes were still bleak.

As they made their way into the house and into the library, where the fire had been built up again and was giving off a welcome warmth, Vanessa felt a heavy sense of foreboding.

Crispin would surely never come for Margaret. But if she married Viscount Lyngate, entirely for the sake of her sisters and brother, life would lose all meaning for her.

*They* were not Margaret's reason for living. *Hope* was that, even if it had all but been snuffed out over the four years of Crispin's absence.

Hope was what gave meaning to all lives.

Margaret could *not* be allowed to marry Viscount Lyngate. Perhaps he would not even offer, of course, but Vanessa was dreadfully afraid that he would. And if he did, she feared that Margaret would say yes.

Feared for Margaret's sake.

*Only* Margaret's?

But the question, verbalized in her mind, took her by surprise and shook her somewhat. What possible personal objection could she have to his marrying Meg? Or anyone else for that matter? It was true that she had *al-*

*most* fallen in love with him at the Valentine's assembly, but even then she had realized that there was far more in him to repel her than there was to attract.

It just was not fair that he was so very, very good-looking.

But even if she *were* in love with him—which she certainly was not—she must surely be the very *last* woman he would ever think of marrying.

He must not be allowed to offer for Meg, though—she might accept him.

There must be a way of stopping him. She was just going to have to think what it was before it was too late, Vanessa decided.

Though she was already convinced that there *was* only one possible way.

An *impossible* way more like.

# 9

ELLIOTT had made a firm decision.

He was going to marry Miss Huxtable. If she would
have him, that was, but he really could not see any reason why she would not.

It made a great deal of sense that they marry each
other. And his mother approved of her. She had liked all
the Huxtables, in fact. She had found them amiable and
unaffected.

"One thing I am sure you could count on if you were
to marry Miss Huxtable, Elliott," she had said, "is her
loyalty and devotion. And those two qualities almost
invariably deepen into affection and love. I see nothing
but a bright future for you."

She had looked hopefully at him. She had meant, of
course, that his wife's loyalty and devotion would provoke affection and love in *him*.

"I am in total agreement with you, Mama," he had
said.

But love? He had never been in love—whatever that
term meant. He was not *in love* with Miss Huxtable. Or
with Anna, for that matter, or any of the mistresses who
had preceded her or any of the ladies who had occasionally taken his fancy. At least, he did not *think* he had been.
If he sometimes dreamed of finding that elusive magic
*something* that might after all make marriage appealing to

him, he did not expect it. It was never going to happen. But of course there had never been any question of his *not* marrying when the time came. It was one of his primary duties to do so.

The time had come, that was all.

And he would do his duty. And he would be sensible at the same time.

He rode again to Warren Hall the day after his mother's visit there, but this time he went to pay his addresses to Miss Huxtable. He was feeling damnably depressed, if the truth were known. Really, he scarcely knew her, did he? What if . . . ?

But he had never been one to indulge in what-ifs. He could only deal with present reality.

His decision had been made, so here he was.

By the time he rode into the stable yard and turned over his horse to a groom's care, he was feeling decidedly grim, which was not the way one would wish to feel when about to make a marriage offer. He turned his steps resolutely in the direction of the house. He was not going to allow himself to get cold feet at this late stage of the game.

He rounded the corner of the yard and ran almost headlong into Mrs. Dew—of all people to meet when he was feeling irritable. They both stopped abruptly, and he took a step back so that there might be more than three inches of space separating them.

"Oh!" she said.

"I do beg your pardon, ma'am."

They spoke simultaneously.

"I saw you riding up the driveway," she said. "I came to meet you."

He raised his eyebrows. "I am flattered," he said. "Or am I? Has something happened? You look agitated."

"Not at all." She smiled—and looked even more so. "I was wondering if I might have a private word with you."

To deliver another scold? To enumerate more of his shortcomings? To ruffle more of his feathers? To worsen his mood even further?

"Of course." He cupped her elbow in one hand and drew her away from the stables and the house. They began to walk across the wide lawn that led to the lake.

"Thank you," she said.

She was wearing a pale blue dress with a matching cloak, he noticed. Her bonnet was a darker blue. It was the first time he had seen her out of mourning. She looked marginally more attractive than usual.

"How may I be of service to you, ma'am?" he asked curtly when they were out of earshot of anyone at the stables.

"Well," she said after drawing an audible breath, "I was wondering if you would be willing to marry me."

He had already released his hold on her elbow—which was probably a good thing. He might have broken a few bones there when his hands clenched involuntarily into fists. But—could he have heard her correctly?

"Marry you?" he asked in what sounded shockingly like his normal voice.

"Yes," she said. She sounded breathless—as if she had just run five miles without stopping. "If you would not mind terribly, that is. I believe your primary concern is to marry someone eligible, and I do qualify on that count. I am an earl's sister and the widow of a baronet's son. And I think your secondary concern is to marry one of *us* so that you may more easily deal with the problem of bringing us out into society. I know you think you would prefer Meg. I know you do not even like me because I have quarreled with you on more than one occasion. But really I am not quarrelsome by nature. Quite the contrary—I am usually the one who makes people cheerful. And I do not mind . . ."

Her speech, hastily delivered with hardly a pause for breath, trailed off and there was a moment of silence.

No, he had not misheard. Or misunderstood.

He had stopped walking abruptly and turned to face her. She stopped too and looked up at him, directly into his eyes, her own wide. Her face was flushed.

As well it might be.

He could not think of anyone else who had such power to render him speechless.

"Please *say* something," she said when he had not responded within ten seconds or so. "I know this must be a shock to you. You could not have expected it. But *think* about it. You cannot really *love* Meg, can you? You scarcely know her. You have chosen her because she is the eldest—and because she is beautiful. You do not know me either, of course, though you may *think* you do. But really it cannot make much difference to you which of us you marry, can it?"

*I know this must be a shock to you.* Had there ever been more of an understatement? Marry *her*? *Mrs. Dew?* Was the woman quite, quite mad?

She bit her lip, and her eyes seemed to grow even larger as she waited for him to speak.

"Let me get one thing straight, Mrs. Dew," he said, frowning. "Do I interpret your flattering proposal correctly? Are you by any chance offering yourself as the sacrificial lamb?"

"Oh, dear." She looked away from him for a moment. "No, not really. It would be no sacrifice. I believe I would like to be married again, and I might as well marry for convenience, as you would be doing. It really *would* be convenient if we were to marry each other, would it not? It would make things far easier for Meg and Kate—and for Stephen too. And maybe your mother will not mind *too* too much if it is not Meg, though of course I am not as beautiful as she—or beautiful at all, in fact. But I should do my best to see that she approved of me once she had accustomed herself to the idea."

"My mother?" he asked faintly.

"She clearly indicated yesterday," Mrs. Dew said, "that she approved of Meg as a potential daughter-in-law. She did not say so openly, of course, because that was for you to do. But we understood her nevertheless."

*Damnation!*

"Mrs. Dew." He clasped his hands behind him and leaned a little closer to her. "Is this by any chance how you came to marry Dew?"

He had the sensation for a moment that he was falling into her eyes. And then she lowered her lids over them, shutting her soul from his sight. He frowned at the top of her bonnet.

"Oh," she said. "Yes, as a matter of fact it was. He was dying, you see. But he was very young and there was so much he had wanted to do with his life—including marrying me. He loved me. He wanted me. I knew that. And so I insisted that he marry me though he was not willing to trap me, as he put it." Her eyelids came up again, and her eyes looked back into his own. "I made his last year a very, very happy one. I do not deceive myself about that. I know how to make a man happy."

Good Lord! Was this a frisson of sexual awareness he was feeling? Impossible! Except that he did not know what else it could be.

He shook his head slightly and turned away from her to stride onward in the direction of the lake. She fell into step beside him.

"I am sorry." She sounded dejected. "I have made a mess of this, have I not? Or perhaps there *was* no other way I might have approached you or explained myself."

"Am I to understand," he said testily, "that Miss Huxtable will not be disappointed if she discovers that you have stolen me from under her nose?"

"Oh, no, not at all," she assured him. "Meg does not want to marry you, but I am afraid she will if you ask because she has a fearful sense of duty and she *will* insist upon doing what she thinks is right for the rest of us even though there is no real need for her to do so any longer."

"I see," he said, quelling the urge to bellow with rage—or perhaps with laughter. "And she does not wish to marry me because . . . ?"

He slowed his steps and turned his head to look down at her again. He began to wonder if he would perhaps wake up at any moment now to find that he had dreamed this whole bizarre encounter. It surely could *not* be real.

"Because she is dreadfully in love with Crispin," she said.

"Crispin?" He believed he had heard the name before.

"Crispin Dew," she told him. "Hedley's elder brother.

She would have married him four years ago when he purchased a commission and joined his regiment, but she would not leave us. They had an understanding, though."

"If they are betrothed," he said, "why would you fear that she might accept an offer from me?"

"But they are not," she said, "and he has not been home or sent any message to Meg in almost four years."

"Is there something I am not grasping here?" he asked after a few moments of silence. They had arrived at the bank of the lake and stopped walking again. The sun was shining. Its rays were sparkling on the water.

"Yes," she said. "The female heart. Meg's is bruised, perhaps even broken. She knows he will never come back to her, but while she is single there is always hope. Hope is all she has left. I would *really* rather you did not make her an offer. She would probably accept, and she would make you a good and dutiful wife for the rest of both your lives. But there would never be a spark of anything else between you."

He leaned a little toward her again.

"And there *would* be between you and me?" he asked her. He was still not sure if it was anger or a bizarre sort of hilarity he felt at this whole ridiculous conversation. But he suspected that one or the other was about to erupt at any moment.

She flushed a rosy red again as she stared back into his eyes.

"I know how to please a man," she said almost in a whisper and sank her teeth into her lower lip.

He would have thought them the words and gesture of a practiced coquette if it had not been for her blush and her wide eyes. Good God, she was probably as innocent as a babe despite her short-lived marriage to a dying man. Did she really know what she was saying? Did she know she was playing with fire?

"In bed?" he asked her very deliberately.  •

She licked her lips, another provocative gesture that he guessed was unconscious.

"Yes," she said. "I am not a virgin, if that is what you were wondering. Hedley was capable— Well, never mind. Yes, I would know how to please you in bed. And out of it too. I know how to make people cheerful. I know how to make them laugh."

"And I need to be cheered up and to laugh?" he said, narrowing his eyes on her. "And you can make it happen even though I have no sense of humor?"

"Oh, *that*." She looked away from him to gaze out at the lake. "I hurt you, did I not? Somehow that seems to be the worst insult one can cast upon anyone. People will admit to all sorts of vices and shortcomings except a lack of humor. And I did not actually *say* that you had none, did I? I merely said that you never smile. I meant that you take life too seriously."

"Life *is* serious," he said.

"No, it is not." She looked back at him. "Not always or even frequently. There is always something to marvel over. There is always joy to be found. There is always the possibility of laughter in almost any situation."

"And yet," he said, "you lost a husband in a particularly cruel manner. Was not *that* serious?"

"Not a day passed," she told him, her eyes suddenly bright, "in which we did not marvel at the wonder of our world and our life together. There was not a day without laughter. Except the last. But even then he smiled. It was the last expression on his face as he died."

Lord! He did not need this. He waited with some impatience to wake up and find it still early morning with himself still safely in his own bed—preparing to pay his addresses to Miss Huxtable.

"But we have strayed from the point," she said. "*Will* you marry *me* instead of Meg?"

"Why either of you?" he asked her. "Would you not prefer your freedom if I assure you that I will not then pay my addresses to your sister?"

She stared at him again.

"Oh," she said, "you really do not want me, do you?"

*Of course* he did not want her. Good lord! She was surely the last woman on earth he could possibly ever want. She had nothing—*nothing!*—to commend her.

He opened his mouth to confirm her suspicion.

Except one thing—she had *one* thing to commend her. How had his mother phrased it yesterday? *Loyalty and devotion.* That was two things. But she had them both—directed not toward him, but toward her family.

She had realized yesterday from something his mother had said that he was considering offering marriage to her elder sister—and Miss Huxtable had realized it too. Mrs. Dew knew that her sister would accept his offer even though doing so would shatter her already bruised heart. So she had thought desperately of how she might prevent such a disaster. And she had concocted her scheme—instead of taking the easy and obvious course of coming to him today and simply explaining the situation to him. Perhaps she had thought him too much of a monster—or too arrogant!—to listen to reason. However it was, she had decided to offer herself as the family sacrificial lamb. And she had done so even though she had never made a secret of the fact that she disliked and disapproved of him.

And now he was about to humiliate her in perhaps the worst way imaginable. She had offered herself and he was about to spurn the gift—eloquently and brutally.

And serve her right too, he thought nastily, frowning at her.

But he closed his mouth.

"I am not even pretty, am I?" she said. "And I have been married before. It was terribly foolish of me to think that my plan might work and you would be willing to take me. *Will* you promise not to offer for Meg, though? Or Kate either. She needs someone different from you."

"Someone more *human*?" he asked. His eyes narrowed again.

She closed her eyes briefly.

"I did not mean that the way it sounded," she said. "I merely meant that she needs someone younger and . . . and . . ."

"With a sense of humor?" he suggested.

She looked at him and smiled unexpectedly—a smile full of laughter and mischief.

"Do you keep hoping you will wake up and find it is still last night?" she asked him. "*I* do. I have never in my life made such an idiot of myself. And I cannot even ask you to forget this ever happened. It would be impossible to forget."

Yes, it would. He was suddenly angry again.

He leaned forward and set his lips to hers.

She jerked her head back like a frightened rabbit and he raised his eyebrows.

"It is just that I would like a little proof," he said, "that your twice-made boast was not entirely idle."

She looked at him in incomprehension for a moment.

"That I know how to please a man?" Her eyes were huge again, her cheeks aflame.

"Yes," he said softly. "*That* boast."

"It was not a boast."

When he did not move, she lifted her gloved hands to frame his face, raised her puckered lips to his, and kissed him very softly and gently on the lips.

It was the saddest apology for a kiss he had ever been given by any woman who was not either his mother or one of his sisters.

But *that,* he thought as she released him and looked anxiously into his eyes, was *definitely* a frisson of sexual awareness he felt tightening his groin area. More than a frisson, in fact.

Good Lord!

"Hats and gloves *are* an impediment, are they not?" he said, removing his own and dropping them to the grass, and then pulling free the ribbon beneath her chin and sending her bonnet to the ground behind her.

She slid off her gloves, biting her lip as she did so.

"Now," he said, "you can make a less inhibited demonstration."

She framed his face with her hands again—they were warm and soft—and gazed into his eyes until she kissed him.

Her mouth was still softly puckered, but this time she moved it over his lips, parting her own slightly so that he could feel the moist heat within. And her fingers crept up into his hair. She kissed his chin, his cheeks, his closed eyelids, his temples, very softly, very gently. And then his mouth again, touching the tip of her tongue to his lips, running it slowly along the seam.

No other part of her body touched him.

He stood very still, his arms at his sides, his fingers slowly curling into his palms.

And then she was done with her demonstration. She stepped back, and her hands fell to her sides.

"You must understand," she said, "that Hedley had no experience at all before I married him. And I did not either, of course. And he was very, very ill through most of our marriage. I do not . . . I am sorry. It *was* a boast."

He looked downward, stooped to pick up a flat pebble, and turned toward the lake to send it bouncing across the water, leaving tiny whirlpools in its wake.

He had suddenly realized something. It was too late simply to dismiss her preposterous suggestion with the contempt it deserved. He had invited her to kiss him, and she had done so. If he had not exactly compromised her, he had at least toyed with her sensibilities.

There was the small matter of honor to be addressed now.

"Yes, it *was* a boast," he said, turning back to her, speaking almost viciously. "I *am* experienced, you see, Mrs. Dew, and I would make far more demands on a wife than a sick man ever did. I daresay you would retract your kind offer to marry me in a moment if *I* made *you* a demonstration."

"I would *not*," she said, her eyes flashing back at him. "I am not a child. And there is no cause for you to be angry. I have made a perfectly civil offer and you are quite at liberty to say no—though I do hope you would not then offer for Meg after all. *Make* your demonstration and I shall tell you if I wish to retract my offer."

Her nostrils had flared. She was angry.

He reached out and unbuttoned her cloak at the neck. He opened back the garment and sent it to the grass to join her bonnet and gloves.

"You will not be cold for long," he promised her angrily as he unbuttoned his greatcoat—though he did not take it off.

He set his arms about her—one about her shoulders, the other about her waist—and drew her against him. He wrapped his coat about her while lowering one hand to her buttocks and drawing her closer.

"Oh," she said, looking up at him, her eyes wide and startled.

"Oh, indeed," he agreed.

She was very slender. She had little shape—and yet strangely she felt very feminine.

He lowered his head to hers and kissed her. He encountered the soft pucker but would have none of it. He opened his mouth, pressed his tongue firmly against the seam of her lips, and invaded her mouth before she could think of clamping her teeth together.

She made a guttural sound in her throat.

But he was by no means finished with her. He explored the inside of her mouth, stroking against those parts that would inflame her, one hand spread over the back of her head so that she could not pull away.

With his free hand he opened the buttons down the back of her dress until he could nudge the fabric off her shoulders and run both hands along her back and then bring them forward to cup her small, firm breasts, pushed high by her stays. With a finger and thumb of each hand he rolled her nipples until they puckered and hardened.

He kissed her chin and her throat, moving his hands down her body to cradle her buttocks and hold her firm while he rubbed against her with his erection.

And he kissed her mouth again, simulating copulation with his tongue while he felt her fingers twine tightly in his hair.

It had been intended as a sort of lordly demonstration to an impertinent innocent who had played with fire. It had turned into something rather different. He had not expected to become sexually aroused. And if he did not soon put an end to what was happening, he would be laying her down on the grass, late February chill and dampness notwithstanding, and demonstrating something quite different again.

*She* was doing nothing to stop it, dangerous innocent that she was.

Good Lord! This was *Mrs. Nessie Dew*! And it could not possibly be night and just a bizarre dream. It had gone on too long.

He moved both hands to her waist and lifted his head.

She gazed into his eyes, her own darker and deeper than usual. They were really quite blue, he decided. And by far her best feature.

"Your face should always look like this," she said.

"Like what?" He frowned.

"Filled with passion," she said. "You have strong features. They were *meant* to be passionate, not proud and disdainful as they so often are."

"Ah," he said, "we are back to *that,* are we?"

"I *still* do not wish to retract my offer," she said. "You have not frightened me. You are but a man."

She stooped to retrieve her garments and drew her cloak about her shoulders. She shivered, though he was not sure it was from the cold.

"But I know *you* do not wish it," she said. "And it is hardly surprising. I ought to have looked at myself in a mirror when I first thought of it. It does not matter, though. I do not think you will now offer for Meg after all, and that is all that really matters."

She pulled on her bonnet and tied the ribbons beneath her chin.

He turned to face the lake again.

"I am going back to the house," she said. "I am sorry if I have offended you. It is not that Meg dislikes you. It is just that she loves Crispin. I am sure you will have no trouble finding someone eager to marry you when you go to London for the Season."

He raised his eyebrows and turned his head to look over his shoulder. She was still standing there, pulling on her gloves, flushed and slightly disheveled from their embrace.

He wondered suddenly if she knew a pertinent point about him.

"You had ambitions to be a duchess, did you?" he asked her.

She looked blankly at him. "Not really," she said. "Not at all actually. Whatever would I do with a duke? Besides, I do not know any."

"You know a duke's *heir*," he said.

"Do I?"

He continued to look at her over his shoulder until he saw comprehension begin to dawn.

"Mine is a courtesy title," he said. "It is my grandfather's junior title and was given first to my father and then to me on his death. If I survive my grandfather, I will be Duke of Moreland one day."

"O." Her lips formed the letter though he heard no sound. She had turned suddenly pale.

No, she had not known.

"*Now* have I frightened you?" he asked.

"Of course not," she said after gazing at him in silence for a few moments. "You are still just a man. But I am going."

She turned to walk away.

"Wait!" he said. "If you are to marry twice in your lifetime, you really ought to have the memory of one proposal that was made by the man. And I am a proud man, Mrs. Dew, as you have observed. I cannot go through life with a wife who proposed to *me*."

She turned again, an arrested look on her face.

And if it was to be done, it might as well be done properly, he supposed, though he would have done no such thing for Miss Huxtable. He went down on one knee before her and looked up into her eyes.

"Mrs. Dew," he said, "would you do me the honor of marrying me?"

She stared at him for a moment and then—

And then color, animation, and laughter rushed back into her face all at once so that for a startled moment he was dazzled.

"Oh," she said. "Oh, how absolutely splendid of you! You look *very* romantic. But are you quite sure?"

"If I were not," he said irritably, "would I be making such a thorough ass of myself? And would I not be in fear and trembling lest you say yes? Do I *look* as if I am trembling?"

"No," she said, "but you look as if you may have a wet knee. There was rain last night. Do get up."

"Not before I have my answer," he said. "Will you?"

"But of course I will," she said. "Was not *I* the one to ask *you*? You will not be sorry. I promise you will not. I know how to—"

"Make a man happy," he said, interrupting her as he stood again and looked down ruefully at the dark circle of wetness about his right knee. "And what of yourself, Mrs. Dew? Do you believe *I* can make *you* happy?"

"I do not see why not," she said. "I am not difficult to please."

She blushed rosily.

"Very well, then." He bent to the grass to retrieve his discarded garments. "I suppose we ought to go up to the house and tell our news."

"Yes."

She smiled at him again. But just before she took his offered arm, her eyes flickered and looked away from his own. Not, however, before he read something in them that looked very like fear.

It could not be worse than what he was feeling. What the devil had he just done?

Whatever it was, it was irrevocable now.

He was affianced to Mrs. Nessie Dew, for the love of God.

Who irritated him almost beyond endurance almost every time he was in company with her.

Whose very name made him cringe.

Who disapproved of almost everything about him—not that he did not return the compliment.

It sounded like a match made in hell.

He strode off with her in the direction of the house.

# 10

T H E Y walked back to the house in silence.

It had seemed a good idea last night. She had not believed he would refrain from offering for Meg if she simply asked it of him. He would look at her with that hard-jawed, supercilious look of his, and proceed to business. And she *knew* Meg would not say no.

Desperate measures had been necessary, and she had known just what measures they must be.

Something his mother had said had hardened her resolve.

*But you have had your chance, Mrs. Dew. Your elder sister has not.*

It was true. She had had her chance. She had married Hedley. It did not matter that he had lived only a year and had been very ill throughout it. She had had her chance.

Meg must not be deprived of hers, even if that chance appeared to be slim to none.

*She* would marry Viscount Lyngate instead of Meg and give him the wife he needed and give her sisters an easy entrée into society.

She would be the sacrificial lamb—though she had not thought of what she was doing in those terms until *he* had said it.

It did not really matter that neither of them particularly liked the other. That could be changed. If they were married, she would work on making him happy. She would work upon making herself happy too. She had done it before, after all—and in far more difficult circumstances.

And she could not deny that physically she found him very appealing indeed. Peculiar, almost painful things happened to her insides at the very thought of being married to him.

It would not be difficult . . .

Last night it had seemed a good idea. Today she was not nearly so sure.

She was not even marginally pretty, let alone beautiful.

She had had her boast exposed for what it was. How very humiliating it was to compare *her* kiss with *his*.

She knew he had kissed her only to prove a point, not because he had *wanted* to.

She had been left with the feeling that she had unleashed something very dangerous indeed.

Good heavens, she was still aching in places she had not known there were places.

And then there had been the great shock of discovering that he was heir to a dukedom. She had proposed marriage to a future duke!

That meant she was probably going to be a duchess one day.

She was going to be a viscountess as soon as she married and—though she had never until recently ventured more than a few miles beyond Throckbridge—she was going to be presented to the queen, and then she was going to introduce Meg and Kate to society.

And this man was going to be her husband.

If he kissed like that when standing beside a lake in broad daylight, what was he going to do to her when . . .

Well.

She stumbled over the merest tuft of grass, and he pressed her hand more tightly against his side and looked down at her briefly—with a very tight-lipped look as if to say he did not expect such awkwardness from his future duchess.

What were Meg and Kate and Stephen going to say?

What was his mother going to say?

And his *grandfather*?

Why had he turned the tables on her and offered for her? It was the last thing she had expected at that particular point. She had been about to crawl away in search of a deep, dark hole to hide in, preferably forever.

"Mrs. Dew," he said as they stepped onto the terrace. He stopped walking and looked down at her again. "There is still time to change your mind. I have sensed your agitation since we left the lake. Do you *wish* to marry me or do you *not*? You have my word of honor as a gentleman that regardless of your answer I will never marry either of your sisters."

The chance of reprieve!

She gazed up into his eyes and thought quite irrelevantly that whoever had made them blue—God?—had been very clever indeed since one expected dark brown with his Mediterranean complexion.

Yes, she did wish it despite everything. But . . .

"Do *you* wish to marry *me*?" she asked him.

His nostrils flared and his jaw set in a hard line.

"It is not at all the thing, ma'am," he said curtly, "to answer one question with another. I will answer nonetheless. I offered for you. Therefore I wish for a marriage with you. I am not a ditherer, Mrs. Dew. Now I will hear *your* answer."

Ah. A man accustomed to command. He would have the right to command and bully her forever after she married him.

*If* she allowed him to get away with it, that was.

"Of course I wish to marry you," she said. "I was the first to ask, remember?"

"I doubt I will ever forget," he retorted.

And he half bowed to her and offered his arm again.

She chuckled despite herself.

"Was that our first quarrel?" she asked him.

"I would suggest you not even try counting," he said as she took his arm. "Before the nuptials have even been celebrated you may find you cannot count so high."

She laughed outright.

And then sobered again.

"Who is going to tell?" she asked as they climbed the marble steps to the house.

"I will," he said decisively. He sounded grim.

She did not argue. She was massively relieved if the truth were known. However would *she* tell?

Stephen was coming out of the study.

"Ah, Lord Lyngate," he said, "you have arrived at the perfect time. Meg has just sent word that tea is ready in the drawing room. You will join us? And you are wearing *blue,* Nessie. Not gray or lavender today? It is about time, I must say."

As she followed him upstairs with her betrothed, Vanessa wondered if a heart could really beat its way right out of one's chest.

Katherine was sitting by the window, looking

through the fashion plates Miss Wallace had left for her yesterday. Margaret was seated behind the tea tray, wearing her best day dress. She looked very determined and self-conscious when she saw that Viscount Lyngate had come. She must be steeling herself for the offer she thought was coming, Vanessa thought.

"My lord," she said, "you have arrived in time for tea. Will you be seated?"

"I will," he said, "though I would like to say something first that concerns all of you."

Margaret looked openly dismayed—as if she expected a public declaration right there and then. Stephen looked interested, and Katherine looked up from the fashion plate she had been studying.

"Mrs. Dew," the viscount said, "has just done me the great honor of accepting my hand in marriage."

Vanessa wished she had sat down as soon as she was inside the room. But it was too late now. She could only stand where she was on legs that felt distinctly wobbly.

There was a horrible silence that seemed to stretch forever, though it was probably no longer than a second or two.

"I say." Stephen was the first to find his tongue. "Oh, I say, this *is* a surprise."

And he took the viscount's hand in his and pumped it up and down and then caught Vanessa up in a bear hug, grinning at her as he did so.

Katherine jumped to her feet and came hurrying across the room.

"Oh," she cried, "this really *is* splendid. But I did not suspect a *thing*. Ought I to have? Neither of you has given the smallest sign that you have a tendre for each other.

But of course—you danced together at the assembly. And you, my lord, danced with no one else *but* Nessie."

She looked for a moment as if she might rush into his arms, but if she had intended that, she thought better of it and rushed into Vanessa's instead after Stephen had released her.

Margaret remained standing behind the tea tray. Vanessa met her eyes over Katherine's shoulder and saw an expression in them that was impossible to read.

"Nessie?" she said. She did not even look at Viscount Lyngate.

Vanessa crossed the room to her, her hands outstretched.

"Meg," she said, "wish me happy. Wish *us* happy?"

The expression—whatever it had been—was gone, to be replaced by a strained smile.

"But of course I do," she said, taking Vanessa's hands and squeezing them tightly. "I wish you all the happiness in the world. And you too, my lord."

He bowed to her—to the woman he had come here to offer for today.

And then, the announcement having been made and the first outburst of surprise and excitement over with, they all sat and sipped their tea and bit into their cakes as if this were any ordinary afternoon.

Except that the conversation was far from ordinary. Viscount Lyngate told them that he would have a word with his mother, who was intending to leave for London within the week in order to get his sister properly outfitted for the coming Season. She would surely be pleased to take his betrothed too and help her choose her bride clothes and prepare her for her presentation at court after the marriage. In the meanwhile, he would see that the banns were called in both her parish and his own without further delay so that all could be accomplished within the month and in plenty of time before the Season began in earnest.

. . . *within the month* . . .

They all sat politely listening to him—even Vanessa. And they all showed an interest in his plans and made appropriate comments and asked pertinent questions—except Vanessa.

Within half an hour Viscount Lyngate was taking his leave of them all, bowing to each of them in turn, and then taking Vanessa's hand in his and raising it to his lips.

"If I may," he said, "I will come and fetch you tomorrow afternoon and take you to Finchley Park to call on my mother. She will wish it."

"I should enjoy that," she said, stretching the truth so thin that really there was nothing of it left.

And he was gone, taking Stephen to ride a way with him.

Katherine left the room too after another few minutes of excited chatter and several impulsive hugs. She was going to write to her friends in Throckbridge and tell them the news.

Which reminded Vanessa that *she* must write without delay to the Dews. She hoped the news would not upset them too much.

But she would think of that later. She was suddenly alone with Margaret, who was still seated on the same chair though the tea tray had been removed. Vanessa was a few feet away.

Margaret broke the silence.

"Nessie," she said, "what have you done?"

Vanessa smiled cheerfully. "I have affianced myself to a handsome, rich, influential man," she said. "He asked and I said yes."

"Are you sure that is the way it was?" Margaret asked, her gaze uncomfortably direct. "Or did *you* ask *him*?"

"That would be very improper," Vanessa said.

"But not something you have not done before," Margaret reminded her.

"I was happy with Hedley," Vanessa protested.

"Yes, I know." Her sister frowned. "But will you be happy with Lord Lyngate? I have been under the impression that you do not even like him very well."

"I will be happy," Vanessa said, smoothing one hand over the blue fabric of her dress.

"You did it for me, did you not?" Margaret asked.

"I did it because I *wanted* to," Vanessa said, looking at her again. "Do you mind awfully, Meg? Did you really want him for yourself? Now that it is too late, I fear that perhaps you do. Or did."

"You *did* do it for me," Margaret said, clasping her hands so tightly in her lap that Vanessa could see her knuckles turn white. "You did it for *us*. Oh, Nessie, must you make yourself a martyr for our sakes?"

"*You* always do," Vanessa told her.

"That is different," Margaret said. "It is my lot in life to protect you all, to make sure you all have a chance for the best life possible. I so want you all to be happy. You married Hedley for his sake, and now you will marry Lord Lyngate for ours. You *must* not, Nessie. I will not allow it. I will write him a letter and have it taken over to Finchley without delay. I will—"

"You will do no such thing," Vanessa said. "I am twenty-four years old, Meg. I am a widow. You cannot live my life for me. Neither can you live Kate's or Stephen's. It is *not* your lot in life to give up your own dreams and chances of happiness for us. We are all almost grown up. Kate will have all sorts of chances with my sponsorship. And Stephen will be helped to maturity by Viscount Lyngate and Mr. Samson and the tutors who are being hired for him before he goes up to Oxford. It is time you looked ahead to your life on your own account."

Margaret looked stricken. If *only* Crispin had gone off to join his regiment without saying anything to Meg except good-bye, Vanessa thought. She would be over her feelings for him by now.

"Oh, Meg," she said, "it is not that we do not need you any longer. Of course we do. We always will. We need you as our eldest sister. We need your love. But we do not need your *life*. You want us to be happy. Well, we want the same for you."

"I dreamed of you finding love again," Margaret said, tears welling in her eyes. "But a love that could last a lifetime this time. You deserve a happily-ever-after more than anyone else I know."

"And I am not to have it?" Vanessa asked. "Meg, he is heir to a *duke's* title. He told me that earlier. I had *no* idea. Could anything be more dazzling? How could I *not* be happy for the rest of my life? I am going to be a *duchess* one day."

"A *duke*?" Margaret said. "Oh, Nessie, I had no idea either. However will you cope? But of course you will. You are grown up, as you have just pointed out to me. Of course you will cope—and very well too. I wonder if Viscount Lyngate knows yet how fortunate he is to have you."

"I suspect not," Vanessa said, her eyes twinkling. "But he will. I intend to be happy with him, Meg. *Blissfully* happy."

Her sister set her head to one side and regarded her steadily.

"Oh, Nessie," she said.

And then they were both on their feet and in each other's arms, and for some inexplicable reason they were both weeping.

She had just become betrothed, Vanessa thought. Hers were tears of happiness.

Of course they were.

She was going to be married again.

To Viscount Lyngate.

Who could never in a million years love her.

Not that she loved him either, of course, But even so . . .


"What did she say?" Vanessa asked.

She was seated inside Viscount Lyngate's traveling carriage again, but this time she had him for a companion rather than her sisters. They were on their way to Finchley Park, almost twenty-four hours after their engagement. A heavy drizzle misted the windows. She was being taken to call upon his mother.

"She is eager to meet you," he told her.

"But I asked what she *said*." She turned her head to look at him. "She expected you to offer for Meg, did she not? And then you went home and told her you had offered for me instead. What did she say?"

"She was a little surprised," he admitted, "but she

was happy after I had informed her that you were the lady I wished to marry."

"Did you really say that?" she asked him. "And did she believe you? I would wager she did not. And I would wager she was not happy at all."

"Ladies," he said, "do not wager."

"Oh, fiddle," she said. "She is unhappy, is she not? I would rather know now before I meet her again."

He clucked his tongue.

"Very well, then," he said. "She is unhappy—or uneasy, at least. You are not the eldest sister, and you have been married before."

"And I am no beauty," she said.

"What am I to say to that?" he asked, clearly exasperated. "You are not ugly. You are not an antidote."

Loverlike words indeed!

"I will make her like me," she said. "I promise I will. She will like me when she sees that I can make you comfortable."

"Ah," he said. "It is only *comfortable* today, is it? Yesterday you knew how to *please* me and how to make me *happy*."

He was looking at her sidelong. His eyelids were drooped over his eyes again in that disconcertingly slumberous expression she remembered from the assembly.

"And comfortable too," she said firmly.

"Well, then," he said, "I am to be a fortunate man."

"You are," she agreed—and laughed.

"And I would like to have been a spider crawling across the carpet in your drawing room after I left yesterday," he said. "Especially after you and your elder sister were alone together, as I suppose you were eventually."

"She was not upset, if that is what you mean," she said. "At least, not upset that you had offered for me rather than her."

"I am crushed," he said.

"She wishes us well," she told him.

"Now *that*," he said, "I can believe. She is inordinately fond of you. She was not happy, though, was she, to learn that you had offered yourself as the sacrificial lamb for the family."

"I have no intention of being any such thing," she told him. "I am going to be your wife—your viscountess. I am going to learn to do the job well—you will see."

"I am going to be thirty before the year is out," he said. "My primary motive in deciding to marry this year has been to set up my nursery without further delay. There is the need for an heir."

He was looking directly at her from beneath those drooped lids—deliberately trying to discompose her, of course.

"Oh," she said, and knew she was blushing. Her toes curled up inside her half-boots. "But of course. That is perfectly understandable. Especially as you expect to be a duke one day."

"Was there any question," he asked, "of children with Dew?"

She shook her head and bit her lip.

"You told me," he said, "that you are not a virgin and I believed you. But are you perhaps an *almost* virgin?"

She turned her head away sharply. She could not trust her voice. She watched two streams of water snake their way down the side window of the carriage.

It had happened three times in all—*it* being nuptial relations. And after two of them Hedley had wept.

"My apologies," Viscount Lyngate said, setting his gloved hand on her sleeve. "I did not intend to upset you."

"It is quite understandable," she said, "that you would want to know if I am capable of bearing children. As far as I know, I am. I *hope* I am."

"We are almost at Finchley," he said. "You will see it around the next bend."

He leaned across her to wipe the steam off the window with the sleeve of his greatcoat.

It was another gray stone mansion, but this one was older than Warren Hall. It was solidly square with balustrades and statues around the roof and ivy on parts of the walls. It was surrounded by lawns dotted with ancient trees, still bare of leaves. Sheep grazed some distance from the house, probably below a ha-ha. There was another house—it was too large to be called a cottage—some distance away, on the banks of a lake.

There was none of the new splendor of Warren Hall here, but to Vanessa it looked stately and peaceful and welcoming—though that last word reminded her of what she was facing inside its walls within the next few minutes. She sat back in her seat.

"It looks better in the sunshine," he said.

"It looks lovely now," she told him.

She drew a deep breath when the carriage drew to a halt outside the double front doors of the house and let it out on a sigh that was unfortunately audible.

"I suppose," she said after he had descended the steps and turned to offer her a hand, "I ought to have looked beyond the mere request that you marry me to what came next."

"Yes," he agreed as she stepped down, "perhaps you ought. But you did not, did you?"

"And what-ifs are pointless," she said. "You said so yourself the day we arrived at Warren Hall."

"Precisely," he said. "You are stuck with me, Mrs. Dew. And I—"

He stopped abruptly.

"And you are stuck with me."

She often found amusement in the strangest things. She laughed.

It was better for both her spirits and her pride than weeping.

He raised his eyebrows and offered his arm.

# 11

L A D Y Lyngate looked even grander inside her own drawing room than she had in Stephen's. Or perhaps it was just that at Warren Hall she had been merely Viscount Lyngate's mother, Vanessa thought, whereas here she was her soon-to-be mother-in-law.

She was alone. There was no sign of Miss Wallace.

And she was gracious. She greeted Vanessa with apparent warmth and drew her toward a chair across from her own at the fire.

Viscount Lyngate, after presenting Vanessa as his betrothed, was dismissed as if he were quite irrelevant to the discussion to come. He bowed to them both, assured Vanessa that he would return in an hour's time to escort her home, and left the room.

"I suppose," Vanessa said, taking the offensive because she was thoroughly frightened, "you were surprised and none too pleased when Lord Lyngate returned home yesterday to inform you that he had proposed marriage to me instead of to Meg?"

Lady Lyngate raised her eyebrows and looked very aristocratic and very haughty—and very like her son— for a moment.

"I was surprised, yes," she said. "I had thought it was your elder sister to whom he intended to pay his addresses. It seems I was mistaken. I assume he had good reason for choosing you instead. I trust he has also chosen wisely."

Guilt smote Vanessa.

"I will make him happy," she assured the viscountess, leaning slightly forward in her chair. "I have promised him that. I have always been able to make people happy."

But would it be possible with Viscount Lyngate? He would be a definite challenge.

The viscountess looked steadily at her, her eyebrows still raised, but she did not respond. The tea tray was being carried in, and, until the tea had been poured and the plate of macaroons had been passed and the servant had withdrawn, she spoke of the weather and the hope that spring would come at last.

"You have a figure," she said then, "that modern fashion will flatter. It is not voluptuous, but it will look quite elegant when properly draped with silks and muslins. And that blue dress is far more becoming than the gray in which I saw you two days ago, though the design is not fashionable and probably never was. It is very wise of you, of course, to leave off your mourning entirely now that you are betrothed again. We must discover exactly which colors become you best. Pastel shades, I believe, behind which you will not pale into insignificance. And your hair has distinct possibilities, though its present style does not flatter you. We will have it cut and styled by an expert. Your face is prettier when you smile than when you do not. You must cultivate animation rather than fashionable ennui when you are in company. I believe you will take well enough with the *ton*."

Vanessa just stared at her.

"I hope you did not expect that this visit would be a purely social occasion in which we would both mouth meaningless platitudes," the viscountess said. "You are to be my son's bride, Mrs. Dew. What is your Christian name?"

"Vanessa, ma'am."

"You are to be my son's bride, Vanessa. You are to supersede me as Viscountess Lyngate. And one day you can expect to be the Duchess of Moreland. You must be brought up to scratch, then, and there is no time to lose. I found you and your sisters—as well as your brother—quite delightful two afternoons ago, but you will not do for London society, you know. Your manners are pleasing and unaffected, and I believe the *ton* will find your countrified airs charming, but you must learn to dress differently and carry yourself with a more confident deportment and know about *ton* etiquette and the expectations of polite society and the rules of precedence and so on. You will be entering a new world and must not give the appearance of gaucherie. Are you capable of doing all this?"

Vanessa remembered her first meeting with Lady Dew after she became affianced to Hedley. Lady Dew had hugged her and kissed her and wept over her and assured her that she was an angel sent from heaven.

"I have been married to a baronet's son, ma'am," she said. "But Sir Humphrey rarely leaves home—he loves it too much. And I had never been farther than a few miles from Throckbridge until I came to Warren Hall. I am not ashamed of the way I am—or the way Stephen or my sisters are. However, I fully recognize the necessity of adding different qualities now that my circumstances have changed and are to change further. I will be eager and delighted to learn all you are willing to teach me."

Lady Lyngate regarded her steadily while she spoke.

"Then I see no reason why we cannot deal well together," she said. "I will be taking Cecily to town next week to have her fitted for all the new clothes she will need for her come-out Season. You will come with us, Vanessa. You will need bride clothes and a court dress— you will, of course, be presented to the queen soon after your marriage. And I shall spend every available moment of every day instructing you in all you will need to know as my son's wife."

"Will he be coming with us?" Vanessa asked.

"He will certainly escort us," Lady Lyngate said. "He wishes to interview a few of the candidates George Bowen will have found for the positions of tutor to your brother. But he will return almost immediately—he has duties both at Warren Hall and here. *We* will not need him, however. Men can only get in the way at such times. You will not need him until your wedding day."

Vanessa laughed.

"You must know," Lady Lyngate said, looking sternly at her, "that I am going to hold you to your promise to make Elliott happy, Vanessa. He is precious to me. After sowing some very wild oats indeed for a number of years, he has assumed the duties of his rank with diligence and without complaint. Do you have an affection for him?"

"I—" Vanessa bit her lip. "I *esteem* him, ma'am. I will do my best to make him a good wife. And I will expect an affection to grow between us."

Lady Lyngate gazed at her in silence for a few moments.

"I do not believe I misunderstood when Elliott went to Warren Hall yesterday to make his offer," she said. "I believe his intention really *was* to offer for your elder sister. He will not admit it, of course, and I do not expect you would either if I were to ask you directly. For some reason he changed his mind—or was talked into changing it, which does not happen often with Elliott. However, I trust that you have spoken the truth about your feelings for him and your intention to make him happy. It is your best hope of keeping him. Would you get to your feet and pull on the bell rope, if you please? Cecily will be waiting impatiently to be summoned. She wishes to pay her respects to her future sister-in-law."

Vanessa did as she was asked.

"I hope," she said, "*she* was not too disappointed."

"Not at all," the viscountess assured her. "She is supremely uninterested in people as elderly as her brother and even you. What *does* please her is that Elliott will be marrying the sister of Miss Katherine Huxtable, to whom she has taken a great liking."

And so one giant hurdle had been surmounted, Vanessa supposed as she sat down again and awaited the arrival of Miss Wallace. She had been accepted, at least tentatively, by her future mother-in-law. It was now up to her to win full approval.

And next week she would be off to London to be transformed into a lady of the *ton,* into a future viscountess and duchess.

Whoever could have predicted all this just a little over two weeks ago?

And then she heard the echo of words that had been spoken just a minute or two ago.

*After sowing some very wild oats indeed for a number of years . . .*

And of course he had told her yesterday that he was very experienced indeed—*even though he had never been married.*

Was *that* when he had learned to kiss . . .

But this was certainly not the time or place to be remembering the way Viscount Lyngate had kissed her.

Her future mother-in-law had said something else too.

*I trust that you have spoken the truth about your feelings for him and your intention to make him happy. It is your best hope of keeping him.*

Had he still not quite finished with those wild oats, then? Was there a chance that he would stray from her if she did not make him happy?

How terribly naive she was. She knew so little about this world she was entering. Surely society did not condone infidelity in its married members.

She would not be able to bear it if . . .

But how would she ever compete if . . .


Elliott spent almost the entire month before his wedding traveling between Finchley Park and Warren Hall. Normally he would have spent at least a part of March in London, replenishing his wardrobe, reestablishing himself at his clubs, exchanging news and views with his friends and acquaintances, attending any parties that had been organized this early in the year—and putting a glad end to an overlong celibacy with Anna.

But he had needed to spend only one day interviewing the prospective tutors George had lined up for his inspection and visiting his tailor and his boot-maker and dealing with a few other matters of business. There was little else for which to prolong his stay. Anna had chosen to be mortally offended when informed of his imminent nuptials. She had hurled words and a few harder objects at his head. And when she had broken down in tears after a few minutes and would have taken him to her bed, he had discovered that he was not in the mood after all and had made a lame excuse about a forgotten appointment.

He was still not in the mood even later in the evening, when he might have gone back to her—from the house where his mother and betrothed were in residence to his mistress's house. It seemed ever so slightly sordid—a thought quite unworthy of his father's son or his grandfather's grandson.

Just two days after escorting his mother, his youngest sister, and his betrothed to town and settling them at the family town house on Cavendish Square, then, he left for the country again. He would have gone anyway, but his mother had made it clear to him that his presence would be decidedly de trop while she hurried to prepare two young ladies for the coming Season.

He was delighted to go. The conversation ever since they left home—the little he had heard of it anyway—had consisted of nothing but fashions and fabrics and frills and other such faradiddle.

Mrs. Dew's eyes had laughed at him every time he looked at her. He had taken leave of her after those two brief days in London with a bow and very unloverlike haste.

And soon he was going to have to stop thinking of her and addressing her as *Mrs. Dew,* as if she were still someone else's wife. But he would be damned before he would call her *Nessie*.

He had written to his grandfather and had a reply from his grandmother. They were coming to Finchley for the wedding.

It was beginning to feel disconcertingly real.

He rode over to Warren Hall most days, though it soon became apparent to him that he would not need to do so for all of the four years that remained before young Merton achieved his majority. The boy had been taken firmly under the wings of Samson and Philbin, the valet George Bowen had sent from London, a very superior gentleman's gentleman, who was quite prepared to condescend to give his master advice on all matters of appearance and fashion. And Claybourne, the new tutor who would teach him all there was to know about politics and the British aristocracy and what was expected of a member of it took up a large portion of the boy's time as did the thin, bookish, stammering Bigley, the classics tutor. And Miss Huxtable still kept a firm maternal eye upon her young brother.

Perhaps after the Huxtables had been presented in town and had taken their rightful places in society, Elliott sometimes hoped, he would be able to settle back to his own life and find that the whole business of guardianship had become a minor inconvenience of his life.

Except that there was no such thing as his own familiar life to settle back into any longer. He was very soon to be saddled for life with one colossal inconvenience.

He waited for the return of his bride.

In his memory she became thinner and more shapeless, plainer, and more totally insignificant physically every time he thought of her. Her tongue became more impertinent, her frequent smile and her laugh more irritating. Her kiss became more like a child's—or a nun's.

She became less and less appealing.

And he had only himself to blame for the fact that he was to be shackled to her. Good Lord, he could have said no, could he not, as soon as she had asked her preposterous question?

When had he *ever* allowed *any* woman to dictate to him? And about something as major as the rest of his life!

*And you are stuck with me.*

Never had she spoken truer words.

The wedding invitations were sent out, the nuptials and the wedding breakfast organized in lavish detail.

The new facts of his life had taken on a momentum of their own and all he could do was watch helplessly and count down the days.

Easter approached at an alarming speed. His wedding was set for two days after Easter Sunday.


Every night when she went to bed Vanessa expected to lie awake, her senses overloaded with so many new sights and impressions, her mind with so much information. And every night she fell asleep from sheer exhaustion as soon as her head touched the pillow.

She was taken sightseeing and was awed by all she saw—the Tower of London, Westminster Abbey, St. James's Palace, Carlton House, Hyde Park, and a whole host of other famous places she had heard of before but had only dreamed of seeing for herself. She was taken to dressmakers and glove makers and bonnet makers and jewelers and to dozens of other shops until she forgot where she had been and what she had been measured for. Even what had been purchased. She often looked in the drawers and wardrobes in her room at Moreland House and wondered whose nightgowns *those* were or whose satin slippers or whose paisley shawl.

She never wondered about her court dress—the one in which she would be presented to the queen after her marriage. *That* was impossible to forget. For some bizarre reason, the queen insisted upon the fashions of the previous century, and so the dress had to be huge-skirted with an equally huge petticoat and a stomacher and a long train and tall feathers for her hair and other ridiculous accessories.

And Vanessa had to learn to walk in it and back up in it without tripping and toppling backward over the train—one was not, of course, permitted to turn one's back on the queen as one left her presence. And she had to learn to curtsy to the queen until her nose almost touched the floor—but with infinite grace.

She did a great deal of laughing—as did Cecily—while she practiced. Even Cecily's mother sometimes let go of her exasperation at Vanessa's frequent clumsiness and failures and laughed too.

"But you must promise—you absolutely *must*, Vanessa," she said, "not to collapse with mirth if you make a mistake on the day itself, which heaven forbid you will do. But *if* you do, you must efface yourself and make your exit as quietly and unobtrusively as you possibly can."

They all dissolved into laughter again then as they

enumerated and exaggerated all the ghastly things that could possibly go wrong.

"Vanessa," her future mother-in-law said, holding her side when they had finally run out of ideas, "I do not know when I have laughed as much as I have since you joined us."

They laughed a great deal too over the dancing lessons that had been arranged so that Cecily could brush up on her skills but in which Vanessa joined too. She had to learn to waltz. It was a dance she had scarcely even heard of let alone seen performed. But it was not difficult once one grew accustomed to the fact that it was danced exclusively with one partner, whom one held—and who held one—the whole time.

Vanessa had her hair cut. At first the stylist intended merely to take off a few inches, but when he discovered that there was a heavy wave in her hair—though nothing as attractive as Stephen's curls—he cut it short in the newest fashion and styled it in such a way that it bounced about her head and cheeks and could be teased with fingers and tongs into curls and even ringlets for special occasions.

"Vanessa!" the viscountess exclaimed when she saw it. "I *knew* your hair had promise. I told you so, did I not? But I did not fully realize what short, wavy hair would do to fill out your narrow face. It emphasizes the classical lines of your cheekbones and the size of your eyes. Smile for me."

Vanessa smiled and then shook with self-conscious laughter. She felt bald.

"Yes." The viscountess looked critically at her. "You really do look quite pretty. In a unique way. You are an original."

Which Vanessa supposed was a compliment.

She felt bald even so.

All her new clothes were pastel-shaded. The dress she would wear for her wedding was pale green—a lighter shade than the dress Hedley had bought her for the summer fete.

If she had not been so busy every day and so exhausted every night, she might have shed tears over her memories, over the fact that Hedley was not with her to share all the excitement. As it was she ruthlessly suppressed the memories—and the guilt—except when they popped up unbidden.

She also tried to think as little as possible about Viscount Lyngate, to whom she would be married within a month.

In memory he became more arrogant, more supercilious, more morose, more everything that was negative every time she thought of him.

She was going to have to work terribly hard if she hoped to fulfill her promise to make him happy, to please him, to . . . What was the other thing? Ah, yes. To make him comfortable.

And to keep him faithful.

The month galloped along far too quickly. She was not ready. She needed more time.

For what, though?

*For everything!*

But time would not, of course, stand still. The day inevitably came when she found herself in Viscount Lyngate's carriage again with Lady Lyngate and Cecily, headed in the direction of Finchley Park and Warren Hall. Mr. Bowen rode beside them as an escort—he was to be the viscount's best man at the wedding.

In just a few days' time.

The guests would be starting to gather already.

They included Sir Humphrey and Lady Dew and Henrietta and Eva. And Mrs. Thrush.

And the Duke and Duchess of Moreland.

Very soon she would see her betrothed again.

Vanessa's stomach performed an uncomfortable flip-flop, which she attributed to motion sickness.

# 12

THE ladies came home from London three days before the wedding. But very little time, not even the three days, was to be allowed him in order to get to know his bride better, Elliott discovered.

Perhaps it was just as well.

His grandparents had arrived from Kent. His aunts and uncles had come too and his cousins with their families. His paternal cousins, that was. Con, though invited at the request of the Huxtables, had declined. And of course his married sisters had come with their spouses and Jessica's children. Finchley Park seemed very full.

Everyone was delighted with him. But it was his grandmother who put into words what they were all eager to agree with. It was after she had been over to Warren Hall with his grandfather to meet his bride.

"She is not a beauty, Elliott," she said after her return—and in the hearing of all the rest of the family except Jessica's children. "And that is a relief to me. You must have chosen her for qualities of character. She has an extremely pleasant disposition, though she was understandably nervous at meeting Moreland and me. I am pleased that you have shown so much good sense."

"Or perhaps, Grandmama," Averil suggested, "Elliott has fallen in love with her. I must confess I like her exceedingly well though I was rather surprised when I first saw her. She is not the sort of lady I would have expected to attract Elliott. But I could hardly catch my breath for laughing when she was describing her misadventures with the train of her presentation gown. I like someone who can laugh at herself."

"I hope he *is* in love," their grandmother said, looking hard at him. "*Are* you, Elliott?"

He raised his eyebrows and pursed his lips, very aware that every female eye was upon him. "I certainly have a regard for her, Grandmama," he said carefully. "Give me time, and I daresay I will fall in love with her too."

"Oh, men!" Jessica tossed her glance at the ceiling. "Be careful that you do not kill her with your ardor, Elliott."

She was not a beauty, his grandmother had said. No, she was not. But he was shocked nevertheless when he saw her again—in company with his grandparents and his mother and sisters. He scarcely recognized her.

She was no longer wearing mourning—not even the hideous lavender. Neither, he noticed when he glanced at her left hand, was she wearing her wedding ring. She was dressed in a simple but stylish high-waisted dress of pale lemon. Both the color and the design flattered her.

But it was her hair that made her virtually unrecognizable. The new style suited her to perfection. It flattered her face, made it look fuller, less pale. It made her cheekbones more pronounced, her eyes larger. It somehow drew attention to her lips, which were generously sculpted and almost always curved upward slightly at the corners.

He felt that now-familiar but still somewhat puzzling

stirring of desire at the sight of her. For even with the changes she really was no beauty.

But he had no private word with her and would not before the nuptials, it seemed. He was busy with his family, she with hers.

Sir Humphrey and Lady Dew had come with their two daughters. They had brought Mrs. Thrush, the Huxtables' former housekeeper, with them. There were no other guests at Warren Hall, but Sir Humphrey could fill up a house all by himself. And Elliott preferred to keep his distance than be cornered into endless conversation with him.

Actually Elliott was surprised that the Dews had come at all. Would it not be painful for them to see their son's widow remarry?

He endured the final days of his freedom with as much cheerful fortitude as he could muster. There was nothing he could do to avoid his fate now even if he wished to do so. He carefully avoided asking himself if he *did* wish it. It was a pointless question.

He dressed on the morning of his wedding with deliberate care and kept to his own rooms for as long as he was able. It was a ruse doomed to failure. If he was not going down to greet his family, they would—and did—come up to see him.

So he had to endure being hugged and wept over by all and sundry in the narrow confines of his dressing room.

And because it suddenly struck him full force that this was indeed his wedding day, that his life would forever change today, he hugged them all back and wrung his grandfather's gnarled hand.

And finally he was on his way to the small family

chapel in the park at Warren Hall, George Bowen beside him in the carriage.

"Not one word," he instructed firmly when he heard his friend draw breath to speak. "Enough sentimental claptrap has been spoken this morning to give me nausea for a month. Not *one word*."

"How about several, then?" George said with a grin. "Do you have the ring? You were supposed to give it to me after breakfast, but you did not come down to breakfast. You lost your appetite, I daresay. Weddings—one's own wedding, that is—are said to do that."

Elliott dug into a pocket and handed over the ring he had purchased in London.

"The kidneys were particularly delicious this morning," George said, as if to himself. "Nice and greasy, the way I like them."

"If you also like being my secretary," Elliott said, "you will keep such thoughts—and all others for the remainder of this journey—to yourself, George."

His friend chuckled and held his peace.

If Vanessa had hoped to have a private word with her betrothed—and she *had* so hoped—in order to ask him once more if he really minded marrying her or if he would prefer her to grant him his freedom, any such hope was dashed soon after her return from London.

She saw him only twice before her wedding day—once when he escorted the Duke and Duchess of Moreland and his two elder sisters to Warren Hall, and once when he brought his aunts and uncles and their offspring.

He looked positively morose both times, like a dark

and bronzed Greek god who had been expelled from Mount Olympus for some heinous crime.

Both times he conversed with Margaret and Katherine and Stephen and made Vanessa an elaborate and formal bow and asked after her health.

His visits certainly did not aid her digestion as she awaited her wedding day.

Neither did the appearance of the duke and duchess, who were both very gracious and very kind—she almost confided to the duke that it was she who had proposed marriage to his grandson, not the other way around, but Viscount Lyngate was within earshot at the time and she supposed he might be annoyed at what he would surely construe as a slur on his manhood.

But even so, they were a real live duke and duchess. She was awed by them. And she was to marry their heir.

The presence of her mother- and father-in-law and her sisters-in-law did not help either. They were so pleased to see her again and so pleased to be at Warren Hall and to see Meg and Kate and Stephen. And they were so pleased that she was betrothed to Viscount Lyngate. Sir Humphrey even took full credit for bringing them together and told the duke and duchess so—in the viscount's hearing. It was another of those occasions on which Vanessa would cheerfully have sunk through the floor if only it had been possible.

But Vanessa loved the Dews. And she knew they loved her. Soon she would no longer share their name. She would be married to someone else.

Surely they must feel some sadness.

And of course they did. On the night before the wedding, when she was bidding them good night, Vanessa kissed Lady Dew on the cheek and hugged her as she had used to do each night, and she had smiled at Sir Humphrey as she had always done. But then she had hugged him impulsively—very tightly about the neck, her face buried against his shoulder, and had felt as if her heart would break.

"There, there," he said, patting her on the back. "You were good to our boy, Nessie. More than good. He died a happy man. Far too young, it is true, but happy nevertheless. And all because of you. But he is gone now and we must live on. You must be happy again, and we must be happy to see it. Viscount Lyngate is a good man. I picked him out for you myself."

"Papa." She laughed shakily at the absurdity. "May I always call you that? And Mama?"

"We would be mortally offended if you ever called us anything else," he said.

And Lady Dew got to her feet to share the hug.

"When you have children, Nessie," she said, "they must call us Grandmama and Grandpapa. They will be our grandchildren, you know, just as surely as if you had had them with Hedley."

It was almost too much to bear.

Vanessa was glad they stayed out of her dressing room the next morning. Mrs. Thrush insisted upon being there, of course, fussing over Vanessa and getting in the way of the maid who had come down from London to work for Meg and Kate. And everyone else came there.

"Lord, Nessie," Stephen said, looking her up and down in her pale spring-green dress and pelisse with the absurdly festive flower-trimmed straw hat that Cecily had spotted at one of the milliners they had visited in London. Her hair curled and bounced beneath its brim.

"You look as fine as fivepence. And years younger than you did when you went away to London."

He was looking very smart indeed, with far more *presence* than he had had when they left Throckbridge. Vanessa told him so and he waved off the compliment with a careless hand.

Kate was biting her lower lip.

"And to think," she said, "that just a few weeks ago Meg was darning stockings, Stephen was translating Latin texts, I was romping with the infants at school, and you were at Rundle Park, Nessie. And now here we are. And today brings the greatest change of all."

Her eyes filled with tears and she bit her lip again.

"Today," Margaret said firmly, "Nessie begins her happily-ever-after. And she looks absolutely spendid."

She was dry-eyed and rather tight-jawed. But there was such fierce affection in her eyes that Vanessa could not look into them for longer than a few moments at a time for fear of breaking down.

They had sat up far too late last night, Vanessa propped against the pillows of her bed, Margaret seated at the foot, her legs drawn up to her chin.

"I want you to promise me," she had said, "that you will not lose your ability to be happy and to spread happiness about you, Nessie. No matter what. You must not lose yourself. Promise me."

She was afraid that living with Viscount Lyngate would drag at Vanessa's spirit. How foolish she was. The opposite would be true. She would make him smile and laugh. She would make him happy.

She had promised him that she would. She had promised his mother the same thing. More important, she had promised herself.

"I promise," she had said, smiling. "You goose, Meg. I am not going to the guillotine tomorrow. I am going to my own wedding. I did not tell you before, but on the day he asked me to marry him—we were out at the lake—he kissed me."

Margaret stared at her.

"I liked it," Vanessa said. "I really *really* liked it. And I think he did too." That part was probably untrue, but it was not an outright lie because she had not asked him and so did not know for sure. Anyway, he had certainly *wanted* her.

Margaret rocked back and forth, her arms wrapped about her knees.

"I *need* kisses, Meg," Vanessa had said. "And I need more than kisses. I need to be married again. I think sometimes men believe that only they need . . . kisses. But they are wrong. Women have such needs too. I am glad I am getting married again."

And it was not even a complete lie, she had thought. She really did want more of his kisses and more *than* his kisses.

She wanted love and happiness too. If she tried very hard, perhaps she could achieve one of the two.

This morning, though, as Stephen held out his arm and she took it so that he could lead her downstairs and out to the carriage for the short ride to the chapel, she was not so sure that she wanted any of this.

She was going to marry a stranger. A handsome, virile, frowning, impatient, morose, sneering . . .

Oh, dear.

He had also gone down on one knee to propose marriage to her even though it had been unnecessary since *she* had already proposed to *him*—and he had probably ruined his pantaloons on the wet grass in the process.

She settled herself on the carriage seat, leaving room for Stephen beside her, and felt a little as if she *were* on the way to the guillotine after all.

Foolishly, she wanted Hedley.

There were no more than thirty wedding guests all told. Even so, they almost filled the small private chapel.

The nuptial service was not a long one. That fact had always surprised Vanessa at the weddings she had attended—including her own first wedding. And this one was no different.

How could such a momentous and irrevocable change in two lives be effected in so short a time and with such little fuss? The only real moment of drama came with that short pause after the clergyman asked if anyone knew of any impediment to the proposed marriage.

As on all other such occasions that Vanessa knew of, that pause remained unfilled today, and the service swept onward to its inevitable conclusion.

She was aware, as soon as Stephen placed her hand in Viscount Lyngate's, that her own was cold, that his was firm and steady and warm. She was aware of his immaculate tailoring—he wore unadorned black and white, as he had at the Valentine's assembly—of his height and the breadth of his shoulders. She was aware of his cologne.

She was aware of the quickened beating of her heart.

And she was aware of an era slipping away from her as her name changed and she became Vanessa Wallace, Viscountess Lyngate.

Hedley slipped farther into her past, and she had to let him go.

She belonged to this man now.

To this stranger.

She raised her eyes to his as he slipped her new wedding ring on her finger.

How was it possible to marry a stranger?

But she was doing it.

So was he. Did he even realize how little he knew her? Did it matter to him?

The ring safely in place, he looked up into her eyes.

She smiled.

He did not.

And then, a dizzyingly short number of moments later, they were man and wife. And what God had joined together, no man was to put asunder. No woman either, presumably.

They signed the church register and then walked along the short nave of the church together while Vanessa smiled to the left and the right at their guests. Meg was dry-eyed, Kate was not. Stephen was grinning. So was Mr. Bowen. The viscountess—now the *dowager* viscountess—was dabbing at her eyes with a lace-edged handkerchief. The duke was looking at them from beneath craggy eyebrows, a ferocious frown on his face. The duchess was smiling sweetly and nodding her head. Sir Humphrey was blowing his nose.

Everything else was a blur.

The first thing Vanessa noticed as they stepped out of the chapel—she had not noticed on the way in—was that the grass of the churchyard and the hedgerows beneath the trees were dotted with crocuses and primroses and clumps of daffodils.

Somehow spring had arrived late and almost unnoticed. How could she possibly have missed it? It was the end of March already, and spring was always her favorite time of the year.

"Oh," she said, looking up at the man beside her with a bright smile, "look at all the spring flowers. Are they not lovely?"

And the sun was shining, she noticed. The sky was a clear blue.

"The ones in your hat?" he asked her. "They are indeed."

And for one brief moment, before their guests came spilling out of the church behind them, it seemed to her that his eyes came close to smiling.

She laughed at the absurd joke—and felt suddenly breathless and weak-kneed. This man was her husband. She had just promised to love, honor, and obey him for the rest of her life.

"Well, Vanessa," he said softly.

Ah. No one ever called her that—except his mother. How lovely her name was after all, she thought foolishly as she smiled back at him.

They were the last words he spoke privately to her for several hours. Even during the carriage ride to Finchley Park for the wedding breakfast they had company, since the viscount's Aunt Roberta had had quite enough of her sister's whinings about drafts and carriage sickness during the ride to church and chose to ride back with her nephew and his bride. And since she had a word or two of warning to pass along to young Merton about all the pitfalls that would be awaiting him when he stepped into the wicked world of London later in the spring, she insisted that Stephen ride with them too.

The chapel bells pealed joyfully as they drove away.

Vanessa listened to them wistfully. No one else seemed to notice.

Elliott had decided a couple of weeks before the wedding—as soon as he had realized it was an event his whole family would wish to attend, in fact—that he and his bride would not spend their wedding night at Finchley Park. Although the house was large enough to accommodate everyone and he had his own private apartments there, he had no desire to bid everyone good night as he took his bride off to bed or to greet everyone at breakfast the next morning.

He had had the dower house down by the lake cleaned and prepared for them. He had had a few servants moved in there, including his valet and his wife's new maid. And he had announced to everyone at the house that after the wedding breakfast both the dower house and the lake would be out of bounds for three days.

Three days seemed a long time for them to be alone, and he hoped he would not regret his decision—though they could always go back to the house sooner if they became bored with each other's company, he supposed. But he felt the need of a few days in which to establish some sort of relationship with his wife. A sexual relationship anyway even if none other proved possible.

It was late in the evening by the time they left the main house. The revelries were still continuing there as they walked along the path that wound its way between wide lawns toward the lake. It was a night bright with moon and stars. Moonlight gleamed in a wide band across the water. The air was cool, but there was no wind. It felt like spring at last.

It all seemed uncomfortably romantic. Vanessa's arm was drawn through his, but they had not spoken since the flurry of good nights back at the house. He ought to speak. It was unusual for him to feel uncomfortable, tongue-tied.

She was the one to break the silence.

"Is this not beautiful beyond belief?" she asked him. "It is like a fairy wonderland. Is it not *romantic,* my lord?"

He might simply have agreed with her. He had already thought similar things himself. But he chose to take exception to two of her words.

*"My lord?"* he said, irritated. "I am your husband, Vanessa. My name is Elliott. Use it."

"Elliott." She looked up at him.

She was still wearing the green dress in which she had been married. And she had put the absurd straw hat back on for the walk in the outdoors. It was a pretty thing, he had to admit, and became her well.

They had arrived close to the bank of the lake, to where the path bent in order to approach the dower house from the front. For some reason they both stopped walking.

"Do you not appreciate beauty?" she asked him, tipping her head a little to one side.

Another accusation.

"Of course I do," he said. "You have looked very pretty today."

It was only a slight exaggeration. He had found his eyes straying to her even more than was necessary on such a day. She had been bright with animation as she mingled with their guests. She had been vibrant with smiles and laughter.

She had looked happy.

In the moonlight he could see laughter light her eyes now.

"I meant the beauties of nature," she said. "I was not fishing for a compliment. I know I am not pretty."

"You also do not know how to accept a compliment when one is offered," he told her.

The laughter died from her face.

"I am sorry," she said. "Thank you for your kind words. Your mother chose my dress and the color. Cecily chose the hat."

Nobody, he realized with sudden insight, had ever called her pretty. What must it have been like, growing up in a family in which her siblings were all extraordinarily good-looking while she was not? And yet she could still smile and laugh at life.

He set one forefinger beneath her chin and leaned forward to kiss her briefly on the lips.

"Well," he said, "now that I look, I can see that *they* are rather pretty too." The dress and the hat, that was.

"Oh, well done." She laughed. She also sounded rather breathless.

He had been celibate for far too long, he thought ruefully. He was very ready to proceed with the wedding night. Which was, he supposed, a good thing.

"We had better go into the house," he said. "Unless you want more refreshments, I will show you to your room. Your maid will be waiting for you there."

"*My* room?" she said.

"I will visit you there later," he told her.

"Oh." He was certain she was blushing, though the

moonlight hid the evidence from his eyes. She was, he guessed, *very* close to being a virgin.

They were silent again then as they covered the remaining distance to the front door and he opened it to allow her to precede him inside. The caretaker and his wife were in the hallway ready to greet them, but Elliott soon dismissed them for the night.

He led Vanessa up the stairs, well lit by the candles in the wall sconces. She was his wife, he thought. He would bed her tonight—within the next hour, in fact—and for the rest of their lives there would be no one else but her.

It was a private vow he had taken very recently, though he was surprised that it had taken him so long to know his own mind. After his marriage, he had decided even before his return from London, he would be unswervingly monogamous, no matter how satisfying or unsatisfying he found his marriage bed to be. There was too much pain in the alternative.

He had only to look at and listen to his mother and his grandmother to understand that. His father and his grandfather had done them irreparable harm. And both ladies feared he would follow in the footsteps of his ancestors.

He would not. It was as simple as that.

It was not necessarily a happy resolution considering the identity of his bride. But it was a firm one nonetheless.

He stopped outside her dressing room and bowed over her hand as he raised it to his lips before opening the door. Her maid was busy inside there, he could see.

He turned in the direction of his own room.

# 13

VANESSA'S room overlooked the lake. The moon still shone across it in a wide silver band. The view was really quite breathtaking. And the house itself—the little she had seen of it anyway—was lovely.

But her mind was not really on either the moonlight or the house, which she would explore tomorrow.

She was in *her* room.

As opposed to *his*.

Or *theirs*.

She and Hedley had shared a room from the day of their marriage. She had assumed that all married couples did. With Hedley—

But she would not think of him tonight. She must not. She belonged to someone else now.

He had actually called her pretty on the way here. *Very* pretty, to be precise. He had almost joked with her, telling her that her clothes were pretty too—meaning that *she* was prettier, that it was *she* he had noticed first.

What a thorough bouncer! She sighed even as she smiled.

But he *was* capable of humor, even if only of a very dry kind. He was not inhuman.

Well, of course he was not.

She set her forehead against the cool glass of the window and closed her eyes.

The bed behind her had been turned down for the night. She was very aware of its presence. Perhaps she should be lying in it. But she kept remembering how he had accused her a month ago of offering herself like a sacrificial lamb. She would look like one—she would *feel* like one—if she lay there waiting for him.

She felt like a virgin awaiting the deflowering, she thought in some disgust. She was *not* a virgin. She was an experienced woman.

Well, *almost* experienced anyway.

And if her brain did not soon cease its incessant chattering she would surely go mad.

There was a tap on her door and it opened before she could either cross the room or draw breath to call out.

He was wearing a wine-colored dressing gown that covered him from the neck to the ankles. He looked menacing. And gorgeous too, of course.

His face was blank of any nameable expression. His eyelids were half drooped over his eyes, as they had been the first time she saw him. He was looking steadily at her and she could not help thinking of the very different reaction she must be provoking in him.

She did not often wish for the impossible, but just *sometimes* she wished she were beautiful. As she did now, for example.

She was wearing the ice blue silk and lace nightgown that had been chosen specifically for tonight—by her new mother-in-law, not by her. She thought its low neckline too revealing. And she very much feared that if she stood just so to any particular candle, a beholder would be able to see right through it.

She might not have minded so much if there had been something worth seeing.

She hated being self-conscious about her figure—or her lack thereof.

"I suppose," she said, "we will grow accustomed to this."

His eyebrows rose.

"I suppose we will," he agreed as he stepped into the room and came toward her. "You are not *nervous* by any chance, are you? You are the experienced one, are you not? The one who knows how to please a man—in bed."

If that was a joke, she was in no mood to laugh.

"You know that was a boast," she said. "I admitted as much. It would be unkind of you to throw it in my teeth at every turn."

Strangely, he looked even larger and more powerful in dressing gown and slippers than he did in his great-coat and boots. Or perhaps it just seemed so because he was in her bedchamber and it was their wedding night.

"Well, Vanessa." He lifted one hand and cupped her neck and one side of her face with it. "It is time to discover just how much of a boast it was."

He had shaved. She could smell his shaving soap or his cologne. Whatever it was, it was a masculine scent that made her want to keep on inhaling.

She swallowed.

And his lips touched hers. Though it was not really his lips. It was the soft, moist flesh inside them. His tongue pressed hard against her own lips, and she parted them. It pressed deep inside her mouth.

She inhaled sharply through her nose. Sensation darted like an arrow into her throat and downward through her breasts and her abdomen to set up a throbbing between her inner thighs.

She recognized the feeling for what it was—pure,

raw sexual desire. She had felt it out by the lake at Warren Hall the day she asked him to marry her. She had denied it to herself then. It was impossible to do so now.

He drew back his head a few inches, and she realized in some shock that he had not yet touched her anywhere below the neck. He had hardly even *started*.

"It is to be hoped," he said, "that you *do* know how to please me since you are my wife and my bedfellow for life."

His eyes were still heavy-lidded, and the voice he used was a bedroom voice if ever she had imagined one. It was pure velvet.

"The master has spoken," she murmured. "It is to be hoped that *you* know how to please *me,* since you are my husband and my bedfellow for life."

He looked steadily at her for several moments, his face expressionless. And then the hand that had been cupping her face and neck slid lower and along her shoulder beneath her nightgown and on down her arm. The nightgown, having nowhere else to go, went with his hand until her shoulder and breast were exposed.

And then his free hand pushed the garment off her other shoulder, and since it was a loose thing that was anchored in place only at the shoulders, it slithered its way down all the way to her feet.

Only her feet were covered. It was small comfort.

He held her just above the elbows and took a step back.

And looked.

Well, she supposed she had asked for this. She had challenged him and he was giving his answer without the medium of words.

A man's way.

She gazed steadily back into his face as she raised one hand and pulled loose the sash of his dressing gown. It fell open.

He was naked beneath it.

He raised his head to look directly into her eyes again and lowered his arms to his sides. Ah, an invitation. She lifted both arms to push the dressing gown off his shoulders. It fell to the floor without even having to slither its way down.

*Oh, gracious heaven.*

He looked like a classical sculpture of idealized Greek manhood, except that he was no sculpture. He was bronzed from head to toe. His broad, firmly muscled chest was lightly dusted with dark hair. And he was alive and warm—she could feel his body heat even though they stood several inches apart. She could see his chest rise and fall with each breath.

He was slim-hipped and long-legged. His thighs were powerfully muscled.

He was aroused. And that part of him was large and powerful too.

She looked back into his eyes. She had been looking him over as frankly as he had been doing with her, she realized.

How horribly mismatched they were physically.

But he *was* aroused.

She touched her fingertips to his chest and then slid her palms up to rest on his shoulders.

She had never been more terrified in her life.

"It seems," he said softly, "that I have something to prove."

Her inner thighs and the passage within throbbed

with something that felt more like pain than the simple anticipation of pleasure.

"Yes," she said.

But instead of waiting for her to walk toward the bed, he bent down to pick her up and carry her there before setting her down in the middle of the mattress. He peeled back all the bedcovers before joining her there.

Naked flesh had touched naked flesh. She felt as if she were on fire.

He did not extinguish the candles.

This was not, then, something that was going to be accomplished surreptitiously under cover of blankets and darkness.

He lay on his side next to her, raised himself on one elbow, and leaned over her to kiss her again. She opened her mouth to him this time, and when his tongue came inside, she suckled it, then sucked harder to draw it deep and pulsed her teeth against it.

He made a low sound in his throat.

His hand explored her, strong and warm and nimble-fingered. He found her nipples again, as he had by the lake, and rolled them as he had then between his thumb and forefinger, but harder this time until the raw ache she felt below spiraled upward into her throat too.

He ended the kiss and moved his head to one of her breasts, taking it into his mouth, sucking on it, teasing the swollen nipple with his tongue until she buried both hands in his hair and gripped hard.

Not that she had been idle. She had turned half onto her side and moved her leg along his. She moved closer to him and rubbed herself against him, circling her hips as she did so.

And when he raised his head from her breast in order to nuzzle her in the hollow between her shoulder and neck, she took his erection in her hand, caressing him lightly, tightening her fingers about him, causing him to make a sound rather like a growl.

One of his hands was exploring her too, his long fingers pushing between her legs, parting folds, caressing, teasing, reaching up a little way inside her.

She was wet, she realized. She could both feel and hear the wetness.

Desire became pure agony.

And then he turned her onto her back again and came over on top of her. He was big and heavy.

Wonderfully big.

Wonderfully heavy.

His knees pressed between her thighs and pushed them wide. She lifted her legs and twined them about his as he slid his hands beneath her, raised her, and came all the way inside her with one long, firm thrust.

She drew a deep breath and then could not seem to expel it.

There was no pain, but she felt stretched, filled, invaded. She had not known there was so much room inside her.

Foolish thought!

He held still for a moment while he slid his hands free, and she hooked her legs more firmly about his, tilted herself, and relaxed about him. There *was* room, and there would be for what was about to happen, and she wanted to feel the whole of it.

She tightened her inner muscles about him. He was rock-hard.

It was his turn to inhale sharply.

And then he moved.

It was pure, raw carnal delight. Each thrust and withdrawal both aggravated and soothed the ache of her desire. And each thrust came deeper than the last—or so it seemed. There was a rhythm to the act, and Vanessa learned it and adjusted her own movements to it, contracting and relaxing inner muscles to give both him and herself delight.

What she had told him had not been an utter boast.

She *did* know how to please a man.

And he had not boasted at all, of course.

She wanted it to last forever, this sensual delight that was beyond anything she could possibly have imagined. But of course it did not. And finally she was glad it did not. She would, she felt, have gone out of her mind if there had not been a sudden convulsive clenching of her muscles that refused to unclench themselves until something—it was impossible to give it a name—came flowing softly but inexorably up from deep inside where the muscles were and burst through them and through *her* until she was trembling with wonder and then limp with a satiety that also defied words.

He had fallen still, she realized.

But then his hands were beneath her again, and he was pumping into her hard and fast until he stopped abruptly again, deep inside her, and she felt a flow of heat at her core.

She wrapped her arms about him. He was hot and sweaty.

So was she.

How strangely enticing the smell of sweat could be.

She felt suddenly cold when he disengaged from her and moved off her to lie beside her. She shivered, and he reached down and pulled the covers up over them. His one arm came beneath her neck while the other lay heavy across her. And she was warm again.

And sleepy.

And then asleep.

And so it was done.

He was married before the age of thirty, just as his grandfather had expected and he had planned. For convenience he had married one of the Huxtable sisters. Now the other two could make their debut into society and he would feel no further responsibility for them.

He was married, his marriage had been consummated, and soon, it was to be hoped, his wife would be with child. And if he was fortunate, that child would be a boy, and another duty would be done.

*Duty!* It was something that had weighed him down for more than a year now. How he longed sometimes to have his old carefree life back. But it could not be done, and now he had fulfilled his most pressing obligations to his family and his position.

Elliott lay awake for a long time.

Even tonight she had wanted to quarrel with him, staking her claim to be his equal. If she must please him because she was his wife and bedfellow, then *he* must please *her* for the complementary reasons.

She had not been educated in the ways of polite society, of course. If she had, she would have effaced herself and accepted the inequalities in silence and with dignity.

*The master has spoken. It is to be hoped that you know how to please me since you are my husband and my bedfellow for life.*

His lips twitched despite himself.

Vanessa stirred in his arms, muttered something, and burrowed closer.

Strangely, she *had* pleased him.

He was not at all sure why. She had about as unvoluptuous a body as he had ever beheld unclothed or had beneath him on a bed. And she had displayed no really extraordinary skills.

Perhaps it was simply the attraction of novelty.

The novelty of having such a lover would, of course, wear thin very soon. And then? Well, then he would settle into the rest of his life. It was not a bright prospect, though he supposed one must always hope. That was what she had said of her sister, was it not? Something to the effect that hope for the return of the absent military officer was all that gave meaning to Miss Huxtable's life?

Hope.

It was a thin chance for happiness.

"Mmm," she said on a long sigh. Her nose was buried against his chest.

Novelty might as well be enjoyed while it *was* novelty.

He lifted her chin with one hand and kissed her openmouthed.

She tasted of sleep. She smelled of woman and sex. She was warm and relaxed, only half awake.

He turned her onto her back, covered her with his body, spread her legs wide with his own, and buried himself deep in her.

She was hot and wet.

"Mmm," she said again, and her legs came up to twine about his while she tilted her hips to give him deeper access. "Again?"

She sounded sleepy and surprised, and he half smiled in the darkness.

"Yes, *again*," he said against her ear. "What are wedding nights for?"

She laughed softly. Just a few days ago, when she was still in London with his mother, he had remembered her laugh as something irritating. Tonight it was not. It was a low, merry sound of genuine amusement.

It was sexy.

He moved in her with deep, rhythmic strokes, prolonging the encounter for as long as he could, listening to the wet, sucking sounds of their coupling, feeling her smooth, wet heat about the near-pain of his erection, knowing the relief of having a woman again after a long dearth.

She clung to him with her legs, spread her hands over his buttocks, and held herself open and relaxed. She made no other moves of her own. It was clever—or innocent. It gave him more time to savor the satisfaction of sex.

But after several long minutes, he became aware that she was no longer passive. Her inner muscles had tensed, and her hands were straining against his buttocks as if to hold him deep and prevent his withdrawal.

He quickened and deepened his strokes until he felt her sudden shudder of release a few moments before his own came.

He must remind her, he thought just before falling asleep, that he had fulfilled his part of the bargain. He had pleased her.

He woke an indeterminate time later, still on top of her, still inside her. He disengaged and moved to her side.

"I beg your pardon," he said. "I must weigh a ton."

"Only *half* a ton, I believe," she said. "You do not need to apologize. Don't ever apologize."

"Never?" he said. "Not for any reason?"

She sighed sleepily.

"I will have to think about that one," she said. "Perhaps we could arrange our lives so that we never do anything that calls for an apology."

He found himself half smiling again in the darkness—the candle appeared to have burned itself out.

"A happily-ever-after?" he said. "Do you really believe in such a thing?"

"No," she said after giving the question some thought. "And I am not sure I would want it even if it were possible. What else would there be to hope for in life? What else would there be to work toward? I would prefer happiness to a happily-ever-after."

"What *is* happiness?" he asked her.

"A moment of joy," she said without hesitation.

"Only a moment? It sounds not worth working for, then," he said.

"Oh, there you are wrong," she told him. "The whole of life is a single moment. There is nothing else *but* this moment, is there? Always this moment."

In his experience moments passed and were gone forever.

"The whole of life is joy, then?" he said. "It is *all* happiness?"

She could not possibly be *that* naive.

"No, of course not," she said. "But one moment of

happiness can make the whole of life worth living—like leavening in bread. It can show what life can be and is meant to be. It can give one hope in the dark times. It can give one faith in life and the future. Have you *never* been happy, Elliott?"

He felt a huge nostalgia suddenly for the way life had used to be—a long, long time ago. A lifetime ago.

"I was happy enough a few minutes ago," he said.

"You think you are being flippant," she said. "You expect me to scold you for thinking that s—" She drew a breath and rushed onward. "For thinking that *sex* can bring happiness. But it can. Sex celebrates life and togetherness and love."

"I thought," he said, "you did not love me."

That silenced her for a while.

"But I was not the one who said I was happy a few minutes ago," she said.

"*I* was celebrating love, then?" he asked her.

"Oh, you foolish man," she said. "Of course you were. There are many kinds of love. You are not in love with me. You do not even love me. But you love . . . this night."

"Our wedding night," he said. "Sex."

"Yes."

"Sex is love?"

"You want to provoke a quarrel with me," she said, and she lifted herself onto her elbow so that she could prop her head on her hand and look down at him. "Admit it."

*Did* he? Perhaps she was right. Perhaps he was trying to set this night into perspective. He had married a woman today whom he barely knew, who frequently irritated him, who was not even attractive. He had bedded her tonight because it was their wedding night, and he had enjoyed the sex because he had been without a woman since before Christmas.

And even tonight, even now she annoyed him. She was a romantic with her belief in happiness and love. For her even sex was love. She believed there was joy to be found in most of the situations of life.

And yet she had lost a young husband to consumption — a slow and cruel death. Presumably she had loved him.

"You ought to be sleeping, not talking philosophy," he said more harshly than he intended. "I may want you again before the night is out."

"*You* ought to be sleeping too," she said. "Perhaps *I* will want *you*."

He almost laughed aloud. They were back where they had started this night.

"Perhaps," he said, "we ought to do our wanting now while we are both wide awake and our sleeping afterward."

He spread a hand over the back of her head and drew it downward so that he could kiss her.

She stretched one leg across him until she was straddling him, and then she lowered her head so that he could continue to kiss her.

The novelty had certainly not worn thin yet.

And the night was not half over.

# *14*

H A P P I N E S S  did not always come just in fleeting moments. Sometimes it lingered for a while.

Vanessa had no real illusions, of course. This was not a love match and had never been intended as one. He did not love her and she did not love him—not really anyway.

But she *was* infatuated with him, and surely—and strangely—he was with her.

For now anyway. For a short while even if it did not last.

They were to enjoy that most romantic of all interludes in life—a honeymoon.

They made love more times during those three days and four nights than Vanessa could count. Well, not quite. It was thirteen times in all. Afterward, she thought that if she had been superstitious, that number might have struck her as ominous. She ought not to have counted.

She had never enjoyed anything more in her life than those thirteen lovemakings. He was beautiful and virile and skilled and thorough.

But it was not just the lovemaking.

They took their meals together and talked while they ate. They talked of books they had read and discovered that they had read very few of the same ones. But that could be rectified.

"I will read all the books you have read," she said recklessly, "so that we can discuss them."

"I will *not* read everything you have read," he told her. "History was never my favorite subject at school. Instead, you may tell me everything that happened in the past that I need to know."

"Oh, goodness," she said, "wherever would I begin?"

"At the beginning?" he suggested. "With Adam and Eve?"

"I'll start with the Romans in Britain," she said, "since very little is known about the tribes who were here before them. The Romans are fascinating, Elliott. They lived lives that were in many ways more sophisticated and luxurious than ours. And yet we think we live in such an advanced civilization. Did you know, for example, that they knew a way of heating their houses that did not necessitate wood or coal fires in each room?"

"I did not," he said.

He listened with apparent interest while she spoke of Roman Britain and how it had influenced the lives of the British even to the present day.

"Especially in language," she said. "Do you have any idea how many of our words originated from the Latin?"

"Would we be compelled to live in silence if the Romans had not come here, then?" he asked her. "Or, heaven help us, would we all be speaking Welsh or Gaelic?"

She laughed. "Language is an ever-growing thing," she said. "English would just have been different without the Romans."

She suspected—indeed she *knew*—that his knowledge of the past was far more extensive than he admitted to. No educated gentleman could possibly know absolutely nothing about the history of his own country and civilization, after all. But she did not care if he was teasing her with his apparent ignorance. History was something of a passion with her, but she could not always find people who were willing to listen.

Besides, it was interesting to know that he *could* tease.

They spent hours of each day out of doors. The weather was not to be resisted. Although it was still only spring, the sun shone, the sky was cloudless, and there was warmth in the air. They could not have asked for better.

They strolled about the lake and never once spotted another soul. Everyone was indeed respecting their privacy.

They went to the boathouse one day and looked at the boats inside and then took one out onto the water even though it *was* a little chilly out there. Vanessa insisted upon rowing and even got them safely back to shore. But because she had not rowed for years, since she was a girl, in fact, she spent far more time fighting the water and the oars and moving in circles than in skimming gracefully across the lake admiring the view.

"An impressive display," her husband commented after their return. "Perhaps next time you will allow *me* to take the oars to see if I can impress you equally."

She laughed.

"But it was such *fun*, Elliott, you must confess," she said. "Did you fear for your life?"

"I can swim," he told her. "Can you?"

"About as well as I can row," she said, and laughed

again. "I have always been afraid to put my face under the water."

They walked out to the end of the wooden jetty close to the boathouse on another occasion and gazed down into the water at the fish swimming there. He used to dive in as a boy, he told her, and try to catch the fish with his bare hands.

"Did you ever succeed?" she asked him.

"Never," he admitted. "But I did learn something about expending energy on an impossibility."

"That stopped you?" she asked.

"No."

She remembered the stone he had sent skipping across the lake at Warren Hall the day she proposed marriage to him. She had him demonstrate again now and then tried it herself—without any success at all. He tried to teach her, but she could not perfect the sideways flick of the wrist that was apparently the secret to success. When she tried it, she only succeeded in sending her stone straight up in the air so that they both had to duck in order not to be hit on the head when it descended.

She did a great deal of laughing and then watched him show off with a second demonstration.

"Twelve bounces," she said admiringly. "That is a new record."

"Think how much easier your task is now than mine," he said. "I have to reach thirteen to beat my record. You have to reach only one to set yours."

"I think," she said, "that all I have learned is not to expend energy on an impossibility."

She threw one last stone—and it bounced an unmistakable three times. She shrieked with laughter and turned to him in triumph.

"Well," he said, his eyebrows raised. "Maybe I should dive in and see if I can catch a fish."

One of these days, she decided, she was going to make him smile. She was even going to make him laugh. But it did not matter that he did neither. He was enjoying himself as much as she was. She was *sure* of it.

This may not be a match made in heaven, and they may never really *love* each other. But there was no reason at all why they should not be happy together. She had promised him happiness and pleasure and comfort, had she not?

On the third day they walked around to the far side of the lake and came upon a sloping bank that was simply covered with daffodils. It had been hidden from sight from the other bank by a band of willow trees that overhung the water. The yellow trumpets nodded and waved in the sunlight and the light breeze.

"Oh, look, Elliott!" she cried, as if he could possibly not have noticed. "Just look!"

And she went dashing off to run through the daffodils, her arms spread to the sides. She twirled about in the middle of them and lifted her face to the sun.

"Have you ever seen anything more beautiful?" she asked, coming to a halt but keeping her arms raised.

He was standing at the edge of the bank, watching her.

"Probably," he said. "But I cannot for the moment think what it might have been. I believe you must have had secret knowledge of this place, though, Vanessa, and dressed accordingly. It was very cunning and clever of you."

She looked down at herself. She was wearing her lemon-colored dress and pelisse and her straw bonnet.

"I thought you would be impressed," she said, smiling brightly at him.

"I am."

He had come closer while she was looking down. And he kept coming as her smile faded. When he was close enough, he leaned forward and set his lips to hers, and she twined her arms about his neck and kissed him back.

She loved his heavy-lidded look. It made her feel desirable. That he actually found her desirable still seemed incredible to her. But he must. He surely could not be thinking *just* of those heirs for which he had married her. She gazed into his eyes after he had finished kissing her, and smiled again.

It was one of the happiest moments of a happy three days. She almost felt that she was in love with him after all. And he with her.

"Even if family and gardeners had not been given strict orders to stay away from the lake," he said, "this would be a deserted spot. I cannot remember seeing it before at this particular time of the year."

*A deserted spot.*

His meaning was abundantly clear. Vanessa felt the growingly familiar ache between her thighs.

"No one comes here?" she asked him, and licked her suddenly dry lips.

"No one."

And he shrugged out of his coat, spread it on the grass among the daffodils, and gestured toward it.

And they made love in the outdoors, surrounded by the green and gold of springtime, the sun beaming down on them, its rays almost hot in the shelter provided by trees and flowers and the slope of the bank.

It was quick and lusty and wonderfully wicked—for of course someone *could* have come striding into sight at any moment. There was something strangely erotic, she discovered, about making love while almost fully clothed.

"I am going to pick some daffodils for the house," she said when they were on their feet again and had adjusted their clothing. "May I?"

"This is your home," he said. "You are mistress of Finchley Park, Vanessa. You may do whatever you wish."

Her smile broadened.

"Within reason," he added hastily.

"Help me," she said, bending to the daffodils and plucking them by their long stems.

"Is this enough?" he asked after he had picked perhaps a dozen and she had picked more than twice that number.

"Not nearly," she said. "We will pick until our arms can hold no more. We will fill the dower house to overflowing with sunshine and spring, Elliott. Gather some greenery too."

Some time later they staggered back around the lake to the house, their arms laden.

"I hope," she said as they approached the door, "there are enough pots and vases. There must be at least one bouquet for each room."

"The servants will see to it," he said, opening the door with difficulty and standing back for her to precede him inside.

"They will certainly *not*," she protested. "Arranging flowers is one of the finest pleasures of life, Elliott. I will show you. Come and help me."

"I'll come and *watch* you," he said. "You will thank

me for not helping, Vanessa. I have no eye for arrangements."

But he did help nevertheless. He filled the pots with
water and divided the flowers and leaves into groups
and cut their stems according to her directions. And he
helped carry the pots to the appointed rooms and adjusted their positions while she stood back and looked
on with a critical eye.

"One half an inch to the right," she said, gesturing.
"Now one quarter of an inch back. *There!* Perfect!"

He stood back and looked steadily at her.

She laughed. "Perfection ought always to be aimed
for," she said, "even if it is not always possible to
achieve. Anything worth doing ought to be done well."

"Yes, ma'am," he said. "What happens to the flowers
when we return to the main house tomorrow?"

She did not want to return to the house. She wanted
to live here just like this forever and ever. But it had
never been possible—or ultimately desirable—to hold
back time.

"Tomorrow does not exist until it comes," she said.
"We need not think about it today. Today we will enjoy
the daffodils."

"Do you know the poem?" he asked.

"The one by William Wordsworth?" she said. "His
'host of golden daffodils'? Oh, yes, indeed. And now we
know just how he felt when he came upon them."

"We *do* have some reading in common after all,
then," he said.

"Yes, so we do."

Vanessa gazed about happily at the vases full of flowers. And there was one more evening to look forward to
and one more night.

But tomorrow had been mentioned.

Tomorrow they would return to the main house and the rest of their lives.

They would be the same people living the same marriage.

But Vanessa tried not to think about it, nevertheless. When she did, it was with a vague, unnameable sense of foreboding.

They walked back up to the main house after breakfast the following morning under gray skies that threatened rain.

The house was deserted except for the servants and Mr. Bowen. All the wedding guests had been due to leave yesterday, and Lady Lyngate and Cecily had set off for London very early this morning. Vanessa and Elliott were to follow them tomorrow.

Vanessa explored her new bedchamber and dressing room while Elliott was in the study, consulting with his secretary and looking through the letters that had accumulated in three days.

But he was not there long. He tapped on Vanessa's door after less than half an hour and let himself in.

"It is huge," she said, spreading her arms to the sides. "At least twice the size of my room at the dower house."

"Of course," he said, shrugging. "It is the viscountess's room."

The fact that she had moved into a totally different world had still not had time to strike her fully, Vanessa realized.

"I am going to ride over to Warren Hall to see how Merton is getting along with his tutors," he said.

"Would you like to come? If so, we will take the carriage. It would probably be wise anyway. It is going to rain."

"Of course I want to come," she said.

Time had seemed suspended during their brief honeymoon. She had spared hardly a thought for her sisters and brother—or for anyone else. The dower house and the lake had been her world, and she and Elliott had been the only two people who existed in it.

Like Adam and Eve in the Garden of Eden.

Now suddenly she realized that three whole days had passed, and she was eager to see her siblings again.

By the time they arrived at Warren Hall the first few drops of rain were falling, and a gusty wind had cooled the air.

How fortunate they had been to have those three days of glorious spring weather, Vanessa thought. The change now made them seem somehow unreal and far away—as if they had ended weeks ago instead of just this morning.

Margaret was alone in the drawing room. She curtsied to Elliott and hugged Vanessa tightly. Their guests had left yesterday, she told them. Stephen was downstairs in the library with one of his tutors, having returned late from a morning ride with Mr. Grainger and been soundly scolded for it. Katherine had gone out for a walk.

"Though I hope she comes home soon," Margaret said, glancing at the window, which was spotted with rain. "Before she gets a soaking."

She looked listless and a little pale, Vanessa thought as they both sat down by the fire and Elliott went off to the library.

"Are you well, Meg?" Vanessa asked. "Is something wrong?"

"Absolutely nothing." Margaret smiled. "And you, Nessie? How *are* you?"

Vanessa leaned back in her chair.

"Has the weather not been wonderful?" she said. "The dower house at Finchley is *such* a pretty place, Meg, and the lake is lovely. We went boating and yesterday we picked dozens of daffodils without coming even close to denuding the bank on which they bloomed. We set a bowl of them in each room of the house. They looked quite splendid."

*"We,"* Margaret said. "Is all well, then, Nessie? You have no regrets? But you *look* happy."

"Well, of course," Vanessa said, "real life is about to intrude. We will be going to London tomorrow, and I will be presented to the queen next week—a mildly terrifying prospect. And there will be numerous people to meet and places to go and . . . Well, and so on. But of course I have no regrets, you goose. This was something I wanted to do. I told you that from the start."

"Oh, Nessie." Margaret leaned back in her chair, looking weary again. "If *you* can only be happy then *I* will be happy too."

Vanessa looked closely at her. But before she could ask her again what was the matter—clearly *something* was—the door opened and Katherine came inside, all bright eyes and rosy cheeks.

"Ho," she said, pressing one hand to her bosom, "I am breathless. I did not know whether to take shelter in the chapel when it started to rain or make a run for it to the house."

"I take it you ran," Vanessa said, getting to her feet.

"And now I am glad of it." Katherine came hurrying across the room to hug her sister. "I saw Viscount Lyngate's carriage outside the door and hoped he had brought you with him."

"He did," Vanessa said, smiling.

"I cannot tell you how handsome you both looked on your wedding day," Katherine said as they took a seat. "Did you enjoy the three days by the lake?"

"I did indeed," Vanessa said, hoping she was not blushing. "It is an idyllic place. I would have been perfectly happy to remain there forever. Did you enjoy having company for a few days?"

Katherine leaned forward in her chair suddenly, her face lighting up with excitement.

"Oh, Nessie," she said, "you are not the only one to marry recently. Has Meg told you? A letter for Sir Humphrey and Lady Dew was sent on here from Rundle Park and fortunately arrived just before they left yesterday morning. *Did* Meg tell you?"

"She did not."

Vanessa glanced at her elder sister. She was sitting back in her chair, holding the arms, a half-smile on her lips.

"It was from Crispin Dew," Katherine said.

"Oh, Kate," Vanessa cried, "he has not been *wounded,* has he?"

But then she remembered how this conversation had started and darted another look at Margaret.

"No, nothing like that," Katherine said. "He has just *married.* She is a Spanish lady. There was a great deal of excitement here before the carriage left for Throckbridge, as you can well imagine. Though Lady Dew was sad that she had been unable to attend the wedding. As were Eva and Henrietta."

"Oh," Vanessa said, her eyes locked on Margaret's. Her sister looked back at her, that ghastly half-smile still on her lips.

"I have been teasing Meg," Katherine said. "I remember that when I was a girl she and Crispin used to be rather sweet on each other—just as you and Hedley were."

"I have told Kate," Margaret said, "that I cannot even remember clearly what he looks like. And that was all *years* ago. I wish him every happiness with his new bride."

And then Stephen and Elliott came to join them in the drawing room and they all drank coffee and ate sweet biscuits and talked, among other things, about London, where they would all be settled within the next week.

They would not stay for luncheon, Elliott said when they were invited. He had some business to attend to on his estate during the afternoon.

Margaret, Stephen, and Katherine all came downstairs to see their sister and brother-in-law on their way though they did not step out onto the terrace as the rain had settled into a steady downpour.

There was not one moment in which Vanessa might have had a private word with Margaret. Or if there were—they might have held back on the stairs and let everyone else move out of earshot—then Margaret pointedly avoided it.

One of life's great ironies, Vanessa thought as she climbed into the carriage and Elliott took his seat beside her. She had married him four days ago in order to leave her sister free to hope.

But now all hope had been shattered forever.

It would have been far better for Meg if Crispin Dew had been killed in battle.

One hated to think such a horrible thing, but even so . . .

"You are feeling homesick?" Elliott asked as the carriage moved off down the driveway.

"Oh." She turned her head and smiled brightly at him. "No, of course not. Finchley Park is my home now."

She held out her hand and he took it and held it on his thigh while they proceeded homeward in silence.

Would she be married to him now, she wondered, if Crispin's letter had arrived five or six weeks ago instead of just yesterday?

Or would it have been Meg sitting where she was now?

She could feel the warmth of his thigh through his pantaloons and her glove, and she was secretly glad that the letter had not come sooner.

How *could* he? How could Crispin Dew have treated Meg so shabbily?

She leaned slightly sideways and took comfort from the solidity of Elliott's shoulder. She swallowed hastily when she heard a gurgle in her throat.

# 15

VANESSA was still feeling depressed. It was not something she allowed herself to feel very often. There was almost always something to do, someone with whom to talk, something to think about, something to read that would elevate her mood. And there was almost always something to wonder at, something to smile over, something to laugh about.

Laughter was so much better for the soul than glumness.

But just occasionally depression hit like a stone wall. Usually it was because there was more than one cause and it was virtually impossible to avoid.

Her honeymoon had come to an end. And though the unexpected happiness that had filled her days and nights at the dower house and the lake might surely be brought back to the main house with her and taken to London tomorrow, she could not rid herself of the notion that now all would change, that she and Elliott would never again be as close as they had been there.

If that had been all, of course, she would have firmly shaken off any low spirits that threatened. It was up to her to see to it that her marriage worked. If she expected things to change for the worse, then almost certainly they would.

But Elliott had gone off for the afternoon to take

care of some estate business. It was perfectly understandable. She did not expect him to go walking and boating and picking daffodils with her every afternoon of the rest of their lives. But it was a bad time just now today for her to be left alone.

Crispin Dew had married a Spanish lady in Spain.

Meg must be desperately, devastatingly unhappy, but there was absolutely nothing Vanessa could do to help her. The suffering of a loved one was in many ways worse than one's own suffering because it left one feeling so very helpless. She knew that from bitter experience.

And of course *that* thought, the thought of Hedley, sent her running up to her bedchamber and rummaging through her large trunk, which had been brought over from Warren Hall but not yet unpacked because it was to go to London tomorrow. Just where she had placed it with her own hands after carefully wrapping it, she found the object she had almost decided to leave behind. It was only at the last moment that she had slid it down the left front corner.

She sat down on a love seat and opened back the velvet cloth that kept the treasure safe from damage. And she gazed down at the framed miniature of Hedley that Lady Dew had given her after his death.

It had been painted when he was twenty, two years before Vanessa married him, and just before it became obvious that he was really very ill indeed.

Though the signs were apparent even then.

She ran one finger about the oval frame.

His eyes were large, his face thin. It would have been pale too if the painter had not added color to his cheeks.

But even then he had been beautiful, as he had to the end. His had been a delicate beauty. He had never been robust. He had never been able to participate in the more boisterous games of the other children in the neighborhood. Though strangely he had never been teased or victimized by them. He had been widely loved.

*She* had loved him.

She would have died in his place if it could have been done.

Those large, luminous eyes gazed back at her now from the portrait. So full of intelligence and hope.

*Hope.* He had not given it up until close to the end, and when he had finally let it go, it had been with grace and dignity.

"Hedley," she whispered.

She touched a fingertip to his lips.

And she realized something. Apart from one fleeting memory on her wedding night, she had not thought of him at all during the three days at the lake.

*Of course* she had not. It would have been dreadful if she had. She had been there with her new husband, to whom she owed her undivided loyalty.

But even so . . .

Until very recently it had seemed inconceivable that a single day could ever go by without her thinking of him at least a hundred times.

Now three days had slipped by.

Three days in which she had been blissfully happy with a man who did not even love her. Whom she did not even love.

Not as she had loved Hedley anyway. It was impossible to love any other man as she had loved her first husband.

But she had never been able to know with Hedley the sort of sensual happiness she had just experienced with Elliott. By the time of their marriage his illness had rendered him all but impotent. It had been a terrible frustration for him, though she had learned ways to soothe and satisfy him.

And now she had found sexual satisfaction with another man.

She had not thought of Hedley for three whole days — no, four by now.

Would she eventually forget him altogether?

Would it be to her as if he had never existed?

She felt a deep welling of grief and a sharp pang of guilt, which was all the worse for the fact that it was quite unreasonable. Why should she feel guilty about putting behind her memories of her first husband when she was married to a second? Why should she feel as if she were cheating on a dead man? Why should she feel as if she were hurting him?

She felt all of those things.

*You must go on with your life, Nessie,* he had told her during the final few days of his life while she held his hand and dabbed at his feverish face with a cool cloth. *You must love again and be happy again. You must marry and have children. You must. Promise me?*

She had called him a goose and an idiot and flatly refused to make any promises.

*Oh, not a goose, please, Nessie,* he had said. *A gander if anything, but not a goose.*

They had both laughed.

*Keep on laughing at the very least,* he had said. *Promise me you will always laugh.*

*Always when something is funny,* she had promised and

had held his hand against her lips while he fell into an exhausted half-sleep.

She had laughed a few more times in the next few days but not for a long time after that.

"Hedley," she whispered again now and realized she could no longer see the portrait clearly. She blinked the tears from her eyes. "Forgive me."

For doing what he had begged her to do—for living again and being happy. For marrying again. For laughing again.

And for forgetting him for almost four whole days.

She thought of the vigor of Elliott's lovemaking and circled her palm over the miniature. Somewhere she had crossed over a border between depression and something more painful, something that tightened her chest and made breathing difficult.

If Hedley had just once been able . . .

She closed her eyes and rocked backward and forward.

"Hedley," she said again.

She sniffed as the tears flowed, tried to dry them with the heels of her hands, and then felt around for a handkerchief. She had none yet was feeling too inert to get up to fetch one.

She gave in to a terrible self-pitying despair.

Finally she sniffed again, swiped at her nose with the back of her hand, and decided that she must get up, find a handkerchief, give her nose a good blow, and then wash her face in cold water to obliterate the signs that she had been weeping.

How awful if Elliott were to see them! Whatever would he think?

But just after she had set the miniature down on the

cushion beside her a large handkerchief appeared over the back of the seat, held in a large masculine hand.

Elliott's.

He must have come through his dressing room and hers—the door was behind her back.

For a moment she froze. But there was nothing else to do for now than take the handkerchief, dry her eyes with it, blow her nose, and then think of some plausible explanation.

But even as she took the handkerchief from his hand she was very aware of the miniature lying faceup on the seat beside her.

There was really very little that needed doing. Elliott had worked hard to get everything done before his wedding, knowing that soon after he would be leaving for London and staying there for a few months.

He was finished in less than an hour, and the courtesy call he then decided to make on a tenant who was also something of a friend of his had to be cut very short when he discovered the man and his wife were not at home.

He was quite contented to return to the house much sooner than expected. Thus far he was pleased with his marriage. Indeed, he had been surprisingly reluctant to leave the dower house this morning. He had felt absurdly as if some spell were about to be broken.

There was no spell to break, of course, and no magic involved in anything that had happened. He had had a regular bed partner for three days and four nights and the sex had been surprisingly good. A woman's body did not have to be voluptuous in order to be desirable, he had discovered.

It had not been just the sex, though. His wife had decided not to quarrel with him during those three days, and he had found her company congenial.

Good Lord, he had allowed her to row one of the boats—with him in it—even though it was obvious she had no skill whatsoever at the oars. He had allowed her to murder his ears with shrieks of laughter when by sheer accident she had sent a stone skipping three times across the lake. And he had—heaven help him—gathered more daffodils than he had known were in existence anywhere in the world and had then run and fetched for her as she filled the dower house with them a mere few hours before they were to leave there.

He was ever so slightly charmed by her, he realized.

And there was no reason that things should change drastically for the worse now that they were back at the main house and on their way to town tomorrow.

Perhaps after all they could enjoy a decent marriage.

And so instead of just coming home early, he actually *hurried* home, ignoring the inner voice that told him there were other tenants upon whom he might have called.

They had had sex yesterday among the daffodils, he and Vanessa. If the weather had just held they might have gone back there today—to gather daffodils for the main house. As it was, there was the bed in her bedchamber to try out for the first time, and what better time to do that than a rainy afternoon when neither of them had anything better to do?

She was not in any of the downstairs rooms. She

must be in her bedchamber already. Perhaps she was lying down, catching up on some missed sleep.

Elliott took the stairs two at a time, though he did go into his own dressing room first to dry his hair and haul off his boots without stopping to ring for his valet. Vanessa's dressing room adjoined his own. He crossed through it, treading quietly in case she was asleep—though it was going to give him great pleasure to wake her in a few minutes.

The door into her bedchamber was slightly ajar. He opened it slowly without knocking.

She was not in bed. She was sitting on the love seat, her back to him, her head bent forward. Reading? He contemplated tiptoeing up to her and setting his lips against the nape of her neck.

How would she react? With a shriek? With laughter? With shrugged shoulders and a sensual sigh?

She sniffed.

A wet sniff.

And then it was perfectly obvious that she was weeping. She did it with deep, grief-stricken sobs.

Elliott froze in place. His first instinct was to stride forward to scoop her up into his arms while demanding to know what had happened to upset her so. But he had never been much good at embroiling himself in female emotions. What he actually did was move forward more slowly and quietly. He was making no attempt to hide his presence, but she was too preoccupied to notice him.

And then, just as he was about to set one hand on her shoulder and squeeze it, she set something down on the cushion beside her, and he found himself looking down at the miniature portrait of a delicate, almost pretty young man.

It took Elliott less than a moment to realize that the young man must be Hedley Dew. His predecessor.

He found himself suddenly angry.

Furiously angry.

*Coldly* angry.

He drew a clean handkerchief out of his pocket and held it out without a word.

She dried her eyes and blew her nose while he walked farther into the room. He took up a stand before the window, his back to her, his hands clasped behind him. He gazed out through the rain at the park. Off to one side was the lake with the dower house on its near bank.

He did not turn his head to look in that direction. Indeed, he did not really see anything at all beyond the window.

Why he was quite so angry he did not know. They had entered this marriage without illusions. It had been basically a marriage of convenience for both of them.

"I suppose," he said when the blowings and snifflings had stopped, "you loved him more than life."

He did not even try to hide the sarcasm from his voice.

"I loved him," she said after a lengthy pause. "Elliott—"

"Please," he said, "do not feel that you must now launch into an explanation. It is quite unnecessary, and would almost certainly involve nothing but lies."

"There is nothing about which I *need* to lie," she said. "I loved him and I lost him and now I am married to you. That says it all. You will not find me—"

"And you saw fit to bring his portrait into my home," he said, "and to weep over it in private."

"Yes," she said. "I brought it with me. He was a large part of my past. He was—and is—a part of *me*. I had no idea you would be home so soon. Or that you would come to my room and enter without even knocking."

He swiveled right about and stared stonily at her. She was still sitting on the love seat, his handkerchief balled in her hands. Her face was red and blotchy. It was not a pretty sight.

"I need to *knock*," he asked her, "before entering my wife's rooms?"

As she was in the habit of doing, she answered his question with one of her own.

"If I entered *your* rooms without knocking," she said, "would you be annoyed? Especially if you were engaged in something you would prefer I did not see?"

"That," he said, "is a different matter altogether. Of course I would be annoyed."

"But I am not allowed to be?" she asked him. "Because I am merely a woman? Merely a wife? Merely a sort of superior servant? Even servants need some privacy."

Somehow she was turning the tables on him. *She* was scolding *him*. She was putting him on the defensive.

The last few days, he realized suddenly, had been about nothing but sex. As he had intended. There was no point in being indignant at the discovery of what he had already known—and wanted.

He certainly did not want her in love with him.

But even so . . .

"Your wish will be granted from now on, ma'am," he said, making her a formal bow. "This room will be your private domain except when I enter it to exercise my conjugal rights. And even then I will knock first and you may send me to the devil if you do not wish to admit me."

She tipped her head to one side and regarded him for a few silent moments.

"The trouble with men," she said, "is that they will never discuss a matter calmly and rationally. They will never listen. They always bluster and take offense and make pronouncements. They are the most unreasonable of creatures. It is no wonder there are always the most atrocious wars being fought."

"Men fight wars," he said between clenched teeth, "in order to make the world safe for their women."

"Oh, poppycock!" she said.

She ought, of course, to have kept her head down from the beginning and remained mute while he had his say, except to answer his questions with appropriate monosyllables. Then he might have stalked from the room with some dignity without going off on a dozen verbal tangents.

But she was Vanessa, and he was beginning to understand that he must not expect her to behave as other ladies behaved.

And heaven help him, he had married her. He had no one but himself to blame.

"If you men really wanted to please your women," she said, "you would sit down and talk with them."

"Ma'am," he said, "perhaps you think to distract me. But you will not do so. I do not demand what you cannot give me and what I do not even want—I do not demand your love. But I do demand your undivided loyalty. It is my right as your husband."

"You have it," she told him. "And you do not need to frown so ferociously or call me *ma'am*, as if we had just met, in order to get it."

"I cannot and will not compete with a dead man," he said. "I do not doubt that you loved him dearly, Vanessa, and that his passing at such a young age was a cruel blow to you. But now you have married me, and I expect you to appear in public at least to be devoted to me."

*"In public,"* she said. "But in private I need not show devotion? In private I can be honest and show indifference or dislike or hatred or whatever else I may be feeling?"

He gazed at her, exasperated.

"I wish," she said, "you would let me explain."

"About what I encountered when I *invaded your privacy* and came in here?" he asked. "I would really rather you did not, ma'am."

"Crispin Dew is married," she told him.

He could only gaze mutely at her. Was this a massive non sequitur, or was there some sort of logical connection in his wife's convoluted mind?

"Kate told me this morning," she said. "Lady Dew had a letter from him while she was still at Warren Hall. He married someone in Spain, where his regiment is stationed."

"And I suppose," he said, "your elder sister is heartbroken. Though why she should be I do not know. If he has been gone for four years without a word to her, she ought to have expected something like this."

"I am sure she did," she said. "But thinking you expect something and having it actually happen are two different things."

A thought struck him suddenly.

"She might have married me after all, then," he said.

"Yes," she agreed.

He saw the connection at last.

"You realized it while I was gone this afternoon," he said. "You realized that that letter had come too late. You might have been saved from making yourself into the sacrificial lamb."

"Poor Meg," she said, neither admitting nor denying the charge. "She loved him so very much, you know. But she insisted upon staying with us when he wanted her to marry him and follow the drum with him. She would not let me take her place."

"Not on that occasion," he said. "But this time she was given no choice. You spoke to me before she knew what you intended to do."

"Elliott," she said, "I *wish* you would not interrupt so much."

"Ha!" He sawed the air with one hand. "Now *you* are the one who wishes to make a pronouncement and does not wish to discuss anything in a rational manner."

"I am merely trying to explain," she told him.

He clasped his hands behind him again and leaned a little toward her.

"Explain, then, if you must," he said. "I will not interrupt again."

She stared back at him and then sighed. Her hands had been twisting the handkerchief. She set it firmly aside, caught sight of the miniature, still lying faceup on the cushion beside it, and turned it over.

"I was afraid I would forget him," she said. "And I realized that it was desirable I forget him. I am married to you now and owe you what I gave him—my undivided attention and loyalty and devotion. But I was afraid, Elliott. He was my life for the one year of our marriage, just as you will be my life for much longer, I hope. I need to forget him, but it seems wrong. He does not deserve to be forgotten. He loved me more than I thought it possible to be loved. And he was only twenty-three when he died. If I forget him, then love can die too—and I have always believed that love is the one constant in life, the one thing that can never die, in this life or through eternity. I was weeping because I need to forget him. But I do not want to do it."

He had told her he would not compete with a dead man. But he was going to be doing just that anyway, was he not?

A woman, it seemed, could not be commanded not to love. Just as she could not be commanded to love.

"I will take the portrait back to Warren Hall," she said. "Better yet, I will send it to Rundle Park. Lady Dew gave it to me after Hedley died and will be glad to have it back, I daresay. I ought to have thought to give it to her before my wedding to you, but it did not occur to me. I will keep my marriage vows to you, Elliott. And I will not weep over Hedley again. I will tuck him away in a secret corner of my heart and hope that I will not entirely forget him."

Her marriage vows. To love, honor, and obey him.

He did not want her love. He did not expect her obedience—he doubted she would be able to give it anyway. That left honor.

Privately she had promised him more—comfort, pleasure, and happiness. And somehow she had given all three during the three days following their nuptials. And he, like a fool, had taken without question.

She had merely been fulfilling a promise.

And though he did not doubt that she had taken

sexual pleasure from him, he understood now that she had merely been feasting upon the sensual delights of which her first husband's illness had deprived her.

It had all been about sex.

Nothing else.

As it had for him. As he had intended and wanted. He had not wanted more than that.

Why the devil, then, even though his anger had largely dissipated, was there a heavy ball of depression weighting down his stomach?

She would keep at least some of their marriage vows.

So too, heaven help him, would he.

Hedley Dew, he did not doubt, would never be mentioned between them again. She would love him in the secrecy of her heart and give her dutiful loyalty to her second husband.

He bowed again.

"I will take my leave of you, ma'am," he said. "I have some business to attend to. May I suggest that you bathe your face before showing it to any of the servants? I shall see you at dinner. And later tonight I shall visit your room briefly before returning to my own to sleep."

"Oh, Elliott," she said, "I have made a wretched mess of trying to explain to you, have I not? Perhaps because I cannot adequately explain even to myself. All I do know is that it is not quite what you think or quite what I have been able to put into words."

"Perhaps at some time in the future," he said, "you will find yourself able to write a book. A lurid novel would suit you—something filled with baseless passion and emotion and bombast."

He was striding across the room as he spoke. He let

himself in to her dressing room and shut the door firmly behind him before crossing into his own dressing room and shutting that door too.

He was angry again. He had the feeling that somehow she had made a fool of him. She had not allowed him to vent his displeasure at finding her thus or to lay down the law to her about what he expected of her and their marriage. Instead she had led him into numerous verbal labyrinths and made him feel like a pompous ass.

Was that what he was?

He frowned ferociously.

Was one supposed to take one's wife into one's arms and murmur sweet, soothing nothings into her ear while she wept her heart out over the man she loved— who just happened not to be him?

And dead.

Good Lord!

Devil take it, what was marriage leading him into?

He glanced through the window of his bedchamber and noticed that the rain, if anything, was coming down harder than it had been half an hour before. And the wind was swaying the treetops.

It looked like just the weather he needed.

Ten minutes later, he was riding away from the stables again on a fresh and eager mount.

His destination?

He had no idea. Just somewhere far away from Vanessa and his marriage. And from that wretched portrait of a delicate and pretty boy, against whom he would not wish to compete even if he could.

She might love him with his blessing.

To hell with her.

And Hedley Dew too.

When he recognized the essentially childish bent of his thoughts, he urged his mount into a gallop and decided not to go around the hedgerow that was in front of him but to go straight over it.

If one was going to be childish, one might as well be reckless too.

It was all absolutely awful.

For one thing her face would not seem to return to its normal self. The more she dabbed at it with cold water and smoothed it with cream, the more puffy her eyes seemed to look and the more ruddy her cheeks.

Finally she gave up and sallied forth into the rest of the house with a springy step and a bright smile though there were only the walls and the pictures and marble busts to see her.

He returned home and arrived in the drawing room with only moments to spare before he had to lead her into the dining room for dinner. They made stilted conversation for a whole hour for the benefit of the butler and attendant footman. During all of which time Vanessa did not believe she once let her smile slip.

They sat in the drawing room afterward, one on each side of the fire, reading. She counted the number of times he turned a page during the next hour and a half—four times. Each time she remembered to turn a page of her own book too and change position and smile appreciatively at the page in front of her.

It was only after the first half hour that she realized she had picked up a book of sermons.

She converted her smile into something more thoughtful.

It was at about the same moment that she suddenly wondered exactly why he had walked into her bed-chamber without knocking this afternoon—and why he had returned home early. Had he come to—

But when she glanced at him, he was frowning at his book and looking anything but loverlike.

When bedtime finally came, he escorted her to the door of her dressing room, bowed over her hand, and asked—oh, yes, he really did!—if he might be permitted to wait upon her in a short while.

When he came, she was lying in bed, wondering what she could say or do to improve the situation. But all she did was smile at him until he blew out the candle—the first time he had done that.

He proceeded to make love to her without kisses or caresses, swiftly and lustily. It was all over long before she could even think of preparing herself for the pleasure that had always come during their thirteen previous encounters.

All she was left with was the ache of an unfulfilled longing.

He got up from the bed immediately afterward, pulled on his dressing gown, and left via her dressing room.

And before he closed the door he thanked her.

He *thanked* her.

It felt like the final insult.

And it *was* insulting. All of it. It was intended to be, she suspected.

If she wanted to be his wife merely for convenience and the procreation of children, his behavior this evening and tonight had told her, then he was quite happy to give her what she wanted.

Men were *so* foolish.

Or, if that was too much of a generalization and un-just to countless thousands of innocent male persons, then she would amend her thought.

Elliott Wallace, Viscount Lyngate, was foolish!

Except that it was all her fault.

Though he did not know it and would never ever ad-mit to it, he was hurt.

But she did not know quite what to do about it. Do something she must, though. She owed him better than to be crying over another man a mere four days after marrying him.

She owed him what she had promised him. She would owe it even if she had *not* promised.

Besides, she was not content to let the memory of her honeymoon fade into the past, something sweet that could never be repeated. She had been happy for those three days, and she was as certain as she could be that he had been happy too—though doubtless he would never admit to that particular sentiment even under torture.

They had been happy.

Past tense.

It was up to her to make it present tense with bright prospects for the future too.

For both their sakes.

## 16

I T W O U L D have been quite easy to settle into what was really only half a marriage. Vanessa soon came to suspect that most marriages, at least those of the *ton*, were little more than that.

It was what one might expect, of course, in a segment of society in which most marriages were arranged.

But she had known a different type of marriage, however briefly, and could not be content now with only half a one.

After they moved to London she saw very little of Elliott. He went out after breakfast and did not return until late afternoon. And even when he was at home, so were his mother and youngest sister.

The only time Vanessa was really alone with him was at night, when they went through the brief ritual of lovemaking—if it could be called that. He was trying to beget an heir with her, and she was trying to enjoy the short encounters. She hoped he was having more success than she was. He always returned to his own room as soon as he had finished. Always he thanked her as he left.

He treated her with civility, but it was cold enough to draw a sigh and a comment from his mother after he had left the breakfast parlor one morning.

"I *so* hoped Elliott would be different," she said.

"Different?" Vanessa looked at her with raised eyebrows.

"The Wallace men are always as wild as sin before they marry," the dowager said, "and meticulously respectable afterward, at least as far as outward appearances go. They always choose their brides with care and treat them with unfailing courtesy ever after. They never marry for love. It would be beneath their dignity and would restrict their freedom too much to allow themselves to feel any such emotion. It is difficult for a man to break with family tradition, especially when the family is as illustrious as this one is. I thought Elliott might do it, though. Perhaps one always believes one's son will be different from his father. And of course one always wishes desperately for his happiness."

It was a chilling speech.

"I still intend to make him happy," Vanessa said, leaning forward across the table. "It is I who have made him *unhappy*, you see. Or at least I have wounded his pride or something else that is important to him. Three days after our wedding he gathered daffodils with me—great armfuls he could hardly see around. And when we returned to the dower house he filled the pots and vases with water for me and helped sort the flowers and carry them into each room and position them in just the right place and at just the right angle."

"Elliott did this?" The dowager looked surprised.

"And the very next day," Vanessa said, "he found me in tears. I was weeping over a portrait of my late husband because I had been happy for three whole days and felt guilty and feared I might forget him."

"Oh, dear," her mother-in-law said, frowning. "Did you explain to Elliott?"

"I did," Vanessa said. "At least I *think* I did. I was not sure how to explain it even to myself. But clearly he did not understand. I will make him happy yet, though. See if I don't."

It would have been very easy just to fall into the busy pattern that life took on as soon as they arrived in town. There were a hundred and one things to do every day—go shopping, go to the library, pay afternoon calls with her mother-in-law and sister-in-law, call upon her siblings after they had arrived at Merton House on Berkeley Square, pore over the masses of invitations that arrived at the house every day and ponder which she wished to attend—after her presentation to the queen, of course. And there was that presentation to think about and worry about—and the ball that would follow it in the evening. It was a ball intended primarily for Cecily's come-out, but in a sense it would be Vanessa's too—and Meg's and Kate's.

There were people to meet and faces and names to memorize.

Most of them were female pursuits. Indeed, it seemed to Vanessa that ladies and gentlemen of the *ton* lived largely separate existences and came together only for social events like balls and picnics and concerts. The come-out ball would be one such occasion.

She might have thrown herself into the new life and virtually ignored Elliott, who did she knew not what with his days.

But she missed him. They had talked a great deal during the three days of their honeymoon. They had done things together. They had made love frequently and at satisfying length. They had slept together.

It had been a less-than-ideal relationship even then.

She had felt his reserve, his unwillingness to unbend and simply enjoy life. She had noticed that he never smiled or laughed. But it had been only a partial reserve. It had seemed to her that those had been happy days for him too, even if he would never have used that exact word.

At the very least then there had been the hope of more.

Now he was *not* happy—not when he was at home anyway.

And it was all her fault.

She *might* have been contented with half a marriage, then, and she *might* have been contented with the busy nature of her days.

But she was not.

On the morning of the day before her presentation, she heard him leave his dressing room. It was still very early. He always got up early in order to spend some time in the office with Mr. Bowen before going about whatever business kept him from home for the rest of the day.

His mother and sometimes even Cecily took breakfast with him. So did she, but there was no chance of any private conversation there.

Vanessa hurried into her dressing room, hauling off her nightgown as she went. She did not ring for her maid. She washed quickly in cold water and dressed hastily in a pale blue day dress. She pulled a brush through her hair, checked herself in the full-length mirror to make sure she did not look an absolute fright, and followed her husband downstairs.

He was in the study next to the library, as she had expected. He had a letter open in one hand though he was not reading it. He was talking with Mr. Bowen. Dressed immaculately in riding clothes and top boots, he looked very handsome indeed.

He turned as she appeared in the doorway and his eyebrows lifted in evident surprise.

"Ah, my dear," he said. "You are up early this morning."

He had taken to calling her *my dear* in public. It seemed ludicrously inappropriate.

"I could not sleep," she said, and smiled. She nodded to Mr. Bowen, who had risen to his feet behind the desk.

"How may I be of service to you?" Elliott asked.

"You may come into the library or the morning room with me," she said. "I wish to speak with you."

He inclined his head.

"I will dictate an answer to this one later, George," he said, waving the letter in his hand before setting it down on the desk. "There is no particular hurry for it."

He took her by the elbow and led her into the next room, where a fire was already burning merrily in the hearth.

"What may I do for you, Vanessa?" he asked, indicating a leather chair beside the hearth and going to stand before the fire himself, his back to it. He was all courtesy with a hint of impatience.

She sat down.

"I thought we might talk," she said. "We hardly ever have the chance to talk to each other anymore."

He raised his eyebrows again. "Not at dinner?" he asked her. "Or in the drawing room afterward?"

"Your mother and sister are always present too," she said. "I meant alone, just the two of us."

He regarded her steadily. "Do you need more

money?" he asked. "You may ask George for that any-time. You will not find me tightfisted."

"No, of course not," she said, waving a dismissive hand. "I have not spent any of what he gave me two days ago. Oh, except for the subscription cost at the library. I looked around the shops, but there was really nothing else I needed that would not have been a point-less extravagance. I already have more dresses than I have ever owned in my life."

He continued to look down at her and she realized at what a disadvantage he had set her—deliberately? She was seated while he stood. He towered over her.

"It was not about money I wished to speak," she said. "It was about us—about our marriage. I think I hurt you."

His eyes grew cold.

"I believe, ma'am," he said, "you do not possess the power to do that."

It was proof positive that she was right. People who were hurt often felt the need to strike back—only even more viciously.

"If that was all you wished to say," he said, "I will bid you—"

"Of course it is not all," she said. "Good heavens, Elliott, is the rest of our married life to proceed this way, as if we are nothing to each other but coldly polite strangers? Just a few days ago you were skipping stones across the water at Finchley Park and I was rowing us in circles and we were gathering daffodils. Did all that mean nothing to you?"

"You surely did not expect that those days would be more than a mildly pleasant interlude before the real business of the rest of our married days began, did you?" he asked her.

"Of course I did," she said. "Elliott—"

"I really must bid you good morning," he said. "May I escort you to the breakfast parlor? Perhaps my mother will be down by now."

He offered his arm.

"Those three days and nights—*four* nights—were the most wonderful of my whole life," she said, leaning forward a little in her chair and fixing her eyes on him.

She watched him inhale, but she swept onward before he could say anything else.

"I loved Hedley," she said. "I *adored* him, in fact. I would have died in his place if I could. But I was never *in* love with him. I was never—" She swallowed awkwardly and closed her eyes. She had never said any of this aloud before. She had tried very hard not even to think it. "I was never aroused by him. I never wanted him in *that* way. He was my dearest friend in the world."

There was a horrible silence.

"But he was dreadfully in love with me," she said, laboring onward. "Not because of my looks, of course. I think it must have been my cheerfulness and laughter and my willingness to be with him. He was so very ill and weak. If he had been robust and healthy, I daresay he would not have loved me at all even though he had always been my friend. He would have fallen in love with someone who was prettier."

Still he said nothing, and she had stopped looking up at him. She gazed at her hands, which were now tingling with pins and needles.

"You are big and strong and healthy," she said. "What happened between us was . . . well. I have never enjoyed anything so much in all my life. And then afterward, when we had returned to the main house and I had learned about Crispin and realized how dreadfully unhappy Meg must be and then you were gone for the afternoon and I was alone and it was raining—well, *then* I remembered Hedley. And I remembered that I had pushed his portrait down the side of my trunk when I left Warren Hall and I went and got it. I thought of him and I mourned his early death and the fact that I had never loved him in the way he thought I did. I felt guilty for having enjoyed myself so much with you when I had never really enjoyed myself with him. And then I felt guilty for feeling guilty—for I ought not to feel guilty at enjoying myself with my new husband, ought I? Indeed, I ought to *try* to enjoy myself. And here I am getting tied up in words again just when I so much want to explain myself clearly to you."

She stopped—and listened to him inhale deeply and then exhale.

"I am no good at dealing with Cheltenham tragedies, I am afraid, Vanessa," he said. "I am to feel gratified, am I, that you were not in love with Dew though you loved him? There *is* a difference, I take it? I am to be doubly gratified that you felt such eager lust for me during the three days following our marriage—such eager *satisfied* lust—that you completely forgot the man you loved, but with whom you were never *in* love?"

He had succeeded in making her confession seem trivial. She had bared her soul to him, and it had left him cold.

She raised her eyes to his. He was looking steadily back.

"You are *not,* it is to be hoped, in love with *me,* are you?" he asked her.

She hated him at that moment.

"No, of course not," she said. "I married you in order to help my sisters gain an entrée into society, just as you married me to solve the problem the three of us posed for you and to beget your heirs. But even a marriage of convenience need not be an unhappy marriage, Elliott, or a marriage in which the partners rarely speak or spend time alone together. I want us to have a workable marriage. I know you might have chosen someone far lovelier and more suitable than me if you had waited, but it was you who chose not to wait. What else was I to do when you came to offer for Meg but offer myself instead?"

He regarded her with narrowed eyes.

"It is probably as well that we are *not* in love with each other," she said. "Then we might not even try to be happy. We might rely upon the feeling of euphoria that being in love doubtless brings and not bother to work at building any sort of lasting and amicable relationship. But we can be happy again if we try."

*"Again?"* He raised his eyebrows. "And what does this *trying* involve, Vanessa? If you expect me to bare my feelings at every turn, you are doomed to disappointment. That is something strictly for females."

"Well, for a start," she said, "surely you do not need to be from home all day every day. Neither do I. Sometimes we could do something together that will bring us both pleasure."

"Like going to bed?" he asked.

She would not look away from his eyes though she felt her cheeks grow hot again.

"For longer than five minutes at a time?" she said. "*That* would be something. Though a workable relationship must rely upon more than just that. There is to be tomorrow night's ball, of course, but that is only *one* thing, and it is sure to be dreadfully formal. But every day there is a pile of invitations that I look through with your mother. May *we* perhaps decide together upon a few that would suit us both?"

He inclined his head, though he did not say anything.

"Marriage is not easy to accustom oneself to," she said. "And I think it is often worse for the man. Women are used to being dependent, to thinking of others as well as themselves. Men are not."

"We are selfish bastards, then?" he asked her.

She was horribly shocked. She was not sure she had ever heard that word spoken aloud before now.

She smiled slowly.

"If the cap fits . . ." she said.

For a moment there was a gleam in his eyes that might possibly have been amusement.

"Have you seen the Towneley collection at the British Museum?" he asked her.

"No," she said.

"They are classical sculptures brought from the ancient world," he said. "Some ladies will not go to see them, and some men will not take them even if they wish to go. They have not been provided with clothes, you see, and are shockingly naked. They provide a marvelous glimpse into one of the world's greatest civilizations, though. Do you wish to go?"

She stared at him.

"Now?"

"I suppose," he said, his eyes moving over her, "you will wish to have breakfast first and change into something more suitable."

She jumped to her feet.

"How soon do you want me to be ready?" she asked him.

"In one hour's time?" he suggested.

"I will be ready in fifty-five minutes," she promised, and she flashed him a bright smile before turning to hurry from the room and dash up the stairs.

She was going to go out with Elliott!

He was taking her to see the Towneley collection, whatever that was. She did not care. She would look at a field of mud if that was where he chose to take her—and delight in it too.

She paused when she was inside her dressing room and had rung for her maid.

He had asked her if she was in love with him—adding that he hoped she was not.

*Was* she?

It would add an unfortunate complication to a life that was already proving difficult.

*Was* she in love? With Elliott?

She could not answer the question. Or would not.

But suddenly she felt the ache of tears at the back of her throat and behind her eyes.

"I have sorted through the post," George Bowen said when Elliott returned to the study. "The invitations for the ladies to look at are in this pile. The letters I can deal with myself are here. The ones that need your attention are there. The one on top—"

"—will have to wait," Elliott said without glancing at the pile—or at his secretary. "I will be spending the morning with her ladyship."

There was a short pause.

"Ah, quite so," George said, making a great to-do of straightening the third, small pile.

"I will be taking her to see the Towneley collection at the British Museum," Elliott said. Later, he wished he had not added the next words. "It is her wish that we do some things together."

"Some wives are funny that way," George said as he mended a pen though there was no sign that he intended to put it to any immediate use. "Or so I have heard."

"I need to go upstairs and change," Elliott said.

"You do." His friend looked him critically up and down. "A suggestion, Elliott, if I may?"

Elliott had already turned toward the door. He sighed and looked back over his shoulder.

"I suppose the museum and the collection was your idea," George said. "And a fine one it was too. But take her to Gunter's afterward. I daresay she has never tasted an ice. It will please her. She will see it as a romantic gesture on your part."

Elliott turned fully to face his secretary again.

"And you are suddenly an expert in romantic gestures, George?" he asked.

His secretary cleared his throat.

"One does not need to be," he said. "One has only to observe ladies to understand what pleases them. And your lady is easy to please, I would wager. She is a cheerful little thing—even when there is not much to be cheerful about."

"You are wishful of making a point, George?" his employer asked with ominous calm.

"The trouble with you," George said, "is that you do not have a romantic bone in your body, Elliott. The only thing you have ever known to do with a woman you fancied is to bed her. Not that I blame you. I have often envied you, if the truth were known. But the fact is that ladies need more than that or at least— Well, never mind. But they are romantically inclined and it behooves us to give them what they want at least occasionally—if they belong to us, that is, and are not merely mistresses."

Elliott stared at him.

"Good God!" he said. "What the devil have I been harboring beneath my own roof in the guise of a secretary?"

George had the grace to look apologetic, though he did not remain mute.

"The sculptures first, if you really must, Elliott," he said. "I believe your lady has the fortitude not to need smelling salts there. I believe she will even enjoy them. But take her to Gunter's afterward, old chap."

"This early in the year?" Elliott asked.

"Even if it were January," George assured him. "And especially after she has been all alone for four days— except for the other ladies, of course. And married for only a little over a week."

"You are impertinent," Elliott said, his eyes narrowing.

"Only observant," his friend said. "You had better go up and change before breakfast."

Elliott went.

He was not in the best of moods as he climbed the stairs to his room—though he had not been in the best of moods for six days. Not when he was at home, anyway. He had been happy enough at his clubs, at Tattersall's, at Jackson's boxing saloon, mingling with his friends and acquaintances, talking on congenial topics like the government and the wars and the upcoming races and boxing mills.

He was convinced that he had made the biggest mistake of his life when he had allowed Vanessa Dew to talk him into marrying her.

Though if it had not been her, it would have been someone else soon. And if he had not married either her or her sister, then the Huxtable ladies would still be like a millstone hanging about his neck.

She had *loved* Dew, for the love of God, but had not been *in* love with him. What the deuce was *that* supposed to mean? She had not enjoyed her sexual encounters with Dew, though the poor devil had probably been too ill to give her a good time. On the contrary, she had enjoyed her beddings with *him*—until she had remembered her dead husband and got herself caught up in a web of grief and guilt so tangled that his head spun at the thought of even *trying* to unravel it—*not* that he intended to try.

He wondered if there could be a more muddle-headed female in existence than his wife and seriously doubted it.

But she had thought the three days and four nights following their wedding the most wonderful of her life.

That was mildly gratifying, he supposed.

Good Lord, did she expect him to *talk* about every small problem that might arise in their marriage for the rest of their lives? Were they going to *analyze* everything to death?

Was life going to become hopelessly complicated?

*Of course* it was. He was *married*, was he not? And to Vanessa, of all people.

And now he was to give up a perfectly decent morning of reading the papers and conversing at White's Club in order to take her to enjoy a cultural experience. And *that* was to be followed by ices at Gunter's.

Not that he had to take her there. He was not about to allow his secretary to dictate his every move, was he? And scold him for neglecting his wife?

But it appeared that taking Vanessa to Gunter's was the romantic thing to do.

Good Lord!

Had she not at one time promised to make him comfortable?

Thus far he was finding marriage the most uncomfortable thing he had ever experienced or dreamed possible.

Though those first few days had been somewhat enjoyable, he had to admit. More than *somewhat*, in fact.

Either way he was in this marriage for life.

It seemed like a damnably long time.

He rang the bell for his valet.

# 17

VANESSA enjoyed looking at the sculptures. She spent a great deal of time gazing at them all one at a time, quite unabashed by their nakedness and undeterred by the fact that most of them were mere fragments.

"I cannot believe," she said at one point, "that I am actually looking at objects created during such ancient civilizations. It all quite takes one's breath away, does it not?"

But she did not fill the time with chatter, Elliott was interested to find. She gave her undivided attention to the collection. Until, that was, he became aware that she looked at him from time to time rather as she was looking at the exhibits—with a steady, critical gaze. He noticed because *he* was looking at *her* as much as he was viewing the pieces—he had seen them before, after all.

She was wearing pink, a color that ought to have looked dreadful on her but did not. It made her look delicate and feminine. It made her complexion look rosy and vibrant. It made her look really quite pretty.

Of course the clothes were all expertly styled and her absurd little bonnet was in the height of fashion.

He intercepted one of her looks and raised his eyebrows.

"They are all very white or gray," she explained, "as

if the ancient Greeks and other Mediterranean races were pale. But they could not have been in real life, could they? I suppose these were all painted once upon a time in vibrant colors. They must have looked like you. They must have been dark-complexioned like you only more so because they lived under the hot sun all the time. They must have been even more beautiful than they look here."

Was that a compliment? he wondered. And was she calling him *beautiful*?

"All of that is your heritage," she said later, as they left the museum. "Do you feel a tug at your heartstrings, Elliott?"

"I believe," he said, "it is an organ that comes without strings attached."

He was rewarded for his sorry attempt at a joke with a wide, delighted smile.

"But yes," he said, "I am always aware of my Greek heritage."

"Have you ever been to Greece?" she asked.

"Once as an infant," he told her. "My mother took Jessica and me to visit our grandfather and numerous other relatives. I remember little except large, noisy family gatherings and bright sunshine and deep blue water and getting lost in the Parthenon because I would not obey instructions to stay at my mother's side."

"Do you never think of going back?" she asked as he helped her into the carriage.

"Yes," he said. "But I did not do it when I could. Now, since my father's death, I am too busy here. Besides, Greece is a very volatile part of the world politically."

"You ought to go anyway," she said. "You still have family members there, do you?"

"Too numerous to count," he said.

"*We* ought to go," she said. "It would be like a honeymoon again."

"Honeymoon?" It was a word that had always made him cringe. "*Again?*"

"Like the three days at the dower house," she said. "They were good, were they not?"

That had been a *honeymoon*?

"I have estates to run," he said. "And I have just become guardian to a seventeen-year-old boy who has much to learn before he can assume the full exercise of his duties."

"And it is the beginning of the Season," she said as the carriage moved off down Great Russell Street, "and Meg and Kate need to be introduced to society."

"Yes," he agreed.

"And you need to set up your nursery without further delay."

"Yes."

He glanced at her sidelong. She was looking ahead and smiling.

"They are not good enough excuses," she said.

"*Excuses?*" He raised his eyebrows again.

"Your family members are growing older over there," she said. "Is your grandfather still alive?"

"Yes."

"And life goes by very fast," she said. "Just yesterday, it seems, I was a girl, yet now already I am approaching my middle twenties. You are almost thirty."

"We are practically in our dotage," he said.

"We will be before we know it," she said. "If we are

fortunate enough to grow old, that is. Life should be lived and enjoyed every moment."

"And to the devil with duties and responsibilities?"

"No, of course not," she said. "But sometimes it is easier to shelter behind those duties than to admit that our presence is not always indispensable and to step out into life and live it for all it is worth."

"Forgive me," he said, frowning, "but have you not lived all your life thus far in Throckbridge and its environs, Vanessa? Are you qualified to advise me to throw duty and caution to the winds and embark on the first ship leaving for Greece?"

"But I am no longer there," she said. "I chose to move to Warren Hall with my sisters and brother even though it was all a great unknown. And then I chose to marry you—and heaven knows *you* are a vast unknown. Tomorrow I am to be presented to the queen. Then I will be attending Cecily's come-out ball and introducing Meg and Kate to the *ton*. And then a thousand and one other such events. Am I frightened? Yes, of course I am. But am I going to do it all? Absolutely."

He pursed his lips.

"I think," he said, "we will not be going to Greece anytime soon."

"No, of course we will not." She turned her head to smile dazzlingly at him. "For there *is* duty, and I know I must learn that this new life does not mean total and endless freedom. But we must not be oppressed by duty, Elliott. I think perhaps that is what you have allowed to happen since your father died. There can be joy even in a dutiful life."

He wondered suddenly if that was a description of her first marriage. Had she not really been happy, but had forced herself to be joyful? And if he was not careful, he was going to become as tortured by words as she was. What *was* the difference between happiness and joy?

"And one of these days," she said, "when there is nothing urgent to keep you at home and Stephen is capable of looking after his own affairs, we will go to Greece and meet your family and have a second honeymoon. And if we have children by then, they will simply come with us."

She had her head turned to look at him. She blushed suddenly, realizing perhaps what she had just said. Though why she needed to blush after almost two weeks of regular intimacies with him he did not know.

"The carriage is stopping," she observed, looking out through the window beyond his head. "But we are not home yet."

"We have arrived at Gunter's," he told her. "We are going to have an ice here."

"An ice?" Her eyes widened.

"I thought you might like refreshments after trudging about the museum looking at cold marble and breathing in old dust for a whole hour," he said. "Though you actually enjoyed it, did you not?"

"An *ice*," she said without answering his question. "I have never tasted one, you know. They are said to be absolutely divine."

"Nectar of the gods?" he said as he handed her down to the pavement. "Perhaps. You may judge for yourself."

It was easy to become jaded with the luxuries and privileges of one's life, Elliott thought over the following half hour while he watched his wife taste and then savor her ice. She ate it in small spoonfuls and held the ice in her mouth for several seconds before swallowing. For the first few mouthfuls she even closed her eyes.

"Mmm," she said. "Could anything possibly be more delicious?"

"I could probably think of a dozen things *as* delicious if I set my mind to it," he said. "But *more* delicious? No, I doubt it."

"Oh, Elliot," she said, leaning toward him across the table, "has not this been a *lovely* morning? Was I not right? Is it not fun to do things together?"

*Fun?*

But as he thought of the morning at White's as it might have been, he realized that he did not feel unduly deprived. He really had rather enjoyed the morning, in fact.

As they were leaving Gunter's, they ran into Lady Haughton and her young niece, who were being escorted inside by Lord Beaton.

Elliott bowed to the ladies and nodded at Beaton.

"Oh, Lady Haughton," his wife said, "and Miss Flaxley. Are *you* coming to have ices too? We have been to the British Museum to look at the ancient sculptures there, and now we have been here. Is it not a *beautiful* day?"

"Ah, Lady Lyngate," Lady Haughton said, smiling— something she did not often do. "It is indeed a lovely day. Have you met my nephew, Lord Beaton? Lady Lyngate, Cyril."

Vanessa curtsied, smiling brightly at the young dandy.

"I am very pleased to meet you," she said. "Have you met Viscount Lyngate, my husband?" She laughed. "But of course you must have."

"The female population of London has just gone into collective mourning, Lyngate," Lady Haughton told him. "And you must expect many envious glances during the coming Season, my dear. You have stolen one of the most eligible bachelors from the marriage mart."

Vanessa laughed.

"My brother is in town too," she said, looking at Beaton. "He is the new Earl of Merton and is only seventeen years old. I am sure he would be delighted to make the acquaintance of a somewhat *older* young man, my lord."

"I shall look forward to the pleasure, ma'am," he said, making her a bow and looking gratified.

"Will you be attending the ball at Moreland House tomorrow evening?" Vanessa asked. "I will introduce him to you there, if I may. Are you *all* planning to attend?"

"We would not miss it for the world," Lady Haughton said while Beaton bowed again. "*Everyone* who is anyone will be there, Lady Lyngate."

"I can see," Elliott said a few minutes later, when they were inside the carriage and on the way home, "that you have made several acquaintances already."

"Your mother has been taking me about with her," she said. "I have been trying to memorize names. It is not always easy, but fortunately I remembered Lady Haughton and Miss Flaxley."

"It would seem," he said, "that you do not need me for company after all, then."

She turned her head to look steadily at him.

"Oh, but, Elliott," she said, "they are all just *acquaintances*. Even your mother and Cecily and Meg and Kate and Stephen are just *family*. You are my *husband*. There is a difference. An enormous difference."

"Because we go to bed together?" he asked her.

"Oh, you foolish man," she said. "Yes, because of that. Because it is a symbol of the intimacy of our relationship. The total intimacy."

"And yet," he reminded her, "you do not like me walking into your private apartments without knocking. You have insisted that you need some privacy, even from me."

She sighed.

"Yes, it is a seeming contradiction, is it not?" she said. "But the thing is, you see, that two people can never actually become one no matter how close they are. And it would not be desirable even if it were possible. What would happen when one of them died? It would leave the other as half a person, and that would be a dreadful thing. We must each be a whole person, and therefore we each need some privacy to be alone with ourselves and our own feelings. But a marriage relationship *is* an intimate thing for all that, and the intimacy ought to be cultivated. For the relationship ought to be the best of all relationships. What a waste to live two almost totally separate lives when the chance is there for one of the greatest joys of life together."

"You have obviously given a great deal of thought to this subject," he said.

"I had much time for thought when—" She did not complete the sentence. "I have had much time for thought. I know what a happy marriage is." She turned her face away from him and gazed out the window. She spoke so softly that he could barely decipher the words. "And I know what a happier marriage could be."

How had they got onto this subject? How did he get onto *any* subject with his wife?

One thing was becoming very clear to him. She was not going to allow him to settle into any comfortable sort of married life that might somehow resemble his bachelor existence.

She was going to force him to be happy, damn it all.

And joyful.

Whatever the devil difference there might be between the two.

Heaven help him.

"Elliott," she said as the carriage drew up before the house. She set one gloved hand on his sleeve. "Thank you so very much for this morning—for the museum, for the ice. I have enjoyed myself more than I can say."

He lifted her hand to his lips.

"Thank *you*," he said, "for coming."

Her eyes twinkled with merriment.

"This afternoon you may be free to do whatever you wish," she said. "I am going shopping with Meg and Kate. Cecily is coming too. I will *not* suggest that you accompany us. I will see you at dinner?"

"You will," he said. He spoke impulsively. "Perhaps you would arrange to have it served early. You may like to go to the theater this evening. Shakespeare's *Twelfth Night* is being performed at the Drury Lane. Perhaps Merton and your sisters would care to join us in my private box there."

"Oh, Elliott!" Her face lit up with such pleasure that he was dazzled for a moment. "I really cannot think of anything I would like more. And how *good* of you to invite my brother and sisters too."

He was still holding her hand, he realized. And his

coachman was standing beside the carriage door, holding it open. He had already put down the steps. He was staring straight ahead down the street, the suggestion of a smirk on his lips.

"I shall be home in time for an early dinner, then," Elliott said after he had climbed down and held out a hand to help Vanessa descend.

Her smile was warm and happy.

And she did indeed look rather pretty in pink.

Just a couple of months ago an assembly at Throckbridge had seemed the pinnacle of excitement. Yet now, Vanessa thought as they all took their seats in Elliott's box, here they were, she and her brother and sisters, attending the performance of a Shakespeare play in the Theater Royal, Drury Lane, in London. And tomorrow there was to be her presentation to the queen and then a grand *ton* ball in the evening.

And this was all just the beginning.

Sometimes she *still* expected to wake up in her bed at Rundle Park.

The theater was filling with ladies and gentlemen who were dazzling in the splendor of their muslins and silks and satins and jewels. And she and her siblings actually belonged in such company. Vanessa was even sparkling along with everyone else. She was wearing the white gold chain with a multifaceted and indecently large diamond pendant that Elliott had brought home with him during the afternoon and clasped about her neck just before they left the house. The diamond was catching the light whichever way she turned.

"Even without the play," Katherine said to Cecily,

though her voice carried to all of them, "this would be a memorable evening of entertainment."

"It would indeed," Cecily agreed fervently, fanning her face and gazing down into the pit.

The pit was where unattached single gentlemen usually sat to ogle the ladies—the dowager had told Vanessa that. She had been perfectly right. And *they*—or Meg, Kate, and Cecily anyway—were the subject of much of that attention. Some of the gentlemen were even using opera glasses to magnify the view. Meg and Kate were wearing new gowns, both blue, Kate's pale, Meg's darker. Both looked outstandingly lovely. So did Cecily in white.

Vanessa turned her head to smile happily at Elliott, who was seated beside her.

"I knew they would all attract attention," she said. "Kate and Meg and Cecily, I mean. They are so lovely."

She was holding a fan in one hand. He took her free hand and set it on his sleeve. He kept one hand over it.

"And you are not?" he asked her.

She laughed.

"Of course I am not," she said. "Besides, I am a married lady and of no interest to anyone."

His eyebrows rose.

"Not even to your husband?" he asked her.

She laughed again.

"I was not fishing for a compliment," she said. "Of course, if you wish to pay me one anyway . . ."

"With a smile on your lips and in your eyes," he said, "and clothed in that particular shade of green, you look like a piece of the springtime, Vanessa."

"Oh, well done," she said. "Are you about to add that so does every other lady present?"

"Not at all," he said. "No one else does. Only you. And springtime is everyone's favorite season, you know."

Her smile faded slightly and for a moment she felt a desperate yearning for she knew not what.

"Is it?" she said softly. "Why?"

"The renewal of life and energy, I suppose," he said. "The renewal of hope. The promise of a bright future."

"Oh."

She was not sure she made any sound. Was it a compliment? But of course it was. Had he meant by it all she dreamed he meant? Or had he merely found a deft way of avoiding telling her quite bluntly that no, indeed, she was not as lovely as her three companions?

Their eyes locked and he opened his mouth to speak again.

"Oh, I say," Stephen said suddenly, sounding as exuberant as he had looked since the moment of their arrival at the theater, "there is Cousin Constantine."

"*Where?*" Katherine and Cecily asked together.

Stephen indicated a box almost directly across from theirs, and Vanessa looked and saw that sure enough, there was Constantine Huxtable with a party of ladies and gentlemen. He had seen them too and was smiling and raising a hand in greeting as he tipped his head sideways to listen to something the lady next to him was saying. She too was looking across to their box.

Vanessa waved back with her fan hand, smiling brightly.

"It is to London he came, then," she said to Elliott. "He is accepted here?"

"Although he is illegitimate?" he said. "But of course. He is the son of a former Earl and Countess of Merton and was raised as such. There is no real stigma on his name. It was just that legally he could not enjoy the privileges of the eldest son."

"Does he have any money?" she asked. "I mean did he inherit anything?"

"His father provided for him," he said. "Not lavishly, but adequately."

"That is a relief to know," she said. "I did wonder, especially after we arrived at Warren Hall and effectively turned him out of his home."

"Con will always find a way of looking after himself," he said, both his eyes and his voice hardening. "You must not worry about him, Vanessa. Or pay him too much attention."

"He *is* our cousin," she said.

"A relationship that is best forgotten," he assured her. "And *he* is best ignored."

She frowned at him.

"But unless you give me a good reason," she said, "you cannot expect me to ignore him just because you hate him. I do not believe there *is* a good reason."

He raised his eyebrows, his eyes still cold. But at that very moment a sudden hush descended on the theater. The play was about to begin.

Vanessa's mood had taken a downward turn. She was very much afraid that the evening had been at least partially ruined. Her hand was still on Elliott's arm, and his hand still covered it, but there was no real warmth in either and she wondered if it had been a move designed for the benefit of the audience rather than a spontaneous gesture of affection.

She glanced at Margaret, who was smiling, her attention already fixed upon the stage. She had scarcely stopped smiling since her arrival in London. The expression was like a mask. Vanessa could only imagine what lay behind it. Meg was studiously avoiding all personal conversation.

And then the play began.

And all else was forgotten.

There were only the actors and the action and the play.

Vanessa leaned forward in her seat, unaware of either her surroundings or her companions, unaware of the arm she gripped a little more tightly, unaware that her husband beside her watched her almost as much as he did the performance.

It was only later, when the interval began, that she leaned back in her chair and sighed.

"Oh," she said, "have you ever seen anything more wonderful in your life?"

It was clear that four of her companions had not. They were all eager to talk, to exchange impressions, their voices bright with enthusiasm. Even Meg's smile looked genuine.

"I suppose," Vanessa said, turning to Elliott, who had not joined in the hubbub, "you have seen a thousand performances just like this and have become quite jaded."

"One never becomes jaded by good theater," he said.

"And is this good?" Katherine asked.

"It is," he said. "And I agree with everything that has been said during the past minute. If you wish, we may all step outside the box to stretch our legs before the next act begins."

The corridor outside was crowded and noisy as

people greeted one another and commented upon the performance.

Elliott introduced his party to a few of his acquaintances, and Vanessa was gratified to note the interest with which everyone greeted Stephen as soon as they knew who he was. Even in such a glittering setting he looked bright and golden and handsome, she thought fondly—and very youthful. More than a few ladies stole second and even third glances at him.

And then Constantine appeared among the throng. He must have circled half about the theater with the express purpose of greeting them. He had on his arm the lady who had been sitting beside him in his box. She was extremely lovely, Vanessa noticed with interest. She had shining blond hair and a figure to rival even Meg's.

"Ah, cousins," Constantine said when he was close enough to make himself heard. "Well met."

They all exclaimed with delight—except Elliott, of course, who made a stiff half-bow.

Cecily squealed with delight and caught his free arm and clung to it.

"*Con!*" she cried. "Is this not *wonderful*? I am *so* happy you are here. You must not forget my come-out ball tomorrow evening. You promised me a set."

"I believe, Cece," he said, "it was *I* who begged *you* for a set. I will hold you to your promise to reserve one for me, though. Doubtless you will be swarmed by young cubs when the time comes. And so will my cousin Katherine."

He grinned at Kate and even winked.

"Lady Lyngate, Miss Huxtable, Miss Katherine Huxtable, Miss Wallace, Merton," Constantine continued, "may I have the pleasure of introducing Mrs.

Bromley-Hayes to you? I believe you and the lady have an acquaintance already, Elliott."

There was an exchange of bows and curtsies and polite greetings. She was a married lady, then, Vanessa thought. Or perhaps a widow. She and Constantine made an extraordinarily handsome couple.

"My congratulations to you, Lord Merton," the lady said, "on your recent inheritance. And to you, Lord and Lady Lyngate, on your recent marriage. I wish you all the happiness you deserve."

She had a low, musical voice. She was smiling at Elliott and wafting a fan languidly before her face. It must be very pleasurable, Vanessa thought, to be that beautiful.

"I say," Stephen said, "have you ever seen a more impressive performance than this?"

They talked about the play until it was time to return to their respective boxes.

Elliott did not take her hand again, Vanessa noticed. His eyes were like flint, and his jaw was hard set. He drummed his fingers slowly on the velvet armrest of the box.

"What were we expected to do?" she asked him softly. "Ignore our own cousin when he was civil enough to come around to greet us?"

He turned his eyes on her.

"I have not uttered one word of reproach," he told her.

"You do not need to," she said, unfurling her fan and cooling her face with it. "You look thoroughly bad-tempered. Whatever would Mrs. Bromley-Hayes have thought if we had given them the cut direct?"

"I would not know," he said. "I am not privy to the lady's thoughts."

"Is she a widow?" she asked him.

"She is," he said. "But it is quite unexceptionable, you know, for married ladies to be escorted to social events by gentlemen who are not their husbands."

"Is it?" she said. "Must I cultivate the acquaintance of some obliging gentleman, then, so that you may be saved the bother of taking me to the museum and Gunter's and the theater and other places?"

"Who said it was a bother?" He removed his hand from the armrest and turned to her. He set her hand on his sleeve again and patted it with his own. "Are you trying to provoke me into a quarrel, by any chance?"

"I prefer your irritability to your coldness," she said, and smiled at him.

"And I have only the two moods, do I?" he asked her. "Poor Vanessa. However are you to make such a man happy? Or comfortable? However are you to give him pleasure?"

He was looking very directly at her with what she thought of as his bedroom eyes. His eyelids were half drooped over them. She felt a thrill of sexual awareness, which had seemed somewhat pointless since the end of their honeymoon.

"Oh, I will think of ways," she said, leaning a little toward him. "I am endlessly inventive."

"Ah," he said softly just before the play resumed.

She enjoyed the rest of the performance. She watched it with avid attention. But she was no longer as absorbed in it as she had been earlier. She was terribly aware, though she did not once turn her head to look, of her husband's fingers stroking lightly over the back of her hand and sometimes along the full length of one of her fingers.

She desperately wanted to be in bed with him—though bed since their honeymoon had lasted for five minutes from start to finish, if that.

Had he been flirting with her just now?

It was a ludicrous idea. Why would Elliot of all people flirt with *her*?

But what else could he have been up to except flirtation?

# *18*

AFTER dismissing his valet for the night, Elliott stood for a long time in his bedchamber, looking out through the window onto darkness, the fingers of one hand drumming on the windowsill. A night watchman made his round of the square, his lantern swaying as he walked. Then he passed on elsewhere and again there was darkness.

Elliott wondered if it had been deliberate. It was just the sort of thing Con *would* do. It was the sort of thing they might have done together once upon a time, during Elliott's irresponsible youth. Afterward they would have derived enormous amusement from the memory of the discomfiture of their victim. Though he could not remember anytime when they had been deliberately malicious, involving an innocent who might get seriously hurt.

*Would* Vanessa be hurt? He suspected that she might.

How could Con have known, though, that they would be at the theater this evening? Elliott had not known himself before making the impulsive suggestion at the end of the morning's outing.

But of course Con had *not* known for sure. He could have made several educated guesses, however, of places Elliott and Vanessa were likely to appear over the next week or so. It certainly would have been no secret that they were in London. If they had not been at the theater this evening, then they would surely be at this function or that soon.

Yes, it had been deliberate. Of course it had. Had there really been any doubt?

Had it been deliberate on Anna Bromley-Hayes's part too, though? That was the more pertinent question.

But if it had not been, why had she come during the interval to meet his party and be introduced to his wife? If it had not been deliberate, would she not have avoided such a painful encounter?

Yes. It had been deliberate. He would have expected better of her but had no right to demand it. He had undoubtedly hurt her. He had disregarded her feelings and presented her with a fait accompli quite without prior warning.

And good Lord, was this Vanessa's influence, this new tendency of his to analyze everything, to wonder about people's *feelings*?

However it was, his wife and his ex-mistress had not only come face-to-face but had also been introduced. It had been an excruciatingly embarrassing moment for him and doubtless equally intriguing to a number of the onlookers.

All of which Con would have known in advance. And Anna too.

Revenge had been of more importance to Anna, it seemed, than good taste or personal dignity.

She had been looking her loveliest and most ravishing. Con had been at his most charming and his most mocking—both very familiar facets of his character to

Elliott. He had never expected during his youth, though, that one day he would be one of Con's victims.

Vanessa would surely be waiting for him, he thought suddenly, bringing his mind back to the present. He was probably keeping her awake. If he was not going to go to her tonight, he ought to have told her so.

Was he really not going to her then?

He had actually enjoyed the day—morning and evening—right until the moment when young Merton had called their attention to the presence of Con in the box opposite and Elliott had looked and seen not just Con, but Anna too beside him. His eyes had met hers, and he had read a challenge there despite the distance between them.

He had been enjoying himself until then. For some odd reason he had been enjoying his wife's company. There was something inexplicably fascinating about her.

His fingers drummed harder against the windowsill for a moment.

He moved away from the window and wandered through to his dressing room, leaving the door open so that the light from the candle would shine in.

What he ought to do was walk firmly into Vanessa's room and tell her what she wanted to know. She wanted him to give her a good reason for his quarrel with Con, a good reason for her to avoid him. He should simply give it to her. Con was a thief and a lecher. He had robbed his own brother, who had trusted him totally but had not been mentally capable of knowing that his trust was being abused. And he had debauched servants of the house and other women of the neighborhood, something no decent gentleman would ever do.

But how could he tell Vanessa, any more than he had ever been able to tell his mother or his sisters—even though he had sometimes reasoned that they *ought* to know for their own good? How could he betray his *own* honor as guardian to Jonathan? How could he breach the confidentiality of such a trust? Besides, he had no incontrovertible proof. Con had not denied the charges, but he had not admitted to them either. He had merely lofted one eyebrow and grinned when Elliott confronted him, and had invited him to go to the devil.

How could one blacken someone's name to another person when one only had suspicions, no matter how certain one was that those suspicions were well founded?

Dash it all, it was *still* hard to accept that Con was capable of such villainy. He had always been up for any mischief and tomfoolery and devilry—but so had Elliott until fairly recently. He had never been a rogue, though.

And it was hard to accept that Con could hate him so much—and that he could be willing to risk hurting Vanessa in order to demonstrate that hatred.

He opened the door into his wife's dressing room. The door into her bedchamber had been left partly open, something she had done each night since demanding that he knock upon closed doors. There was the glow of candlelight beyond it.

He went to stand in the doorway, remembering another occasion when he had done so without an invitation. This time, though, she was asleep in bed.

He crossed the room and stood looking down at her. Her short hair was untidy and spread about her on the pillow. Her lips were slightly parted. In the light from the single candle her cheeks looked flushed.

She looked slight, girlish. Her breasts scarcely lifted the sheet that had been pulled up over them. Her arms and hands were slender.

For an unguarded moment he thought of Anna and made the contrasts. But strangely they were not thoughts he had to make any great effort to suppress.

There was something about Vanessa. She was not beautiful. She was not even pretty. She was plain. But there was something . . . She was not voluptuous. If there was an antonym for that word—he could not think of any at the moment—then she was that. There was nothing about her that should be sexually appealing.

And yet somehow there was.

He had desired her almost constantly during what she called their honeymoon—ghastly word! He had desired her every night since even though he had made their encounters brief and businesslike because . . .

Well, *why* exactly? Because she still loved her dead husband and he felt slighted? Hurt? No, certainly not that. Because he had wanted to punish her, to make her feel that she had only one function in his life?

Was he really so petty? It was an uncomfortable thought.

He desired her now. He had done all day, in fact— right from the moment she had appeared unexpectedly in George's office doorway before breakfast.

What *was* it about her?

He set two knuckles against her cheek and drew them lightly across it.

She opened her eyes and looked sleepily up at him— and smiled.

That was definitely a part of her appeal, he decided. He had never known anyone else whose eyes smiled almost constantly with genuine . . . what? Warmth? Happiness? Both?

Was she happy to see him? When his behavior toward her in the bedchamber for the last several nights had been little short of insulting?

"I was not sleeping. I was merely resting my eyes," she said, and laughed.

And there was her laugh too. Genuine. Warm. Almost infectious.

Some people seemed to have been born happy. Vanessa was one of them. And she was his wife.

He undid the sash of his dressing gown and shrugged out of it. He was wearing a nightshirt, something he had done each night since coming upon her in tears that afternoon at Finchley. He pulled it off now and dropped it to the floor while she watched him.

He lay down on his back beside her, one forearm over his eyes. Was there such a thing as a good marriage? he wondered. Was it possible? The thing was that no one in the *ton* ever expected it, not if goodness equated happiness anyway. Marriage was a social bond and often an economic one too. One looked elsewhere for sexual pleasure and emotional satisfaction—if one needed it.

His father obviously had. And his grandfather.

She was lying on her side, he was aware, looking at him. He had left the candle burning tonight.

"Elliott," she said softly, "it has been a lovely day. It is one I will long remember. Tell me it has not been an utter bore for you."

He removed his arm and turned his head to look at her.

"You think me incapable of enjoyment?" he asked her.

"No," she said. "But I wonder if you are capable of enjoyment with *me*. I am not at all lovely or sophisticated or—"

"Has no one ever called you lovely?" he asked her before she could think of another derogatory word to apply to herself.

She was silent for a moment.

"You," she said, "at the Valentine's ball." She laughed. "And then you added that every *other* lady was lovely too, without exception."

"Do you love springtime?" he asked her. "Do you think it loads the world with a beauty not found in any other season?"

"Yes," she said. "It is my favorite season."

"I called you a piece of springtime this evening," he said. "I meant it."

"Oh." She sighed. "How lovely. But you *have* to say such things to me. You are my husband."

"You are determined to see yourself as ugly, then?" he said. "Has anyone ever called you that, Vanessa?"

She thought again.

"No," she said. "No one in my world would have been so cruel. But my father used to tell me that he ought to have called me Jane since I was his own plain Jane. He said it with affection, though."

"With all due respect to the late Reverend Huxtable," he said, "I do believe he ought to have been hanged, drawn, and quartered."

"Oh, Elliott." Her eyes widened. "What a dreadful thing to say."

"If I were still unmarried," he said, "and had to make a choice among you and your sisters based upon looks alone, I would choose you."

Her eyes filled with laughter again, and her lips curved into a smile.

"You are my gallant knight," she said. "Thank you, sir."

"I am not a simple mix of coldness and irritability, then?" he asked her.

The laughter held.

"Like all humans," she said, "you are a dizzying mix of things and you ought to take no notice of me when I say you are all one thing or even all of two or three things. I daresay you are thousands of things and I will discover hundreds of them during our marriage. But not all. We can never know another person completely."

"Can we know even ourselves?" he asked.

"No," she said. "We can always take even ourselves by surprise. But would life not be dull if we were all unfailingly predictable? How would we ever continue to learn and grow and adapt to new conditions of our life?"

"Are we talking philosophy again?" he asked her.

"If you ask questions," she said, "you must expect me to answer them."

"You know how to change me for the better," he said.

"Do I?" She looked uncomprehendingly at him.

*"I will think of ways. I am endlessly inventive."* He quoted the words to her, just as she had spoken them at the theater earlier.

"Oh." She laughed. "I really did say those things, did I not?"

"While you were lying here just now," he said, "not sleeping but resting your eyes, were you *thinking*? Were you being *inventive*?"

She laughed softly.

"If you were not," he said, "I believe I am doomed to be cold and irritable for the rest of the night. I shall lie here and see if I can sleep."

He closed his eyes.

He heard her laugh softly once more, and then there was silence—until he felt the mattress sway and he heard the unmistakable rustlings of a nightgown being removed. She had worn it for the last several nights, just as he had worn his nightshirt.

He was instantly aroused. He lay still as if he slept.

After a while he felt her hand against his chest, her fingers circling and caressing, moving up to his shoulder, down to his navel.

But the use of one hand did not satisfy her. She lifted herself onto her knees beside him and leaned over him, using both hands to caress him and then her nails and her lips and breath and teeth.

He kept his eyes closed and concentrated upon keeping his breathing even. She was marvelously skilled after all.

She blew warm air into his ear before licking behind his earlobe and then drawing it into her mouth and sucking and pulsing her teeth about it.

Her hands circled his erection and circled until they touched him, featherlight, and stroked him and closed about him. The pad of her thumb rubbed lightly over the tip.

It took all the power of his will to lie still.

She was exquisite. She was pure magic.

And then she was straddling him, her thighs hugging his hips, her small breasts brushing against his chest, her fingers twining in his hair, her mouth kissing his eyes, his temples, his cheeks, until she reached his lips.

He opened his eyes for the first time.

Her own were shimmering with tears.

"Elliott," she murmured, her tongue licking his lips and then sliding inside. "Elliott."

He caught her by the hips then, found her entrance, and pulled her down hard onto him even as she pressed downward.

She cried out, a high, keening sound, and there followed a hot frenzy of thrusting and riding that took them both over the edge of passion before there was time to settle to any rhythm.

She was weeping openly, he realized when he had stopped throbbing and his heart had stopped thundering in his ears. She was sobbing against his shoulder, her knees still hugging his waist, her hands still buried in his hair.

At first he was alarmed, even angry. For of course she had made love to him—up to a point—as she must have made love to her first husband, whose desperate weakness had rendered him virtually unable to perform. She had taught herself all those marvelous skills for the benefit of a dying man whom she had loved.

Except that she had not been *in* love with him. She had not *desired* him. She had pleasured him because she loved him.

He was beginning to understand something of the fine distinctions of meaning.

How blessed it must be to be loved by Vanessa Wallace, Viscountess Lyngate.

His wife.

He did not grow angry. For he recognized the tears

for what they surely were—happiness that all the work she had put into foreplay was rewarded by the pleasures of full intercourse both given and received. And if there was some grief mingled in for the husband who had not been able to enjoy the completion of what she had done for him, well it would be petty to take offense.

Hedley Dew, poor devil, was dead.

Elliott Wallace was not.

He hooked the sheet with one foot and pulled it up over them both. He dried her eyes with one corner of it.

"Elliott," she said, "forgive me. Please forgive me. It is not what you think."

"I know," he said.

"You are . . . oh, you are so very gorgeous."

*Gorgeous?* Well.

He lifted her head from his shoulder and held her face framed in both hands. She sniffed and laughed.

"I look a dreadful fright," she said.

"Vanessa," he said, "I want you to listen to me. And I insist that you believe me. I will make it a command, in fact, one you must obey. You are beautiful. You are never to doubt it ever again."

"Oh, Elliott," she said, sniffing once more, "how very splendid of you. But you really do not need to—"

He set the pad of one thumb over her lips.

"*Someone* needs to tell you the truth," he said, "and it might as well be your husband. You have been coy with your beauty. You have hidden it from all except those who take the time to bask in your smiles and look deeply into your eyes. Anyone who *does* take the time will soon uncover your secret. You are *beautiful*."

Good Lord, where was all this coming from? He could not possibly *believe* it, could he?

Her eyes had filled with tears again.

"You are a kind man," she said. "I would never have suspected it until this moment. You can be cold and you can be irritable and you can be kind. You *are* a complex man. I am so glad."

"And gorgeous?" he said.

She laughed and hiccuped.

"Yes, and that too."

He drew her head down onto his shoulder again and then straightened her legs on either side of his. He caught at the blankets and covered them more warmly.

She heaved a sigh of apparent contentment.

"I thought you were not coming tonight," she said. "I fell asleep worrying about tomorrow."

Tomorrow? Ah, yes, her presentation to the queen. One of the most important days of her life. And then that infernal ball in the evening.

"All will be well," he assured her. "And I thought you were just resting your eyes."

"Mmm," she said. "I am *so* tired."

She yawned out loud and was almost instantly asleep.

They were still joined.

She weighed almost nothing at all. But she was warm and smelled enticingly of soap and sex.

*Beautiful?*

*Was* she beautiful?

He closed his eyes and tried to picture her as he had first seen her, standing with her friend at the Valentine's ball, dressed in a shapeless lavender gown.

*Beautiful?*

But then he remembered that as soon as he had led her into the dance and the music began, she had smiled and glowed with happiness. And when he had made that sorry joke about *all* the ladies, as well as her, being dazzlingly lovely, she had thrown back her head and laughed, not at all chagrined that the compliment did not apply to her alone.

And now she lay naked and relaxed and asleep in his arms.

Beautiful?

Certainly there was *something* about her.

He followed her down into sleep.

Because she was a married lady and not simply a young girl making her debut into society, Vanessa was not compelled to wear white. It was a good thing too. She looked a positive fright unless there was *some* color in her clothing.

Her satin skirt, falling from her natural waistline and arranged over huge hoops, was a pale ice blue. So was her stomacher, though it shimmered with reflected light as it was heavily embroidered with silver thread. The lace petticoat worn over the bodice and skirt and pulled open to the sides to reveal the latter, was of a slightly darker blue, as were her long train and the lappets that fell behind her from the silver-embroidered band she wore about her head. Pale blue and silver plumes waved above her head. Her long silver gloves reached above her elbows.

"Oh my," she said, looking at herself in the pier glass in her dressing room when her maid was finished with her, "I really am beautiful. Elliott was quite right."

She laughed with delight because she really did think she looked her very best. She ought to be able to dress thus always. She ought to have been born fifty years sooner than she had been. Except that then she could have been Elliott's grandmother, and she would have hated that.

"*Of course* you are beautiful," Katherine cried, stepping forward to hug her sister, though she did so very gingerly lest she crush something. "I do not care how many people scoff at the necessity of wearing such old-fashioned styles for the benefit of the queen. I think they are glorious. I wish we still wore them every day."

"Which is just what I was thinking," Vanessa said.

But Margaret had heard something else in her sister's earlier words.

"Viscount Lyngate said you are beautiful?" she asked.

"Last night," Vanessa admitted as she straightened the seam of her left glove. "He was being foolish."

"He was being very *perceptive*," Margaret said with feeling. "All is going well, then, Nessie?"

Vanessa smiled into her sister's anxious eyes. He really had been very *foolish* last night. She did not know what had got into him. But whatever it was, it had left a glow of happiness in her this morning. He had commanded her to think of herself as beautiful—and she had promised during their nuptials always to obey him.

Foolish man!

She had woken early this morning as she had fallen asleep, warm and comfortable on top of him, his arms about her, her cheek cradled against his shoulder. And he had still been inside her, except that he had grown long and hard again. And, sensing that she had awoken, he had rolled her over onto her back without disengaging from her, and made swift love to her before returning to his own room.

For once he had not thanked her as he went. She was so glad.

She had not seen him since. Her maid had brought her breakfast in bed—on his orders apparently—and she had been in her dressing room ever since, her mood oscillating between excitement and a horrible anxiety. Her mother-in-law and Cecily had been in and out, observing the progress her maid had been making. Meg and Kate had arrived to see her on her way to court. Stephen had also come to the house. He was downstairs with Elliott. They were both going to court too. Elliott was going to present Stephen to the Prince of Wales at one of his levees.

"Kate was right," Margaret said. "You really *are* looking lovely, Nessie. And it is not just the clothes. If Lord Lyngate has put that glow in your face, then I will forgive you for proposing marriage to him."

"You did *what*?" Katherine looked at her with startled eyes.

"We both knew he was coming to make an offer for Meg," Vanessa explained hastily. "Meg did not want him. I did. And so I offered him my hand before he could offer his to Meg."

"Oh, Nessie!" Katherine's eyes brimmed with laughter. "How could you do anything so bold? But why did you not want to marry Lord Lyngate, Meg? He is gloriously handsome among other assets. I suppose you felt that you must stay with Stephen and me a little longer."

"I have no wish to marry," Margaret said firmly. *"Anyone."*

They were interrupted at that moment by the return of the dowager and Cecily. Cecily squealed with delight.

The dowager looked upon Vanessa with approval and nodded her head.

"You will do very well, Vanessa," she said. "We were quite right about the color. It makes you look youthful and delicate and really quite pretty."

*"Beautiful,"* Katherine said with a fond smile. "We have already agreed, ma'am, that she looks beautiful."

"An opinion with which I fully concur," Vanessa said with a laugh. "Now if I can just contrive to keep my plumes above my head rather than over my eyes and not to fall all over my train while in Her Majesty's presence, I shall be entirely pleased with myself."

"And *you* look lovely too, ma'am," Margaret said politely and quite truthfully.

Vanessa's mother-in-law was dressed in wine red, a shade perfectly suited to her dark Mediterranean coloring. She was to be Vanessa's sponsor this morning.

"You do indeed, Mother," Vanessa said with a warm smile.

It was time to leave. It certainly would not do to arrive late for the most important appointment of her life.

The others stood back at the head of the stairs so that she could precede them down. She could see why as soon as she began the descent. Elliott and Stephen were standing in the hallway, looking up.

"Oh, I say, Nessie," Stephen said, admiration in his eyes. "Is that really you?"

She might have said the same of him. He was dressed in a dark green well-tailored coat with gold-embroidered waistcoat and dull gold knee breeches. His linen was sparkling white. He looked taller, more slender, than ever. His hair had been tamed but already showed signs of fighting back. His eyes burned with the intensity of suppressed excitement.

But in truth Vanessa had less than half her attention to spare for her brother. For Elliott too was dressed for a court appearance.

He had not seen her court finery until now. But she *had* described the clothes to him. She had told him the colors. He wore a pale blue coat with silver breeches and a darker blue silver-embroidered waistcoat. His linen matched Stephen's in whiteness.

The pale colors that he wore looked nothing short of stunning with his dark Greek looks.

It was a pity, she thought, they would not be appearing together at court. But perhaps it was as well. Who would be able to drag their eyes away from him in order to spare her a glance?

He stepped forward to the foot of the stairs and held out a hand for hers. She set her own in it and laughed.

"Look at us," she said. "Are we not all splendid indeed?"

He bowed over her hand and raised it to his lips before looking directly into her eyes.

"I suppose we are," he said. "But you, my lady, are beautiful."

If he kept saying it, foolish man, she was going to start believing it.

"I think so too," she said, batting her eyelids at him.

And then they were on their way, though it took a ridiculously long time to get the ladies and all their finery into the carriage.

"I think after all," Vanessa said after waving to Margaret and Katherine and Cecily, "I am glad I was born in this age and not in one when clothes like this were worn every day."

"I am glad of it too," Elliott said from the seat opposite, where he sat with Stephen, his eyelids half drooped over his eyes.

Was it possible, Vanessa wondered as she smiled back at him, that she was beginning to live a happily-ever-after? Not that she really believed in such a thing. But was it possible that she was to have a happy marriage? Was it possible that she could fall in love with her husband? Well, of course *that* was possible. It had happened already, in fact. It was impossible to deny it to herself any longer. Could she also *love* him, though?

More important, was it possible *he* could ever love *her*? Or at least feel something of an affection for her?

Did he already feel it?

This morning everything seemed possible. Even that she would not make an utter cake of herself in the presence of the queen.

And yes—this morning even happily-ever-after seemed possible. And even desirable.

Outside the sun shone from a blue sky. There were some clouds on the horizon, but they were too far away to cause concern. They would not bring rain soon enough to ruin the morning.

## 19

A L L went smoothly during Vanessa's presentation at court. She did not draw any undue attention to herself. She curtsied correctly without losing her balance or disappearing entirely inside her hooped skirt. And she backed out of the royal presence without once tangling her feet in her train.

In between times she gazed at the queen and wanted to pinch herself so that she could believe all this was really happening. She was actually in the same room as England's queen. The queen actually *looked* at her when she was presented and addressed a few remarks to her—Vanessa could never afterward remember exactly what was said.

It was a relief when the ordeal was over. At the same time, it was an event that Vanessa knew she would never forget even if she lived to be a hundred.

In the meanwhile Stephen had been presented to the Prince of Wales, who had actually engaged him in conversation for several minutes. There was nothing so very remarkable about that, of course. Stephen was the Earl of Merton after all. But it was still hard to believe.

How could all their lives have changed so drastically in such a short time?

It was a question Vanessa kept asking herself as she dressed for the ball in the evening—a real *ton* ball in

London during the Season. The ballroom at Moreland House had been decorated to resemble a garden complete with masses of pink and white flowers and greenery. The twin chandeliers had been cleaned and polished and fitted with new candles and raised to hang below the coved, gilded ceiling. The air had been filled with enticing aromas all day as the supper banquet was being prepared. And a full orchestra of professional musicians was already in place on the dais when she descended to the ballroom after dinner to join Elliott, her mother-in-law, and Cecily in the receiving line.

Her brother and sisters had come for dinner, and Margaret and Katherine were in the ballroom before her. Margaret was wearing a gown of shimmering emerald green, Katherine a delicate muslin gown of white embroidered all over with tiny blue cornflowers. How different they looked from usual, how much more elegant and poised and . . . expensive.

"I wish there were a more powerful word than beautiful," Vanessa said, looking fondly from one to the other of them. "You would both be that word."

"Oh, Nessie," Katherine said, "do you sometimes long for Rundle Park as I sometimes long for my class of infants? This is all absolutely terrifying as well as being more exciting than anything else so far in my life."

Vanessa laughed. Yes, sometimes she *did* long for home, though she was no longer sure where that was. The cottage in Throckbridge? Rundle Park? Warren Hall, Finchley Park? The dower house? Perhaps home was really not a place at all but wherever one felt most sense of belonging. Perhaps home now was wherever Elliott and she happened to be together.

Oh, dear, she really must be in love.

"I am very happy for you, Nessie," Meg said. "This is all yours, and you have a good marriage to go with it. It *is* good, is it not?"

She looked at her sister almost pleadingly.

"It is good," Vanessa said, smiling at her and daring to hope that she spoke the truth. Her relationship with Elliott would doubtless suffer numerous other growing pains, but surely the worst was over. The possibility for happiness or at least for contentment was surely there.

There was no time for further thought or conversation. The first guests were arriving, and Vanessa had to hurry to join the receiving line.

For the next half hour or so she smiled and exchanged greetings with a seemingly endless line of guests, most of whom she had not seen before. All were the very cream of society. She tried desperately to commit faces and names and titles to memory, though she suspected it was a hopeless task.

"You will get to know everyone soon enough," Elliott said, moving his head closer to hers during a brief lull in the arrivals. "You will meet the same people at almost every function you attend during the coming weeks."

She smiled gratefully at him. Obviously he did not expect the impossible from her. He was looking enormously handsome in black and white again. She would have told him so earlier when he appeared in her dressing room to escort her downstairs to dinner, but he had spoken first. He had told her how pretty she looked in pink. He had actually used that word—*pretty*.

She did not believe him, of course—or that she was beautiful. But it felt *so* good to hear the words anyway.

She was starting to feel both pretty and beautiful in Elliott's presence.

If she had told him after that how handsome he looked, it would have seemed that she was merely feeling obliged to return the compliment.

"I wish," he said now, "I could lead you into the opening set, Vanessa, but I must do that with Cecily."

"Of course you must," she said. "It is *her* come-out, not mine. We have already talked about it. I can wait until later."

But how lovely it would be . . . They had danced the opening set at the Valentine's assembly.

"Come," he said when it seemed that all the guests had arrived, "I will introduce Lord Bretby and his brother to your sisters."

"And then ask Meg and Kate quite pointedly in their hearing if they are engaged to dance the opening set?" she asked.

He looked at her blankly for a moment, and then there was a gleam of understanding and perhaps amusement in his eyes.

"Ah," he said, "memories of Sir Humphrey Dew and a certain assembly at Throckbridge."

"I wished," she said, "that a deep hole would open at my feet and swallow me up."

"Dear me," he said, "was I such an undesirable partner, then?"

She laughed and took his offered arm.

Lord Bretby and Mr. Ames needed no such hint. Lord Bretby solicited Meg's hand for the opening set, and Mr. Ames did the like for Kate.

How easy it had been, Vanessa thought. Her sisters

were launched into society, and all *she* had had to do was marry Elliott.

Stephen was in attendance too. Everyone had agreed that it was quite unexceptionable for him to put in an appearance at a ball in his brother-in-law's house despite his youth. He was looking extremely handsome, Vanessa thought as she approached him with Elliott, and very intense. And he was attracting a great deal of attention. A number of the very young ladies in particular were eyeing him with considerable interest.

But the receiving line had been disbanded a little too soon, it seemed. There was another couple just arriving.

"Oh, famous!" Stephen said as Vanessa turned her head to look. "Here comes Cousin Constantine. And he has Mrs. Bromley-Hayes with him."

Vanessa heard the sharp intake of Elliott's breath and looked up at him. His eyes were fixed on the doorway. They were cold with rage. His jaw was hard set.

"Oh, you *knew* he was coming, Elliott," she said, tightening her hand about his arm. "Cecily wanted him here. He was invited."

"But *she* was not," he said curtly.

Mrs. Bromley-Hayes was wearing a shimmering gown of a golden fabric so diaphanous that it clung to every curve of her body and looked almost transparent. It was cut low at the bosom—as was the fashion, of course. Perhaps it was only the magnificence of the bosom itself that made the fact more noticeable than it was with other ladies present. Her thick, shining blond hair was piled high and unadorned. It did not need adornment.

Vanessa sighed inwardly. And she had dared to feel pretty in pink?

"We must go and greet them," she said, urging Elliott in the direction of the door. She smiled warmly in greeting. Constantine was a cousin and she liked him despite Elliott's warnings.

"Ah, cousins," he said, bowing low. "I do apologize for being rather late. It took me a while to persuade Anna that she would be welcome here despite the fact that by some oversight she did not receive her invitation."

"But *of course* you are welcome," Vanessa said, reaching out a hand to the lady. She had lovely hazel eyes, and Vanessa suspected that she had used some cosmetics to enhance the darkness of her lashes. "Do come and enjoy yourself, Mrs. Bromley-Hayes. The dancing is about to begin. Elliott is to dance the opening set with Cecily since this is her come-out ball. I am going to ask Stephen—"

But Constantine had lifted one hand, palm out.

"Vanessa," he said, "do not, I beg of you, dance with a mere brother. Dance with me instead."

She looked from him to Mrs. Bromley-Hayes in some surprise, but the lady did not look in any way annoyed. She was smiling at Elliott.

"Thank you, Constantine," Vanessa said. "That would be very pleasant. But are you going to feel obliged to spend half your evening dancing with all your cousins, poor man? I know you have promised to dance with both Cecily and Kate, and they are unlikely to let you forget."

"And there is Margaret too," he said. "I am the most fortunate man in the room, not being in need of an introduction to any of the loveliest ladies present. Has

Elliott thought to compliment you on your appearance? You are looking very fine indeed."

"He has," she said. "He has told me that I look pretty in pink."

She laughed, half in amusement and half in embarrassment that she had said so in the hearing of a lady who did not need any reassurance.

"And I like your hair that way," Constantine said.

"You will excuse me," Elliott said curtly and abruptly. "I must go and lead Cecily out and get the dancing started."

Vanessa turned her head to smile at him, but he was already gone.

Mrs. Bromley-Hayes was strolling away to join a group close by.

"It was a horrible oversight on my mother-in-law's part not to have invited her," Vanessa said as Constantine led her onto the dance floor. "She said she had invited simply everyone."

"Perhaps not *quite* an oversight," Constantine said. "Although Anna is a perfectly respectable widow, she also has something of a reputation for being sometimes, ah, overfriendly with certain gentlemen."

For a moment Vanessa did not comprehend his meaning, but then she did and felt intensely uncomfortable.

"Oh," she said.

*Overfriendly.* The lady sometimes took lovers? It was no wonder the real sticklers of society, like the dowager viscountess, forgot to include the lady in their invitations.

Was Elliott aware of her reputation? But of course he must be. Was that why he was angry, then? This was, after all, a ball in honor of his youngest sister, who was a mere eighteen years old.

"It was naughty of you, then," she said, "to persuade her to come here with you, Constantine. Perhaps you ought to apologize to my mother-in-law."

"Perhaps I ought," he said, his eyes laughing at her.

"But you will not," she said.

"But I will not."

She tipped her head to one side and regarded him closely. He was still smiling, though there was that edge of something almost mocking in the expression that she had noticed on other occasions. And there was a suggestion of hardness there too though she had not noticed that before. Constantine Huxtable, she suspected, was a very complex man whom she really did not know at all and probably never would. But he *was* a cousin and he had never been unkind either to her or to her siblings.

"Why do you and Elliott hate each other so much?" she asked. Perhaps *he* would tell her.

"I do not hate him at all," he said. "But I offended him, you see, when Jon was still alive. I used to encourage the boy to tease him, not realizing that he would take the whole thing so seriously. He used to have a sense of humor before my uncle died and left him with so many responsibilities. He used to be up for all sorts of larks. But somewhere along the way he lost the ability to laugh at himself—or at anything else for that matter. Perhaps you will help him regain his sense of humor, Vanessa. I do not hate him."

It all sounded very reasonable. But as she stood in the line of ladies and watched him take his place opposite her, she could not help feeling that there must be more to it than that. Elliott was moody and often irritable and downright morose. She herself had accused him of lacking a sense of humor. But he would surely not still hate Constantine with such passion just because once upon a time Jonathan had been encouraged to make something of a fool of him.

Then the music began and she gave herself up to the almost unbelievable joy of dancing at an actual *ton* ball. She looked about her, feasting her eyes on all the flower arrangements, breathing in their scents, and smiling at all their guests.

Her eyes met Elliott's at the head of the line, and it seemed to her that he looked at her with the intensity of ... Well, not of love exactly. But of *something*. Fondness, perhaps? She smiled dazzlingly at him.

Ah, yes, she thought, theirs really was turning into a good marriage.

She was happy.


Elliott was so furious that he was surprised he had been able to cling to some control.

His first instinct had been to ask her to leave—to ask them both to leave.

To *demand* it, in fact.

To have them tossed out.

To do it himself.

But how could he do any of those things without creating a very public scene? They had timed their arrival with care—late but not too late. They had known he would not make a scene before so many people—and in his own home.

Nevertheless, a large number of the people present must *know*. Including his own mother!

No decent gentleman would ever invite his mistress—even his *ex*-mistress—into his own home. Especially when his wife was there, for God's sake. And his mother and his sisters.

Of course Con knew too—and it was Con who had brought her. He was as much to blame as she was. Probably more so. It was the sort of bold idea he was far more likely to have concocted than she.

Elliott tried to give his full attention to Cecily during the opening set. She was bright-eyed and nervous and chattery. This was, after all, one of the most important nights of her life. After dancing with him, she would dance with a succession of eligible young men, all carefully picked out for her by their mother. One of them might be her future husband.

But it was hard not to let his attention stray. What was Con saying to Vanessa? It appeared to be very little. He was smiling at her, and she was positively sparkling—as she had at the Throckbridge assembly. Con could not have said anything to upset her, then.

Anna was not dancing. She was standing on the sidelines, part of a group but not paying attention to the conversation of its members. She was fanning her face languidly and half smiling and watching him dance. She was not even trying to disguise that fact.

She was wearing the gold gown he had bought her last year because it was daring almost to the point of vulgarity and he had told her that only she of all the women he knew had the figure to do it justice. She had always worn it in private, for his eyes only, when they had dined together or sat together in her boudoir.

He must assiduously avoid her for the rest of the evening, he decided, and hope that would be the end of the matter. He would try to see to it that Vanessa avoided her too.

Good Lord, how avidly interested half the guests must be, watching and waiting and—for the malicious element—*hoping*.

She was not to be so easy to avoid, however. As soon as he had finished dancing with Cecily, Con came to claim her hand for the second set. Vanessa was with her brother and sisters, introducing them to Miss Flaxley, Lord Beaton, and Sir Wesley Hidcote. Lord Trentam, Jessica's husband, spoke in Vanessa's ear even as Elliott looked, and she smiled at him and set a hand on his sleeve. Apparently he was asking her for the next set.

And then Anna appeared at Elliott's side before he could make any move to avoid her, waving her fan languidly before her face, still half smiling. He had little choice but to bow politely to her and listen to what she had to say.

"I fear, Elliott," she said in her low, musical voice, "that you must have taken mortal offense."

He raised his eyebrows.

"I believe," she said, "one of my slippers hit you on the shoulder. I had forgotten when I threw it that it was one of the pair with the sharp heels. Did I hurt you?"

"Of course not," he said.

"I have a volatile temper," she said. "But you have always known that. You have always known too that it cools as quickly as it flares. You ought to have returned later that very day. I was expecting you."

"Were you?" he said. She had forgotten, perhaps,

that her temper had cooled even before he left on that occasion.

"But of course."

"I was busy," he said. "I have been busy ever since."

"Have you? Poor Elliott," she said. "Doing your duty? It must have been a sad chore."

He raised his eyebrows again.

"It cannot have been much of a pleasure," she said, laughing that low laugh that had always been able to raise his temperature a notch.

"Indeed?" he said.

"Pleasure and duty were never a good mix," she said, "which is why a marriage between you and me would not have worked well. It was wise of you to have seen that before I did. When may I expect you?"

He had thought their affair firmly at an end. But the words had never been spoken, had they? They had quarreled on other occasions and had always ended up together again.

"I am a married man, Anna," he said.

"Yes, you poor man." Her eyes regarded him over the top of her fan. "But all is not lost. I am here to comfort you and I bear you no ill will. Tomorrow afternoon I could be free if I need to be. *Do* I?"

"You have misunderstood me," he said, well aware that this conversation had already gone on long enough to have attracted attention and speculation. "I meant that I am a *married man,* Anna."

She stared at him and fanned her face harder.

"You *cannot* be serious," she said. "Elliott, she is an absolute fright! She is a *joke!*"

"She is *my wife,*" he said firmly. "I will bid you a good evening, Anna. There is something I need to attend to."

He strode off in the direction of the card room but turned at the last moment to make off for the library instead. He needed a few moments alone before returning to his guests.

He ought, he supposed, to have made himself clearer during his last visit with Anna. They had been together for all of two years before that. She had deserved better of him. She had deserved a face-to-face termination of their affair.

But Con—Con had done this deliberately. Which was fair enough, perhaps, if his only motive had been to annoy Elliott. But it was *not* fair to risk involving Vanessa. And to insult his own aunt and cousins by bringing sordidness into Elliott's home.

Anna had disappeared by the time he returned to the ballroom ten or fifteen minutes after leaving it. She had not danced at all.

It was to be hoped that now all was over between them.

Though he did wonder if perhaps he owed her a formal visit within the next few days. She had never done anything to deserve shabby treatment—except perhaps last evening and tonight.

Vanessa was enjoying herself very much indeed. She had danced every set, which was extremely gratifying considering the fact that she was a married lady and was surrounded by numerous other ladies who were younger or lovelier than she was.

More important, Meg and Kate had danced every set too. So had Stephen. And Cecily, of course—once with Stephen—though that was no surprise. The girl was both young and lovely and this was her come-out ball. She had also been brought up to just such a life as this. She was attracting a great deal of male attention, and she was holding court as if she had been doing so forever.

And now one of the two waltzes that had been planned for the evening was coming up. The dowager had decided to include them in the evening's program despite the fact that Cecily would not be allowed to dance either since young ladies needed the approval of one of the patronesses of Almack's before waltzing at a public ball. Kate ought not to dance it either, it had been decided in advance, though it would be quite un-exceptionable for Meg as an older lady to waltz if she wished—and if she was asked. As it would for Vanessa, of course.

Vanessa and Cecily had been giving lessons to Meg, Kate, and Stephen, though it would perhaps be more accurate to say that Cecily had taught Stephen while Vanessa had concentrated upon her sisters.

No less a person than the Marquess of Allingham had solicited Meg's hand for the dance. It was really very gratifying even if he *was* half a head shorter than she. Cecily and Kate were part of an animated group of very young people who would amuse themselves while their elders danced.

Vanessa hoped someone would ask her to waltz. Though most of all, of course, she hoped—

"Ma'am," someone said from behind her shoulder with stiff formality, "may I hope that I am not too late to be granted the honor of leading you into the waltz."

She turned her head and smiled brightly, happier than she had been all day.

"You are *not* too late, sir," she said. "I will indeed waltz with you."

She set her hand on his sleeve.

"Oh, Elliott," she said, "is this not the most wonderful evening ever?"

"Probably," he said as he led her onto the floor, "if I were to give the matter deep thought I would remember another evening or two that were equally wonderful. But certainly not more so."

"You always say something like that." She laughed. "I have only recently learned the steps. I hope I do not trip all over my feet. Or, worse, yours."

"We both know you weigh a ton," he said. "I would be doomed to walk around with flattened toes for the rest of my life."

"*Half* a ton," she said. "You must not exaggerate."

"But if I were to allow you to trip over my feet," he said, "I would have to judge myself a clumsy oaf and go home and shoot myself."

"You *are* home," she reminded him.

"Ah," he said. "So I am. I am reprieved, then."

It was one of the happier surprises of her marriage to find that she could talk nonsense to Elliott and he would talk it right back.

"Are you still angry at Constantine's coming and bringing Mrs. Bromley-Hayes with him?" she asked. "He explained about her reputation, which I daresay you are aware of. But I was happy to see you talking with the lady, Elliott. That was kind of you. She left very early. I hope she did not feel unwelcome."

"Let us not talk of the lady or Con, shall we?" he said. "Let us enjoy the waltz instead."

"I hope," she said, "I do not—"

But he leaned so close to her as he set one hand behind her waist and took her hand with the other that she thought for one startled moment that he was going to kiss her right there in the middle of his own ballroom with surely half the *ton* looking on.

"You will *not* make a cake of yourself," he told her. "Trust me. And trust yourself."

She smiled.

"I believe," he said, "I told you earlier that you look pretty. I was mistaken."

"Oh," she said.

"You do not look pretty," he said. "You look *beautiful*."

"Oh," she said again.

And then the music began.

She had loved the waltz from the moment she began learning it. She had thought it daring and romantic and graceful and . . . Oh, and a whole host of other things.

But she had never waltzed at a real ball until now.

And she had never waltzed with Elliott until now.

She had never before waltzed among flowers and perfumes and the myriad colors of the silks and satins and muslins and lace of dozens of guests or among the sparkle of jewels in candlelight or the glow of the candles themselves. She had never before waltzed to the music of a full orchestra.

She had never before waltzed with the man she loved.

For of course she was more than just *in* love with Elliott.

He led her into the steps of the waltz and she instantly forgot her fears of bungling them and making an idiot of herself.

She forgot that she was not really beautiful, that he

did not really love her. She waltzed and it seemed to her—or would have if she had paused for conscious thought—that she had never enjoyed anything more in her whole life.

She kept her eyes on her husband's face—dark-complexioned, classically handsome, blue-eyed—and smiled at him. And he looked back at her, his eyes roaming over her features.

She felt beautiful.

She felt cherished.

And she felt all the splendor of her surroundings as they swung about her in loops of light and color—and saw only Elliott.

She smiled more dazzlingly.

And finally, at last, oh, at last, his eyes smiled into hers and his lips curved upward ever so slightly at the corners.

It was surely the happiest moment of her life.

"Oh," she said when it was obvious the music was coming to an end—and she realized it was the first sound either of them had uttered since the waltz began. "Is it over so soon?"

"It is," he said. "I forgot to give the orchestra leader instructions to keep on playing forever."

She laughed into his eyes, where the smile lingered.

"How remiss of you," she said.

"Yes."

It was time for supper, and they were forced to separate in order to mingle with their guests.

But Vanessa would remember this evening, she thought, as one of the most memorable occasions of her life. Even apart from its other attractions, it was the evening during which she had fallen all the way in love with Elliott—so deeply, in fact, that there could no longer be any distinction between being *in* love with him and *loving* him with all her being and for all time.

She spared a regretful thought for Hedley and then nudged it gently away.

That was then.

This was now.

And *now* was a very good time in which to be living.

# 20

VANESSA walked over to Merton House on Berkeley Square the following afternoon to call upon her sisters. They were both at home, though Stephen was out. He had gone with Constantine to look at sporting curricles, though in Margaret's opinion he was far too young to be thinking of tooling around in such an impractical and potentially dangerous vehicle.

"I do fear," she said as they all took a seat in the drawing room, "that he might turn into a wild young man. He is vastly impressed with London and everyone he has met here so far. And the trouble is that everyone is impressed with him too, even gentlemen several years older than he is. They will lead him astray if they can."

"He is merely fluttering his wings, Meg," Katherine assured her. "He has not even spread them yet. But it is inevitable that he will. We must trust that he has a steady enough character that he will not turn irresponsibly wild."

"I have to agree with Kate," Vanessa said. "Stephen must be allowed to be a young gentleman just like every other, Meg, and find his own way to being the person he wishes to be."

"Oh, I suppose you are both right," Margaret conceded with a sigh. "Indeed, I *know* you are. It is just that he is still so very young. He is too young to be here, where there are so many distractions and temptations."

"If it is any consolation," Vanessa said, "Elliott takes his responsibility to our brother very seriously. He will keep a careful eye on him in that male world into which we cannot intrude. And it is into that world that he has retreated himself this morning, wise man. The conversation at breakfast was of nothing but balls and beaux and conquests. Cecily has received no fewer than five bouquets from gentlemen with whom she danced. She has declared herself an unqualified success, and we have all agreed with her."

"And you thought to escape by coming here?" Katherine said. "Have you looked about you, Nessie?"

Vanessa did so now and laughed. Meg had always kept the house full of flowers in season, but never with so many lavish bouquets as adorned the room today.

"*More* success?" she said. "And *more* beaux?"

"Singular in my case," Margaret said. "The white roses are mine. The Marquess of Allingham was kind enough to send them. All the other bouquets are Kate's—four of them."

"I was never more surprised in my life," Katherine said. "I felt like a country cousin last evening despite all my finery. This is all quite absurd."

"Not at all," Vanessa said. "Both of you were more lovely than anyone else last evening and attracted a great deal of interest."

"Because of Stephen," Margaret said.

"Well, yes," Vanessa conceded. "Without Stephen we would all be back in Throckbridge living our old lives. But even there you both had more than your fair share of admirers. Enough of such talk, though. It is a lovely day. Shall we go for a walk in the park?"

It was a welcome suggestion to two country ladies. And Hyde Park was large enough to seem like a good chunk of the countryside dropped right into the middle of busy London.

They strolled along some of the quieter paths there, avoiding the crush of riders and carriages and strollers in the more fashionable area.

"The Marquess of Allingham has invited Meg to drive here with him tomorrow afternoon," Katherine said.

"Has he?" Vanessa looked at her elder sister, impressed. "And have you agreed to come here with him, Meg?"

"I have," she said. "It was obliging of him to ask. He is a widower, you know."

"And you, Kate?" Vanessa asked, smiling. "Did you meet anyone special at the ball last evening?"

"Everyone was special," Katherine said predictably. "I had a truly lovely time. But is it not wonderful to be walking here in the quiet of the park and breathing in the smells of grass and trees? I miss Warren Hall. And I *do* miss Throckbridge so very much."

"We will grow accustomed to this new life," Vanessa said. "And there will be so much to do over the next few months and so many new things to see and experience that there will scarcely be a moment in which to fret and feel homesick."

"Constantine is going to take me to the Tower of London later this week," Katherine said, "and anywhere else I wish to go. I like him exceedingly. I wish we had known him all our lives. I wish we had known Jonathan."

"Yes," Margaret and Vanessa both agreed.

They strolled onward, not talking all the time. They were all familiar enough with one another that they could be perfectly comfortable with silence, especially when there were the beauties of nature to enjoy.

Vanessa continued to relive yesterday—her presentation at court, the ball, her waltz with Elliott. The night with him.

It surely would be quite impossible to be happier than she had been then and was now today, she thought. She had danced only once with Elliott last evening, but it had been enough.

She would always remember their first waltz together.

And exhausted as they both ought to have been after such a busy day, they had made love over and over again through the night.

She was really quite tired today. But sometimes tiredness itself could be almost pleasurable.

She was three days late with her courses. *Only* three days. She must not hope too strongly. But even so, she was usually very regular.

But she did hope . . . Oh, she *hoped*.

Finally their route brought them close to the busy part of the park, the area where the whole of the fashionable world promenaded each afternoon.

The Marquess of Allingham was the first to stop to pay his respects to them. He was alone in a high-perch phaeton.

"Lady Lyngate, Miss Huxtable, Miss Katherine," he

said, touching the brim of his tall hat with his whip. "How do you do?"

They assured him that they were doing very well indeed and Margaret thanked him for his flowers.

"Word has it," he said, "that there is a chance of rain tomorrow."

"Oh," Margaret said, "that would be a disappointment, my lord."

"Perhaps," he said, "if your sisters can spare you, Miss Huxtable, you would care to take a turn with me now this afternoon. I will return you safely to your own door within the hour."

Margaret looked inquiringly at her sisters.

"But of course you must go, Meg," Vanessa said. "I will walk home with Kate."

The marquess descended from his perch and handed Margaret up to the high seat beside his own.

"I am glad," Vanessa said as she and Katherine watched them drive away, "that she is willing to enjoy the company of someone else."

"Someone else?" Katherine asked.

"Other than Crispin Dew," Vanessa said. "She has loved him all her life, you know. She would not marry him when he asked because of us. But they had an understanding when he went away."

"Nessie!" Katherine cried, clearly stricken. "And he has just married a Spanish lady. Oh, poor Meg! I really had no idea. And to think that when we heard the news at Warren Hall, I teased her about being a little sweet on him when she was a girl. How that must have hurt!"

"You cannot be blamed. Meg never was one to talk about herself or to display her feelings for all to see," Vanessa said. "I believe I was her only confidante as a girl, though now she does not confide her deepest feelings even in me. I will be happy if she finds someone else to love this Season or next."

"Perhaps the marquess?" Katherine said. "He is not terribly handsome, is he, but he seems amiable enough. And he can be no more than ten years older than Meg."

"And he *is* a marquess," Vanessa said, smiling. "How blasé we are becoming about such things already."

"He is not a prince, though," Katherine said, and they both laughed and walked on.

Cecily was out walking with a group of young ladies, their maids trailing along some distance behind. They stopped to talk with a couple of young gentlemen on horseback as Vanessa and Katherine approached—Vanessa recognized them from last night's ball. Greetings were being exchanged with much merry laughter.

Cecily smiled brightly at them and invited them to join her group.

"We are going to walk down to the Serpentine," she explained.

"Oh, I would love to see the water," Katherine said.

Vanessa would too—but preferably not in company with such an exuberant crowd of young ladies. She must be getting old, she decided ruefully.

"*You* go," she urged Katherine. "I must be getting home anyway. Perhaps Elliott will be there. Cecily and her maid will surely accompany you home."

"But of course we will," Cecily said. "I *wish* you had brought your brother with you."

"Yes, indeed," one of the other young ladies said. "He is quite divine. Those curls!"

There was a flurry of giggles.

Vanessa watched them go on their way. But she was

now without either companions or a maid and must not
dawdle. Perhaps she would lie down for an hour when
she got home and catch up on some of the sleep she had
missed for the last two nights. Unless Elliott had come
home, of course. And then perhaps . . .

She quickened her pace.

Three ladies were approaching in an open barouche,
all of them with bonnets or hats that were extremely
fashionable. Vanessa looked admiringly at them until
the lady who sat with her back to the horses turned her
head, and Vanessa saw that she was Mrs. Bromley-
Hayes.

The lady saw her at the same moment, and they
smiled warmly at each other.

"Oh, do stop," Mrs. Bromley-Hayes called to the
coachman as the barouche drew abreast of Vanessa.
"Lady Lyngate! The very person I have been hoping to
see today. I must thank you for being so gracious last
evening. It was a splendid ball, was it not? I would have
stayed longer if I had not had another engagement elsewhere."

"Oh," Vanessa said, "I am so glad to hear that. I
hoped you did not feel unwelcome. It was an unfortunate oversight that your invitation was not sent out."

"That is kind of you," the lady said, and looked at her
companions. "I am going to walk with Lady Lyngate for
a while. Do go on without me. I shall find my own way
home."

The coachman jumped down from his perch, and
soon Mrs. Bromley-Hayes, looking fashionable and
startlingly beautiful, was at Vanessa's side and taking
her arm so that they could stroll onward together.

"Elliott said you were tired after yesterday," Mrs.

Bromley-Hayes said. "But it is good to see you out and enjoying the air this afternoon."

*Elliott?*

"You have seen him today?" Vanessa asked.

"Oh, yes, of course," the lady said. "He called on me earlier as he often does."

*Why?*

"Did he?" Vanessa said.

"Oh, you need not worry," the lady said with a light laugh. "The Wallace men are always very discreet, you know, and unscrupulously loyal to their wives in public. Elliott will never embarrass you. And you will have his home and his heirs. You already have his title. Indeed, Lady Lyngate, *I* am the one who should envy *you*. You need not envy *me*."

What was she saying? But even an imbecile, or even someone who had lived a sheltered existence in the country, could not possibly mistake her meaning.

She was Elliott's mistress!

*Although Anna is a perfectly respectable widow, she also has something of a reputation for being sometimes, ah, over-friendly with certain gentlemen.*

The words Constantine had spoken last evening came back to Vanessa as clearly as if he were walking beside her speaking them now.

As did Elliott's anger at seeing the lady in his ballroom when she had not been invited.

*Of course she had not been invited.*

"Oh, dear," Mrs. Bromley-Hayes said now, a suggestion of laughter in her voice, "never tell me you did not *know*."

"I believe," Vanessa said through lips that felt stiff

and did not obey her will very easily, "you were depending upon my not knowing, ma'am."

"I forgot," the lady said, "that you have come recently from the country and have never mingled with polite society. You cannot be expected to know its secret workings. Poor Lady Lyngate. But even you, surely, cannot believe that Elliott married you for any other reason than convenience."

Of course he had not. He had not even dreamed of marrying her until *she* had asked *him*.

"You have only to look at yourself in a glass," Mrs. Bromley-Hayes continued. "Which is not to say that you are ugly. You are not, and you must be commended for dressing as well as you can given your figure. But Elliott has always been renowned, you know, for his exquisite taste in women."

The wife and the mistress were walking side by side and arm in arm, Vanessa thought, in surely the most public afternoon location in London. The picture they presented to everyone else in the park must be ludicrous indeed. And of course, everyone else must *know*. Only she had not until a few moments ago.

"Exquisite in what way?" she asked.

It was the best she could do without any chance to think of any better or more cutting reply. Her head buzzed as if it were inhabited by a hiveful of bees.

The lady laughed low.

"Ah," she said, "the cat *does* have claws, does it? But come, Lady Lyngate, there is no reason we cannot be friends. Why let a man come between us? Men are such foolish creatures. We may need them for certain things—well, for *one* thing at least—but we can live far more happily without them most of the time."

"You will excuse me now," Vanessa said, drawing her arm free. "I was on my way home when I met you. I am expected."

"By Elliott?" The lady laughed. "Poor Lady Lyngate. I doubt it. I very much doubt it."

"Good afternoon to you," Vanessa said, and hurried off through the throng, looking neither to right nor to left.

From the jumble of her mind certain thoughts popped out, clear as day, one at a time.

The fact that she was plain.

That Elliott had called her beautiful, rather as one would soothe a child with insincere flatteries.

That until she had confronted him two mornings ago, he had been from home all day every day following their arrival in London.

That his mother had said at some time during the first few days here that she had hoped he might be different from his father.

That his frequent lovemaking had nothing to do with love and everything to do with begetting his heirs.

That he had spent a few minutes last evening talking with Mrs. Bromley-Hayes before she left.

That seeing her at the theater had discomposed him and set him to drumming his fingers on the armrest of their box.

That he and Constantine had a quarrel—and it was Constantine who had brought the lady to meet them at the theater and to appear at the ball last evening. To embarrass Elliott.

That he had seen and talked with Mrs. Bromley-Hayes today and told her that *she*, Vanessa, was tired.

Like a child who had been given too many treats the day before.

That he was enormously handsome and attractive and could not possibly be satisfied with a wife such as she.

That she was a fool and an idiot.

Naive, gullible, stupid.

Unhappy.

Wretched.

Almost unable, long before she reached home, to continue setting one foot in front of the other.

Fortunately—*very* fortunately—he was not at home when she arrived there. Her mother-in-law was in the drawing room, the butler informed her, entertaining a few callers.

Vanessa walked past the drawing room, treading lightly lest she be heard. She continued on up to her room, made quite sure that both her bedchamber and dressing room doors were tightly shut, climbed into bed fully clothed except for her shoes and bonnet, and pulled the covers up over her head.

She wished she could die then and there.

She fervently wished it.

*Hedley,* she whispered.

But even that was unfair. She had been unfaithful to the man who had loved her with his whole being—with a heartless man who did not even know the meaning of love.

And who happened also to be her husband.

Incredibly, she fell asleep.


Elliott had spent an hour at Jackson's boxing saloon, drawing more than one protest from his sparring partner for treating the bout as if it were a real fight.

He had spent fifteen minutes at White's Club and then left despite the fact that a group of acquaintances whose company he usually enjoyed had called him over to join them.

He had ridden aimlessly about the streets of London, avoiding the park or any areas where he was likely to run into someone he knew and be forced to stop to make polite conversation.

But finally he returned home. George Bowen was still in his office. He pushed a dauntingly thick pile of mail his employer's way when he went in there. Elliott picked it up and leafed through the letters, all of which needed his personal attention. If they had not, of course, George would have dealt with them and not bothered him.

"Her ladyship is at home?" he asked.

"Both their ladyships are," George said. "Unless they have crept out down the servants' stairs without my seeing them."

"Right." Elliott set down the pile and made his way upstairs.

He could not rid himself of the notion that he had hurt Anna. She had been very quiet during his visit. She had listened to him with a half-smile on her lips. And then she had told him that his visit had been quite unnecessary, that she had realized last evening how fortunate she was to be free again to pursue a friendship with someone else. Two years was quite long enough for any relationship, was it not? Freedom was what she valued most about her widowhood. And their liaison had grown somewhat tedious, would he not agree?

He had *not* agreed—it would have been tactless. Besides, their affair had not grown tedious to him, only . . . irrelevant. But that was not something he could say to her either.

He had Vanessa to thank for the fact that he had been bothered all day by the possibility that he had hurt Anna. Vanessa and feelings! He had never particularly bothered himself with people's feelings before meeting her—including his own.

She was not in the drawing room. Neither were his mother or Cecily.

She must be in her bedchamber, he decided after going upstairs and ascertaining that she was not in her dressing room. But the door into the bedchamber was shut. He tapped lightly on it, but there was no answer. That was where she was, though, he would wager. She was probably fast asleep.

He smiled to himself and decided not to knock more loudly. He had kept her up for much of last night after a busy day. Or she had kept him up. They had kept each other up.

It still surprised him that he could find her so appealing sexually. She was not at all his usual type of woman. Perhaps *that* was the appeal.

He wandered downstairs again and looked through some of his letters, though he was unable to dictate replies to any of them. George had finished work for the day and had disappeared.

He went back upstairs and shaved and changed. It was almost time for dinner by that point, but still there was no sound from Vanessa's room. Perhaps she was not even there. Perhaps George had been wrong and she was still out, though where she was likely to be at this hour he did not know.

He tapped on her door again and, when there was no reply, he opened it cautiously and looked in.

The bed was rumpled. There was a lump in the middle of it, which he guessed to be his wife though no part of her was visible.

He stepped into the room and moved around the bed closer to the lump. He lifted a corner of the covers. She was curled up into a ball, fully clothed, her hair rumpled, the one cheek that was visible flushed.

She *must* have been tired. He smiled.

"Sleepyhead," he said softly, "you are in danger of missing dinner."

She opened her eyes and turned her head to look up at him. She began to smile. And then she turned sharply away and curled into a tighter ball.

"I am not hungry," she said.

Did her flush denote a fever? He touched the backs of his fingers to her cheek, but she batted at his hand and turned her face even farther into the mattress.

He raised his hand, leaving it suspended above her.

"What is the matter?" he asked her. "Are you unwell?"

"No."

"Something has happened?" he asked her.

"Nothing." Her voice was muffled by the mattress. "Go away."

He raised his eyebrows and set both hands behind his back. He stood looking down at her.

*"Go away?"* he said. "You are lying here when it is almost dinnertime? Yet nothing has happened?"

A thought struck him suddenly.

"Your courses?" he asked her. "Have they begun?"

"No."

Was *that* the trouble, then? But it was supposed to be *morning* sickness, was it not?

"Vanessa," he said, "will you look at me?"

"Is that a command?" she asked him, turning over almost violently onto her back and glaring up at him through untidy hair. Her clothes were twisted about her. "Yes, my lord. Whatever you say, my lord."

He frowned.

"I think," he said, "you had better tell me what has happened."

And he felt a sudden sense of foreboding. *Con.*

"I will not share you," she said, pushing her hair back from her face with one forearm. "You may say I have no choice since I have married you. And you may say that I am obliged to obey you and grant you your conjugal rights whenever it pleases you to exercise them. But if one person can break vows, then so can the other even if she is merely a woman and therefore a nonperson. I shall scream very, very loudly if you ever try touching me again. It is no idle threat."

Ah, yes. Con.

"I can see it is not," he said. "Of what do I stand accused?"

"Of harboring a mistress when you are a married man," she said. "It does not matter that she is beautiful while I am not. You knew that before you married me. And it does not matter that it was *I* who asked *you* to marry me. You might have said no. But you did not. You married me. You made sacred vows to me. And you have broken them. You will not be my husband ever again, except in name."

"Are you quite sure," he asked, shaken and slightly

angry too, "that Con gave you accurate information, Vanessa?"

"Ha!" she said. "You are going to try to deny it, are you? Were you or were you not at Mrs. Bromley-Hayes's house today?"

Ah. Not Con after all.

"You see?" she said when he did not immediately reply. "You cannot deny it, can you?"

"Anna called here?" he asked.

*"Anna,"* she said scornfully. "And she calls you *Elliott.* How cozy! I met her in the park. Go away. I do not want to see you again today. I wish it might be never."

"Will you let me explain?" he asked her.

"Ha!" she said again. "Go away."

"You wished to explain yourself when I discovered you weeping over your dead husband's portrait," he reminded her, "and I did eventually listen to you. Things are not always as they seem to be."

"She is *not* your mistress?" Her voice was more scornful than before.

"No," he said.

"Ha! Mrs. Bromley-Hayes is a liar, then?" she asked him.

"I do not know what she told you," he said.

He waited.

She flung back the bedcovers and swung her legs over the far side of the bed. She got to her feet and smoothed her hands over one of her smart new walking dresses, which was going to need far more than hands to make it look presentable again. She passed her fingers through her hair, keeping her back to him.

"I am listening," she said.

"Anna was my mistress for most of last year and the

year before," he told her. "If that fact offends you, Vanessa, I am sorry about it, but I cannot change what is in the past and would not if I could. I was not married then. I did not even know you then."

"I do not suppose I would have provided powerful competition even if you had," she said.

"When I brought you and my mother and Cecily to town before our wedding," he said, "I called on Anna to tell her that I was to be wed. She quarreled violently with me and I left. I thought that was the end of the matter, but it seems it was not. She appeared at the theater two evenings ago and at the ball last evening and I realized that I had not looked her in the eye and told her specifically that our affair was at an end. And so I called upon her today to do just that."

"And you also told her I was tired after yesterday," she said.

He hesitated.

"I suppose I did," he admitted.

"How dared you even mention my name to her," she said, turning around and looking him very directly in the eye.

"I am sorry," he said. "It was indeed in poor taste. Did she lead you to believe that we are still lovers, Vanessa? On the assumption that you would never confront me but would allow the lie to fester in your mind? She does not know you at all well, does she? We are not lovers and have not been since I affianced myself to you. I would not have expected her to be capable of such spite, but apparently she is. I am sorry from my heart that you have been hurt by all the sordidness of the end of an affair."

"Do you *possess* a heart?" she asked him. "You spent

last night in this bed with me. I thought you were coming to care for me. But the first thing you did this morning was go to your mistress."

"I called upon my *ex*-mistress, yes," he said. "I have explained why I felt it necessary to go there."

"But you did not feel it necessary to tell me you were going?" she asked.

"No," he said.

"Why have you ended the affair?" she asked him.

"Because I am married."

She smiled fleetingly.

"Not because you are married to *me*?" she asked him. "Just because you are married? Well, that is something, I suppose. It is admirable, perhaps. But how soon will it be before this noble sense of morality wears thin and you take another mistress?"

"Never," he said. "Not as long as we both live."

"I suppose," she said, looking down at her hands, "you had other mistresses before her."

"Yes," he said.

"All beautiful, I suppose."

"Yes."

"How can I—" she began.

He cut her off, speaking rather harshly.

"Enough of this, Vanessa," he said. "*Enough!* I have told you that you are beautiful and I have not lied. Even if you cannot trust my words, surely you cannot disbelieve my actions. Does my lovemaking not tell you that I find you both beautiful and irresistible?"

Her eyes filled with tears and she turned sharply away again.

Her insecurities about her looks ran very deep, he realized. Probably she did not even realize it herself.

She had cultivated cheerfulness as an antidote. But when she was robbed of good cheer, she was defenseless against hurt.

"I *wish* she had not been your mistress," she said. "I do not like her. I cannot *bear* the thought of you—"

"And I cannot bear the thought of you with young Dew," he said, "different as the circumstances are, Vanessa. I suppose we would all like to believe that our life's partner comes to us as fresh and new as a babe, that there has been no one else but only us. But that is impossible. You had done almost twenty-four years of living before you met me. I had done almost thirty before I met you. Yet if neither of us had done that living, we would not be as we are now. And I like you as you are now. I thought you were starting to like me."

She sighed and dropped her head.

"Whose idea was it to approach us at the theater and to come to the ball last night?" she asked him. "Hers? Or Constantine's?"

"I do not know," he said. "Both, probably. I ought to have robbed them of power by immediately telling you all: *Oh, by the way, that lady sitting next to Con is my ex-mistress, who perhaps does not even know that she is an ex. I am sorry, but I promise to be a good boy for the rest of my life.* It would have solved a lot of headaches, would it not?"

She turned her head over her shoulder and half smiled at him though her face was wan.

"It would have ruined the play for me," she said.

"Would it?"

She nodded.

"And has the knowledge now ruined your marriage for you?" he asked her. "Has it ruined the rest of your life?"

"Elliott," she said, "you *are* telling me the full truth?"

"I am." He looked steadily back at her.

She sighed and turned to face him fully again.

"I have never believed in or even wanted a happily-ever-after," she said. "How foolish of me to have believed yesterday and this morning that I had found it after all. I had not. But no, nothing has been irrevocably ruined. I will live on. *We* will. Do you really find me irres— Do you really find me a little bit attractive?"

"I do," he said. He could have stridden around the bed at that point and caught her up in an embrace, but it might have been the wrong thing to do. She might have doubted his sincerity. "But I did not use the word *attractive,* accurate though it would be. It is also tame. I used the word *irresistible*."

"Oh," she said. "I really do not know why. I look a fright." She looked down at herself.

"At this precise moment you do," he agreed. "If there were mice in the house, they would surely be frightened away after one glimpse of you. Outdoor clothes were not meant to be worn in bed, you know. And hair was meant to be brushed every few hours."

"Oh," she said, and laughed—a rather thin, tremulous sound.

"Let me ring for your maid," he said. "I'll go down and tell Mama and Cecily that they do not have to starve tonight after all, that you will be down within half an hour."

"It will be a Herculean task," she said as he came around the bed and made for her dressing room, "to make me presentable in just half an hour."

"Not really," he said, pulling on the bell rope and

turning his head to look at her. "All you really have to do is smile, Vanessa. Your smile is pure magic."

"I ought to call your bluff, foolish man, and come downstairs with you now, then, smiling," she said. "Your mother would have a fit of the vapors."

"I will return in twenty-five minutes," he said as he stepped inside his own dressing room and closed the door.

He stood against it for quite some time, his eyes closed.

He had much atoning to do. He had hurt too many people recently. He had been hurt himself during the past couple of years by people he had trusted so he had turned to stern duty and turned his back on love—and on laughter and joy.

He had hurt people anyway.

*Love and laughter and joy.*

All of them embodied in the wife he had married so unwillingly and so cynically.

He had married a treasure he did not at all deserve.

What had she said a few minutes ago? He frowned in thought.

*I have never believed in or even wanted a happily-ever-after. How foolish of me to have believed yesterday and this morning that I had found it after all.*

She had been happy yesterday and this morning. Happily-ever-after happy.

Dear God!

She had been happy. But *of course* she had.

So had he.

# 21

VANESSA had expected her task of introducing her sisters to the *ton* to be an onerous one. She was as new to society as they were, after all, even if she *was* married to a viscount, heir to a dukedom. She knew practically nothing and no one.

But it turned out not to be very difficult after all. All that had been needed was her respectable position as a lady married to a gentleman of the *ton*. Elliott more than qualified in that role.

They were something of a curiosity, the three sisters. Vanessa because she had recently married one of England's most eligible bachelors. Margaret and Katherine because they were the sisters of the new Earl of Merton, who had turned out to be very youthful and very handsome and very attractive despite—or perhaps because of—a certain lack of town bronze. And Margaret and Katherine had the added attraction of being rare beauties.

The *ton*, Vanessa soon learned, was always avidly interested in seeing new faces, hearing new stories, getting wind of new scandals. The story of the new earl and his sisters having been found in a remote country village, living in a cottage smaller than most people's garden shed—the *ton* also had a strong tendency to hyperbole—captured the collective imagination and fed drawing-room conversations for a week or more. As did the fact that one of those sisters had captured the hand, if not the heart, of no less a personage than Viscount Lyngate. She was *not* a beauty, and therefore one must not suppose that it was a love match—though if it was not, it was strange that he had not married the *eldest* sister. And there was a positive swell of interest when word spread that Mrs. Bromley-Hayes had been dropped like a hot brick as Viscount Lyngate's mistress after she was seen in company with the viscountess one afternoon in Hyde Park.

The viscountess's prestige rose significantly.

The Huxtables were invited everywhere fashionable people were invited—to balls, soirees, concerts, picnics, Venetian breakfasts, dinners, theater parties . . . The list was endless. They could, in fact, have been busy merrymaking every day from morning to night. Well, perhaps not morning as they defined it. Most people slept until past noon, having danced or played cards or conversed or otherwise diverted themselves almost all night long.

It amused Vanessa to discover that an invitation to breakfast actually was an invitation to a meal beginning in the middle of the afternoon. It amazed her that most people seemed perfectly content to begin their day in the afternoon and end it early in the morning.

What a sad waste of daylight and sunshine!

She accompanied her sisters to numerous entertainments, but she did not have to make any great effort to introduce them to people whose names she often could not recall herself or to find conversational groups for them to join or partners for them to dance with. As Elliott had predicted, they met the same people almost wherever they went, and names, faces, and titles soon became more familiar.

Margaret and Katherine soon acquired friends and acquaintances, and each very quickly had a court of admirers—as did Vanessa herself, to her great amazement. Young gentlemen whose names she scarcely remembered asked her to dance or offered to fetch her refreshments or to escort her on a stroll about a garden or dance floor. One or two even offered to drive her in the park or to ride on Rotten Row with her.

It was not an uncommon occurrence, of course, for married ladies to have their cicisbei. And she remembered Elliott telling her at the theater that it was quite unexceptionable for a married lady to be escorted in a public place by a man who was not her husband.

It spoke volumes to Vanessa about the state of marriage among the *ton,* though she had no wish to behave as others did. If Elliott could not be with her, she preferred the company of her sisters or her mother-in-law to that of some strange gentleman.

She was not unhappy during the weeks following her presentation at court.

She was not particularly happy either.

There had been something of a reticence between her and Elliott since the day on which she had confronted him over the matter of Mrs. Bromley-Hayes. They were not estranged. He accompanied her to many entertainments, especially in the evenings. He conversed with her whenever the opportunity presented itself. He made love to her each night. He slept in her bed.

But there was . . . something. Some sense of strain.

She believed him, and yet she was hurt. Not hurt

that he had had a mistress before marrying her—that would have been unreasonable. Hurt perhaps because he had visited his ex-mistress after marrying her and would have said nothing to her if she had not found out on her own. And hurt perhaps because Mrs. Bromley-Hayes was beautiful in every imaginable way—physically at least.

There was nothing wrong with her marriage, Vanessa kept telling herself. There was only everything right with it, in fact. She had a husband who paid attention to her, who was faithful to her, who had sworn to remain faithful. She was well blessed. What more could she ask for?

*His heart?*

If one had the moon and the stars, must one be greedy for the sun too?

It seemed that the answer was yes.

Katherine treated her court of admirers much as she had done in Throckbridge. She smiled kindly and indulgently upon them all, granted them all equal favors, *liked* them all. But when asked, she would admit that there was no one special among them.

"Do you not *want* someone special in your life?" Vanessa asked her one morning when they were taking a brisk walk through an almost deserted park.

"Of course I do," Katherine said with something of a sigh. "But that is it, you see, Nessie. He must *be* special. I am coming to the conclusion that there is no such person, that I am looking for an impossibility. But that cannot be so, can it? Hedley was special to you, and Lord Lyngate is. How I envied you when I watched you waltzing together at Cecily's come-out ball. If it has happened to you twice, is it too much to ask that it happen to me just once?"

"Oh, it will," Vanessa assured her, taking her arm and squeezing it. "I am glad you will settle for no less than love. And what about Meg?"

Their sister was not with them. She had gone to Hookham's library with the Marquess of Allingham.

"And the marquess, you mean?" Katherine said. "I do believe he is seriously courting her."

"And will she have him?" Vanessa asked.

"I do not know," Katherine admitted. "She seems to favor him. Certainly she pays no attention to anyone else, though there are several eligible and personable gentlemen interested in her. She does not behave as if she were in love, though, does she?"

It was true. Meg was far more concerned with trying to control Stephen's movements and with encouraging Kate to enjoy herself as much as she was able and with assuring herself that Vanessa was happy than with forging a new life for herself.

Yet the marquess, who really was an amiable gentleman, was very attentive.

And Crispin Dew was married. There was no point in pining any further for him. Ah, easy for *her* to say, Vanessa thought.

"Meg never will talk about herself, will she?" Katherine said. "I have never particularly noticed before, but it is true. That is why I never knew about Crispin Dew, I suppose. Oh, Nessie, did she care for him so very much?"

"I fear she did," Vanessa said. "But perhaps given time she will find someone else. Perhaps he will even be the Marquess of Allingham. She seems to enjoy his company."

But it was a hope soon to be dashed.

When Vanessa arrived at Merton House one afternoon a week or so later, she found Stephen in the hallway, about to go out with Constantine. They were to go to the races. He was frowning.

"Dash it all, Nessie," he said, "when will Meg learn that she is my sister, not my mother? And when will she learn that I am seventeen years old, going on eighteen, and far too old to be kept in leading strings?"

"Oh, dear," she said, "what has happened?"

"Allingham came here earlier," he said, "and asked to speak with me. It was dashed decent of him since I *am* only seventeen and he must be twice that and Meg is twenty-five. He came to ask my permission to pay his addresses to her."

"Oh, Stephen," Vanessa said, clasping her hands to her bosom. "And . . . ?"

"And of course I said yes," he said. "I was delighted actually. He does not have the best of tailors or bootmakers, perhaps, but he rides to an inch and is reputed to be the devil of a fine fellow and it doesn't really matter that he is not very tall. He has *presence*. And Meg has spent enough time with him in the last few weeks, the Lord knows. One could be forgiven for thinking that she would welcome an offer from him."

"But she did not?" she asked.

"Refused him out of hand," he said.

"Ah," Vanessa said. "She was not fond enough of him after all, then?"

"I dashed well don't know," he said. "She refuses to say. Says that has nothing to do with anything. She had made that infernal promise to Papa and she is going to keep it, by God, until I am twenty-one and Kate is married."

"Oh, dear," Vanessa said. "I thought perhaps she would consider that things have changed somewhat."

"As they dashed well have," he said. "I am *Merton* now, Nessie. I have land and a fortune and a *life*. I have new friends. I have a future. It is not that I don't love Meg. It is not that I am not grateful for all she has done for me since Papa died. I will *never* forget, and I will *always* be grateful. But I resent having to account for my every movement every single hour of the day. And I resent being made the cause of her rejecting the best marriage offer she will probably ever have. If she does not like him well enough, then fine. I applaud her having the gumption to refuse him. But if it is not that . . . If it is just me . . . Ah, this must be Constantine."

He brightened considerably.

Vanessa had no wish to come face-to-face with their cousin. She patted Stephen's arm.

"I'll see what she has to say," she said. "Have fun."

"Oh, I will," he said. "Constantine is a capital fellow. So is Lyngate, Nessie, I must confess. He keeps an eye on me, it is true, but he does not try to put leading strings on me."

He left the house without waiting for Constantine to knock on the door.

Margaret was tight-lipped and uncommunicative when Vanessa arrived in the drawing room and explained that she had just been talking with Stephen.

"The trouble with our brother," Margaret said, "is that he thinks his new circumstances have added four years or so to his life. But the truth is, Nessie, that he is still a boy, and a boy who is becoming more rebellious by the hour."

"He is a boy who perhaps needs a somewhat less firm hand on his reins," Vanessa suggested.

"Oh, not you too," Margaret said, clearly exasperated. "He should be at Warren Hall with his tutors."

"And soon he will be," Vanessa said. "He also needs to become acquainted with the world that awaits him when he reaches his majority. But let us not quarrel over him. The Marquess of Allingham has paid his addresses to you?"

"It was very obliging of him," Margaret said. "But I have said no, of course."

"Of course?" Vanessa raised her eyebrows. "I thought perhaps you were growing fond of him."

"Then you thought wrongly," Margaret said. "You of all people ought to know that I cannot even consider marriage until I have fulfilled the obligation to our family that I took on eight years ago."

"But Elliott and I live close to Warren Hall," Vanessa said. "And Kate will reach her majority in a few months' time. Stephen will be at university for most of the next several years. By that time he will be a full adult."

"But that time is not yet," Margaret said.

Vanessa tipped her head to one side and regarded her closely.

"Do you not *want* to marry, Meg?" she asked. *"Ever?"*

Crispin Dew had much to answer for, she thought.

Margaret spread her hands on her lap and contemplated the backs of them.

"If I do not," she said, "the time will come when I will have to live at Warren Hall with Stephen's wife as the mistress. Or at Finchley Park with you. Or with

Kate somewhere and *her* husband. I suppose the time will come when I will marry anyone who is kind enough to offer. But not yet."

Vanessa stared at her bent head. There was a lengthy silence.

"Meg," she said eventually, "Stephen probably does not know about . . . about Crispin, unless Kate has said anything to him. He thinks your refusal of the Marquess of Allingham is all about *him*."

"And so it is," Margaret said.

"No, it is not," Vanessa said. "It is about Crispin."

Margaret lifted her head to look at her, a frown creasing her brow.

"Stephen needs to know that," Vanessa said. "He needs to know that he is not responsible for keeping you from happiness."

"Stephen *is* my happiness," Margaret said fiercely. "As are you and Kate."

"And so you put fetters upon all of us," Vanessa said. "I love you dearly, Meg. I love Kate and Stephen too. But I would not describe any of you as *my happiness*. My happiness cannot come from another person."

"Not even Lord Lyngate?" Margaret asked her. "Or Hedley?"

Vanessa shook her head.

"Not even Hedley or Elliott," she said. "My happiness has to come from within myself or it is too fragile a thing to be of any use to me and too much of a burden to benefit any of my loved ones."

Margaret got to her feet and walked to the window to stare down on Berkeley Square below.

"You do not understand, Nessie," she said. "*Nobody* understands. When I made my promise to Papa, I knew

I was making a twelve-year commitment—until Stephen reached his majority. I am eight years into that commitment. I am not going to shrug free of the remaining four years just because our circumstances have changed, just because you are happily married and Kate is being courted by half a dozen or more eligible gentlemen and Stephen is chafing at the bit to be free. Or because I have had a good offer and might go off to Northumberland to begin a new life and leave Kate and Stephen to your care and Lord Lyngate's. This has *nothing* to do with Crispin Dew. It has nothing to do with *anything* except a promise freely made and gladly carried out. I *love* you all. I will *not* abandon my duty even if Stephen finds it irksome. I *will* not."

Vanessa moved up beside her and wrapped an arm about her waist.

"Let's go shopping," she said. "I saw the most glorious bonnet yesterday, but it was royal blue and would not suit me at all. It will look quite ravishing on you, though. Come and see it before someone else buys it. Where is Kate, by the way?"

"She has gone for a carriage ride with Miss Flaxley and Lord Bretby and Mr. Ames," Margaret said. "I have more bonnets than I know what to do with, Nessie."

"Then one more will be neither here nor there," Vanessa said. "Let's go."

"Oh, Nessie." Margaret laughed shakily. "Whatever would I do without you?"

"You would have more room in your wardrobe, that is for sure," Vanessa said, and they both laughed.

With a heavy heart, though, Vanessa arrived home at Moreland House a couple of hours later. The unhappiness of one's loved ones was often harder to bear than one's own, she thought—and Meg was undoubtedly unhappy.

Not that *she* was unhappy. It was just that . . .

Well, it was just that she had known delirious happiness during her honeymoon and again for a few days before and after her presentation. And that happiness had made her greedy for more.

She could not force herself to be contented with a marriage that was just workable and agreeable.

She was, of course, almost certain that she was with child. Perhaps *that* would make a difference. But why should it? She was merely performing the function for which he had married her.

But oh, dear—she was pregnant with Elliott's child and her own. With *their* child. She so desperately wanted to be happy again. Not just happy within herself, despite what she had said to Meg earlier. She wanted to be happy with *him*. She wanted him to be ecstatic with joy when she told him. She wanted . . .

Well, she wanted the sun, of course.

How very foolish she was.

There were not many free evenings. It seemed like a rare treat when one occasionally presented itself.

On one such evening Cecily had gone to the theater with a group of friends, under the chaperonage of the mother of one of them. Elliott retired to the library after dinner. His mother, who sat drinking tea and conversing with Vanessa in the drawing room, could not hide her yawns and finally excused herself, pleading total exhaustion.

"I feel," she said as Vanessa kissed her cheek, "as if I could sleep for a week."

"I daresay one good night of uninterrupted sleep will suffice," Vanessa said. "But if it does not, then I will chaperone Cecily at the garden party tomorrow and you may have a quiet day. Good night, Mother."

"You are always so good," her mother-in-law said. "How very glad I am that Elliott married you. Good night, Vanessa."

Vanessa sat alone for a while, reading her book. But the growingly familiar feeling of slight depression settled upon her and distracted her attention from the adventures of Odysseus as he tried to return to Ithaca and his Penelope.

Elliott was downstairs in the library and she was up here in the drawing room during a precious evening when they were both at home. Would this be the pattern of their married life?

Would she *allow* it to be?

Perhaps he would come up here if he knew his mother had gone to bed and she was alone.

Perhaps he would resent her going down there.

And perhaps, she thought finally, getting resolutely to her feet and keeping one finger inside the book to mark her place, she ought to go and find out. This was her home too, after all, and he was her husband. And they were not estranged. They had not quarreled. If they drifted apart into a distant relationship, then it would be at least partly her fault if she had not tried to do something about it.

She tapped on the library door and opened it even as he called to her to come in.

There was a fire burning in the hearth even though it

was not a cold evening. He was seated in a deep leather chair to one side of it, a book open in one hand. The library was a room she loved, with its tall bookcases filled with leather-bound books lining three walls and its old oak desk large enough for three people to lie across side by side.

It was far cozier than the drawing room. She did not blame Elliott for choosing to sit here for the evening. Tonight it looked more inviting than ever. So did he. He was slightly slouched in his chair. One of his ankles was resting on the knee of the other leg.

"Your mother is tired," she said. "She has gone to bed. Do you mind if I join you?"

He scrambled to his feet.

"I hope you will," he said, indicating the chair opposite his own, on the other side of the fire.

A log crackled in the hearth, sending a shower of sparks upward into the chimney.

She sat and smiled at him and then, because she could not think of anything to say, she opened her book, cleared her throat, and began to read.

He did likewise, without the throat clearing. He no longer slouched. He had both feet on the floor.

Her seat was too deep for her. She either had to sit with straight back against the rest and feet dangling a few inches off the floor or with feet flat on the floor and back arched like a bow against the rest or with feet flat on the floor and back ramrod straight and unsupported.

After a few minutes, during which she tried all three positions and found none of them comfortable, she kicked off her slippers, curled her feet up on the seat beside her, settling her skirt about her as she did so, and nestled the side of her head against the wing of the chair. She gazed into the fire and then glanced at Elliott.

He was looking steadily back at her.

"It is not ladylike, I know," she said apologetically. "My mother and father were forever telling me to sit properly. But I am short and most chairs are too large for me. Besides, I am comfortable like this."

"You *look* comfortable," he said.

She smiled at him and somehow neither of them resumed reading. They just looked at each other.

"Tell me about your father," she said softly.

She had kept remembering his mother telling her that she had hoped he would be different from his father. Elliott never spoke of him.

He continued to stare at her for a while. Then he turned his gaze on the fire and set his book down on the table beside him.

"I adored him," he said. "He was my great hero, the rock of my existence. He was the model of all I aspired to be when I grew up. Everything I did was done to please him. He used to be away from home for long spells at a time. I lived for his return. When I was very young, I used to camp out at the gates of the park watching for his horse or carriage and on the rare occasion when he came while I was there, I would be taken up beside him and made much of before my mother and sisters could have their turn. When I was older and started getting into scrapes with Con, my behavior was always tempered by the fear of disappointing my father or inciting his wrath. When I began sowing wild oats as a young man, part of me worried that I would never be worthy of him, that I would never measure up to the standard he had set."

He was silent for a while. Vanessa did not attempt to say anything. She sensed that there was more to come. There was pain in his eyes and his voice, a frown line between his brows.

"There was never a closer, happier family than ours," he said. "Never a husband more devoted to his wife or a father more devoted to his children. Life was in many ways idyllic despite his long absences. It was filled with love. More than anything else in this world I wanted a marriage and a family like his. I wanted to bask in his approval. I wanted people to be able to say of us, 'Like father, like son.'"

Vanessa let her book close on her lap without marking her place and clasped her arms with her hands, though she ought not to have been cold when she sat so close to the fire.

"And then a year and a half ago," he said, "he died suddenly in the bed of his mistress."

Vanessa stared at him, shocked beyond words.

"They had been together for more than thirty years," he told her, "a little longer than he had been married to my mother. They had five children, the youngest fifteen, a little younger than Cecily, the eldest thirty, a little older than me."

"Oh," Vanessa said.

"He had provided well for his mistress in the event of his death," he said. "He had placed two of his sons in steady, lucrative employment. The third was still at a good school. He had found respectable, well-to-do husbands for his two daughters. He had spent as much of his time with that family as he had with mine."

"Oh, Elliott," she said, so aware of his pain that her eyes filled with tears.

He looked at her.

"The funny thing was," he said, "that I knew about my grandfather and *his* other family. His mistress of more than forty years died only ten years ago. There were offspring of that liaison too. I even knew that it was a sort of family tradition—a way in which we Wallace men proved our masculinity and our superiority over our women, I suppose. But it never once occurred to me that perhaps my father had upheld that tradition too."

"Oh, Elliott." She could think of nothing else to say.

"I believe," he said, "the whole world must have known except me. How I could *not* have known, I do not know. I spent enough time here in town after I came down from Oxford, heaven knows, and I thought I knew everything that was happening among the *ton,* even the seamier goings-on. But I never heard so much as a whisper about my own father. My mother knew— she had always known. Even Jessica knew."

She tried to imagine how his whole world must have shattered just over a year ago.

"Everything," he said as if he had read her thoughts. "Everything I knew, everything I had lived and believed—*everything* was an illusion, a lie. I thought we had our father's undivided love. I thought perhaps I was extra-special because I was the son, the heir, the one who would take his place eventually. But he had a son older than I and one almost exactly the same age and three other children. It was hard to grasp that fact. It is *still* hard. All those years my mother was nothing to him except the legal wife who had provided him with the legal heir. And I was nothing to him except that legal heir."

"Oh, Elliott." She unfolded her legs from the chair, got to her feet, not even noticing her book thudding to the floor, and hurried across to him. She sat on his lap, burrowed her arms about his waist, and nestled her head against his shoulder. "You do not know that. You were his *son*. Your sisters were his *daughters*. He did not necessarily love you the less because he had other children elsewhere. Love is not a finite commodity that will stretch only so far. It is infinite. Don't doubt that he loved you. Please don't."

"All those lies," he said, setting his head back against the chair. "About how busy he had to be in London, about how much he hated leaving, and then about how much he had missed us, how lonely he had been without us, how very glad he was to be back home. All lies, doubtless repeated to his other family when he returned to them."

She lifted her head to look into his face and drew her hands free so that she could smooth her fingers through his hair.

"Don't," she said. "Don't doubt everything, Elliott. If he said he loved you, if you *felt* he loved you, then no doubt he did."

"The point is," he said, "that none of this is rare. I could name a dozen other such instances without even having to think too hard. It comes of living in a society in which birth and position and fortune are everything and strategic marriages are the norm. It is common to seek sensual delights and emotional comfort elsewhere. It is just that I did not know it of my father, did not even suspect it. Suddenly I was Viscount Lyngate with precious little preparation for all the duties and responsibilities that were now mine—my fault, of course. I had been a careless young blade for far too long. And suddenly I was Jonathan's guardian. All of which I would have handled, suddenly and unexpectedly as they had come to me. I was my father's son, after all. But just as suddenly and unexpectedly I was—"

"Robbed of your memories?" she suggested when he stopped talking abruptly.

"Yes. Made to realize they were all false, all a mirage," he said. "I was cut adrift in a world I did not know."

"And," she said, "all the joy and love and hope fled from your life."

"All the stupid, naive idealism," he said. "I became a realist very fast, almost overnight. I learned my lesson quickly and well."

"Oh, you poor, foolish man," she said. "Realism does not exclude love or joy. It is made up of those elements."

"Vanessa," he said, lifting a hand and setting the backs of his fingers against her cheek for a moment, "we should all be as innocent and optimistic as you. I was until a year and a half ago."

"We should all be as *realistic* as I," she said. "Why is realism always seen as such a negative thing? Why do we find it so difficult to trust anything but disaster and violence and betrayal? Life is *good*. Even when good people die far too young and older people betray us, life is good. Life is what we make of it. We get to choose how we see it."

She kissed him softly on the lips. But she would not belittle a pain he had still not come to terms with even after well over a year.

"And then you lost your closest friend too?" she said softly. "You lost Constantine?"

"The final straw, yes," he admitted. "I suppose I was partly to blame. I marched over there, to Warren Hall, with crusading zeal to do my duty by Jonathan, quite prepared to ride roughshod over everyone involved with him if necessary. Perhaps I would soon have learned to be less obnoxiously zealous if all had been as it ought. But it was not. It quickly became apparent to me that my father had trusted everything to Con and that Con had taken advantage of that trust."

"In what way?" she asked him, her hands framing his face.

He sighed.

"He stole from Jonathan," he said. "There were jewels. Heirlooms. Almost priceless ones, though I daresay they did bring a handsome price. Most of them had disappeared. Jonathan knew nothing of them when asked, though he remembered his father showing them to him at one time. Con would not admit to taking them, but he would not deny it either. He had a look on his face when I spoke to him about them, a look with which I was long familiar—half mockery, half contempt. It was a look that told me as clearly as words that he had indeed taken them. But I had no proof. I did not tell anyone. It was a family shame that I felt obliged to hide from the world. You are the first one to know. He was *not* a worthy friend. I had been as deceived by him all my life as I had been by my father. He is not a pleasant character, Vanessa."

"No," she agreed sadly.

He closed his eyes. His hand fell to his side again.

"Lord," he said, "why have I burdened you with all this sordid family history?"

"Because I am your wife," she said. "Elliott, you must not give up on love even though it seems as if everyone you loved betrayed you. Actually it was only *two* people out of everyone you have known, precious as those two were to you. And you must not give up on happiness even if all your happy memories seem to be hollow ones. Love and joy are waiting for you."

"Are they?" He looked wearily into her eyes.

"And hope," she said. "There must always be hope, Elliott."

"Must there? Why?"

And then, as she watched, her palms still cupping the sides of his face, she saw tears well into his eyes and spill over onto his cheeks.

He jerked his head away from her hands and uttered an oath that ought to have brought color to her cheeks.

"Damn it," he said, following up the first oath with a milder one. He was feeling around for a handkerchief and found one. "Dash it all, Vanessa. You must excuse me."

He was trying to lift her off his lap, push her away, exclude her. But she would have none of it. She wrapped both arms about his neck, drawing his face down to her bosom.

"Don't shut me out," she said against his hair. "Don't keep on shutting me out, Elliott. I am not your father or Constantine. I am your wife. And I will never betray you."

She turned her face to rest one cheek against the top of his head as he wept with deep, obviously painful sobs and gasps.

He was going to be terribly embarrassed when he

stopped, she thought. He had probably not shed a tear for years. Men were foolish about such things. It was a slur on their manhood to weep.

She kissed his head and one temple. She smoothed her hands through his hair.

"My love," she murmured to him. "Ah, my love."

## 22

ELLIOTT had reserved a box at Vauxhall Gardens. An evening at the famous pleasure gardens just south of the River Thames was something not to be missed when one was in town during the Season, and Vanessa's face had lit up with anticipated pleasure as soon as he asked her if she would like to go there.

Pleasing his wife had become of great importance to him. So had the certain kind of love he felt for her. He could not—or would not—put a name to it. He was surely not *in* love with her—it was too trivial a term. And as for simply loving—well, he had come to distrust love and did not want to put his feelings for Vanessa into that fragile category.

He trusted her. It seemed to him that her life must always have been characterized by the unconditional love she gave freely to all who were close to her, whether they deserved it or not.

He did not deserve her love, heaven knew.

And yet he knew that in her own way she loved him.

She had left him on that evening in the library as soon as he had finally got himself under control, and she had never alluded to the horribly embarrassing incident since. She had given him time and space in which to recover himself and heal.

And heal he did. He came to understand that love—

if he dared use that word—did not reside in any one person. His father had let him down. So had Con. But *love* had not.

Love remained to him both as something other people gave him and, more important, as something he was capable of giving.

He was going to love his own children with a steadiness upon which they could rely for as long as he lived. And their mother would teach them, by example if not in words—though there doubtless *would* be words in plenty—that love was something that lived deep inside everyone, a bottomless well, something that could give a happy bent to their lives even during dark and difficult days.

And those children—or the first, at least—would not be too far in the future. Vanessa, he realized, must be with child even though she had not chosen to tell him yet. She had not had her courses since their marriage.

He was beginning to feel a cautious contentment with his marriage.

The visit to Vauxhall had not been arranged purely for Vanessa's benefit, however. It was mainly for Miss Huxtable and young Merton, who were going to go back to Warren Hall within a few days. Vanessa and Elliott were going with them, but as soon as Elliott had seen the boy properly settled with his tutors again, they would return to London for the rest of the Season.

Elliott had been feeling a little concerned by the ease with which the boy had taken to London. He was still years too young to enter fully into the life that would eventually be his, but he had made a number of older friends, both male and female, and was out and about most days—riding in the park, or going to the races, or examining the horses at Tattersall's, or attending the surprisingly large number of social events to which he was invited.

He was too young, and he was perhaps an easy prey to men like Con, who often accompanied him. It was time for him to be reined in and returned home, where his education would resume until he went up to Oxford.

Surprisingly, Merton had been quite willing to go. He put up no fight whatsoever when Elliott took him aside to broach the subject with him.

"I cannot join any of the gentlemen's clubs yet," he said, counting the points off on his fingers, "and I cannot buy horses or a curricle or a dozen and one other things without your permission, and I cannot take my seat in the House of Lords or attend any of the most interesting of the balls and soirees. And it has become very clear to me that there are a million things I need to learn before I am allowed to do all these things. Besides, I miss Warren Hall. I scarcely had time to start to feel at home there before coming here. I will be glad to go back."

The boy was going to go through a wild period before too many more years had passed, Elliott was sure. But he would come through it all relatively unscathed, it was to be hoped. He had a good character beneath all his restless energy, the result of a good upbringing.

His eldest sister insisted upon going back to the country with him. She had made her debut in society, she told Elliott firmly when he suggested that she did not need to go with Merton since he would have his tutors to keep a firm eye upon him. She could now mingle with the *ton* whenever she was so inclined—*if* she ever felt so inclined. She was very glad she had come to London for a part of the Season, but her place was with Stephen, and for the next several years, anyway, until he married, her place was at Warren Hall as its mistress. And she was not needed in London with her younger sister, as Kate was to move to Moreland House, where she would be well chaperoned by the dowager Lady Lyngate until Vanessa returned from the country.

She was not to be shaken from that resolve.

It was Vanessa who told Elliott about Allingham's offer and her refusal of it. It would have been a brilliant match for her, but according to Vanessa, her sister still carried a torch for her faithless military officer and perhaps always would.

Katherine Huxtable had wanted to return to Warren Hall too when she first knew of her brother and sister's plan to go there. She missed the quiet of the countryside, she explained. But Cecily and Vanessa between them persuaded her to stay. She had a host of admirers and would-be suitors—as many as Cecily, in fact. Perhaps, Elliott thought, she did not realize quite how fortunate she was. Many young ladies who were making their debut would have given a great deal to have just half as many.

But one thing was growingly apparent to Elliott. Life might have changed almost beyond recognition for the Huxtables, but it had not changed them. They would adjust—they were already doing so. But they would not be spoiled.

At least, he *hoped* that applied to Merton as well as to his sisters.

The evening at Vauxhall was planned, then, as a farewell party for Merton and Miss Huxtable. Elliott's mother, Cecily, Averil and her husband, and of course Katherine Huxtable were of the party too.

Elliott had chosen an evening when there was to be dancing and fireworks. And as good fortune would have it, it was an evening on which the sky remained cloudless after dark and the air remained almost warm and the breeze was only strong enough to cause the lanterns in the trees to sway slightly and send their colored lights and shadows dancing through the branches and across the numerous paths along which the revelers strolled.

They approached the gardens by river and stepped inside just as darkness was falling. The orchestra was already playing in the central rotunda, where they had their box.

"Oh, Elliott," Vanessa said, holding tightly to his arm, "have you ever seen anything lovelier?"

Vanessa and her superlatives! Nothing was ever just simply lovely or delicious or enjoyable.

"Than the gown you are wearing or your newly cut hair?" he asked, looking down at her. "Yes, I have seen something lovelier. Infinitely lovelier, in fact. *You!*"

She turned her face up to his and the familiar laughter lit it from within.

"How absurd you are," she said.

"Ah," he said, recoiling. "Did you mean the gardens, by any chance? Yes, I suppose they are rather lovely too now that I spare them a glance."

She laughed outright, and Miss Huxtable turned her head to smile at them.

"Happy?" he asked Vanessa, touching the fingers of his free hand to hers on his arm.

Some of the laughter faded.

"Yes," she said. "Oh, yes, I am."

And he wondered if this was it—the happily-ever-after at which he had always scoffed and that even she did not believe in. Something that had crept up quietly on them, something that did not need to be put into words.

Except that it would be strange indeed if Vanessa did not somehow *find* words and force him into finding some too.

He grimaced inwardly and then smiled to himself.

"Oh, look, Elliott," she said. "The orchestra and the boxes. And the dancing area. Will we dance? Outdoors, under the stars? Could anything be more romantic?"

"Absolutely nothing I can think of," he said, "except that the dance be a waltz."

"Oh, yes," she said.

"Oh, good," young Merton said at the same moment, his voice bright with enthusiasm. "There is Constantine with his party. He said he would be here this evening."

Vanessa was so deeply in love that it was almost painful. For though she had answered truthfully when Elliott had asked her unexpectedly if she was happy, it had been only partly the truth.

He had not said anything since that night in the library, and she had been left to wonder if he resented her, if he felt she had humiliated him by forcing tears from him and refusing to leave when he had wanted her to.

Not that he *behaved* as if he were resentful. There had been a certain tenderness in his manner to her in the week since—and even greater tenderness in his lovemaking. And perhaps actions really did speak louder than words.

But she needed the words.

He had not said *anything*.

She was not one to brood, however. Her marriage was many times happier than she had expected it to be when she had taken the desperate measure of proposing marriage to him so that he would not offer for Meg. She would be content with things as they were for the rest of her life if she must.

But oh, how she longed for . . . Well, for *words*.

How could she possibly be anything but nine parts out of ten happy, though, when she was at Vauxhall Gardens with everyone who was most dear to her in life?

They strolled along the main avenues of the gardens as a group, drinking in the sights of trees and sculptures and arched colonnades and colored lanterns and fellow revelers, breathing in the scents of nature and perfumes and food, listening to the sounds of voices and laughter and distant music.

They feasted upon sumptuous foods, including the wafer-thin slices of ham and the strawberries for which Vauxhall was famous. And upon sparkling wines.

They conversed with numerous acquaintances who stopped briefly outside their box.

And they danced—all of them, even the dowager.

Waltzing beneath the stars was every bit as romantic as Vanessa had dreamed it would be, and it seemed to her that she and Elliott did not remove their eyes from each other while they performed the steps. She smiled at him, and he gazed back at her with that look in his eyes that surely was tenderness.

She would believe it was that. Words really were unnecessary.

But perversely, though she was mostly happy, and that was happier than any mortal could expect to be in this life for longer than a few moments at a time, there *was* that one other part to mar her joy. And it was not entirely due to Elliott's failure to say anything of any great significance since that evening in the library.

For Constantine was here—as he was at almost every other entertainment she attended. And avoiding him was as much of a strain this evening as it had been for the last week and more.

He was as smiling and charming as ever. And as attentive, despite the fact that he had come there with another party. He talked with Stephen for a while and danced with Meg. He took Cecily and Kate for a stroll, one on each arm, and did not reappear with them for half an hour. Vanessa would have been downright uneasy if the girls had not been together. As it was, she felt—well, annoyed with him and annoyed with herself. For though she had every reason to warn her brother and sisters against him, she had not done so. She would have had to mention Mrs. Bromley-Hayes if she had, and his theft at Warren Hall when Jonathan was still alive. She was unwilling to mention either, so she had said nothing.

She had avoided Constantine on her own account, though he always smiled at her and would have approached, she knew, if she ever gave him the slightest encouragement. She could have avoided him for the rest of the Season, she supposed, especially as she was going to be away from London for the next week or so. But avoidance had never been her way of dealing with life. When he returned Cecily and Kate to the box and would have returned to his own party, Vanessa leaned forward in her seat. Elliott was talking with a few of his male acquaintances.

"And will you walk with me too, Constantine?" she asked.

He smiled warmly at her, and it struck her that it was a great pity she had lost a cousin so soon after finding him. He was undoubtedly capable of great charm. He bowed to her and offered his arm.

"It would be my pleasure," he said. As soon as they had moved away from the box, he bent his head a little closer to hers. "I thought you had fallen out with me."

"I have," she said.

His face was grave, but his eyes laughed in the lamplight as they turned onto a broad avenue. He raised his eyebrows, inviting an explanation.

"It was not well done," she said, "to introduce Mrs. Bromley-Hayes to me and my brother and sisters and Cecily at the theater. And it was not well done to bring her to Cecily's come-out ball. I expected better of you. You are our *cousin*."

Some of the laughter had faded from his eyes.

"It was not," he agreed. "I apologize, Vanessa. My intention was never to hurt you or your family. Or Cece."

"But you did," she said. "Cecily and Stephen and Meg and Kate do not know that they were exposed to a tasteless indiscretion for all the *ton* to see. But I do. And I was the one most affected, apart from Elliott, whom I assume you deliberately set out to embarrass. Did you assume, Constantine, that I would not confront Elliott with what I learned from Mrs. Bromley-Hayes the day after the ball, though she lied to me? Did you assume that our marriage would be damaged from deep within, rather as a tumor might silently destroy the body? If you did, you assumed wrongly. My marriage has not been destroyed and my happiness has not been dimmed. Though it has in one way. I was happy to discover you when we came to Warren Hall. I instantly loved you as a cousin and I soon liked you as a person. I would have been your friend for the rest of your life and welcomed your friendship for the rest of mine. We could have been *family*. But you maliciously destroyed any such chance, and I am sorry for it. That is all I have to say."

All the laughter was gone from his eyes now as he maneuvered her to one side of the path so that they would not be mowed down by a boisterous group that was approaching from the opposite direction.

"Anna *spoke* to you?" he asked. "She told you that she was still Elliott's mistress, I suppose? She would not have expected that you would confront him with your knowledge and discover her lie so soon. I am sorry."

She looked reproachfully at him but said nothing.

"And I must confess *my* lie," he said after a short silence. "For of course I *did* hear about your meeting with Anna in the park. She told me herself. I am sorry, Vanessa. I really am. My quarrel is with Elliott, and I chose to embarrass him without ever considering the harm I would be doing you too. Believe me, that was never my intention."

"You have a quarrel with him because he knows you for who you are," she said. "I side with him, Constantine. And your apology means nothing to me. I hope I will never see you again. I will never voluntarily speak with you again."

"*Who I am,*" he said with soft emphasis as they stopped walking. "A thief and a debaucher, I suppose."

A *debaucher*? Was there something else Elliott had not told her, then? But if there was, she did not want to know.

"Yes," she said. "And you cannot deny the charge."

"Can I not?" He smiled, a tight, mocking expression.

She gazed up at him as someone jostled her in passing, hopeful that against all reason he would offer some explanation.

"You are quite right," he said instead, making her an elegant bow. "I cannot deny either charge, Vanessa, and *will* not. And so I must stand a villain in your eyes. And you are at least partly justified in your opinion of me. I will return you to your box, if I may. I do not suppose you wish to walk farther with me."

"I do not," she said.

They turned to walk back the way they had come, not touching or speaking. But they had not gone far before Vanessa could see Elliott striding toward them, a frown on his face.

"I return your viscountess unharmed," Constantine said when they came up to him, all the mockery back in his face and his voice. "Good evening to you, Vanessa. And to you too, Elliott."

And he strolled away without a backward glance.

"It was I who invited *him* to walk with *me,*" she explained. "I have been avoiding him. But I realized I needed to tell him how disappointed I was with his behavior at the theater and at Cecily's come-out ball. I needed to tell him why I will not speak to him again except as strict courtesy dictates. And I needed to tell him that I *know* about him. He mentioned debauchery as well as theft."

"Ah, yes," he said, taking her arm and leading her off the main avenue onto a narrower, more shaded path. "But you need not know about that, Vanessa. Ah, but I suppose you do. There are young women in the neighborhood of Warren Hall, some of whom were once servants at the house, who are now bringing up their illegitimate children alone."

"Oh," she said. "Oh, no."

"Oh, yes, I am afraid," he said. "But let us not speak anymore of Con, Vanessa. Tell me about Hedley Dew instead."

She turned her face toward him in the darkness.

"About Hedley?" she said, sounding surprised.

"After I spoke to you about my father," he said, "it struck me that you now knew a secret part of myself that you ought to know as my wife. Hedley Dew is, I believe, the secret part of yourself and perhaps there is more about him that you need to tell me."

The path had narrowed, and he released her arm in order to set his about her shoulders and draw her against his side. She was slender and warm, and it occurred to him that he had come to find her body infinitely enticing. Her hair smelled of some subtly fragrant soap.

"He was delicate and dreamy all his life," she said. "He always preferred to sit in some secluded, scenic spot outdoors and talk than to join the other children in their boisterous games. I befriended him at first because I felt sorry for him—I would rather have joined in the games. But he knew a great deal—he was intelligent and he read voraciously—and he dreamed big dreams. As he grew older, he included me in those dreams. We were going to travel the world and immerse ourselves in the cultures of all sorts of people. He . . . He *loved* me. He had the loveliest smile, Elliott, and eyes one could fall into. He had *dreams* one could fall into."

They came to a wooden seat beside the path and he drew her to sit on it. He kept his arm about her.

"And then one day I woke up from those dreams," she said, "to the realization that reality was a far harsher thing. He was ill. He was probably dying. I think I knew that before almost anyone except perhaps him. And he wanted me. He loved me. I loved him too, but not in *that* way. My parents had always told me that I would probably never marry because I was so much plainer than Meg and Kate and other girls from neighboring families. I *wanted* to marry, though, and of course Hedley was a dazzlingly good catch—he was Sir Humphrey Dew's son. He lived at Rundle Park. I do not think even so that I would have married him if he had not needed me. But he did. Marrying him was one thing I could give him, one dream of his that I could bring true for him. It was so obvious that none of the others would come true."

She was shivering and her hands fidgeted in her lap. There was pain in her voice. He withdrew his arm from about her, shrugged out of his evening coat, and set it about her shoulders, holding it in place with his arm.

"I did not want to do it," she said. "He was ill and dying and I was neither. I . . . did not find him attractive despite his great beauty. I have felt so much guilt over that. I told so many lies. I told him over and over again that I adored him."

"And you regret that?" he asked her.

"No!" she said vehemently. "What I regret is that I could never make it the truth. Oh, that is not quite true either. I *did* adore him. I loved him with all my heart and soul. But I did not *love* him."

Even just a few weeks ago he would have shaken his head with exasperation at such muddle-headedness. Now strangely he knew exactly what she meant. He could understand the fine distinctions between different kinds of love.

"What you *did* give him," he said, "was the best of all loves, Vanessa. It was the pure gift of a love that gave and gave and took nothing in return."

"Except that I did take too," she said. "He gave as much as I did, Elliott. He taught me so much about living life one day at a time, about finding joy in small things and laughter in the face of tragedy. He taught me about patience and dignity. And he taught me not to cling. He taught me how to let go, how to . . . He told me before he died that I must love again and marry again and be happy again. He told me I must always laugh. He—" She swallowed, and he could hear the gurgle in her throat.

He buried his nose in her hair and kissed the top of her head.

"He loved me," she said. "And I loved him. I *did*. I am sorry, Elliott. I am truly sorry. I *did* love him."

He set his free hand beneath her chin and lifted her face to his. He kissed her, tasting the salt of tears on her cheeks and on her lips.

"You must never apologize for that," he said against

her lips. "And you must never deny it to yourself. Of course you loved him. And I am glad you did. You would not be the person I have come to know you as if you had not loved him."

Her hand came up to cup the side of his face.

"You are not still *terribly* sorry you married me?" she asked him.

"Was I ever?" he asked her.

"I think you were," she said. "You would never have chosen me left to yourself. I am plain, and I quarreled with you a number of times."

"I suppose you *were* something of a pest," he said, "now that you remind me."

She choked with laughter—as he had intended.

"But never plain," he said. "Just beauty in disguise. And no, I am not sorry, terribly or otherwise. I am not sorry at all."

"Oh," she said, "I am so glad. I have made you comfortable, then? And a little bit happy?"

"And a little bit pleasured?" he said. "All three in fact, Vanessa. And you?"

"And I am happy too," she said, kissing him softly on the lips with the old pucker.

It never failed to arouse him.

It was time for some grand declaration, he supposed. It was the time when, if he were not already married to her, he ought to go down on one knee with a flourish, take her hand in his, declare his undying love, and beg her to make him the happiest of men.

Since they *were* already married, he ought to—

There was a loud crack and whoosh from somewhere close by, and his thoughts were shattered as Vanessa shot to her feet.

*What the devil?*

"The fireworks!" she cried. "They are beginning, Elliott. Oh, do let us hurry and go and see. Look!" She pointed upward to a fountain of red sparks that had appeared above the treetops. "Have you ever heard or seen anything more exciting in your life?"

"Never," he said with a grin as she found his hand in the darkness and drew him—in his shirtsleeves—along the path at a smart trot.

# 23

T H E day before her brother and sisters left for the country, Katherine moved into Moreland House, from where she would continue participating in the activities of the Season with Cecily under the chaperonage of Cecily's mother until Vanessa returned. She was quite cheerful about the move, though part of her wished she were going home with everyone else, she told Vanessa and Margaret.

Vanessa sat down in her bedchamber to have a private word with her just before leaving the following morning. She wanted to warn her sister to be careful of Constantine, though it was a difficult thing to do as she did not want to disclose specifics of her misgivings about him.

"He is a number of years older than you, Kate," she said, "and very handsome and charming. He is an experienced man about town. I fear he may be something of a . . . Well, something of a rake. It would not be wise to trust him implicitly just because he is our second cousin."

"Oh, you need not concern yourself, Nessie," Katherine said with a laugh as she seated herself in the middle of her bed and hugged her raised knees. "I know you have not liked Constantine lately because Lord Lyngate has a quarrel with him. I do not know what that is about, and I do not want to know—it is between the two of them. But our cousin is as strict a chaperone as you could possibly be—or Meg or Lady Lyngate."

Vanessa raised her eyebrows in some surprise.

"Chaperone?" she said.

"Cecily can be a little wild when she is out of her mama's sight or yours and Lord Lyngate's," Katherine said. "She expected that when she was with Constantine she would be able to stop and talk with any gentleman with whom she has even the slightest acquaintance and walk with him while I stayed with Constantine. I even suspect that some of those chance meetings were trysts that had been arranged beforehand. But our cousin will have none of it, and though he is very good-humored and never makes Cecily cross, he makes it quite clear that she will not do anything in his company that she would not do in her mama's. And he has been concerned enough to point out to both of us those gentlemen whose advances we ought not to encourage. Perhaps he *is* a rake when in different company—many gentlemen are, I believe. But with us he is always the soul of honor and propriety."

"Is he?" Vanessa said. "I am glad to hear it."

And she was more than ever sorry that his quarrel with Elliott had provoked him into such spite against *her*. She was sorrier still that he had behaved so dishonorably at Warren Hall when Jonathan was alive. But of course he was not a monster and she must not expect him always to be villainous.

"Don't ever allow yourself to be alone with him, though, Kate," she said.

"*He* would never allow it even if I would," her sister said. "Besides, Nessie, he too is going away within the next few days. He has purchased a house and land in Gloucestershire and is going to settle there."

"Is he?"

"I will miss him," Katherine said. "I like him exceedingly well."

He was certainly not poor, then, Vanessa thought. But surely his father had not left him a large enough fortune to enable him to buy an estate of his own. Then she remembered the money and jewels he had stolen, and she sighed aloud.

"He had a talk with Stephen when they were riding in the park together one morning," Katherine said. "He advised him to return to Warren Hall and apply himself to his studies and to learning all there is to know about the running of his properties and the responsibilities of his position. There will be time enough later, when he has reached his majority, to sow a few wild oats, he told Stephen, and to enjoy his life to the full. Though he must always remember that he is the Earl of Merton and strive to be worthy of the position. Stephen told me all about it. And then the very next day Lord Lyngate also suggested to him that he go back home. Stephen admires and respects them both enormously. Is it not a shame that they hate each other?"

"Yes," Vanessa said with another sigh.

Would she ever understand Constantine? It was so much more comfortable to be able to divide people into heroes and villains and expect them to play their allotted part. What happened when someone fit into both categories?

But it was one of those unanswerable questions with which life abounded.

"It is time to go," she said, getting to her feet and

hugging her sister when she scrambled off the bed. "Elliott will be waiting for me. We will be back within a week or ten days. Do enjoy yourself until then, Kate. I will miss you."

"And I you," Katherine said, clinging to her for a moment. "I often think of that day when Tom Hubbard brought word to the school that there was a viscount staying at the inn in Throckbridge and I hurried home to tell you and Meg and to speculate on why he was there. And then we went to the assembly and he danced only with you. And the next day he came to the cottage to change all our lives. I sometimes wish none of it had happened, Nessie, but life cannot be held back from taking its course, can it? And everything has certainly turned out happily for you."

"It has," Vanessa agreed.

"And sometimes I am not sorry at all," Katherine said. "Sometimes I think that this new life will turn out happily for *all* of us if we just have the courage to grasp what it offers."

Vanessa smiled at her.

"Of course it will," she said, thinking rather sadly of Meg. "That is what life is for."

She linked her arm through Katherine's as they descended the stairs to the waiting carriage.


It had not really been necessary to come into the country in person in the middle of the Season, Elliott soon discovered. Merton was cheerfully resigned to returning and immersing himself in his various studies. And his eldest sister was quite capable of seeing that his attention did not stray too far from duty. Samson and the butler and housekeeper between them had kept house and estate running smoothly, and both tutors were eager to take their pupil in hand again.

But perhaps duty to his position as guardian of the boy had been only an excuse. It was not that he did not enjoy being in London for the Season. Or that he did not enjoy being there with Vanessa. But he had kept remembering the few days following their wedding—their honeymoon as she had once called it—with some nostalgia. They could not have stayed longer at the dower house—duty had called them to London. But he would have *liked* to stay longer.

A man ought to be allowed to spend sufficient time alone with his bride to get to know her thoroughly, to become comfortable with her, to enjoy himself with her.

To fall in love with her.

It was perhaps unwise to try to recapture the magic of those days.

It was *probably* unwise.

They had both spent the bulk of the first day home at Warren Hall. They had not promised to return on the second day, though they had said that they *might* go. It was a sunny day with very little wind. It was really quite hot. It was a perfect day for a ride over to Warren Hall, or for a drive there in an open vehicle.

It was a perfect day . . .

"Do you really *want* to go to Warren Hall today?" he asked Vanessa at breakfast. "Or would you prefer a quiet day at home? A stroll down to the lake, perhaps."

"Together?" she asked him.

"Together, yes."

"I daresay Stephen will be busy all day," she said. "It

may be wise not to disturb him. And Meg was planning to spend all morning with the housekeeper and all afternoon—weather permitting—seeing what can be done to improve the rose arbor. The weather does permit."

"It would be best, then," he said, "if we did not disturb her either."

"I think so," she agreed.

"The lake, then?"

"The lake."

She smiled at him suddenly, that bright expression that involved not only her mouth and eyes, but every part of her right down to her soul—or so it seemed. It always dazzled him.

"Yes," she said, "let's go to the lake, Elliott. Even though the daffodils will no longer be blooming."

"But nature never leaves us bereft," he said, "no matter what the season."

Good Lord, he would be writing poetry soon if he was not careful. But his words proved prophetic. The daffodils were, of course, long gone, but in their place were the bluebells, growing even more lavishly on the far riverbank and carpeting the slope on which the daffodils bloomed in spring.

"Oh, Elliott," she said as they walked along the banks. "Could anything be lovelier?"

Everything within sight was blue or green, from the water to the grass to the flowers to the trees to the sky. Even her dress was cornflower blue, and her straw bonnet was trimmed with blue ribbons.

"The daffodils were *as* lovely," he said, "but not lovelier."

"Elliott." She stopped walking and stepped in front

of him. She took both his hands in hers. "I was happier here for those three days than I have ever been in my life. Though that cannot be quite true because I have been happy since too. I am happy now. I want you to know that. I promised *you* happiness, but I am the one who has been most blessed."

"No, you are not." His hands closed firmly about hers. "If you feel blessed, Vanessa, you cannot feel more so than I do. And if you are happy, you cannot be happier than I."

Her eyes widened and her lips parted.

"I am happy," he said, lifting her hands one at a time to his lips.

For once he seemed to have rendered her speechless.

He was inclined to remain so himself. But if he did not say it now, perhaps he never would. And such things were important to women, he believed. Perhaps they were equally important to men.

"I love you," he said.

Her eyes brightened—with tears, he realized.

"I love you," he told her again. "I am head over ears in love with you. I adore you. I *love* you."

She was biting her lower lip.

"Elliott," she said, "you do not need to—"

His forefinger landed none too gently across her lips.

"You have become as necessary to me as the air I breathe," he said. "Your beauty and your smiles wrap themselves about me and warm me to the heart—to the very soul. You have taught me to trust and to love again, and I trust and love *you*. I love you more than I have ever loved anyone. More than I knew it was possible to love. And if you think I am making an ass of myself with such romantic hyperbole just because I want to make you feel better about admitting that you are happy, then I am going to have to take drastic measures."

Her face filled with laughter—and radiance. Two tears spilled onto her cheeks. She blinked away any others that might have followed.

"*What?*" she asked him.

He smiled slowly at her, and realized he was doing it—letting go his final defenses against the dangers of loving—when her own smile was arrested and she freed her hands and cupped his face gently with them.

"Oh, my love," she said. "My love."

The same words she had spoken that night in the library while he wept. He had scarcely heard them then, but he heard their echo now. She had loved him for a long time, he realized. It was in her nature to love, but she had chosen to love *him*.

"Do you have something to tell me?" he asked her.

She tipped her head to one side.

"The baby?" she said. "There will be a baby, Elliott. Are you happy about it? Perhaps it will be your heir."

"I am happy about the *baby*," he said. "Son, daughter—it really does not matter." He leaned forward and touched his forehead to hers.

She slid her arms up about his neck and leaned into him.

"I am glad it is *here* we have spoken of it for the first time," she said. "I am glad it is *here* you have told me you love me. I will always, always love this place, Elliott. It will become sacred ground."

"Not too sacred, I hope," he said. "It has just occurred to me that it has not rained for several days and that the ground will be dry. And this is a secluded spot. No one ever comes here."

"Except us," she said.

"Except us."

And the gardeners who prevented this part of the park from becoming too overgrown and wild. But all the gardeners were busy with their scythes today, cutting the grass of the large lawn before the house.

He took off his coat and spread it on the ground among the bluebells, perhaps in the very same spot where they had lain among the daffodils during their honeymoon.

And they lay down among the blooms and made quick and lusty and thoroughly satisfying love.

They were both panting when they had finished, and they both smiled when he lifted his head to look down at her.

"I suppose," he said, "I am going to have to pay for this. You are going to make me gather an armful of bluebells for the house, are you not?"

"Oh, more than an armful," she said. "*Both* arms must be laden and full and overflowing. There has to be a vase of bluebells for every room in the house."

"Heaven help us," he said. "It is a mansion. The last time I tried counting the rooms, I found I could not count that high."

She laughed.

"We had better not waste any more time, then," she said.

He got to his feet, adjusted his clothing, and reached down a hand for hers. She clasped it and he drew her up and into his arms. They hugged each other for several wordless moments, but not for too long.

There were flowers to be gathered. The house was to overflow with them.

Their *lives* were to be brimful and overflowing, he suspected—and always would be.

What else could a man expect when he was married to Vanessa?

He grinned at her and set to work.

# ABOUT THE AUTHOR

MARY BALOGH is the *New York Times* bestselling author of the acclaimed Slightly novels: *Slightly Married, Slightly Wicked, Slightly Scandalous, Slightly Tempted, Slightly Sinful,* and *Slightly Dangerous,* as well as the romances *No Man's Mistress, More Than a Mistress,* and *One Night for Love.* She is also the author of *Simply Perfect, Simply Magic, Simply Love,* and *Simply Unforgettable,* a dazzling quartet of novels set at Miss Martin's School for Girls. A former teacher herself, she grew up in Wales and now lives in Canada.

Visit our website at www.bantamdell.com.

# AUTHOR'S NOTE

The plot of a book almost invariably covers several days or weeks or months—or even years. It is impossible, then, for a writer to include every moment of that time in the book. She must select. How delightful it is, though, to be given a chance to go back to fill in some of the missing moments, as I am doing here with *First Comes Marriage*.

*First: It is late one afternoon when Vanessa realizes that Viscount Lyngate is about to propose marriage to her sister. He must be stopped at all costs. Meg will accept out of a sense of duty to her family, but she loves Crispin Dew. By the following afternoon Vanessa has found a solution and proposes marriage to Elliott herself, before he can propose to Margaret. She could not possibly have slept during the intervening night, could she? What agonizing thoughts went through her mind during all those sleepless hours? It might have been something like this . . .*

His dark eyebrows arched over his blue eyes, and those intensely blue eyes gazed into hers with astonishment and warm ardor. He looked more handsome than ever. More Greek than ever.

More *gorgeous* than ever.

"Do you mean," he asked her, "that you would have me, after my less than gallant behavior at the Valentine assembly and since? You would forgive me? You would *marry* me?"

He had taken a step closer so that she had to tip back her head slightly in order to look back into his eyes. She could smell his cologne—his very *masculine* cologne.

"I would," she said and then smiled as the ardor deepened in his eyes. "Forgive you, that is. What is there to forgive, after all? You were merely being yourself. I am above being offended by such foolishness."

Ardor was replaced by anxiety. He reached out a hand, as if for hers, but she kept her own hands clasped at her waist. His hand trembled.

"But you will marry me too?" he asked. "You have just said you will. I have hardly dared hope . . . I did *not* hope. I knew myself wholly unworthy. I chose your elder sister instead."

No. Vanessa frowned at the canopy above her head as she lay flat on her back in her bed, still wide awake though she had heard the clock in the hallway strike two quite a while ago. No, she could not have him say that. It was quite offensive to Meg. Meg was just as worthy as she. More so. *Far* more.

"But you will marry me too?" he said, starting again and omitting any mention of Meg. "You just said so. Or were you merely teasing me, cruel heart?"

That was better. She liked the *cruel heart* bit. She lofted her nose slightly in the air, though she also smiled half tenderly at him. He really did look very anxious, the poor dear. Almost abject.

"Why *should* I marry you?" she asked him, still ignoring his outstretched hand—and the fact that really she had just asked *him* to marry *her*.

"So that your sister will not have to?" he said, but he quickly realized it was the wrong thing to say. This was the dream Viscount Lyngate, after all, not the real man, who was far, far different and would doubtless say something a great deal more cutting than that, horrid man. "And because I admire you and . . . "

She looked hard at him and willed him to do better.

He took a step forward, both hands outstretched now. His eyes were smoldering. His voice, when he spoke, had dropped at least half an octave in tone. It trembled with the sincerity of a deeply felt passion.

" . . . and have done so in secret from the moment my eyes first alit upon you in the assembly rooms at Throckbridge and I thought I was looking at the other half of my soul." That was a nice touch. It made her eyes feel quite misty. "And because my devotion has grown—if it were possible—with every passing day since then. Because your beauty outshines that of any woman I have ever known. Because your character surpasses even your beauty. Because I adore you. Because I *love* you. Tell me, cruel heart, that you offered yourself to me in matrimony not only because you wished to save your sister but because you return my regard in some small measure, even though you can never equal it. No one can. No one has ever loved or will ever love as I love."

He was overdoing things a bit, perhaps, especially the beauty part, but never mind. Vanessa smiled damp-eyed up at the canopy. Her toes curled under her bare feet. She sighed deeply and aloud.

He took her hands and warmed them in his own. His eyes blazed hotly into hers. She could feel his breath against her lips though he maintained an *almost* decorous distance from her.

And she relented—though of course she *was* the who had proposed marriage to *him*. He was.

all, more gorgeous than a Greek god because he was dark-complexioned and warm-blooded and blue-eyed and . . . Well. And she had *almost* fallen head over ears in love with him at the assembly and would have done if he had not looked about him with such stuffy arrogance. That was all forgotten for the moment, though.

"I could not *bear* it," she said, and paused to recover from the catch in her voice. "I could not *bear* it if you were to marry Meg. My heart would be broken. Life would have no further meaning to me. I would want to die. I lo—"

He kissed her with hot ardor and her knees buckled under her. It was a good thing she was lying down. She hugged her pillow, which she stopped kissing after a mere few moments since really it could not be mistaken for a man's hot lips. She cast it aside and gazed up into the darkness again.

What absolute twaddle.

What utter poppycock.

If she *was* going to ask him to marry her instead of Meg—and she had decided during the past several hours that there really was no satisfactory alternative—she must do it coolly and calmly as if she were making him a mere business proposition. As, of course, she would be doing. She would be offering herself for his comfort and pleasure and convenience, and she would make him see that really it was a very sensible offer. He was bound to see it. He would . . .

He would probably fall down with derisive laughter and drum his booted heels on the floor and roll around with mirth, holding his sides and trying to catch his

uld not. Not Viscount Lyngate. He proba-
en know what laughter *was*.

He would fix her with a stare from those very blue eyes of his and she would feel icicles growing from her chin and her eyebrows and her nose. He would look at her as if she were a worm beneath his feet and then sweep her aside in order to find Meg and proceed with his plans.

Oh, dear, this was all very like a mouse planning to challenge an elephant to a duel.

She being the mouse, of course.

Perhaps there was another way out.

Perhaps Meg could be persuaded to say no.

No, she could not. When Meg saw family duty as the issue, she could be as solid and immovable as the Rock of Gibraltar.

Perhaps Stephen could have a word with Viscount Lyngate.

No, it would be unfair to ask it of him—he was only seventeen years old.

Perhaps she could send word to Finchley Park in the morning that Meg had a touch of smallpox or typhoid.

That they *all* did.

He would be horrid enough not to believe her.

The clock struck three.

Perhaps she could simply intercept his arrival tomorrow—assuming it was tomorrow he planned to come with his offer—and tell him the truth and appeal to his better nature.

She doubted he had one.

Perhaps she could . . .

Oh, but she had been over all this at least a dozen times since coming to bed.

She must get some sleep, or she would be so haggard and muddle-headed tomorrow—or did she mean day?—that she would not be able to do anything

She closed her eyes resolutely.

"I admire your courage more than I can say," he said in that half-an-octave-lower-than-normal voice, carrying her hand to his lips and holding it there with both hands. "And your beauty and your devotion to your family. I pledge you my love until my dying day. Allow *me* to offer *you* my hand and my heart, Mrs. Dew. May I have the great honor of calling you Vanessa?"

"Yes," she said, "as long as you never call me Nessie."

"Never," he promised with fervent ardor. "Never, my love."

He really sounded very convincing when he spoke in that voice.

*And next: What about Elliott? He did not love Margaret, but he thought she would be a tolerable bride—even though by marrying her he would also be acquiring that pestilential Mrs. Dew as a sister-in-law. Yet on the very day he was to propose to Margaret, he found himself accepting an offer from Mrs. Dew instead. How did he feel afterward, as he rode home to Finchley Park? Perhaps something like this . . .*

"Hell and damnation." That was the mild—the *very* mild—introduction to a lengthy outpouring of oaths and blasphemies that must have come close to singeing the grass on either side of the driveway down which he rode.

Away from Warren Hall.

Away from his betrothed.

But not forever, alas.

he beautiful and refined and sensible Miss

the plain and outspoken and outrageous

Good Lord! Damn and blast! He wasted another diatribe on the empty air before passing through the gates of the park and proceeding along the village street, scowling at any persons who looked as if they might smile and touch a forelock to him or drop a curtsy.

"I was wondering if you would be willing to marry me," she said.

She was looking plain and dowdy, even if her blue dress *did* become her rather more than the habitual gray or lavender attire. She looked abject and hopeful. She had probably never even *heard* of good manners or proper decorum or acceptable etiquette.

He raised his eyebrows and looked her directly in the eye.

"I would not," he said curtly. "If you will excuse me, ma'am, I will proceed on my way to the house."

No, better to kill with kindness. Better to show up bad manners with good.

"I would not, ma'am," he said coolly, trying again. He bowed and offered his arm. "May I escort you to the house?"

Of course, those who knew nothing of good manners would not recognize them even when they saw them demonstrated. And escorting her to the house would be giving her an opportunity to renew her outrageous request. Why not wither her with eloquence?

Let's start again.

"I was wondering if you would be willing to marry me," she said, as he rode clear of the village and set his horse's head for home and sanity. No, not sanity. There would never again be any of that in his life.

"*Marry* you?" he said, raising a suddenly acquired quizzing glass to his eye. "Marry *you*, Mrs. Dew? I mi be persuaded to jump into a fiery furnace or an i if thereby I might be of service to humanity or some small portion of it for which I cared. I might be willing to give up my title and fortune if by so doing I could eradicate poverty and suffering from the earth. I might be persuaded to do any number of unlikely, unpleasant things in a good cause. Marrying you would never be one of them. Even if you were the only woman on earth capable of giving me heirs. Even if you were the only woman on earth full stop. You will excuse me now, ma'am?"

He executed a deep and elegant bow and turned to leave.

*That* would teach her.

Who had ever *heard* of a *woman* proposing marriage to a *man*?

But he made the mistake of looking into her face before stalking away in the direction of the house—and he could see that her eyes were large with unshed tears and that her lower lip was trembling.

"Don't cry," he said softly. "I did not mean a word of what I said. Tell me what this is all about."

He reached out a hand toward her, and she placed her own in it—a small, trembling hand.

"You are going to offer for Meg," she said. "I cannot bear it. I really cannot when I adore you so much. Give me a chance to—"

It was a good thing Elliott had ridden clear of the village. He pulled back on the reins of his horse, which almost reared in surprise and alarm, and he spoke aloud
oath he knew.

devil . . . ?

only one answer to the question she had
ne-word answer.

"I was wondering if you would be willing to marry me."

*"No!"*

That was all. And if he had not been taken so much by surprise—he might have been knocked flat with the proverbial feather, in fact—it was the answer he would have given.

But he *had* been taken by surprise.

"*Marry* you?" he had said instead, making a question of his response and so giving her all the opportunity she had needed to reel him in.

He had actually listened to her.

He had actually *kissed* her.

He had actually . . . No, he had not.

Yes, he had. He had actually *wanted* her.

He shuddered and scowled.

And then he had—devil take it, he would rather obliterate that memory for all time, though he suspected it would be popping into his mind at regular intervals during the next fifty years or so, if he should be so unfortunate as to live so long. Then he had *gone down on one knee* to propose marriage to her.

What a shudderingly awful thing to have done.

And she had *laughed* at him.

Worse, she had said yes.

Why did the English language possess so few satisfyingly profane words?

*She had said yes.*

She kissed like a novice.

At least—it was *one* consolation—he would be ridding her of one half of her ghastly name. *Dew* would be gone. He wished it were the *Nessie* part instead.

He was going to marry *Nessie Dew*.

Now *there* was a pleasant thought to bring home with him.

And *how* was he going to explain to his mother that he had ridden off to affiance himself to Miss Huxtable and was riding back affianced to Mrs. Dew?

Perhaps, he thought hopefully, he would wake up at any moment to find this all a bizarre dream.

Dreams did not come this bizarre.

This was reality, right enough.

If *First Comes Marriage* stole your heart,
get ready to fall in love with
the next book in Mary Balogh's series
featuring the extraordinary Huxtable family.

## Then Comes Seduction

KATHERINE'S STORY

Available from Dell in paperback April 2009

And make sure to be on the lookout for
the following books in the series . . .

## At Last Comes Love

MARGARET'S STORY

Available from Dell in paperback May 2009

## Seducing an Angel

STEPHEN'S STORY

Available from Delacorte in hardcover June 2009

Turn the page for a sneak peek inside

# Then Comes Seduction

by Mary Balogh
Coming April 2009

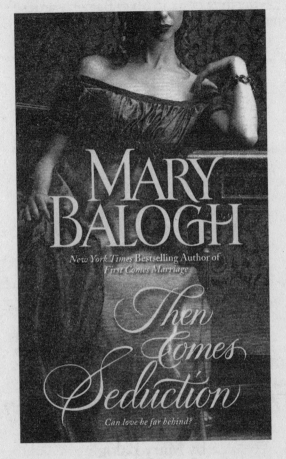

# MARY BALOGH

*New York Times* Bestselling Author of
*First Comes Marriage*

# Then Comes Seduction

*Can love be far behind?*

# THEN COMES SEDUCTION

## on sale April 2009

"Miss Huxtable," he said, moving his head even closer to hers and turning it so that he could look into her face, "do you never feel even the smallest urge to live adventurously? Even dangerously?"

She licked her lips and found that even her tongue was rather dry. Had he been reading her mind this evening?

"No, of course not," she said. "Never."

"Liar." His eyes laughed.

*What?* She felt the beginnings of outrage.

"Everyone wants some adventure in life," he said. "Everyone wants to flirt with danger on occasion. Even ladies who have had a sheltered, very proper upbringing."

"That is outrageous," she said—but without conviction. She could not look away from his eyes, which gazed keenly back into hers as if he could read every thought, every yearning, every desire she had ever had.

He laughed again and lifted his head a little away from hers.

"Yes, of course it is outrageous," he agreed. "I exaggerated. I can think of any number of people, both men and women, who are staid by nature and would sooner die than risk stubbing a toe against even the smallest of adventures. You are not, however, one of those people."

"How do you know?" she asked him, and wondered why she was arguing with him.

"Because you have asked the question," he said, "instead of pokering up and staring at me in blank incomprehension. You have become defensive. You know that I speak the truth but are afraid to admit it."

"*Really?*" she said, injecting as much frost into the one word as she could muster. "And what adventure is it that I crave, pray? And with what danger is it that I wish to flirt?"

Too late she wished she had used a different word.

His head dipped closer to hers again.

"*Me,*" he said softly. "In answer to both questions."

A shiver of horrified excitement convulsed her whole body, though she hoped it was not visible. Everyone, she realized, had been perfectly right about him. Constantine had been right. Her own instincts had been right.

He was a very dangerous man indeed. She ought to pull her arm free of his *right this moment* and go dashing after the others as fast as her legs and the crowds would allow.

"That is . . . preposterous," she said, staying instead to argue.

Because danger really was enticing. And not so very dangerous in reality. They were on the grand avenue at Vauxhall, surrounded by people even if their own party was proceeding farther ahead with every passing minute. Danger was only an illusion.

"I speak of your deepest, darkest desires, Miss Huxtable," he continued when she did not reply. "No true lady, of course, ever acts upon those, more is the pity. I believe any number of ladies would be far more interesting—and interest*ed*—if they did."

She stared at him. She glared at him—at least, she hoped she did. Her cheeks were uncomfortably hot. So was all the rest of her. Her heart was pounding so hard she could almost hear it.

"You most of all," he said. "I wonder if it has ever occurred to you, Miss Huxtable, that you are a woman of great passion. But probably not—it would not be a genteel admission to make, and I daresay you have not met anyone before now who was capable of challenging you to admit the truth. I assure you that you *are*."

"I am *not*," she whispered indignantly.

He did not answer. His eyelids drooped farther over his eyes instead, and those eyes laughed. The devil's eyes. Sin incarnate.

Suddenly and so unexpectedly that she almost jumped with alarm, she laughed. Out loud.

And she realized with astonishment and no uncertain degree of unease that she was actually almost *enjoying* herself. She knew that she would relive this part of the evening in memory for several days to come, perhaps weeks. Probably forever. She was actually talking with and *touching* the notorious Lord Montford. And he was actually flirting with her in an utterly outrageous way. And instead of being paralyzed with horror and tongue-tied with enraged virtue, she was actually laughing and arguing back.

They had stopped walking. Although her arm was still drawn through his, they were standing almost face to face—and therefore very close together. The crowds of revelers flowed around them.

"Oh, how very wicked of you," she was bold enough to say. "You have quite deliberately discomfited me, have you not? You have deliberately maneuvered me into hotly denying a quality of which we all wish to think ourselves capable."

"Passion?" he said. "You *are* capable of it, then, Miss

Huxtable? You admit it? How sad it is that a gentle up-bringing must stamp all outer sign of it from a lady."

"But it is something she must display only for her husband," she said and felt instantly embarrassed by the ghastly primness of the words.

"Let me guess." He was more than ever amused, she could see. "Your father was a clergyman and you were brought up listening to and reading sermons."

She opened her mouth to protest and shut it again. There was no smart answer to that, was there? He was quite right.

"Why are we having this conversation?" she asked him, about five minutes too late. "It is very improper, as you know very well. And we have not even set eyes upon each other until tonight."

"Now *that*, Miss Huxtable," he said, "is a blatant bouncer for which you will be fortunate indeed not to fry in hell. Not only have you set eyes upon me before tonight, but you have done so quite deliberately and with full awareness on more than one occasion. My guess is that Con's warnings against me—I do not doubt he *did* warn you—have had the opposite effect from what he intended, as a man of his experience ought to have known. But before you swell with indignation and perjure your soul with more lies, let me admit that since I am aware of your observing me before tonight, then of course *I* must have been observing *you*. Unlike you, though, I have no wish to deny the fact. I have seen you with increasing pleasure. You must realize how extraordinarily lovely you are, and so I will not bore you by going into raptures over your beauty. Though I will if you wish."

He raised both eyebrows and gazed very directly into her eyes, awaiting her answer.